The Second Mile

Ron and Janet Benrey

BROADMAN
&HOLMAN
PUBLISHERS

Nashville, Tennessee

0-8054-2558-6

Published by Broadman & Holman Publishers,
Nashville, Tennessee

Dewey Decimal Classification: 813
Subject Heading: FICTION

Unless otherwise stated all Scripture citation is from the NIV,
the Holy Bible, New International Version, copyright © 1973,
1978, 1984 by International Bible Society. Also used is the
King James Version of the Holy Bible.

1 2 3 4 5   06 05 04 03 02

IN MEMORIAM

Irwin & Polly Benrey
Ron's parents

ACKNOWLEDGMENTS

We were blessed by many people who walked the second mile for us when we wrote this book. Our writing group, the Annapolis Mystery Writers, cheerfully read our initial drafts and made invaluable suggestions. A hearty thank you to Ray Flint, Christiane Carlson-Thies, Mary Ellen Hughes, Trish Marshall, Sherriel Mattingly, and Marcia Talley.

We're also grateful to Janis Whipple and Kim Overcash for expertly editing the manuscript and overseeing production . . . to Joyce Hart, our agent (and friend) for her encouragement . . . and to Dr. Henriette Taarwaarbeek, M.D., for once again helping separate medical fact from fiction.

Prologue

THE MAN SITTING AT THE COMPUTER BEGAN TO TYPE:

> To My Family, Friends, and Coworkers: By the time you
> read this letter I will be dead.

Was that an appropriate way to announce a suicide? The man
didn't feel sure. He had never seen a real suicide note before and wondered if the opening should have a less somber tone. He stared at the
screen for a moment, then decided that the tenor of the farewell message wouldn't make any difference. "It's close enough for government
work," he murmured. "Everyone will get the idea."

The man glanced at his wristwatch. *11:35 P.M.* In twenty-five minutes the clock-thermostat would switch on the apartment's gas-fired
heating system. Almost immediately the disconnected chimney pipe
would begin to fill the apartment with carbon monoxide. Thirty minutes later the air in the bedroom would be fully saturated with a lethal
dose of the odorless, colorless gas. He was running out of time; he had

to finish typing this note quickly and then print a copy to place on the bed table.

When he looked back at the words on the screen, however, a new problem caught his eye. The greeting wasn't quite right. *Only a handful of people will ever read this note,* he thought—*certainly not all my family, friends, and coworkers.* The police could hardly be expected to communicate what they would find. *A pity,* he thought, *because the more people who see the note, the better.*

The man began to smile, delighted with the brilliant idea that had popped into his head. *Why not send everyone an electronic-mail copy of the suicide note? Why not make the letter public right from the start?* It was so simple. He could format the note as an E-mail message. Then, with a few mouse clicks, he could direct the E-mail program to broadcast the message to the immediate world at an appropriate time, say 2:00 A.M.—long after the carbon monoxide had finished its job.

A suicide note "spam." That will keep people at Campbell & McQueen talking for weeks.

The man chuckled as he opened the E-mail program:

SUBJECT: My Final Decision

Dear Family, Friends, and Coworkers: By the time you read this message, I will be dead.

The *very* few of you who actually care about me know how much I hate the stress at Campbell & McQueen Precision Components. Well, I put up with it for seven solid weeks, but today the pain became impossible to bear— along with most of the people at C&M. So I have arranged a *permanent* resignation from my job and from my stupid life.

To Anne Goodwin, my wonderful mother, all I can say is, sorry, Mom! I think we both knew that this might happen some day.

To Karen Constantine, my dear fiancée, I hope you will move beyond me without too much bitterness. I never wanted to hurt you.

To my handful of friends at C&M, remember me kindly—if you can!

Barry Goodwin

The man at the computer still wasn't satisfied. Something was missing. He reread the message twice before he spotted its weakness: The tone seemed too mellow. The note needed a hefty dose of anger to balance the calmness, maybe even a squirt of petty hatred.

Who is worthy of loathing? Who deserves to be skewered by a man about to commit suicide?

He rocked back in his chair and closed his eyes. The ideal target would be someone connected to Campbell & McQueen—someone whose name everyone would recognize—someone who made a credible enemy. Someone like . . . *Pippa Hunnechurch.*

Another brilliant idea! Pippa Hunnechurch was an outsider. A perfect person to hate. A perfect person to blame for an unexpected suicide.

The man continued typing:

P.S. If you want to blame someone for what I've done, blame Pippa Hunnechurch. It's her fault that I ended up in a job that was all wrong for me. She knew that I don't handle stress well, but she kept pushing me to join C&M. Pippa Hunnechurch messed up my life!

"Should I add another exclamation point?" the man murmured. "No. It's just right."

The one remaining chore was to create the list of recipients on the To: line. He began by typing everyone@campbellmcqueen.com, a blanket E-mail address that would automatically send a copy of the message to every C&M employee. Next, he opened the E-mail program's "Contacts" file and found addresses for Anne Goodwin and Karen Constantine. He copied them to the To: line.

Pippa Hunnechurch should get a copy too.

The man appended pippa@pippahunnechurch.com to the end of the list of addresses and checked his wristwatch again. *11:51.* He configured the E-mail program to broadcast the message in 129 minutes.

Well done, he told himself, and then he began to laugh.

Oh, to be a fly on the wall when folks access their E-mails tomorrow morning.

Chapter One

I HAVE DINED AT MAISON PIERRE, the most expensive restaurant in Ryde, Maryland, a total of three times since I launched Philippa Hunnechurch & Associates, Executive Recruiters.

The first occasion was a Sunday brunch to congratulate myself for having the nerve to start my own business.

The second was a welcome-aboard dinner for Gloria Spitz, my one and only "associate."

The third—an expense-account lunch—turned out to be the last meal I shared with Barry Goodwin, a week before my first techie recruit went over the edge and killed himself.

It was a Monday in early December, and Maison Pierre was stylishly decked out with European Christmas wreathes and handmade angel candles. I spotted Barry sitting at a quiet corner table the moment I entered the chic dining room. His shock of carrot-red hair stuck out among the soft pastel colors of southern French decor like a bouquet in a bathtub. I waved at him, he nodded, and the beaming restaurateur,

Pierre Renauld himself, led me to my chair with practiced Gallic court-
liness, complete with a discreet kiss on my hand.

"Thanks for coming," Barry said as I sat down. "I apologize for not
giving you more notice."

"No apologies are necessary. I'm always delighted to break bread
with one of my recruiting success stories."

He let out a soft groan and turned his attention to his menu, a tall,
foil-covered extravaganza embossed with an enormous *fleur-de-lis*. I
studied the reflections of our angel candle on the gold foil and wondered, *What on earth has happened?*

I waited patiently while a hovering busboy filled my glass with mineral water, stocked my side plate with enticing miniature baguettes, and
positioned a dish of butter swirls in easy reach. When he left, I said in
my most caring voice, "Tell me Barry—how have you been?"

His answer was a muffled "Not that good!" projected through the menu.

Barry sounded even more melancholic than when he had telephoned me early that morning and commanded, without any preliminary greeting, "Meet me at Maison Pierre today for lunch. I need to talk
to you about my job as soon as possible. It's *really* important."

Both the unexpected directive and Barry's apparent urgency took
me by surprise. When I pressed for an explanation, all he would say
was, "I can't discuss it over the phone. I want to see you in person."

"And so you shall," I replied cheerfully, trying to ignore the alarm
bells that clanged from ear to ear. We agreed to meet at noon. I rang off
with an anxious feeling that stuck with me the rest of the morning.

Barry's odd behavior in person did nothing to allay my concerns.
Hiding behind a menu was certainly not the sort of performance I ex-
pected from the spanking new director of corporate communications at
Campbell & McQueen Precision Components, Incorporated.

Campbell & McQueen is hardly a household name, but the company is quite well-known to those who build aircraft, design space
satellites, and perform open-heart surgery. C&M began as a specialist

manufacturer of high-precision parts molded of engineering plastics and then used its molding skills to develop a line of medical prostheses—most notably replacement heart valves. C&M employed about eight hundred people and was headquartered in an upscale industrial park in the southwest corner of Ryde, not far from Route 50-301.

C&M had become Hunnechurch & Associates's newest client the previous summer. Sidney Monk, the company's vice president of human resources, asked us to recruit—I quote from his assignment letter—"an energetic public relations person with a solid technical background in plastics. We want a corporate communicator who truly appreciates the technology of making precision molded parts."

Gloria had bubbled with excitement. "If we can hit a home run on this one, we'll get a dozen more juicy assignments. I have great vibes about Campbell & McQueen, Pippa."

My friends call me Pippa because my full name seems to go on forever: Philippa Elizabeth Katherine Hunnechurch. I am a Brit by birth, a resident of Ryde by choice, thirty-seven by the inexorable march of time, and a "headhunter" by occupation.

A *good* headhunter.

I landed Barry Goodwin in only seven weeks—a feather in my cap because this was my first try at recruiting a techie. During my three previous years as a headhunter, I had searched for accountants, sales managers, mid-level executives, and the occasional attorney—but never a technologist. Barry broke the pattern. He held both a bachelor's and a master's degree in materials science and had worked as a plastics engineer. He loved plastics with the ardor of a teenage groupie and had written a flock of technical magazine articles about molding technology. Furthermore, Barry had recently earned a second master's degree in business administration with an emphasis in marketing and public relations, which made him a perfect candidate for C&M.

Sidney Monk swooned when I presented Barry. He was interviewed by C&M's senior executives and hired in less than a week, near record time for the company. He had now been on C&M's payroll for forty-six days, and according to the glowing report Sidney had given me scarcely a week earlier, was "fitting in like a hand inside a rubber glove."

So why the long face?

Barry was still holding his menu high when the waiter arrived to take our orders.

"I can't decide what I want," he said.

"In that event," I said, "have the specialty of the house. Coquille Chesapeake is similar to Coquille St. Jacques, but it's made with lump crabmeat instead of scallops. *Everyone* loves it."

Barry clapped the menu shut. "Sure. Why not?"

The waiter shot Barry a twisted smile before he walked away. I imagined him mumbling, *sacré bleu!* at the outrage of a patron treating Pierre's *specialité* with such indifference.

At that moment Barry Goodwin, who was thirty-five years old, made me think of a petulant child—the kind of kid who would stomp his feet then lock himself in the bathroom. It was a side of Barry I had not seen before, one that raised my hackles.

"You are plainly upset about something," I said as I prepared to sample a baguette. "I assume you asked me here to explain the problem."

He didn't hesitate for an instant. "To be honest, Pippa, I can't stomach C&M's business practices. I intend to quit."

Quit?

The *Q* word hit me with the force of a well-thrown punch. I coughed the morsel of baguette I had just bitten halfway across the table, then spent the next thirty seconds sipping water and clearing my throat.

"Are you *OK?*" Barry asked in a voice that sounded more amused than concerned.

"Fully OK," I said, although both my mind and heart were racing.

Let me explain the shock to my system. My headhunting contract is a fairly traditional affair. A clause on the second page explains that we will send an invoice for our services when the recruit joins the company but that the client need not pay the bill until the new employee has completed sixty days of work. This reasonable "no-risk guarantee" protects my client should a candidate be fired for cause or unexpectedly leave the company.

I had never experienced a situation where the clause might be invoked, but it seemed to be happening now. Hunnechurch & Associates's "home run" was in danger of becoming a strikeout. If so, we would lose a fat fee—and blot our reputation inside Campbell & McQueen.

I had regained most of my composure when I asked, "Can you be more specific, Barry? What kinds of business practices have upset you?"

He stared at his bread and butter plate. After what seemed an eternity, he shook his head. "I can't tell you the details, without . . . well, without hurting people who have enough to worry about right now. What I can say is that C&M does things that are both illegal and immoral."

I chose my words carefully. "That comes as an enormous surprise to me. After all, C&M is one of the most respected companies in its field."

"How do you think I feel?" Barry spoke loud enough to make several heads turn in the dining room. He realized his gaffe and cranked his voice down to a loud whisper. "I planned to spend the rest of my career at C&M. I never would have accepted the offer if I had known the company played fast and loose with critical quality specifications."

"I still don't grasp what C&M has done wrong."

"Good! I told you more than I meant to."

"Have you spoken to anyone at the company about your . . . concerns."

"Like who?"

"Why not Sidney Monk? He strikes me as a pillar of integrity."

"Sidney doesn't know anything about plastics. He's like you. He'll never understand what I'm talking about."

I ignored the slight. "But you report to Hilda McQueen. She's the president and chief operating officer—and a Ph.D. chemist. I'm confident that she would want to be warned about shoddy business practices going on in her company."

Barry glared at me. "You just don't get it, do you? Hilda already knows what's happening. I'm pretty sure that she's responsible."

"I see," I said, not sure what else to say.

"No! You don't see! If Hilda is a crook, it stands to reason that Richard Campbell, our esteemed chairman and chief executive officer, is also involved. The whole executive suite has to be corrupt."

"Blimey!"

"Yeah. Blimey."

I placed my hand on top of his. "Don't take this the wrong way, but is there any chance that you are mistaken?"

He snatched his hand away and slapped the table with his palm, making our cutlery rattle. "Do you think I'm stupid? Do you think I'm blind? C&M is cheating its . . ." Barry reached for the right word, "customers big-time."

My brain struggled to wrap itself around his accusations. Could someone who worked at C&M for so short a time have discovered such serious wrongdoing? It didn't seem possible, but what else could explain his vehemence and determination?

I remembered another name. "Is Jerry Nichols part of this . . . *conspiracy?*"

Jerry was Campbell & McQueen's master molder. I had spent several days with him at the start of my search to learn some of the vocabulary of plastics technology. I had promptly forgotten most of the arcane words he defined for me.

Barry reacted with an angry toss of his head. "No. Jerry isn't involved, but he has stuck his head in the sand. He refuses to acknowledge that a problem could exist."

I took his hand again; he didn't object. "When do you intend to submit your resignation?"

"I don't know—probably not for another month or two."

I'm sure I gawked at Barry. "Let me get this straight. You have witnessed unethical behavior at C&M that reaches to the boardroom and has caused you profound distress, yet you plan to work on for another month or two. Why?"

He looked me straight in the eye. "I'm *not* leaving C&M until I have solid evidence of what's going on—enough to get the problem fixed, maybe even enough to send people to jail. That means I have to keep doing a bang-up job as director of corporate communications." He had begun to sound like the chipper technical whiz I had interviewed four months earlier. "Next week I'll throw the best darn news conference Ryde has seen this year. C&M is going to announce an expanded line of heart valves. I'll send you an invitation."

"Please do." Now it was my turn to stare at a bread-and-butter plate. Barry obviously felt better after sharing his lurid accusations with me, but I was bewildered by his finger pointing, his mood swing, and his intended course of action.

Is my first techie a nutter?

The waiter delivered two giant ramekins piled high with Coquille Chesapeake. Barry dug in and seemed to enjoy every mouthful, while I had all but lost my appetite. I poked at my food and ate what I could, but our bizarre conversation kept getting in the way. I finally asked the waiter for a doggy bag to pack up more than half of my lunch. He provided one, along with a disapproving glower.

When I reached for the check, Barry said, "This is C&M's treat." He tucked his American Express card into the folder and pushed it toward the edge of the table.

A few minutes later we stepped into the cool December air on High Street.

"Thanks for the lunch, Barry," I said.

"Don't thank me, Pippa. We've just enjoyed some of C&M's ill-gotten gains."

I watched him walk away past several holiday shoppers, his red hair as bright in the sunlight as the holiday packages people carried.

Chapter Two

I WALKED NORTH ON RYDE HIGH STREET, swinging my doggy bag, trying to fathom what a company that makes fancy plastic parts can do that is both "illegal and immoral." When I ran out of ideas, I began to think about how best to respond to the dilemma that Barry Goodwin had created for Pippa Hunnechurch & Associates. Campbell & McQueen would pay our full recruiting fee in a few weeks, believing that Barry had signed on as a long-term employee, but I knew that he planned to resign in "another month or two."

It's a simple question, Hunnechurch. Are you going to cash the check when it arrives?

According to our contract, our obligations and no-risk guarantee expired at the end of Barry's sixtieth day on the job. From that point forward, he became C&M's bother—no matter what his actions.

Except you know what the blighter intends to do.

My knowledge had created a large stumbling block in my conscience. To begin with, we Hunnechurches have a well-developed British sense of fair play. Moreover, my inborn reluctance to cheat had recently been bolstered by a refresher course in Christian morality at the Ryde Fellowship Church.

Blast you, Barry! Why did you have to tell me you intend to quit? Or that C&M might be a less-than-honest enterprise?

That was a second ethical issue for me to ponder. If C&M was really the sort of company that played fast and loose, how could I take on any other assignments? It would be unprincipled to knowingly place other recruits into Barry Goodwin's situation.

I enjoyed a bracing hike while I grappled with my problems. My office was a mile away from Maison Pierre, on the northernmost end of Ryde High Street, in a restored, five-story, eighteenth-century leather warehouse. A developer had gutted the historic redbrick building and filled it with two- and three-room office suites, that now housed a dozen dentists of varied specialties, a smattering of CPAs and lawyers, several management consultants, four graphic designers, three public relations agencies, two real estate appraisers, and one headhunting firm—mine.

I had decided to hoof it to lunch that day chiefly because parking is tight on Ryde High Street during the Christmas shopping season. However, the shining sun, the blue sky, and the crisp air on the walk back turned out to be more important rewards. I felt so frisky after my twenty-block walk that I forsook the elevator and strode up the three flights of stairs to reach my office.

Thus energized, my mind should have automatically answered the simple question that poked at my scruples, but when I pushed open my office door, I still had no idea how to react to Barry's announcement.

Gloria was talking on the phone when I entered the office. She jammed the receiver back onto the cradle as soon as she saw me.

"Did you hang up on someone?" I said.

"A friend from church who can wait until later," she replied. "I'm dying to hear what happened during your lunch with Barry."

Gloria is twenty-four years old, has blonde hair and slate blue eyes, and judging from the number of heads she turns, is widely recognized as a knockout by the men in our building. She also has a brilliant smile, which she cranked up to full power as she asked, "So, what did Barry have to say?"

"Not much, actually. We talked about his job. He seems to be feeling the odd concern." I didn't want to share my conundrum with Gloria until I devised a solution. I tried to change the subject. "Did anyone call me while I was out?"

"Nope. It's been dead quiet." She waited until I hung my topcoat in the reception room closet, then changed the subject back. "What kind of concerns did Barry bring up?"

It was the intensity of her voice that ignited my suspicions. "Wait a blooming minute," I said. "Why are you so interested in Barry Goodwin?"

"Professional curiosity." Her glance flicked away from me. "I wondered how he was doing, that's all."

"Right!" I moved to her desk. "You are curious merely because Barry is our client and you are my associate headhunter?"

"Yep."

"No other reason?"

Now it was Gloria's turn to become evasive. "What's in the bag? I know it's food."

"Coquille Chesapeake."

"Yummy!"

I held it behind my back. "You can have it—if you tell me why you are interested in Barry Goodwin."

"Well, the truth is, I like him."

"Like him, as in girlfriend likes boyfriend?"

"No silly—I find Barry to be an amiable and honorable person. In short, a nice guy."

I peered at her. "How is that possible? If memory serves, you met him once for about thirty seconds. I did most of the interviewing while you were off shooting machine guns and missiles—or whatever you do at Maryland Army National Guard summer camp."

Few people realize it when they first encounter Gloria, but she is an authentic weekend warrior, a technical sergeant who takes great pride in her military service. Fewer still would guess that Gloria is licensed to carry a firearm in Maryland and that she occasionally moonlights as a bodyguard for Collier Investigations, a private detective agency in Baltimore. She has shepherded several movie stars when they have made films in and around Baltimore.

Instead of answering my question, Gloria delved into a drawer and pulled out a colorful catalog. "We have more important things to talk about than Barry Goodwin," she said with a sniff. "I was productively engaged while you were lunching in posh surroundings."

I quickly decoded the upside-down lettering: *Soderberg Office Furniture.*

"You landed a new client?"

"Nope. I chose new furniture for this room. We have made do with bits and pieces from your old office long enough."

"I disagree. A young company must be frugal."

"Frugality is great, but my desk and credenza are close to being disreputable."

I stood back and began to peruse Gloria's credenza. The finish had seen better days, and the top showed more scratches than shine. My eyes stopped moving when they reached a teapot wrapped with a cozy.

"Is there tea in that teapot?" I asked.

"Your favorite Darjeeling blend. Brewed less than half an hour ago."

"Bless you!" I poured myself a cuppa in one of the C&M mugs we'd been given by Sidney Monk. "I take it you have a specific new desk in mind."

Gloria opened the catalog and tapped a photograph. "This one!"

Her finger rested on a medium sized desk with a dark cherry finish, five drawers, and a scratch-resistant top—sold as a set with a matching credenza. I winced when I read the price.

"You are much too good-looking to hide betwixt eleven hundred dollars worth of cherry veneer."

"Thank you, but my workstation is the first thing our candidates see when they enter the office. We have to make a good impression. We do, after all, represent our clients."

I had to admit that Gloria's present desk was as battered as her credenza. "You may have a point, but the idea of spending more than a thousand dollars on furniture leaves me breathless."

"May I remind you that Hunnechurch & Associates has become the leading executive recruiter in Ryde? We are working on two active searches. . . . We have been promised a juicy assignment from Liberty Construction, . . . and we have billed Campbell & McQueen a princely sum. The check should arrive in a week."

Unless I withdraw my bill. I had to make a decision before C&M sent the check.

I must have frowned because Gloria asked, "Are you OK? You look annoyed."

"In truth, I am a bit annoyed—at Barry Goodwin."

She abruptly became solemn. "Why are you mad at Barry?"

"I have been holding out on you, for which I apologize. Barry dropped a bombshell at lunch. He is unhappy at C&M and plans to resign sometime in the future."

"What do you mean *sometime in the future?*" Gloria knocked over her own mug of tea.

We attacked the spill on Gloria's less-than-pristine desktop from two sides with paper towels. As we mopped up the last of the Darjeeling, she smiled guiltily at me. "I've been holding out on you too," she said. "That was Barry on the phone when you came in."

"Ah."

"I know about his moral crisis. As it happens, I urged him to tell you."

"Why didn't you warn me that Barry was unhappy at C&M?"

"I couldn't. He talked about himself in a confidential setting."

"You sound as balmy as Barry. Start explaining! From the beginning!"

Gloria shook her head. "I can't tell you everything."

"Then tell me what you can." I sat down on the well-padded Victorian sofa opposite Gloria's desk and sipped my tea.

"When Barry moved to Ryde, he joined Ryde Fellowship Church."

"Really? Then why haven't I ever seen him in church?"

"He goes to the eight-fifteen service. You go later."

"Quite right!" There seemed no point in arguing that eleven o'clock is—and shall always be—the proper starting time for church on Sunday. Gloria and I had frequently debated the point since I became a member of Ryde Fellowship. "Continue, please."

"Well, Barry joined my Wednesday evening small group. A couple of Wednesdays ago, he shared a personal concern with the group."

"And?"

"That's all I can say. Barry asked that the discussion stay within our small group. Everything we share is confidential."

"Heavens, Gloria. You're not a priest."

"True, but I'm a Christian who made a promise I don't intend to break. However, I knew you would want to know, and that's why I suggested that he bring the matter to your attention."

"And so he did. He claims to have uncovered slapdash, possibly criminal business practices at Campbell & McQueen."

I studied Gloria and saw no reaction on her face.

I went on. "He believes that senior management is responsible."

Still no reaction.

I kept talking. "Barry refused to tell me the particulars of what he found."

Gloria's eyebrows twitched. I know that twitch.

"Blimey!" I said. "He wouldn't tell you either."

"No. He told us that he had to keep the details secret—at least for now."

"I can deduce the rest. Barry asked for the group's counsel. He wanted to know if should he resign from C&M."

Gloria shrugged.

"I infer from your shrug," I said, "that the group advised him to resign immediately."

Gloria sighed. "Does he really plan to hang on?"

"For at least a month or two."

"That puts us on the spot, doesn't it?" she said. "Can we take C&M's money?"

"That's the very question I have been wrestling with since noon."

Gloria's telephone rang. She looked at me. "We might as well take the call," I said. "I'm ready to think about something other than quandaries of principle."

"Philippa Hunnechurch & Associates," she announced calmly. "This is Gloria Spitz."

Her face lit up. She blushed, she giggled, and then she put her hand over the mouthpiece.

"It's James," she crooned.

I flew into my office and snatched up the receiver.

"What did you say to my nubile associate, Mr. Huston?"

"A gentleman—most especially a southern gentleman—never repeats words of affection spoken in private to a lady." James Huston's mellifluous drawl poured into my ear like melted butter. "However, it is common knowledge that your associate is one of the two most alluring headhunters in this here United States. Need I identify the other?"

"You sir, are incorrigible."

"I ma'am, am coming to Maryland."

"When?"

"In two weeks."

My heart leapt. *Two weeks that would pass much too slowly.*

I had met James a year ago. We became fast friends, despite the fact that he lived more than six hundred and fifty miles away, in Atlanta, Georgia.

"Another seminar?" I asked.

James was an international marketing consultant who complemented his consulting practice by teaching business people the secrets of selling overseas. His seminars attracted overflow audiences in Atlanta; now he was bringing them north.

"Three," he said. "One in Washington, D.C., one in Baltimore, and the third in Ryde—at the Waterside Hotel, which is scarcely two miles from your abode."

"Wonderful!"

"I scheduled my last seminar on the afternoon of Thursday, December twentieth, and I don't have to be back in Atlanta 'til after the New Year, so . . ."

"We can spend the holidays together!"

"And most evenings too. Assuming, of course, that your prior commitments permit."

"I will make them permit," I said, blithely unaware that the tumult of the following week would capsize every priority in my life. I opened my desk calendar and began to X out *Friday, December 21,* and the days that followed. I stopped scribbling when the penny dropped.

"Friday, December twenty-first, is your birthday!" I squealed.

"Yeah, but it's no big deal. As I told you . . ."

"I *know* what you told me, James," I cut in. "Because your birthday is so close to Christmas, your parents gave you one set of presents each year and you rarely had a separate birthday party. However . . ."

"However *what?*" he cut in.

"However, I am not your mother or father. In light of your attainment of another milestone, you will have a proper celebration this year."

"Don't remind me!" James bellowed.

"There is nothing wrong with being forty-three years old."

"Oh, yeah? Let's see how much you like it when the time comes and you are no longer the international stunner you are today."

"My thanks, gallant sir, for noticing."

"I will do more than merely notice. I shall react."

James sounded a loud wolf whistle, and I began to laugh. I see myself as more pretty than stunning. I have prominent cheekbones, a longish nose, blue eyes that sometimes seem gray, and a classic peaches-and-cream complexion—all in all, a typical English face. My hair is naturally dishwater blonde; I keep it mid-length and simply styled.

Our mirth expelled all thoughts of Barry Goodwin from my mind, but then James asked innocently, "How's business?"

I didn't mean to let out as big a sigh as I did.

"Oh, oh!" James said. "Is this a predicament you can discuss with me?"

I thought for a moment. "Certainly. Perhaps you can suggest a way out."

I sketched the situation for James, without identifying C&M or Barry by name. "And so you see," I finished up, "we're in an ethical pickle."

"Not really."

"Pardon?"

"Two months from now is a long time. You really don't know what will happen. Your recruit may change his mind, get fired for cause, even get hit by a truck. Your so-called ethical dilemma is based on speculation and conjecture—not fact."

"I suppose so, but Gloria and I have our consciences to deal with."

"No problem. *If* your man should quit next year, offer to find a replacement at a reduced fee. Your client will be delighted, and your consciences will be clear."

"There's still the matter of the shaky business practices."

"*Alleged* shaky business practices. You haven't seen any evidence of the company's wrongdoing. It seems to me that your client, a well-regarded company, is more worthy of trust than your candidate—at least until he produces the so-called proof he intends to gather."

I started chuckling.

"What's so funny?" James asked.

"Me! I feel like a dodo. Your strategy is brilliant. Have you ever thought of becoming a business consultant?"

"On that ridiculous note, it's time for me to get back to work."

I put down the phone feeling at peace with the world. James had sliced through the Gordian knot with one elegant stroke. We would collect our fee for the work we did, then offer C&M a discount should Barry actually follow through on his threat to resign.

Gloria poked her head around the doorframe.

"Delicious!" she said, waving the empty container that had held my Coquille Chesapeake.

"Oh my. I'm suddenly starving. I didn't eat much at Maison Pierre."

"Want me to send for a sandwich from the coffee shop on the corner?"

"I'll do it. You order the desk and credenza."

"Really?" She beamed at me.

"Really."

"While I'm at it, let's replace the decrepit sofa I look at eight hours a day."

"Over my dead body. My venerable Victorian sofa—with its soft and soothing padding—is like an old friend. Where is your loyalty? Where is your sense of tradition?"

Gloria smiled. "It was worth a try. You're usually a pushover after chatting with James."

She breezed out of my office before I could devise a suitable reply. I leaned back in my chair and watched as the line-in-use light on my telephone blinked on. I wondered when our new furniture would arrive. I also wondered why my feeling of unease had returned.

Chapter Three

A FAXED INVITATION to attend Campbell & McQueen's news conference was the next-to-last communication I received from Barry Goodwin. He had scribbled on the cover note, "This should be a fun hour—artificial heart valves are more interesting than you probably think!"

His sales pitch was unnecessary. I try to attend my clients' media events whenever I'm invited because it's good sense to grab every opportunity to wave the Hunnechurch & Associates flag in front of senior executives. This news conference had the added attraction of seeing Barry in action and having another face-to-face meeting with him. Six days had passed since our luncheon, and I was fully caught up in James's hopeful notion that Barry might rethink his conclusions about C&M's business practices.

I would soon know differently.

The news conference was scheduled to begin at nine o'clock on Monday morning. At eight thirty-five, I parked my red Miata roadster in the underground parking lot beneath the Waterside Hotel at One Ryde High Street. In keeping with its seventeenth-century roots, Ryde's chief thoroughfare is a meandering boulevard that resembles a large *C* when seen from above. Its foot runs east to west, its midsection south to north, and its top west to east. The Waterside—an eight-story glass-walled tower—sits at the very toe of the foot, next to the Magothy River, on land that once held the Customs House and the terminal for a ferry that in the nineteenth century linked the north and south shores of the river.

The "Today's Events" sign in the lobby confirmed that the "Campbell & McQueen Meeting" would take place in the Magothy Lounge—the hotel's rooftop restaurant that overlooks the river.

A burst of sunshine greeted me when the elevator doors swooshed open on the eighth floor. It was certainly a nice morning to look down at Ryde Old Port and the Magothy River. The muddy blue of the water mirrored the diluted blue of the December sky and set off the browns (and occasional greens) of the land. I spent a few moments ogling the fancy houses on Gibson Island across the river and the pricey yachts secure in their cradles onshore at the Ryde Marina.

An administrative assistant who worked with Barry Goodwin was on duty behind a registration table. "Hi, Nancy," I said. "How many reporters are inside?"

"A dozen so far, Pippa," she replied. "Media people show up early if you feed them, and Barry arranged for a fabulous continental breakfast buffet." She stood up and pressed a nametag on the right lapel of my blue wool jacket. "Grab some food before it's gone."

One end of the Magothy Lounge had been rearranged to create a kind of theatre, with several rows of chairs facing a raised platform made of portable scaffolding. A long banner over the improvised stage shouted, *Campbell & McQueen—A World Leader in Precision Plastics and Medical Prostheses.*

The promised breakfast buffet filled a long table on the other side of the room. It was loaded with croissants, bagels, donuts, pastries, miniature quiches, and many kinds of fruits, but all I wanted was a fresh cuppa. I drowned a tea bag in steaming water, added a splash of milk, and wondered for the umpteenth time why restaurants in America serve brewed coffee but not brewed tea.

Thus engaged in musing, I didn't see David Friendly come up behind me until I caught his reflection in the well-polished hot water urn.

"Something is seriously wrong!" he said with mock alarm. "Headhunters *never* start work before 10:00 A.M."

"True on many mornings, but like you, I couldn't resist a free breakfast." I tipped my head toward the plateful of goodies precariously balanced in David's hands along with a large glass of orange juice and a mug of coffee. "You still have room for a slice of quiche if you perch it carefully between the bagel, the croissant, and the raspberry danish."

"That sounds like jealousy talking," David said. "I can't help it if my metabolism is faster than yours."

"It's terribly unfair that you and Gloria are lean, mean, calorie-burning machines, while I—"

"While you, what?"

"Never mind." I stood up straight to my full five-foot-eight-inch height and sucked in my stomach. "Let's find somewhere to sit."

David Friendly—the business reporter for our local newspaper, the *Ryde Reporter*—had become one of my best pals on this side of the pond. He jokingly labeled himself "the media midwife who slapped the newly born bottom of Hunnechurch & Associates," because the story he wrote a week after I opened my doors helped attract my first three corporate clients. David tends to use medical metaphors, possibly because Joyce, his wife, is a nurse.

I call David a pal rather than a friend to emphasize that we never were—nor will be—anything more than great buddies. As David (who adores Joyce) puts it, "We love each other, but we don't *love* each other."

Several small tables were set up in an alcove beyond the breakfast buffet. We chose the most secluded and sat down.

"I'm the bearer of an invitation," he said. "Joyce and I want you to have Christmas dinner with us."

"Oh my! I haven't even thought about Christmas day."

"We figured as much."

I paused to find the best way to explain that James was coming to town for the holidays. David misread my hesitation.

"We *really* want you to come," he said. "You won't be *any* trouble. The truth is, Joyce and I have a special mission this year. Our goal is to de-Scrooge one overworked, high-powered executive. We've chosen you to receive a triple helping of Christmas spirit along with a heaping plate of Joyce's famous fried turkey."

"How would you feel about de-Scrooging *two* high-powered executives?"

David blinked. "Boy, do I feel dumb. Of course James Huston is invited! We'll have a Christmas to remember. In fact, both of you can also spend Christmas Eve at our house. We'll do carols and evening service and tree-trimming and eggnog—the whole works."

"Slow down, Mr. Friendly. I will convey your kind invitation to James, and we will think on it."

"Think all you want, but keep this in mind—if you don't come, Joyce will kill me. She has access to sharp instruments and powerful medications."

"Speaking of medical things," I said, "What did you think of the media kit that Barry Goodwin put together for this conference?"

"It's the best I've ever seen out of C&M. Barry certainly knows his plastics technology."

"By any chance, have you dealt with him directly?"

"Sure. I called him when I included C&M in an overview of Ryde companies and again when I heard a rumor that C&M would soon be acquired by a larger company." David took a bite of bagel, then said, "Have you heard the rumors that C&M is about to be acquired by another company?"

"Nary a word, but I dearly hope that your tittle-tattle is wrong. I am working to develop C&M as a long-term client. A new corporate parent would mean new people in high places. I would have to start marketing the company all over again."

I reached over to David's plate and broke off a chunk of croissant.

"Help yourself," he said with a smirk.

I ignored the jibe. "About Barry . . . how would you rate his performance as a director of corporate communications?"

"Professional and responsive." David peered at me over his coffee cup. "Now you've got me curious. Why all the questions about a candidate who has been hired? Is there something about Barry you haven't told me?"

"Off the record?"

"Sure. Friend to friend."

"I have my suspicions that he is unhappy at C&M."

"What could possibly make him unhappy? He has a plum job at a successful company that is soon to be part of a much larger corporation." David shrugged. "I'm afraid those rumors about C&M being acquired are pretty solid."

"Rats!" I made a mental note to revise our marketing strategy. "In any event, Barry claims not to like C&M's business practices, although he refused to tell me the specifics of what is bothering him."

David stared thoughtfully at his danish for a moment, then shook his head. "That makes no sense to me. C&M is a squeaky clean company—always has been. In fact—"

An amplified voice interrupted David. "Good morning, ladies and gentlemen. Will everyone please find a seat? We plan to begin in exactly five minutes."

We both looked toward the temporary stage. Barry Goodwin was standing at the podium, holding a microphone.

"That's my cue," David said. "See you later."

The reporters, including David, took seats toward the front. I maneuvered around two TV camera operators who were setting up tripods and made for the last row of chairs where two C&M people I knew were sitting.

"Hi, Pippa!" said Sidney Monk, C&M's vice president of human resources. He extended his hand and tried to smile, but his mouth refused to cooperate. Sidney's small eyes, sharp nose, and thin lips gave him a perpetual sour grapes expression—in complete contrast to his everyday personality. Sidney was one of the most jovial VPs I knew.

"You certainly look spiffy," I said. Like many high-tech companies in Maryland, C&M had adopted a casual dress code. Sidney wore slacks and a sweater most days. Today he sported a dark gray suit, striped blue shirt, and red tie.

"A man with no hair left has to wear power clothing," said a voice further down the row.

The speaker was Jerry Nichols, C&M's master molder, who looked like a distinguished yachtsman in his blue blazer and white turtleneck. Jerry's full head of salt-and-pepper hair was closely cropped, which suited his square, craggy face.

"Sit between us," Sidney said, "before I am forced to kill the company's most valuable employee with my bare hands."

"How long have you two worked together?" I asked, although I knew the answer.

Their replies were nearly simultaneous.

"I knew him before the resin fumes rotted his brain," Sidney said.

"I can remember when he had hair," Jerry said.

Sidney and Jerry are, of course, great friends. C&M legend has it that Jerry was the first person Sidney hired when he was appointed to the junior post of assistant human resources manager some twenty-five years earlier.

Sidney touched my arm. "This is Barry Goodwin's first real news conference. You must feel like a mother watching her child at a piano recital."

This good-intentioned bit of small talk made me shudder. I turned my head away, hoping Sidney wouldn't notice. I willed myself not to cry. But for a silly accident, I might have attended a piano recital that very day in England. If Peggy were still alive, she would be eleven—a fine age for one's public debut.

Stop it Pippa! Not here! Not now!

Sidney touched my arm again. "Actually, there's Barry's real mother, sitting next to Diane Dupont."

I took a deep breath to calm myself and quickly identified Anne Goodwin, a woman of about sixty, whose hair was only slightly less coppery than Barry's. She was conversing with Diane Dupont, Sidney's deputy, although Anne seemed to be doing most of the talking. Diane, who holds the title of manager of human resources, sat as still as a rock, staring straight ahead, her shoulders stiff and unyielding. I couldn't see her face, but it was clear that she wasn't enjoying the chat.

At nine on the dot, Barry tapped his microphone to signal the audience and waited patiently for the room to fall silent.

"Good morning," he said. "My name is Barry Goodwin. On behalf of everyone at Campbell & McQueen, I thank you for coming this morning. We promise you a fascinating hour."

Barry looked and sounded remarkably at ease—not at all like a man who didn't like the company he worked for.

"C&M was founded more than twenty-five years ago to manufacture precision parts made of high-performance engineering plastics. Ten years ago we began to manufacture replacement body parts. Today we are pleased to announce the opening of a brand new production facility to manufacture our CM-7 molded artificial heart valve. As many of you know, the CM-7 recently completed its clinical trials and received Food and Drug Administration approval. The best way to introduce our latest product is to show it to you in actual use."

Barry clapped his hands like a magician, and three things happened: A motorized movie screen descended from the ceiling above the stage; waiters pulled dark draperies across the Magothy Room's massive windows; and someone turned off the overhead lights.

An electronic projector filled the screen with images of an operating table and overhead lights. A male narrator intoned, "We are guests in the operating theater at Ryde General Hospital."

The scene switched to a close-up of a circular thingamabob—not much larger than a quarter—held between two fingers wearing latex gloves. "This is the CM-7 molded aortic heart valve manufactured by Campbell & McQueen. A surgeon is about to implant this device into the heart of a thirty-four-year-old man whose own aortic valve was damaged by a weight-loss medication that proved to have unfortunate side effects. In medical terminology, the patient's aortic valve became incompetent."

The image changed again, this time to a cartoon animation of a human heart. "Because the incompetent valve leading to the aorta does not close completely during each heartbeat, there is a backflow of blood into the heart. Consequently, the patient's heart is unable to pump the required amount of blood through his body when he is active. Merely walking across a room causes him to experience shortness of breath, dizziness, chest pain, pounding heartbeat, and severe fatigue."

The cartoon faded, and we were looking inside the patient's rib cage at the actual open-heart surgical procedure. The narrator continued, "The surgical team has stilled the patient's heart so that the diseased valve can be replaced. The man is being kept alive by a heart-lung machine that is circulating oxygenated blood through his body."

"Oh boy!" Sidney whispered to me. "We served these reporters a huge breakfast. I hope they have strong stomachs."

The final scene was a shot of the patient walking smartly along Ryde High Street, waving at the camera, a happy grin on his healthy face. The narrator added, "This patient has returned to the vigorous lifestyle he enjoyed before his heart valve was damaged. The prognosis is excellent for a long, full life."

The lights in the room flashed on, and the screen whirred back into the ceiling. Barry moved back to the podium. "It is now my pleasure to introduce two world leaders in advanced plastics technology who will tell you more about the CM-7 heart valve and then answer any questions you have. Richard Campbell is our chairman. Dr. Hilda McQueen is our president."

I don't know if anyone else noticed, but to my ears Barry sounded much less enthusiastic as he spoke the names of the two executives. He had used the right words to introduce Richard and Hilda, but his spirit seemed elsewhere. He didn't wait for them to reach the podium as a good master of ceremonies should but simply stepped off the side of the raised platform and took a seat in the front row.

I had met with Hilda McQueen several times to discuss her specific requirements for a director of corporate communications and get her reactions to different candidates, but I had talked to Richard Campbell only once. Hilda was in her late fifties, medium height, with well-coiffed brunette hair, and got up in an elegant green silk dress that clung to her trim figure. Richard was older—mid sixties, I knew from his corporate biography—tall, heavyset, with thick silver hair, wearing an obviously custom-tailored suit that must have cost thousands. There was a smattering of applause as they climbed the two steps leading up to the portable stage.

Richard spoke first. He explained that CM-7 heart valves are molded much like ordinary plastic parts—a process that dramatically lowers the cost. When Hilda took over to describe the manufacturing procedure in detail, I began to lose interest and feel hungry.

Sidney turned his head when I quietly pushed my chair rearward.

"Bailing out?" he whispered.

"I have a sudden craving for a doughnut," I whispered back.

"Me too. Let's go to the breakfast buffet."

I tiptoed around my chair, Sidney close on my heels. The level of Hilda's amplified voice diminished as we approached the food table, but we could still hear everything being said at the podium.

"I admit it, Sidney," I said after I selected a lovely sugared donut. "High pressure injection molding is not a topic of great curiosity to me."

He chuckled. "Hilda is a fabulous chemist, but . . ."

"I've heard she can be a tad long-winded."

"Today more than ever, because we're all really proud of the CM-7."

"Do that many people need artificial heart valves?"

"No, but C&M plans to roll out an armada of molded plastic body parts. Finger joints. Knee joints. Even replacement hips. Today, the heart—tomorrow, the whole body."

What use is a donut without tea to dunk it in? I made another cup while Sidney buttered an English muffin and Hilda finished her lecture. Richard took over the microphone and invited the reporters to ask questions. I found myself paying attention once more.

A woman asked, "How many Maryland jobs will the CM-7 create?"

"Perhaps twenty at first," Richard answered. "We hope hundreds in years to come."

A man asked, "How many CM-7 heart valves have you distributed?"

"We delivered most of our initial production run—approximately three thousand valves—to hospitals throughout the United States. We also shipped a few to leading health care facilities in Europe, Asia, and Australia."

"I have a follow-up question," the same man said. "Why only three thousand? That's a small number compared to the tens of thousands of artificial heart valves produced by other firms."

Richard smiled. "I hope you noticed that I said *initial* production run. The CM-7 valves we've delivered to date were custom molded in our prototype molding shop during the past six months. Each month we produced a batch of five hundred essentially handmade valves to get ready for the big day when we received FDA approval. At the same time, we were building our new production facility that will manufacture hundreds of CM-7s each day. Campbell & McQueen is ready to deliver prosthetic valves as fast as the orders arrive."

David Friendly stood up. "Can you comment on the safety of the CM-7? Other artificial heart valves have failed in service, and, of course, we all have heard of the problems attributed to silicone implants."

"I'm glad someone asked that question," Richard said. "We are confident that the CM-7 is the most reliable artificial heart valve ever made—thanks to its design, materials, and manufacture. Campbell & McQueen is committed to the highest standards of quality. We are proud of our hard-won reputation for excellence; but even more important, we are committed to the people we help."

David went on, "Those are nice words, Mr. Campbell, but heart valves are not like other medical devices. A failure can . . . well—"

"A failure can cause sudden death," Richard interrupted. "We're well aware of that—more so perhaps than you give us credit for. We understand the responsibility we have accepted."

David didn't have a chance to say anything else because a man standing in the shadows at the side of the room bellowed, "C&M makes wonderful heart valves!"

Two dozen heads swung in unison. Richard Campbell laughed. "OK, Scott. The time has come to introduce you to our guests. Everyone—the strapping fellow with the booming voice is Scott Wilkens. You saw his heart being worked on a few minutes ago. Scott now leads a normal life. In fact, he has returned to his job at United Parcel Service."

Scott stepped out of the shadows. He was the man who had waved to the camera, but now he looked even healthier than he had on the screen. Someone began to applaud, and most of the audience joined in.

Not Barry Goodwin, however. He quietly slid off his chair and walked to the side of the room. I thought he was getting ready for the next part of the news conference—until I saw the expression of fury on his face. His ears had become as red as his hair.

Anne Goodwin realized that something was wrong. She rose and tried to intercept him, but he gently moved her aside and continued out of the improvised theater.

Barry shot past me without a sideways glance, but he stopped when Sidney Monk said softly, "Calm down. A man in your position shouldn't look so angry."

"Of course I'm angry!" Barry hissed in reply. "I decided that Scott Wilkens would not be invited to this news conference. I made that perfectly clear to everyone."

"Yes, you did, but Hilda overruled your decision. Scott called her yesterday and said that he really wanted to attend. She chose not to hurt his feelings. After all, he's the star of the video you projected."

Barry threw up his hands. "Fine!" he said. "Now I know where I stand." He spun on his heels and returned to the news conference.

I remember thinking, *Dear Lord, . . . Barry Goodwin can be a severe pain in the bum.*

Chapter Four

SIDNEY MONK AND I left the Magothy Lounge together before the news conference ended—he to prepare for a mid-morning staff meeting at Campbell & McQueen, me to spend a fretful morning in my office. As we rode down in the elevator, Sidney smiled at me and said, "Stop looking like the world ended. No one cares if your kid blew a gasket in the wings. He played great during the piano recital."

I felt in no mood to explain why my mind was tightly wrapped around the axle of Barry Goodwin's erratic behavior, so I ignored the first two-thirds of Sidney's remark. "I thought he did a fine job too," I said. "The news conference was put together beautifully."

"Yep. Barry is a good worker. He really cares, which is why he sometimes gets overly passionate if things don't go according to his expectations."

"Ah. You've seen him upset before."

Sidney shrugged. "Once or twice. But this time he had good reason to get mad. Hilda didn't tell Barry why she overruled his decision not to invite Scott Wilkens."

The elevator door opened at the garage level. "Rank hath its privilege," I said.

"Not in this case!" Sidney underscored his reply with a brusque wave of his hand. "There were sound reasons for bringing Scott to the conference. Hilda couldn't explain them to Barry, and I can't explain them to you."

I took a stab in the dark. "Do the reasons have something to do with the rumored acquisition of C&M by another company?"

Sidney winked. "You didn't hear *me* say anything like that, Ms. Hunnechurch."

We went our separate ways—Sidney sliding into a lush new Mercedes, me squeezing into my trusty, five-year-old Miata. I drove along Ryde High Street wondering how often Barry Goodwin became "overly passionate" without reason since he joined C&M. Was it only "once or twice"? Or did Barry blow his top every time he became frustrated? When I stopped at the traffic light a block away from my office, an additional question popped into my head: How would the impending acquisition of C&M alter my relationship with the company?

Gloria, as always, displayed a wise pragmatism. "It makes no sense to ask yourself questions you can't possibly answer," she said as she poured a hot cuppa for me, "especially when you still haven't bought Christmas gifts for your mother, your sister, and your brother-in-law, and considering that you are running out of time to have them shipped to England. Take your mind off C&M—spend the day shopping."

Late that morning, I decided to take her advice.

"Ta ta!" I said. "I am off to Mulberry Alley."

One of the reasons I fell in love with Ryde on my first visit is Ryde High Street. On it you can still find a goodly assortment of real shops, with real glass windows, in front of real sidewalks, filled with real people browsing. Yes, we have malls outside the city, but happily they have not destroyed Ryde's small downtown shopping district. I mentioned that Ryde High Street is shaped like a C; my favorite shops are clustered on either side of the bottom "elbow," where the street makes a sharp turn.

Jutting off from the tip of the elbow is a short, stubby lane called Mulberry Alley, which houses a dozen trendy boutiques that offer the same kind of merchandise—and price tags—you will see on Rodeo Drive in Beverly Hills. I felt confident that one of them would have an item suitable for my finicky sister, Chloe.

Chloe is, as the old saying goes, easily satisfied by the best of everything. It is an odd trait in a woman who is married to a clergyman and grew up in the same hardworking English household I grew up in. Nonetheless, I have learned over many Christmases that one must shop carefully for Chloe Hunnechurch-Parker, and with considerable creativity.

Chloe, Stuart, and Mum live in Chichester, a small city in Sussex County, in the south of England—a cosmopolitan place where you can purchase most of the goods that are available in the States. Chloe has come to expect something "colonial"—a decidedly *American* gift that can't be bought at the shops on East Street in Chichester.

The afternoon sped by, and the watery December sunlight faded. By five-thirty I ran out of steam. I had found an elegant leather-bound journal for Stuart (a want-to-be writer) and a piece of Navaho Indian pottery for Mum (a collector with eclectic tastes)—and arranged for them to be express shipped to England. I also bought a lovely Icelandic sweater for Gloria, which I carried with me. However, I found nothing suitable for Chloe. Her perfect gift would have to wait for another shopping expedition.

I was back at "Hunnechurch Manor" by six, cheerfully footsore, no longer worrying about Barry Goodwin. My home is a narrow, two-story row house that is old enough to be listed in the Ryde Historical Society Registry. It's on Magothy Street—about a dozen cross streets up from the river. I had bought the house more than four years earlier when I still worked nine-to-five as a "junior in-house personnel recruiter" for

CentreBank in Baltimore. The ground floor (the "first floor" as people say on this side of the pond) contains a small living room, a smaller dining room, and an even smaller kitchen that overlooks a tiny garden behind the house. Upstairs are two small bedrooms and a wee bath. The only thing large about Hunnechurch Manor is the whopping mortgage held by Ryde Savings Bank. Be that as it may, I love every insufficient square inch of floor space.

I moved into the kitchen and turned on the lights. Winston chirped at me; I whistled back.

Winston is a budgie (a.k.a. a parakeet) who has light blue feathers, a bright yellow beak, and a loyal disposition. I dropped the drawbridge door on his cage and said, "There you go, matey. Enjoy your evening walkies."

Winston perched in the opening and began his leaving-the-cage warm-up routine. Left wing lift. Right wing lift. Left leg stretch. Right leg stretch.

"That's the spirit," I said. I knew that Winston, budgie of habit that he is, would eventually join me. He and I often share what's on my plate.

That evening Winston and I enjoyed the dinner special at Hunnechurch Manor, a frozen entrée and a tossed salad—a simple meal that went perfectly with the entertainment I chose, a three-hour marathon of Christmas episodes from British sitcoms, broadcast on public TV.

I retired feeling Christmassy and content. I even set my alarm clock for eight o'clock. Why not? Tomorrow was a quiet day on my calendar. I had no reason to be at my office before nine-thirty. I drifted off with my mind full of cheerful thoughts, without an inkling of the tragedy taking place across town.

———————

I awoke at seven the next morning to a heavy-fisted knocking on my front door. I looked out the bedroom window and immediately recognized Gloria's enormous four-wheel-drive Dodge pickup truck parked on Magothy Street.

I raced downstairs in my nightgown and bathrobe, unlocked the front door, and found Gloria scowling at me. The tears in her eyes were running down her cheeks.

"Why don't you have a doorbell?" she snapped.

"Because this house was built in 1867, when doorknockers were all the rage."

"Like I care! Give me your car keys. Quick."

"My car keys? You want to borrow the Miata . . ."

I never really got the last syllable out. Gloria had spotted my purse sitting on the walnut buffet table in my hallway. She pushed past me, grabbed my purse, and moved back to the doorway before I could regain either my balance or composure.

She turned to me and shouted. "I'll be back in ten minutes. Read your E-mail while I'm gone, and keep this door locked!"

"Read my E-mail?" I said bewilderedly. Her answer was to slam the door shut behind her.

One of my recent investments had been a lightweight portable computer to use on business trips or whenever I brought work home. I had no idea what was going on, but I decided the best course of action was to follow Gloria's shouted commands. I turned the deadbolt on the door and set up the laptop on my dining room table in easy reach of a power outlet and a telephone jack. Four minutes later I was downloading my E-mail messages. I had a total of five, but the last on the list caught my attention:

From: Barry.Goodwin@Campbellmcqueen.com
Subject: My Final Decision

I remember thinking when I read the *Subject* line that Barry must have finally cut through his confusion. He had obviously made a decision about resigning, or not resigning, from C&M. *Good!* Either way, Hunnechurch & Associates would be able to move forward. I felt a mixture of curiosity and relief as I double-clicked the message listing to read it.

SUBJECT: My Final Decision

Dear Family, Friends, and Coworkers: By the time you read this message, I will be dead.

The *very* few of you who actually care about me know how much I hate the stress at Campbell & McQueen Precision Components. Well, I put up with it for seven solid weeks, but today the pain became impossible to bear—along with most of the people at C&M. So, I have arranged a *permanent* resignation from my job and from my stupid life.

To Anne Goodwin, my wonderful mother, all I can say is, sorry, Mom! I think we both knew that this might happen some day.

To Karen Constantine, my dear fiancée, I hope you will move beyond me without too much bitterness. I never wanted to hurt you.

To my handful of friends at C&M, remember me kindly—if you can!

Barry Goodwin

P.S. If you want to blame someone for what I've done, blame Pippa Hunnechurch. It's her fault that I ended up in a job that was all wrong for me. She knew that I don't handle stress well, but she kept pushing me to join C&M. Pippa Hunnechurch messed up my life!

Thinking back to that morning, I have to admit that Barry's postscript hit me even harder than his suicide note. I don't know how long
I stared at the screen, nor can I begin to catalog the different emotions
I felt, but Gloria told me that I had "a look of horror" on my face when
she let herself into the house with my keys. All I really remember is that
she pulled a chair next to mine, put her arm around my shoulders, and
we cried together for a while.

"I don't suppose," I finally said with a sniffle, "that this is some kind
of cruel hoax."

She shook her head woodenly. "Have you ever met Dennis Marsh,
the tall, thin tenor in the church choir?"

"I know who you mean. He stands in the back row."

"Dennis is the computer guru who takes care of C&M's internal networks. He arrives at work at five o'clock every weekday morning so he
can check out the network servers and switches and a lot of other hard-
ware I don't understand. He was the first C&M person to read Barry's
message. Naturally, he tried to reach Barry, but he gave up trying at five-
thirty and called the police. Then he phoned me. Dennis is a member
of my Wednesday evening small group too."

"So he knew about Barry's concerns."

"Yep. I have his permission to tell you that he argued with Barry at
our last meeting. Dennis has worked at Campbell & McQueen for six
years. He told Barry that the company is too straight laced to do anything
shoddy or criminal."

"How did Barry react?"

"Badly. He stood up and left without saying good-bye to anyone. He
had an ugly expression on his face. Pure anger."

I sighed. "I've seen that expression."

"Anyway, after Dennis called me, I threw on my clothes and drove
to Barry's apartment building. I got there at about six-thirty. There were
two fire engines, an ambulance, and three grim-looking cops out
front—plus a half-dozen people wrapped in blankets, standing on the

sidewalk. I hung around for a while and managed to talk to a guy in a blanket who happens to be Barry's next-door neighbor. He was awakened by the fire department at 6:00 A.M. and ordered to evacuate his apartment."

"An evacuation? Why?"

"My question exactly. The word on the street is that Barry sabotaged the gas-fired furnace in his utility room by disconnecting the chimney pipe and sealing all the vents. When the furnace switched on, it filled the apartment with carbon monoxide. A cop told my guy that Barry is dead. The cop also said it's a miracle that no one else in the building was poisoned by leaking carbon monoxide and that Barry's apartment didn't blow up. It seems the stuff is flammable as well as deadly."

I nodded mechanically while my mind chewed on the details. *Sabotage. Furnace. Carbon monoxide. Flammable. Deadly. Death.*

Gloria said a few words I didn't catch.

"Pardon?"

"I said, then I came over here."

"And for some reason, you borrowed my car."

"I *moved* your car, from the front of your house to a parking garage on Ryde High Street."

"What for?"

"So that visitors will think you aren't home." She hesitated. "Barry's suicide—and his E-mail message—will be big news in a couple of hours. People will want to talk to you."

"Oh my! Anyone who sees the note will think I drove Barry to suicide." The impact of what she said finally sunk in. "What kind of people will want to talk to me?"

"Reporters mostly, but maybe the police."

"Blimey!"

"You can't hide forever, but we can make you hard to find for most of today. We'll ignore the doorknocker and let the answering machine take care of the phone. The idea is to give you enough time to absorb what happened and figure out what you want to say. The essence of good strategy is to fight battles on your own terms."

A picture flashed in my mind of Barry Goodwin tapping away at his computer, composing his suicide note, E-mailing it far and wide.

Why blame me for messing up your life?

I had recruited Barry fair and square. Of course, it was "my fault" that he took his job at Campbell & McQueen. That's the whole point of headhunting. I had told him about the opening and explained why I thought it was a good match for his skills and experience. Barry agreed immediately. He asked me to present him to C&M. He willingly went to three different interviews and became ecstatic when Hilda McQueen offered him the post, then eagerly accepted the job without any prompting from me.

"The E-mail message doesn't read like the Barry I saw yesterday," I said to Gloria. "He was furious; he nearly stormed out of the news conference. The note seems so . . . so *deliberate.*"

"That doesn't surprise me," she replied. "He wrote the note knowing that he was about to die. I'm sure people get very deliberate when they write their last words."

"Perhaps, but the postscript makes no sense. I didn't ruin Barry's life. Why punish me?"

"You're not his only victim," Gloria said. "If you check the 'To:' list, you'll see that Barry E-mailed the note to his mother and to his fiancée."

"Oh my! I can't imagine him doing such a hateful thing."

"I agree. He never seemed mean or vindictive." She sniffed. "I called Reverend Clarke at his home. He'll try to reach Mrs. Goodwin before the police do—or before she logs on to her E-mail account. She lives in Easton, on the Eastern Shore. Pray God the traffic isn't heavy on the Chesapeake Bay Bridge this morning."

"What about Karen Constantine?"

"We don't know how to find her. She's not in the phone book. Reverend Clark is going to ask Mrs. Goodwin . . ."

She stopped in mid-sentence, half-turned away from me, and wiped her eyes. It suddenly dawned on me that Gloria was hurting too. Focused as I was on my own shredded feelings, I forgot that Gloria had lost a friend.

"Forgive me," I said. "I've been a dolt. You've done yeoman's duty taking care of me, while I haven't even asked how you feel."

"I feel lousy, Pippa. I want to keep so busy that I can't think about the awful thing Barry did. Otherwise, I'll crumble into a million pieces."

We both heard a knock on my front door. Gloria tiptoed down the hallway and into the living room where you can see the door from the window. She tiptoed back and whispered, "It's David Friendly."

"Let him in. He has two strong, sympathetic shoulders we can lean on."

I had just made my biggest mistake of the day.

Chapter Five

I REALIZED THAT DAVID had not come as a friend when he didn't give me his usual affable hug. He stopped at the entrance to my dining room, his media credentials hanging from a lanyard around his neck, a grim expression on his face. He noticed my laptop computer, wavered a moment, then said, "Gloria is here, and your computer is on. I assume you have heard about Barry Goodwin's death?"

I nodded.

"Well then—I have several questions about your professional relationship with Mr. Goodwin."

I stood there like a fence post, trying to make sense of the thousand miles of distance I could hear in David's voice. I had lost my best pal on a day when I really needed his companionship.

"Whoa!" Gloria said as she stepped between us. "You didn't tell me you're on duty. Pippa isn't talking to reporters this morning."

David scowled at Gloria. He started to say something to her but must have thought better of it. Instead, he looked at me uncomfortably. "Coming here like this wasn't my idea. If you want me to leave, I will."

I drew my bathrobe tighter around my middle and retied the belt. "I haven't had my morning tea yet. Follow me into the kitchen. I'll put on the kettle, and we'll see about your questions."

Gloria led the way. David followed her, and I trailed behind, wondering if I should send him on his way. David was a fine reporter; he knew how to be a really tough interrogator.

Think about it, Pippa. If you have to face reporters, perhaps it's best to start with someone you know.

My kitchen table is a petite oval four-seater made of walnut. Gloria positioned herself on the left side and David on the right. They proceeded to glare at each other.

"You guys sit down and play nice," I said. I moved to the sink and filled my electric kettle with cold water. "David, what do you have in mind?"

"Hold on," Gloria said. "I want to ask David a question first. It's 7:30 A.M. How did the business reporter of a twice-weekly local newspaper get here so quickly when the cops arrived at Barry Goodwin's apartment only an hour-and-a-half ago? I doubt the police went out of their way to notify the *Ryde Reporter.*"

Gloria was right. It was way too early for David Friendly to be covering Barry Goodwin's suicide. I spun around to face him and accidentally banged the kettle against the faucet. A gobbet of cold water sloshed out of the spout and splashed down on my bare toes, but I ignored the abrupt chill. "How did you find out about Barry?" I said. "Your name wasn't on the list of people who received his suicide E-mail."

David looked first at Gloria then at me. "Fortunately, it wasn't, but someone at Campbell & McQueen called Leonard Smithson at his home a few minutes before seven o'clock. He told him about Barry then faxed him a copy of the suicide note. Lenny contacted a captain he knows at the Ryde Police Department. He acknowledged that they had responded to a death that was being treated as a suicide."

"Who is Leonard Smithson?" Gloria asked.

"The publisher of the *Ryde Reporter,*" I said as I plugged in the electric kettle. "David's boss."

"Who made the call?" Gloria pressed on.

"He refused to identify himself," David said, "but Lenny's Caller-ID box confirmed that the call—and the fax—both came from inside C&M."

"I'm sure it wasn't anyone we know," Gloria said to me. I needed a moment to figure out that "anyone we know" was Gloria's friend, Dennis Marsh.

David was still wearing his winter trench coat—an elderly tan Burberry in need of both a cleaning and a pressing. He reached into the deep right side pocket and pulled out a copy of the *Ryde Reporter.* "What really infuriates Lenny," he said, "is that Barry Goodwin killed himself several hours *after* our Tuesday edition went to press." He slid the folded paper to my side of the kitchen table. "My lead story in the business section is about Campbell & McQueen. I used a lot of the information presented at yesterday's news conference, and I quoted Barry Goodwin extensively. I even gave Pippa Hunnechurch & Associates a friendly mention."

"In that event," I said to David, "you have my blessing to remove your coat."

He smiled, twisted out of his coat, and said, "We only publish twice a week. By the time our Friday edition hits the street, Barry's suicide will be ancient news. Every newspaper and TV station in Baltimore, Annapolis, and Washington, D.C., will have reported the details."

"I get it," I said. "Lenny wants a special feature for Friday."

"I have been instructed to write a human-interest piece—a story that explains *why* Barry decided to kill himself. Lenny ordered me to interview you first."

"I can't imagine why Barry killed himself," I said quickly.

"You can't give me the whole picture; no one can. But maybe I can get some of the pieces from you, then stitch them together with facts I learn from other people who knew Barry."

I put three heaping tablespoons of the strongest Assam tea on my shelf into my largest teapot. This was shaping up to be a many-cuppa morning. I touched the lid of the electric kettle. Warm, but a good five minutes away from boiling.

"What do you think?" I asked Gloria.

"I think you need time to think," she said, "before you answer any questions about Barry Goodwin."

Of course, it was sound advice. I should have listened to Gloria rather than charging ahead without regard to my frame of mind, but that is precisely what I foolishly chose to do.

"I feel fine," I said to Gloria. And then to David: "I am willing to entertain a few reasonable questions about our professional dealings with Barry Goodwin."

He grinned at me. "I knew I could count on you. Thanks." He began to fish around in the Burberry's other side pocket. "Do you mind if I use a tape recorder instead of a notepad? It will speed things up because I write slowly."

"I don't mind."

David's recorder was a small, innocuous, gray plastic object scarcely larger than a candy bar. He set it in the center of the table. I forgot it was efficiently capturing my every word when David asked his first question.

"How long have you known Barry Goodwin?" David said.

"I met him in person in early August. However, I knew *about* him two weeks earlier."

"Was Barry easy to headhunt?"

"To the contrary. I worked especially hard to uncover Barry as a potential candidate."

I didn't mean to sound arrogant, but I had expected David, who understands the world of business, to appreciate how difficult it can be to locate a top-notch manager. Campbell & McQueen had been highly specific in its requirements for a corporate communicator with credentials in both plastics and public relations. One doesn't find a candidate of Barry's education and experience without considerable effort.

Alas, many people think headhunting is easy—a simple chore of making a few telephone calls until an appropriate name magically drops into one's lap. In fact, I invested nearly a week of time at C&M studying plastics technology under the tutelage of Jerry Nichols before I made my first phone call. I spent another week tracking down a likely candidate at a large chemical company in New Jersey who politely explained that she was perfectly happy with her present job and would I please not bother her again.

I widened my search during the third, fourth, and fifth weeks, reaching into every corner of my network of contacts: company executives, trade association managers, and university professors—all to no avail. I also listed the position on my Web site (www.pippahunnechurch.com) and several Internet job-search engines, and placed advertisements in newspapers from Philadelphia, Pennsylvania, to Richmond, Virginia. As before, no response.

I hit pay dirt during the sixth week when a serendipitous follow-up discussion with the president of the Ryde Public Relations Society generated an offhand remark: "You know, now that you mention it, I met a communicator who knows plastics last winter at a conference on the Eastern Shore. I don't recall his name, but I think he was one of the speakers."

I needed one more day to identify Mr. Barry Goodwin, manager of public relations at Flynt Molding in Easton, Maryland, and also the author of a presentation called "Why Nobody Writes Right About Plastics," delivered at the Maryland East Communication Conference the previous January. Six days later, near the middle of the seventh week, I presented his "candidate package" to C&M. It contained Barry's résumé, which I had helped to fine-tune, plus the enthusiastic comments of several colleagues who gave him high marks for his abilities and personality.

I didn't have the opportunity to explain any of this to David. He merely grunted at my initial answer and asked his next question.

"Why did you think Mr. Goodwin was a suitable candidate for the post at Campbell & McQueen?"

"Barry's education and experience were perfect for the job. Two master's degrees. A knowledge of plastics that wouldn't quit. And current experience as a PR manager."

David grunted again. "I'd like to see a copy of Barry's résumé. I can ask C&M, but . . ."

"But it's easier to ask your old pal, Pippa."

"You got it!"

I glanced at Gloria. "Make a note to fax a copy to David when we return to our office."

She frowned at me. "Is that really a good idea?"

"There's nothing in Barry's résumé that can't be made public," I said. "It's wholly accurate. I double-checked the dates and places myself."

"While we're talking about what you did," David said, "did you also speak to any of his references?"

"Every last one! My reputation is on the line when I present a candidate. I always make certain that everything in the candidate package is valid, including references."

"So you verified *everything* Mr. Goodwin told you?"

"Indeed I did. I am exceptionally thorough. Diligence is my stock in trade."

David nodded. "Let's go on to the suicide note . . ."

Gloria interrupted him: "*Shhhh!*" She put her finger to her lips. "Someone's at the front door."

My doorknocker clanged a moment later.

"Where is your car parked?" Gloria whispered to David.

"Across the street, in front of the house with the big Santa Claus," he whispered back.

"Good. No one can tell we're inside."

"Whom are we hiding from?" David asked.

"Other reporters."

He rapped the table lightly with his knuckles. "Serves 'em right!"

My nameless visitor gave up on the doorknocker and began to pound on the door. A few seconds later we heard the covered letter slot in my front door squeak open. "Is Pippa Hunnechurch home?" a male voice shouted through the aperture. "I'm a reporter from the *Baltimore Sun.*"

After two more shouts, the metal flap dropped with a snap.

I stifled a giggle with my hand. Gloria and David shared a silent high-five.

"Moving right along," David said to me more softly than before, "I have a few questions related to the content of the suicide note. Did Mr. Goodwin ever suggest to you that he had problems coping with job-related stress?"

"No. And neither did the people I spoke to about Barry."

"Then why would he write, 'She knew that I don't handle stress well'?"

"The body of the message makes no sense to me. It simply doesn't sound like the Barry I knew, and as for the postscript, well, none of it is true. I found nothing in Barry's background that indicated such a difficulty."

"Really?" David said in a tone that signaled skepticism.

"Really!" I insisted. "Besides, a person allergic to stress doesn't willingly take on the kind of responsibilities that Barry shouldered. He was eager to become C&M's director of corporate communications."

"He did seem a tad frazzled toward the end of yesterday's news conference."

"That's your impression—not mine."

No sooner were the words out of my mouth than I remembered the burst of irate behavior I had witnessed. It was too late to reframe my answer; I let it pass. After all, getting angry at one's boss is not the same thing as being frazzled by stress.

"What about the job itself?" David asked. "Did Mr. Goodwin ever express concerns to you about his position at Campbell & McQueen?"

I tried to keep a poker face. "I prefer not to answer that, David."

"Why? It's a simple yes-no question."

"Perhaps. Nonetheless, I choose not to reply."

"Then he *did* express concerns . . ."

"I have nothing to say on the subject."

David glared at me awhile, then said, "Then let's change subjects. Do you have anything to say about Mr. Goodwin's accusation that you 'ruined his life'?"

"I didn't ruin Barry's life," I said irritably. "I helped to advance his career. That is what headhunters do for good people. You know me well enough not to ask such a horrid question."

David pushed the recorder's *stop* button. "Calm down, Pippa. I'm only doing my job."

"Are you finished doing it in my house?"

"Sure. You've made it abundantly clear that you have no idea why your *ideal* recruit killed himself." David emphasized "ideal" in a way that made me grit my teeth.

He and I stood up together, but Gloria tugged us back down. "Time out! Nobody's leaving until we pray for Barry's family and friends—and maybe for ourselves."

"Sure. Why not?" David said.

"Why not, indeed?" I echoed.

"Then I will lead us in prayer," Gloria said.

We held hands and bowed our heads, and Gloria began. "Father God, we know that you have forgiven Barry Goodwin for taking his own life. We ask now that you comfort his mother and the other members of his family . . . and his loved ones, including Karen Constantine . . . and the many friends he made at Campbell & McQueen." She took a deep breath. "Heavenly Father, we need your comforting too. We ask you to heal our hurts . . . and mend our broken spirits . . . and help us to forgive as you forgive us. In Jesus' name we pray."

I heard the words she spoke about forgiveness, but all I felt was blossoming anger. I was furious with David for asking me his silly questions. Even worse, I was mad at Barry for killing himself—and for pillorying me in his horrible note. I wanted to wring his blooming neck.

When Gloria was finished, I yanked my hands back so quickly that David said, "Let me know when you cool off. I'll find my own way out."

"Use the back door, and please don't return until you stop being a reporter and start being my friend."

My back door is at the opposite end of the hallway that serves my front door. It leads into a small rear garden that is overlooked by my kitchen window. I heard David slam the door, and then I watched him storm away through my herb bed.

Gloria tapped my shoulder. I spun around. "Don't you dare say 'I told you so'."

"Not me. I'm merely wondering when you actually intend to pour some hot water into your teapot. I'm in the mood for a strong cuppa too."

"Blimey! I forgot about the kettle."

Hardly had the boiling water soaked the tea leaves when my phone and doorknocker began to sound at full volume. Gloria lowered the shade in the kitchen window while I fetched two large commemorative mugs from my china cabinet. The gold lettering on their sides read, *Ryde, Maryland—Three Hundred Fifty Years Young*. We enjoyed our brewed Assam tea amid a cacophony of bells, knocks, and shouts.

"They certainly are a persistent bunch," I said.

She shrugged. "A suicide E-mail is something different. Barry Goodwin might get himself on national news. Quite an achievement."

I clasped my hands around my half-empty mug. "I've been thinking about the prayer you just spoke—the part about God forgiving Barry. Do you think that suicide is a sin?"

She shot up straight in her chair. "Of course suicide is a sin! Your life belongs to God. You don't have a right to destroy it. Not to mention that suicide is thoughtless and irresponsible. It devastates the people you leave behind."

I stared at Gloria. "Did I say something wrong?"

She tucked her chin close to her chest. I could see tears in her eyes. "I didn't mean to yell at you," she said. "I'm sorry."

"Tell me what upset you." I reached for her hand and held on tightly. "I'm fine. Forget it."

"Nothing doing! I am not going to lose another friend today. My question caused distress. I can't see why, unless . . ." I hesitated. "Gloria, have you had experience with suicide?"

She sighed. "It's no big secret. My brother Frank killed himself six years ago."

Gloria had never mentioned a brother named Frank, although she often talked about Charles, her older brother who was married and worked as a computer programmer in Minnesota. She stood up and began to pace. "Frank was fifteen when he died. His death came close to tearing our family apart."

I couldn't think of anything to say. Gloria didn't seem to notice.

"My parents almost split up because of him," she went on. "Dad didn't want to talk about the suicide, and Mom couldn't stop. They both blamed themselves for not recognizing the warning signs. Of course, we were all mad at Frank, which made things worse because Christians are supposed to forgive." She shook her head. "Look how I'm acting. The memories can still push my button after all these years."

I refilled Gloria's mug and brought it to her.

"Those reporters had better stay far away from us," I said. "We're both on edge enough to tear them apart."

Gloria and I shared another high-five. This one was exuberant and loud.

Chapter Six

ON WEDNESDAY MORNING Gloria reluctantly agreed to reopen our office.

"I think you should stay away the rest of the week," she had argued, "until the story of Barry's suicide becomes thoroughly old news."

"I don't feel productive working at home," I had countered. "We Hunnechurches are not the hiding type. A Hunnechurch stands her ground. A Hunnechurch looks the bulldog in the eye without flinching—"

"I know, I know," she interrupted. "A Hunnechurch doesn't cower like a trapped rabbit. I've heard your pet British clichés a dozen times."

"You will hear them once an hour until I am back behind my desk."

We compromised. I would leave my Miata parked out of sight, in the garage where Gloria had hidden it. Further, I would tell no one where we were and invite no one to visit our office. Finally, we would do a quick U-turn if the building was still teaming with reporters.

"I accept your terms," I said. "Do I have to sign a contract in blood?"

"You can be a royal pain to protect, Hunnechurch," Gloria said with a shake of her pretty head.

She drove us to the refurbished leather warehouse in her tall white pickup truck. The only media vehicle in sight was a bright orange TV truck from Channel 11 in Baltimore, parked near the front entrance. I scrunched down in the seat as Gloria barreled into the underground garage that had been carved beneath the building when it was restored a dozen years earlier.

"The tall brunette standing next to the TV truck looks familiar," I said. "Did you recognize her?"

"Sure. Veronica Nelson, the station's roving reporter. She's probably getting ready to do an on-location story for the morning news."

"About Barry?"

"More likely about you."

"Blimey!"

We reasoned that Channel 11 had staked out the lobby, so we climbed the fire stairs to reach the fourth floor. The hallway in front of our office was empty, but we found several business cards—all from area reporters—taped to our front door and more cards slipped underneath. Once inside, we decided to leave the curtains drawn.

"Look at our answering machines," I said. We have two, one for Gloria's telephone and one for mine. Their warning lights were blinking rapidly—a signal that both had reached full recording capacity.

"Forget the regular phones," she said. "We'll use our cell phones today."

My first call that morning was to Sidney Monk's direct number. He answered on the third ring.

"Yes . . ." he said, hesitantly.

"It's Pippa."

"I feared you might be a reporter. We are still besieged."

"I suppose you know that someone at Campbell & McQueen faxed Barry's suicide note to the media."

"I do, and I will personally garrote the idiot if we ever identify him."
He paused, then asked. "How are you doing?"

"I feel bruised and befuddled. I can't fathom why Barry used his
parting words to attack me."

I heard him take a deep breath. "The note was weird, I admit.
Although . . ."

"Although what?"

Sidney didn't answer my question. Instead, he said, "Pippa, I have
a meeting with Richard Campbell and Hilda McQueen at nine o'clock
to discuss the situation. That gives me only twenty minutes to get
ready."

I couldn't let him off the hook so easily. "We need to talk, Sidney.
Face-to-face. I presume that C&M wants to replace Barry."

"You presume right," he said, "but let's discuss our replacement
strategy after I've had a chance to take a breath. I am still running in all
directions. So is Diane Dupont. C&M has never before had an employee commit suicide—we're learning how to respond as we go
along."

"I'll keep in touch."

"Same here."

I rang off, not sure what I had accomplished, except perhaps to
keep the lines of communication open. When I put my cell phone
down, Gloria hollered, "Our building is on TV."

Hunnechurch & Associates owns an all-in-one TV set and video
cassette player we use to watch the marketing videos our clients make.
Gloria had set it up on her desk. I arrived in time to see Veronica
Nelson, framed by a redbrick wall, saying, ". . . and despite our frequent tries, we have been unable to reach the woman who was named
in the strange suicide note sent to more than eight hundred people on
Monday morning. Pippa Hunnechurch, reportedly a native of Great
Britain, operates a small executive recruiting firm located in this upscale office building in Ryde, Maryland.

"Commercial colleagues of Miss Hunnechurch report that she has built a moderately successful business by locating hard-to-find executives for local companies—including, of course, Mr. Barry Goodwin, age thirty-five, a native of Easton, Maryland, on the Eastern Shore, who apparently committed suicide on Monday night. Police seem satisfied that the death was a suicide. A source close to the investigation told Channel Six News that Mr. Goodwin had a history of psychiatric treatment. This is Veronica Nelson reporting."

I shouted at the TV screen, "*What* history of psychiatric treatment?"

Veronica didn't answer my question. Her smiling face was soon replaced by a laxative commercial.

I poked Gloria's shoulder blade. "Did Barry tell your Wednesday small group that he was seeing a psychiatrist?"

Her edgy hesitation was as good as a loud yes.

"How long have you known?" I asked.

"Since three Wednesdays ago. I suppose I can talk about it now. It's no big deal—Barry used to visit a shrink on the Eastern Shore. He quit when he moved to Ryde."

"He never told me," I said.

"Why should he? His medical history is private."

"Apparently only to me!" But my heart wasn't in my exclamation. I added, "You are right, of course. Medical treatment is one's own business. I don't investigate that kind of . . ."

Gloria put her finger to her lips. She pointed to our front door and then her ear. She had heard something in the corridor.

Gloria moved to the door silently, then yanked it open. A stocky woman half-tumbled into our office. She scrambled to her feet, smiled at me, and stuck out her hand .

"Sophie Hammond," she said. "I'm a writer for the *Ryde Rebel*. We want to know what *really* happened to Barry Goodwin. For starters, doesn't it strike you as strange that he made you the star of his suicide note?"

The *Ryde Rebel* was a gossipy, alternative tabloid whose stories verged between bizarre and sensational. I cringed when I imagined the kind of story its editors would choose to publish.

Pippa Hunnechurch Hunts Heads for Real in Ryde.

"I have nothing to say about Barry Goodwin," I said coolly, ignoring her hand. "Especially not to a reporter from a sleazy newspaper who has the gall to eavesdrop at my office door."

My insult didn't make a dent. "Cut me some slack, Pippa," she said. "I've camped out in your stairwell for two days. What's the harm in answering a few questions?"

"Let me repeat. I have nothing to say."

"That I *can't* believe. Barry Goodwin publicly accused you of messing up his life. He dropped you in the center of a media feeding frenzy. You must have *some* opinion about his E-mail."

"It is time for you to leave, Miss Hammond."

"Actually, it's Mrs. Hammond, but please call me Sophie."

Gloria intervened. "You heard Miss Hunnechurch, *Sophie*. Take a hike!" She gave Sophie a gentle shove that propelled her into the hallway, then slammed the door behind her.

"Elegantly done," I said to Gloria. "The very last thing we need to do this week is waste time with the bottom feeders of the media food chain."

We puttered around the office for the rest of the day, paying no heed to our twinkling telephone answering machines, catching up on miscellaneous administrative chores like paying bills and filing correspondence. Late in the afternoon Gloria dropped a sheet of paper on my desk.

"Dennis Marsh forwarded an E-mail with the details of Barry's funeral. It's scheduled for Friday morning. There's a viewing tomorrow at the Badecker Funeral Home in Easton. What do you think?"

"I think we go."

"Me too. Should I arrange to have flowers sent?"

"Of course. Commission a decorous wreath from both of us." I stared at the message. The original E-mail, written by Sidney Monk, had been distributed at eight o'clock that morning—nearly an hour before we spoke. Why hadn't Sidney told me about Barry's funeral?

========

Thursday dawned cold and leaden gray, proving that the meteorologists had been right when they forecast that snow would begin to fall before noon. Gloria and I made two spur-of-the-moment decisions. First, we would travel to Easton early rather than late. Second, we would take her big pickup truck with off-road tires because my little sports car could be squirrelly on icy roads.

We set out on Maryland Route 50-301 at nine-thirty. Traffic was light as we headed east over the Chesapeake Bay Bridge. Gloria drove in the rightmost lane, giving me a wonderful view of the bay north of Annapolis. Under different circumstances I would have enjoyed our forty-minute journey to Easton, but that morning my mind kept conjuring up images of Barry Goodwin in a coffin. When I tried to push them away, I would remember the sight—eight years earlier—of two caskets lowered into the ground in a small churchyard near Chichester, England.

The accident had happened in an instant on a narrow road a bit north of the ancient town of Bosham. The morning sun had blinded an old man driving a vintage Austin Mini. He crossed over the centerline and struck our new Ford sedan head-on. My husband, Simon, and my three-year-old daughter, Peggy, were in the front seat—she strapped in with a seat belt as English law requires, playing with her teddy bear—while I enjoyed "Her Majesty's rear seat." They were killed instantly; I survived with a few cuts, a cracked ankle, and a broken heart.

I don't do funerals well any more.

Badecker's parking lot was nearly full. The prospect of a developing snowstorm had apparently encouraged other mourners to come early in the day. The feeble December sun had broken through the clouds, and though its light wasn't strong enough to cast shadows, it cheered me considerably. Gloria finally found a space between a behemoth sports utility vehicle and a dark blue sedan—both with Campbell & McQueen "Executive Parking Area" stickers on their rear bumpers.

"We're definitely in the right place," Gloria said.

"How do I look?" I asked as I descended from the lofty Dodge truck. I unbuttoned my trench coat to show Gloria my dark gray suit. Unbeknownst to me when I bought it, it was made of a fabric that rumpled easily.

"Crisp and uncreased," she replied. "How about me?" She was wearing a midnight blue dress.

"Stunning as always."

We joined a stream of people walking somberly toward the one-story clapboard building that seemed more like a large home than a mortuary. I looked for a familiar face but didn't see one.

The viewing room set aside for Barry was chockablock with people I didn't know. A tall man in a severe black suit intercepted us at the door. "Would you please sign our visitors' book?" he asked in a syrupy voice.

"Write something for both of us," Gloria said softly. "My mind has turned to mush. Even worse, I keep thinking about Frank."

I gave her hand a squeeze—to cover up my failure to remember that Gloria had her own horrid memories to deal with today.

The visitors' book lay open on a narrow table. I found a blank line and wrote: *We knew Barry for only a short while. Nonetheless his death is a great loss to us.* I signed "Pippa Hunnechurch." Gloria added her signature below mine.

We moved toward the front of the room. I caught a glimpse of the bier and several mourners conversing quietly. Among them were Richard Campbell, Hilda McQueen, and Jerry Nichols—C&M's chairman, its president, and its master molder. I was in no mood to talk to them just then, but Hilda spotted me and smiled.

"I'm not ready for the open casket thing yet," Gloria said. "Dennis Morse is in the back corner with other members of my small group. I'll be with them."

Barry's casket was made of polished oak, the interior white satin. I approached it warily and peered inside. Barry's face was rouged and powdered but otherwise serene. He was wearing a dark grey suit, a white shirt, and a red tie. His arms were folded cross-wise, and he clutched two books to his chest. I looked sideways at the titles. One was a King James Version of the Bible, the other a worn textbook on plastics. I felt an upwelling rush of emotion that put tears in my eyes.

"Cheerio, Barry," I whispered. "God bless."

A voice behind me said, "It's sad to see a man with such potential leave us."

When I turned around, I was astonished to see Hilda standing alone. Richard Campbell and Jerry Nichols had moved halfway across the room. I must have looked startled because Hilda asked, "Pippa, do you need to sit down?"

"Not at all," I fibbed quickly. "I expect the sight of so many lovely flowers took my breath away."

"I agree. The flowers are fantastic. The arrangement you sent is toward the left."

I grabbed the opportunity to leave Hilda and proceeded to examine the wall of flowers behind the casket. The biggest display was a garish wicker spaceship filled with carnations, dahlias, and lilies, and sprouting antennae of long-stemmed roses. A card in a plastic holder read: We will miss you, Barry. Your friends at Campbell & McQueen. Further on I found the floral wreath that Gloria had ordered: a large ring of mixed blooms and greenery wrapped with a broad band of purple ribbon. Next to it was a simple spray of lilies. One word was written on the card tucked among the stems: Karen.

I made a mental note to offer my condolences to Karen Constantine. I knew what it felt like to watch the love of your life buried.

"Pippa!"

I spun on my heels to find Gloria with a lanky, dark complexioned man in his late twenties who stood a head taller than me.

"This is Dennis Marsh," she announced.

We exchanged handshakes, then Dennis said, "I think I owe you an apology."

"Me? Why?"

"I goofed on Monday morning. I'm in charge of C&M's networks. I could have prevented Barry's E-mail from being distributed throughout C&M, but I decided to honor Barry's wishes, so I let it go. I now realize it was a mistake."

"I see," I said evenly, biting my tongue, willing myself not to shout, *"You blooming idiot!"*

"Gloria explained the difficulties that my decision has caused you, so please forgive me."

It took me a moment to understand the preamble to his apology. Today was Thursday; Gloria's Wednesday small group had met the evening before. A group of mostly strangers had talked about me the night before.

Should I be mad about that too?

I didn't get the chance to say something foolish to either of them because Gloria broke my chain of thought when she said, "Did you speak to Barry's mother yet?"

"Ah . . . no, I haven't."

"She's sitting on a sofa thataway." Gloria pointed to the left side of the room.

"Then that's where I shall go."

I had never met Anne Goodwin, but her picture had appeared in the *Baltimore Sun,* not far from mine. I also had seen her in person—although from a distance—at C&M's news conference. Today she seemed older, and her mouth was set firm against grief.

"My name is Philippa Hunnechurch," I said as I extended my hand. "Please accept my sincere condolences."

She thrust my hand away. The gruffness of her reaction caught me by surprise.

"I don't need your condolences, Miss Hunnechurch," she said.

The ice in her voice chilled me. The flame in her eyes signaled an emotion that might have been hate. She rose from the sofa. I took two steps backward and bumped into Sidney Monk.

"My son was happy until you interfered with his life," she said. "Why couldn't you leave him alone?"

Her shrill voice carried throughout the room. I could sense people turning to look at us.

"Barry was moved to commit suicide because he hated his work, which is *your* fault. Barry would have stayed in the job he loved if you hadn't pushed him to make a change." Her eyes misted as she spoke. "You thoroughly misjudged Barry. You never took the time to learn his limitations. You shoved him into an inappropriate job so you could earn your thirty pieces of silver."

"Please don't say that, Mrs. Goodwin," I said softly.

She went on. "You've made an appearance—now you can leave. You are no longer welcome here. Don't come to the interment tomorrow."

I stood there, speechless, until Sidney led me away.

Chapter Seven

OUR RETURN TO RYDE took twice as long as our drive to Easton because we traveled through a wind-propelled barrage of plump, moist snowflakes. Creeping ahead at twenty miles an hour gave me the silent time I needed to recover from Anne Goodwin's dreadful rebuke. Gloria, bless her heart, didn't say a word as I sat quietly with my arms wrapped around myself, feeling a chorus of emotions that ranged from befuddlement to humiliation to anger. We reached the Chesapeake Bay Bridge before I finally spoke.

"I can't make sense of this situation," I said. "I truly believe with all my being that I did a conscientious job. Barry Goodwin was a perfect match for Campbell & McQueen. At the same time, I am surrounded by evidence that I made a terrible mistake—from Barry's recent erratic behavior to his horrid suicide note to his revelations to your Wednesday evening small group to Anne Goodwin's tirade. I can't bring both halves of the picture together."

"If a terrible mistake was made, *we* made it. I was with you every step of the way."

"Thank you for being loyal, Gloria, but the world recognizes that I bear the full responsibility—even though I don't know how I made a hash of a straightforward recruiting assignment."

"*We* didn't make a hash of anything." She hesitated. "What happened, I think, is that we didn't go the extra mile for Barry."

"Stuff and nonsense! I talked to a dozen people. I assembled a comprehensive candidate package. I—*we*—did everything required of us."

"How much do you know about the Holy Land in the first century?"

I fought back the exasperation I felt at her sudden shift of gears. "We were talking about Maryland in the twenty-first century."

"Correct, but I'm taking a roundabout route. Answer my question."

"I know that Ancient Judea was occupied by Rome."

"Exactly! The Romans were harsh conquerors. They levied heavy taxes and imposed demeaning laws on the Jews. One of those laws gave a Roman soldier the right to stop any Jewish man in sight and make him carry his military backpack—which weighed about eighty pounds—for a single Roman mile."

"Goodness! What an outrageous idea."

Gloria snickered. "Oh, I don't know about that. There are times when I'd love to order a civilian to tote my National Guard gear for me." She cleared her throat. "However, our Roman soldier and his Jewish draftee made up the cast of characters Jesus was talking about when he said, 'If someone forces you to go one mile, go with him two miles.' It's in Matthew 5:41."

"I've seen the words, but your explanation doesn't make sense. Why should anyone willingly carry a soldier's pack an extra mile?"

"Jesus was telling his followers to go beyond everything required of them." Gloria switched to her bogus English accent to mimic the words I had spoken a moment earlier.

"Even if it's a demeaning requirement."

"That's the point! During the first mile you are a powerless servant; but during the second mile, the *extra* mile, you take charge of the situation. By unexpectedly doing more, you change the rules of the game."

Gloria punctuated her explanation by beeping the Dodge's horn twice.

"We rarely meet Roman legionnaires carrying heavy packs through downtown Ryde," I said.

"Maybe not, but the same principle applies in all the work we do. It's no big deal to deliver the bare minimum that's required. Whenever possible, we should do more."

"How much more? In business one does what a customer requests. What's wrong with meeting a customer's expectations?"

"Nothing—and yet everything. If Anne Goodwin is right, we misjudged Barry and didn't understand his limitations." Gloria reached over and touched my hand. "Think about it! We know how to evaluate the skills of accountants and attorneys, and we're good at checking out sales managers. But Barry was our first techie recruit—our first scientist. Perhaps he deserved special treatment. If we had gone the second mile for him, dug a little deeper, asked some tougher questions, maybe we would have spent this morning somewhere else."

"Are you saying that Hunnechurch & Associates is responsible for Barry's death?"

"No, we're not responsible because we did everything required. That lets us off the hook if anyone wants to blame us. However, we didn't go the extra mile for Barry. If we had . . . well, who knows?"

I felt a stab of annoyance. "You're setting an impossible standard for us. Miles are easy to measure, but our work doesn't have convenient markers. When does one stop doing more as a headhunter? How much inquiry into a candidate's background is finally enough?"

"Beats me! The second mile is one of those recommendations by Jesus that can be tricky to apply in our daily lives. But I've begun to regret that my Wednesday small group didn't pray a little harder for Barry

when we had the chance. And I'm sorry that Hunnechurch &
Associates didn't poke a little further into Barry's life."

"What a lot of twaddle! Do you want the perfect illustration of
someone who went the second mile? I give you Barry Goodwin! He did
a superb job of damaging my reputation. He even killed himself to get
the job done. That's *doing more* with a capital *M!*"

The spiteful words were out of my mouth before I could halt them.
I heard Gloria take a deep breath.

You're in for a tongue-lashing now, which you richly deserve.

Happily, Gloria chose to speak instead of shout. "You seem to understand the concept of the second mile," she said, "but your example
can use a lot of work."

———

Once again, the weather forecasters got it all wrong. Our "major snowstorm" began to peter out at noon, and by 2:30 P.M. an unexpectedly
warm afternoon sun had turned most of the fallen white stuff into gray
slush. The chill in the air was gone, and so was any iciness between
Gloria and me. We were sitting side by side on the Victorian sofa, fine-
tuning the list of potential clients we would try to contact the following week, when someone knocked on our office door.

"Are we here?" Gloria asked. We had been keeping our front door
locked to fend off reporters and curiosity seekers.

I looked at my watch. "Three-thirty on a Thursday afternoon. It
seems a bit late in the day for a member of the press to show up."

"Can I help you?" Gloria shouted at the door.

"Surefire Messenger Service," a woman's voice shouted back, "with
a package for Hunnechurch & Associates."

Our "package" proved to be a large manila envelope with a
Campbell & McQueen logo in the upper left-hand corner. Someone
had pasted two neon-red stickers on the front. One read "Deliver
Immediately," the other "IMPORTANT!"

"Oh, my!" I said. "I don't like the look of this."

Gloria reached for the heavy army-issue survival knife she used as a letter opener and filleted the envelope's flap. Inside was a single sheet of C&M letterhead. On it was a single paragraph of text:

"Dear Miss Hunnechurch" (I read aloud). "We are in receipt of your invoice dated October 22 for executive recruiting services provided by your firm. Please be advised that Campbell & McQueen, Incorporated, on the advice of legal counsel, rejects your demand for payment. The recent suicide of Mr. Barry Goodwin terminates our respective responsibilities under the contract that defines our relationship. Yours truly, Sidney Monk, Vice President of Human Resources."

"Wow!" Gloria said. "Talk about an abrupt letter."

"C&M has every right to refuse payment because Barry won't finish his sixty days on the job. Except . . ."

"What?"

"Except, this letter doesn't sound like Sidney. In fact, the words are *so* not like Sidney that I want to know why he sent it."

I dialed Sidney's direct number.

"We need to chat about the letter," I said without any preamble when he answered.

He startled me by replying, "Come right over. A chat sounds like a fine idea."

"I'm on my way!"

Gloria lobbed her keys to me when I put down the telephone. "You'll need my truck if you are going to visit C&M." She added, "Anything I can do back here?"

"Browse through our finances and figure out how we can tighten our belt. We just lost a fifth of our revenues for the year."

"I think I'll also pray for you, Pippa."

"Do so immediately. I can't imagine what I'm going to say to Sidney when I get there."

Twelve minutes later I presented myself to the receptionist in C&M's well-appointed lobby.

"Tell Sidney Monk that Pippa Hunnechurch is here," I said in a vigorous tone that drained the welcoming smile from her face. She whispered into her phone while I perused the panels of large photographs on display. Creating the lobby "science fair exhibits," as Barry had called them, was one of his first projects as director of communications. The series of photos showed the steps of the molding process—starting with tiny beads of resin, each the size of a grain of rice, and ending with finished plastic parts.

A friendly voice interrupted my perusing. "Hi, Pippa."

I turned. Diane Dupont was standing in the archway that led out of the reception lobby. She was thirtyish and stood five-foot-three, but her simple, straight-line black wool dress—most likely the dress she had worn to Barry's viewing—made her seem taller. Even at a distance, her green eyes signaled a lively intelligence, and her small features gave her face the pixielike quality that vacuumed men to her side.

"Hello, Diane," I said somewhat tentatively. I hoped that Sidney had not changed his mind and sent his loyal deputy to repel the invading headhunter.

Diane beckoned to me. "We have a conference room in the prototype molding shop," she said. "Everyone is waiting for you there. I'll take you back."

We trudged side by side down a wide corridor tiled with shiny vinyl squares, my boots squeaking softly, Diane's gold charm bracelet tinkling melodiously.

"Who is *everyone?*" I asked. "And why are we meeting out back?"

"To answer your first question, 'everyone' is Sidney, plus Richard Campbell, Hilda McQueen, and Jerry Nichols."

"Goodness! I don't want to interrupt a get-together of the corporate brain trust."

"You're not interrupting anything. The nasty letter was Richard's doing, with a little help from Hilda and Jerry. Sidney set up the meeting so that Richard can tell you in person why it was sent. Richard wanted Hilda and Jerry to be there."

My mouth felt dry. My impulsive chat with Sidney had transmuted into a full-blown challenge meeting with senior management, but I wasn't prepared to argue my case, or even explain the reason for my visit.

Stiffen your spine, Hunnechurch. A headhunter must be agile and think on her feet.

Diane went on, "Your second question is trickier to answer. All I can say is that the conference room in the executive suite is full of confidential stuff that you can't see."

"Pertaining, of course, to C&M being acquired by a larger company."

"Whatever," Diane said blithely.

Campbell & McQueen's prototype molding shop was a high-ceilinged factory space the size of a hotel banquet hall, with beige speckled floor tiles and banks of suspended fluorescent lights that cast a blush glow. The powerful aroma in the air—a curious mixture of sweet and acrid—made me sneeze.

"Bless you!" Diane said as she handed me a pair of safety glasses. "That's the smell of hot plastic resin. I'm one of the weirdos who likes the odor; it makes me think of exotic flowers."

I didn't argue, although hot resin smelled like no flower I had ever poked my nose into.

We walked along a wide center aisle, close to laboratory tables laden with glass jugs full of colorful resin beads and past twelve large injection-molding machines arranged in three neat ranks. A dozen or so white-coated technicians toiled at the machines, which thumped, whirred, and occasionally hissed.

"Your injection molding machines resemble miniature steam-powered locomotives," I said. "The nineteenth-century sort."

"They work on a simple principle. We melt the resin beads, squirt the hot goop into metal molds, then let it cool. Out pops a molded plastic part."

"You summed up in a single sentence what Jerry Nichols took four days to explain."

Diane laughed. "You're the one who asked for a crash course in plastics."

"So I did, but you might have warned me about your master molder."

"I distinctly remember telling you that Jerry is a world-famous manufacturing genius who knows more about plastics technology than anyone else at C&M—and who loves to share his knowledge."

"Can I ask you a touchy question?" I said.

Diane stopped walking. "About?"

"About Sidney," I said. "If the letter wasn't Sidney's doing, why did he sign it?"

Diane sighed. "I don't like the way you're being treated by C&M, so I'm going to say something I probably shouldn't. Sidney Monk sincerely believes that to get along you have to go along. He *never* argues with Richard, Hilda, or Jerry. Anything they want is fine with him."

"Oh, dear."

"Sidney is a nice guy and an OK boss, but I wish that he had a backbone."

Diane led me to the far corner of the molding shop, to a small walled-in area—a room within a room. She knocked on the door and turned the knob. I pushed the door open and walked inside. Diane silently pulled the door shut behind me as she left.

The four of them were seated on one side of a rectangular walnut conference table: Sidney Monk, Jerry Nichols, Hilda McQueen, and Richard

Campbell. Richard, obviously in charge, pointed to a chair on the other side and said, "Good afternoon, Miss Hunnechurch. Please be seated."

There were no handshakes, no friendly faces. I might have been a defendant at a trial.

I sat down and Richard went on, "Mr. Monk arranged this meeting after you expressed a desire to review the correspondence that Campbell & McQueen sent you today. Frankly, I think our letter speaks for itself. However . . ."

I took Richard's pregnant pause as a signal that the ball was in my court.

I began by putting on the warmest smile in my repertoire. "Thank you for taking the time to meet with me," I said. "I fully agree that Mr. Goodwin's death eliminates C&M's responsibility to pay my fee. In fact, I had intended to withdraw my invoice. What shocked me was the harsh tone of the letter."

"The tone of our letter also speaks for itself, Miss Hunnechurch." This time Richard didn't hesitate. "It says that we have no further need for your services."

Richard continued to look at me, but the others averted their eyes. Sidney gazed at his wristwatch. Jerry stared at the blank writing pad in front of him. Hilda studied the map of the world that filled the wall to my right.

I tried to keep the quiver out of my voice. "That is most disappointing to hear," I said. "My goal is to build a long, productive relationship with C&M. Can you tell me why you want to dismiss Hunnechurch & Associates?"

"The short of it is, you sold us damaged goods." Richard looked to his right. "Hilda, do you have anything to add?"

Hilda nodded, then slowly turned toward me. "Pippa, I won't be coy with you. Barry Goodwin's suicide triggered an onslaught of unpleasant publicity at a critical time in C&M's history. The irony of the situation is that we also lost the very manager responsible for dealing with the media during a crisis. We have to replace Barry as rapidly as possible."

"I would be pleased to take on the assignment."

"I'm afraid we must decline your offer. We have decided to retain a larger, more experienced recruiting firm—one with the resources to do a more comprehensive investigation before it presents a candidate. Specifically, Nailor & McHale. I'm certain you have heard of them."

Another loss to Nailor & McHale!

I sat upright in my chair. "Certainly you don't fault me for not anticipating Barry Goodwin's suicide," I said quickly.

Hilda took a deep breath. "At first we discounted the accusations in Barry's suicide note. However, additional information we received today has convinced us that you did not perform the scrupulous background examination we expect from an executive recruiter."

"What information? I carefully investigated every detail in Barry Goodwin's résumé."

Richard jumped in before Hilda could answer me. "We are fully satisfied by the definitive proof we have received. I see no particular reason to discuss it further."

His switch to the word *proof* sent a shiver through my body. My reputation as a recruiter is the very bulwark of my business. Something that Campbell & McQueen saw or heard had shattered their faith in me. *But what could it be?*

I looked at Sidney, hoping for a sign of support. All he offered me was a ponderous shrug.

Jerry merely shook his head while continuing to stare at his pad of paper.

Time to leave, Pippa. You are clean out of friends.

I rose with all the dignity I could muster.

"As I said before, thank you for seeing me," I said. "I appreciate your candor, and I make you a promise. I intend to rebuild your confidence in Hunnechurch & Associates."

I doubt that any of the four believed me, which was only fair, considering that I had no idea how I would get the job done.

```
┌─────────────────────────────────┐
│         Chapter  Eight          │
└─────────────────────────────────┘
```

WE HUNNECHURCHES are realistic folk. The more distance I put between Campbell & McQueen and me, the more pointless my bold promise seemed. Richard Campbell had personally handed me my walking papers; he didn't seem the type who reversed his decisions. Worse yet, C&M would soon have a relationship with another headhunting firm. Even if I managed to restore Richard Campbell's confidence in me, Hunnechurch & Associates would be out in the cold. I could imagine Mum throwing back her head and saying, "Trying to undo the past is a foolish waste of energy. Learn from your mistakes and look ahead."

Your worst mistake was agreeing to recruit a technologist.

I decided then and there that from now on Gloria and I would stick with the kinds of assignments and candidates we knew best. Furthermore, we would work only for clients who did things we could understand without several days of on-the-job training. I felt considerably more optimistic as I turned left on Ryde High Street, a block away from the refurbished leather warehouse.

It was five-thirty when I returned the keys to Gloria's truck and summarized the sorry result of my visit to C&M.

"I'll give you a lift home?" she said.

"No. The reporters have lost interest in us. I am going to retrieve my car." I had a pleasant notion. "I deserve a mental battery recharge after this horrendous week. I think I'll play hooky tomorrow."

"You can't. You have an appointment at Mattingly Industries at eleven o'clock to talk about the new sales director they want."

"Remind me what Mattingly Industries sells."

"Custom-made windows and doors."

"That's the ticket! What could be less technological than windows and doors?"

Gloria peered at me. "Have you gone bonkers too?"

"As it happens, I have regained my senses."

"In that case, would you like a lift to your car? The garage is nearly two miles away."

"I shall walk," I declared grandly.

In fact, I strolled down Ryde High Street, making detours into four interesting shops to look for the perfect Christmas gift for my sister Chloe. I rejected an elegant fountain pen (too old-fashioned), a solar-powered wristwatch (not American enough), turquoise earrings (too costly for my budget), and a pair of nifty waterproof sports sandals (the size might not be right).

Tempus fugit, Hunnechurch. It is only twelve days before Christmas and you have to ship the gift to England.

I went to bed early that night and awoke the next morning to find that most of the previous day's snow and slush had disappeared. The thermometer bolted to the outside sill of my kitchen window read 42°F. It seemed too lovely a day to linger indoors until my visit to Mattingly Industries. I decided to drop the Miata's convertible top and go for a brief pedal-to-the-metal drive—my usual escape when I want to clear my head or find a bit of peace. It would be a perfect opportunity to ponder the future of Hunnechurch & Associates.

Winston perched on the table and watched me prepare a breakfast to go: a handful of imported grapes, a buttered English muffin, and a covered travel mug full of strong Assam tea. I peeled a grape for Winston; he pecked at it valiantly with little effect. I cut it into several small pieces and shooed him back into his cage.

As I left Hunnechurch Manor, I found a freshly delivered, Friday morning issue of the *Ryde Reporter* lying on my doorstep. I tucked it behind the Miata's front seat, and for no particular reason decided to begin my feel-better junket by crossing the Chesapeake Bay.

The Chesapeake Bay Bridge is five miles long with few places a state trooper can hide. I swung the convertible top down when I passed the tollgate, tromped on the gas pedal, and (keeping an eye open for unmarked patrol cars) let the speedometer creep past seventy. I sped along, listening to the tires whining on the metal reinforced pavement.

I was chilled to the bone in less than a minute—I had worn a light woolen car coat and a pair of earmuffs, not my heavy winter parka with its draw-stringed hood.

I pulled off Route 50-301 at the eastern end of the bridge and followed the signs to the Bay Bridge Marina. My instantly concocted Plan B was to find a quiet, sun-soaked bench near the water, eat my breakfast, and admire the Chesapeake for an hour or so. The bench I chose was alongside a two-story wooden building that sheltered it from the wind but let the sun do its thing. I could see across the bay all the way to Annapolis. I watched two large, heavily laden containerships steam down the big-ship channel while I nibbled my muffin and sipped my tea. I completely forgot about marketing strategy.

At ten o'clock—convertible top up and heater on—I pointed my Miata back to Ryde. I would stop at my office for the paperwork I needed, then go on to the Mattingly headquarters near Annapolis.

I was one-third of the way across the Chesapeake Bay Bridge when traffic came to a dead halt. I tuned my radio to a Baltimore news radio station and learned that a large truck had overturned on the western end of the bridge. The roadway was strewn with frozen chickens and diesel fuel. I reached for my cell phone and called Gloria.

"Give the folks at Mattingly a call," I said. "I am trapped on the Bay Bridge, stuck behind an accident that may take hours to clean up."

"No problem. Rose Connelly, Mattingly's human resources director, telephoned a half hour ago. She cancelled the meeting."

"Did she reschedule?"

"Nope."

"Well, did she give a reason?"

"Sort of. She said, 'Pippa will understand why.'"

"But I *don't* understand why."

"Want me to call Rose back and ask?"

I thought about it. "No. I'll do it right now. It'll give me something to do while I wait."

"While you're at it, buzz Liberty Construction. Simon Harris called earlier but didn't leave a message."

"Yes, ma'am."

"By the way, if you don't get back before I leave, have a nice weekend."

Then I remembered. "Ah, you're off being a weekend warrior again."

"*Ten hut!*"

"Don't shoot yourself—or any other National Guard chaps—in the foot."

"No chance of that," she said. "This is a short training weekend. Our primary mission is to cohost a Christmas party for disabled kids in Baltimore."

I rang off and dialed Rose Connelly.

"Hi, Rose. It's Pippa," I said. "I'm bewildered by your cryptic message."

After about ten seconds of silence, she said, "I don't want to talk about it now. Call me late next week."

Click.

I stared at my little cell phone and muttered, "What was that all about?"

When I looked up, I could see that several people had stepped out of their vehicles and were standing on the bridge roadway. It's not something one can do every day. Specifically, it's something that one can do officially only during the Bay Bridge Walk in May, when one span of the bridge is turned over to pedestrians.

Why not? You may be here awhile.

I shoehorned myself out of my little sports car, raised my coat collar to shield my neck, and called Simon Harris at Marshall Construction.

"Our senior management met this morning, Pippa," he said. "They have decided to commission Nailor & McHale to find our new controller. We won't need your services."

"But you told me that you preferred using a local recruiting firm. You asked me to send you a contract."

"We reevaluated our position. We decided that we would be safer with Nailor & McHale—a well-established recruiter with an unassailable reputation."

"Did you say *safer?*" I squeaked.

"A bad choice of words, but you know what I mean."

"No. I don't know what you mean."

Click.

The chill I felt as I climbed back into my car had nothing to do with the brisk wind that whipped across the bridge.

None of this makes any sense.

When I turned to latch my seatbelt, I saw the *Ryde Reporter* poking out from behind my seat. *Something to take my mind off business.* I unfolded the newspaper on the passenger seat and browsed the front page. David Friendly's feature article on Barry Goodwin was the lead story:

ANATOMY OF A SUICIDE
Did a Local "Headhunter" Contribute to
the Death of a Tormented Businessman?

I felt my stomach knot. It seemed that David's "human-interest piece" had become an investigative exposé aimed at me.

I began to read. The first half of the article summarized Barry's life story, described his role at Campbell & McQueen, and presented an unadorned, if harrowing, account of his suicide. I let myself relax a bit. Perhaps Lenny Smithson had tacked a garish headline on a straightforward story?

No such luck. The second half of the story went right for my jugular:

> When this reporter asked Miss Hunnechurch how long she had known Barry Goodwin, she replied, "I met him in early August." Mr. Goodwin was hired by C&M less than three weeks later.
>
> Sidney Monk, vice president of human resources at C&M, says, "My understanding is that Miss Hunnechurch presented his résumé to us about a week after she identified him as a potential candidate."
>
> Was a week sufficient time to evaluate Mr. Goodwin's ability to cope with on-the-job stress?
>
> "Absolutely not!" says Dr. Judith Barnard, a Baltimore-based psychologist who serves as a consultant to the *Ryde Reporter.* "Mr. Goodwin's résumé shows a pattern of job changes that demands a detailed investigation as to his

ability to fill a high-stress position. Looking backward, we can see that he was not clearly suited for the job."

Yet, Miss Hunnechurch never doubted that Mr. Goodwin was a suitable candidate for the post at Campbell & McQueen. "Barry's education and experience were perfect for the job," she said. "Two master's degrees. And a knowledge of plastics that wouldn't quit. And current experience as a PR manager."

Dr. Barnard counters, "A person's life on paper never tells the whole story. In Barry Goodwin's case, you have to read between the lines of his résumé, and you have to probe the people who know him best to ascertain his limitations."

When asked if she spoke to Mr. Goodwin's references, Miss Hunnechurch said, "Every last one! My reputation is on the line when I present a candidate. I always make certain that everything in the candidate package is valid—including references. I am exceptionally thorough. Diligence is my stock in trade."

However, when this reporter contacted one of Mr. Goodwin's primary references, a troubling example of lack of diligence emerged. "Pippa Hunnechurch did talk to me about Barry," says Sheila Wade, the owner of Flynt Molding, Easton, Md., Mr. Goodwin's previous employer, "but she didn't ask me any questions about stress. If she had, I would have told her that Barry was a high-strung individual who has a history of anxiety attacks at work."

Mr. Goodwin's suicide note declares that Ms. Hunnechurch "knew that I don't handle stress well." When asked about this, she flatly denied that Mr. Goodwin had ever expressed concerns about his ability to cope with job-related stress. She also stated, "A person allergic to stress doesn't willingly take on the kind of responsibilities that Barry shouldered. He was eager to become C&M's director of corporate communications."

Mr. Gerald Nichols, C&M's master molder and a coworker of Mr. Goodwin tells a different story: "Barry told me that he was worried about taking the C&M job and that he gave his headhunter a heads-up about his anxiety attacks. Barry didn't keep them a secret from anyone. Several of us at C&M knew that he was seeing a psychiatrist and taking medication."

Mr. Goodwin had worked for C&M for only fifty-three days when he killed himself. Yet his business colleagues were able to detect warning signs of stress buildup. "Barry was edgy much of the time," Gerald Nichols reports, "but the past few weeks were worse. He would lose his temper every day and get into fights with people, including our executives. He slammed doors a lot and threw stuff around."

Ms. Hunnechurch acknowledged that Mr. Goodwin recently expressed concerns to her about his position at Campbell & McQueen, but she refused to provide details. Nor would she comment about Mr. Goodwin's accusation that she "ruined his life," other than to say, "I didn't ruin Barry's life. I helped to advance his career. That is what headhunters do for good people."

Mr. Richard Campbell, CEO of Campbell & McQueen, disagrees. "It appears to me that Miss Hunnechurch did not know that her candidate was emotionally ill-prepared to handle a high-stress job. Yet she recruited him for a position that would put him on the front lines of a dynamic, growing company. Executive recruiters earn hefty fees for the work they do. Surely they should be held accountable when their mistakes cause a tragedy."

_____

I heard a horn honking behind me and looked up. The stalled traffic on the bridge had begun to move. I crumpled the *Ryde Reporter* into a ball of waste paper and cranked the Miata's engine. My hand trembled on the steering wheel as I accelerated, angry tears blurring my vision. A tempting notion popped into my head: Proceed directly to the airport and board a plane to England.

Why not go back home? Your career in America is finished.

I broke the speed limit on every road leading back to Ryde. My tires squealed when I swung onto Ryde High Street. I ran the red light at Jefferson Avenue, and I parked my car in a loading zone in front of the pudgy marble and glass building that is home to the *Ryde Reporter.*

I stomped up the stairs and found David Friendly in his office, working at a video display terminal.

"You wretched two-faced rotter!" I bellowed. "You faithless lying blob of treachery! You miserable excuse for a journalist!"

"Please sit down, Pippa" he said, quietly, "and lower your voice. Other people are trying to work."

"How could you publish such drivel at my expense?"

David set his chin in a stubborn line. "My assignment was to write an article about Barry Goodwin's suicide. I interviewed more than a dozen people and collected a notebook full of facts. Many of the statements and facts were about you. I had no choice but to include them in my story."

"You made me look like an incompetent fool." I wagged my finger at him. "Two potential clients just slammed their doors in my face."

"If you have lost business, I'm sorry, but I stand behind my work. If you want to rebut anything I put in the piece, write a letter to the editor. I'll see that it gets published."

The face that I'd once thought of as handsome now looked cruel and callous. David's nose seemed too long, his eyes too close together, and his hair the color of a weasel.

"A most gracious thank you—for nothing!" I snapped. "An abbreviated letter of complaint from me published on page twenty-five of the

Ryde Reporter will hardly undo the damage wrought by your front-page hatchet job."

David stood up. "If you won't sit," he said, "I'll stand."

He tried to take my hand; I crossed my arms.

"I didn't do a hatchet job, as you call it, on anyone," he said. "My article fairly and accurately presented what people told me about Barry Goodwin—and you."

"But what if their assertions aren't true?"

David frowned. "You talk about your reputation, Pippa. Well, I have a reputation too. I'm smart, I'm tenacious, and I care about publishing the truth. I also work hard. Don't blame me because I dug up unflattering information about Barry Goodwin that you should have found."

"Piffle, David. You betrayed my trust and smashed my standing in the business community, even though we are friends. *Correction*—even though we *were* friends." I turned on my heels and moved toward the exit. I shouted over my shoulder, "I shall not, of course, spend Christmas with you, and please cancel my subscription to the *Ryde Reporter.*"

If David replied, I didn't hear him. I stormed out of the building and found a freshly written parking ticket beneath my car's windshield wiper.

The marmalade on the crumpet of a truly rotten morning!

As I stuffed the ticket into my purse, I began to feel painfully alone. It was as if the city of Ryde had become an inhospitable place. All at once I couldn't bear to be seen by the scores of people on Ryde High Street—every one of whom undoubtedly believed that I had done a slack job of recruiting Barry Goodwin.

Chapter Nine

I'VE HEARD IT SAID that there is no such thing as bad publicity. I invite the person who came up with that silly maxim to have the *Ryde Reporter* cast doubt upon his qualifications and ethics. David had eviscerated my hard-won reputation with one quick jab of his journalistic pen—and what does a headhunter have in the world, except her reputation? Hunnechurch & Associates was finished in Ryde, Maryland. Kaput. Dead.

I slunk home late that morning, hung up my business suit, and commenced to anesthetize my mind and memory by doing all the busywork I could invent. I dusted Hunnechurch Manor from top to bottom, I vacuumed, I tidied drawers and closets—but still the sun shone in the sky.

I made myself a pot of Darjeeling tea and read the entire *Baltimore Sun* from front page to last, including the legal notices. At last the day waned.

As evening came, I played with Winston for an hour or so, rolling his little rubber ball along the kitchen floor for him to chase. It was entertaining watching him hop after the ball, his claws skittering on tiles, and he seemed to take pleasure in the extra attention I gave him. Our game came to an abrupt end when the toy rolled under my refrigerator. Winston waited patiently for me to retrieve it. When he figured out that I couldn't, he flew to the top of a cabinet and glared at me.

Curiously, looking up at Winston gave me the idea to pray, although I felt uncertain what to pray about. Was it proper to ask God to change the hearts and minds of my clients? Gloria and Chloe were good at praying; I wasn't. Their impromptu prayers sounded like spur-of-the-moment poetry. Mine often came out as rambling monologues that lacked direction or purpose. Nonetheless, I shut my eyes and took a deep breath.

Father in heaven, I began. *I am in trouble today. I feel alone because I have lost a close friend in Ryde. I don't think I will ever be able to forgive him for the article he wrote. I suppose that I also feel frightened. Everything I've worked so hard for is slipping away. I ask you to stop this from happening, but if you choose not to, I ask for the strength to persevere—no matter what the blighters throw at me. I don't know what else to say, except that I ask for your blessing. In Jesus' name. Amen.*

When my eyes opened, they fell on the snapshot of James Huston that is pinned to my refrigerator door by a magnet shaped like Georgia. I thought about calling James but decided not to. I had too much to share with him to do it over the telephone. Better to wait until next week when he came to town. What's more, I'd almost certainly start blubbering and add to the embarrassment that filled me to overflowing that day.

I watched an old Cary Grant comedy on TV until ten, when I remembered I hadn't eaten lunch or dinner. It didn't seem important. My muscles had begun to ache from all the housework I had done. I went up to bed and fell promptly asleep.

Saturday morning arrived right on schedule, and with it a sense of resignation. Who would care if Hunnechurch & Associates faded away? No one, really. The few clients we had would soon find other headhunters. I lounged in bed until nine-thirty, rereading old issues of *National Geographic,* until I began to feel ravenous. I made myself a breakfast of Irish oatmeal covered with a double dollop of Lyle's Golden Syrup—a self-prescribed dose of comfort food to drive away my gloom for at least an hour or two.

My house was spotless; I needed another chore to keep my mind off myself. I soon found it.

When I washed my breakfast dishes I caught sight of a package of aluminum foil on the shelf above my kitchen sink. I remembered a pressing task that *had* to be done that morning. Buried deep in my refrigerator, at the rear of the bottom shelf, were twelve miniature Christmas puddings, each four inches across and three inches high. Homemade plum pudds are a Hunnechurch family tradition. I had prepared my puddings two months earlier and allowed each to age to spicy perfection—tasty gifts to accompany the Christmas messages I would send to my dearest friends in Ryde. I had posted my other cards a weekend ago, but the pudding cards (as I called them) had been victims of my tumult-filled week.

They won't get them before Christmas if you don't mail the packages today.

Fortunately, I had already bought the Christmas cards, shipping boxes, and labels. All I needed to do was assemble the lot—a four-step process. First, wrap a pudding in foil and tie it up with a ribbon. Second, write a personal message on a Christmas card. Third, pack the wrapped pudding and card in a shipping box, using colored tissue paper as a filler. Fourth, add the appropriate mailing label.

I spread my supplies across my kitchen table. Each Christmas card I wrote brightened my mood a whit—until I reached "Mr. & Mrs. David Friendly" on my list. My mounting good cheer dissolved like a sugar cube in hot tea. I stared at the blank card and wondered what to do. I finally decided to address the message and the label to Ms. Joyce Friendly.

Rotters like David don't deserve a Hunnechurch's famous Christmas pudding.

The main post office on Ryde High Street was open until five o'clock that afternoon. I reached the front of the line a few minutes before three. For a fleeting moment, as I paid for the postage, I basked in the contentment of having completed one's Christmas duties—until I thought about Chloe.

Today is the day you buy her gift.

Yet again, I set out to browse the shops on Ryde High Street, but then I realized that I was approaching the problem from the wrong end. One doesn't browse for Chloe; rather, one decides on an appropriate gift, then locates it.

No sooner had I chosen my new tactic, than inspiration struck. I saw a poster advertising the Ryde Playhouse's upcoming series of Broadway musical comedies. Chloe *loves* Broadway shows, and what could be more American? I sped to Ryde Books & Videos and within ten minutes had purchased "The Rogers & Hammerstein Collection," a boxed set of five videos and arranged for express shipment to England.

Hooray! Now I could enjoy Christmas. At least that's what I thought at the time.

———

I elected not to attend church on Sunday morning. Too many members of the congregation are faithful readers of the *Ryde Reporter.* The thought of their reactions when I walked into the sanctuary gave me pause. I would let memories of the article fade before I darkened the doorway of Ryde Fellowship Church again.

The morning was chill but sunny. I went for a long walk on a hiking path south of Ryde that winds close to the Magothy River. I passed dozens of plump Canadian geese standing in groups of three and four and grazing on what little grass survived into December. I also pondered my future. Before I established my little business, I had worked for CentreBank in Baltimore, as the in-house recruiter of junior personnel. *Perhaps I should find a nine-to-five job in human resources.* Sidney Monk seemed to enjoy his life, and his competence had never been questioned in print by a local business reporter.

I arrived home a little before noon to find the light on my answering machine blinking. For a moment I wondered if a sadistic reporter wanted my reactions to David's article. On second thought, I decided that the local media had written me off. I pressed the play button.

"Hello, Miss H.," a bluff male voice said. "Call my cell phone ASAP." He provided the number. "We need to talk about Barry Goodwin."

The voice belonged to Stephen Reilly, a homicide detective at the Ryde Police Department. I had first met Reilly a year and a half earlier when another headhunter in town had fallen off a party boat and drowned under suspicious circumstances. We were like chalk and cheese back then—two opposite personalities who butted heads—but we began to build a more cordial relationship during the hours we spent working together at the Ryde Chamber of Commerce. I served as the chamber's social chairperson, and Reilly was the police department's liaison to the Ryde business community. We saw each other at least once a month. He had fallen into the habit of calling me "Miss H." I always called him "Reilly."

I dialed his number.

"What are you doing for lunch today?" he asked.

"I have no plans."

"I'll pick you up in fifteen minutes."

"Your message said that we need to talk about Barry Goodwin. Why?"

"Lunch first—then business." He rang off before I could say anything else.

Reilly was driving an unmarked police sedan painted the inevitable plum. "I'm in the mood for a roast beef sandwich at Ruth's," he said as I slipped into the passenger's seat.

"Ruth's is fine with me," I said. Reilly's car reeked of stale cigarette smoke; I tried to open my window, but the pushbutton didn't work.

"So, how are you managing?" he asked.

"As well as can be expected under the circumstances, I suppose."

"I love British understatement." He chuckled. "But I give you fair warning. David Friendly is a good friend of mine. We go way back in this town. If he turns up with a knife in his back, you'll be my prime suspect."

"Charming! I love the emotional sensitivity of Ryde coppers."

Ruth's is a legendary delicatessen that traces its roots to Ruth Rubinsky, an immigrant who sold sandwiches to factory workers during the 1930s from the back of a converted Ford Model A pickup truck. Her illustrious vehicle hangs from the ceiling of the current restaurant on Romney Boulevard. The hostess led us to a booth beneath the right rear fender.

We ordered two jumbo roast beef sandwiches, a pot of tea for me, and a mug of coffee for Reilly. I had managed to eat half of my sandwich when Reilly said, "What's your take on Barry Goodwin? You don't really think he was as batty as everyone insists, do you?"

My amazement sent a crumb of rye bread down the wrong way. "Good heavens!" I said when I stopped coughing. "Why would you ask that of me?"

"Two reasons. First, because you have to be a good judge of people in your business. Second, because I know you don't do sloppy work."

"Ah . . ."

"In fact, given that Miss H. is both perceptive and persnickety, I've been wondering why she would recruit a manager who was visibly loony."

"She wouldn't," I said. "Barry was the epitome of sanity when I met him last summer. He seemed friendly, sensible, well-balanced, temperate. . . . I've run out of adjectives."

"That's what I thought. Yet four months later he's as irritable as a Tasmanian devil. I have two witnesses who saw him toss a chair through a glass-paneled door in Campbell & McQueen's executive suite."

"Blimey!"

"The door belonged to a vice-president named Sidney Monk. Heard of him?"

"Indeed I have. When did this happen?"

"A few hours before Goodwin turned on the carbon monoxide. The word is, C&M management decided to fire him but didn't get the chance before he killed himself. What do you think of that?"

I sighed. "I am mortified by Barry's inexplicable behavior."

Reilly smiled at me. "There's no doubt that Barry had a short fuse and a nasty disposition, but that raises a fascinating question. Do angry people commit suicide?"

I clasped my cup in front of me to hide the pounding of my heart. "Are you suggesting that Barry Goodwin did *not* commit suicide?"

Reilly brought his head closer to mine. "Goodwin had a medical history that is wholly consistent with suicide. He was treated for anxiety and depression for several years, but nobody describes his behavior at C&M as anxious or depressed. The universal consensus is that he was a jerk who kept losing his temper."

"You didn't answer my question."

"Of course not. I can't divulge the results of an ongoing police investigation to a civilian."

"Very funny."

"What I can tell you is that there are a couple of oddities associated with Goodwin's suicide note."

"For example?"

"For example, he didn't leave a handwritten message."

I shook my head. "So what? Barry was a techie; E-mail was his medium. Surely he wasn't the first person to E-mail a suicide note?"

"It happens," Reilly admitted, "though not every day and not to hundreds of people. The fact is, many suicides don't explain themselves. However, when we find a note, we usually can verify the authorship. Here we have nothing. No signature, no handwriting, no fingerprints."

"What is the other oddity?"

"The note is too short and too articulate. In my experience, when a suicide expends the effort to write a suicide note, you generally get a meandering message, not a well-organized one-pager."

"Goodness! I felt the same way when I saw it. It seemed oddly deliberate."

"The writing is extremely deliberate, although the subject matter bounces around."

"How so?"

"Goodwin starts off blaming his job at C&M, but then as an after-thought he blames you."

"Please don't remind me."

"I'd be more convinced if he had settled on one target throughout the message." Reilly stared into his half-empty coffee mug. "I've seen about two dozen suicide notes during my career in homicide—let's say two a year. Most of them were apologetic and usually had statements designed to make suicide not seem so bad. Phrases like, 'I'll meet you in the next life,' or 'I'll be looking down on everything you do.' Only a handful of the notes blamed other people, and those that did were consistent front to back."

"Aren't there mental-health professionals who analyze suicide notes?"

"Sure. I know three forensic psychologists who could tear the message apart and tell me whether or not it contains psychological themes consistent with a genuine wish to die."

"Why not ask one?"

"Because my boss, his boss, and the state's attorney are all satisfied that Barry Goodwin killed himself. It's my gut against everyone else's foregone conclusion."

"In short, you think that Barry was murdered."

Reilly shrugged. "His gas-fired furnace didn't sabotage itself."

"Why tell me all this?"

"I'm grasping at straws. I need ammunition to fight the assumption of suicide. A motive for murder would give me a starting point." Reilly tapped the top of my hand with a finger. "Do you know of *any* reason someone would want to kill Goodwin—other than his lousy personality?"

"Oh dear! It never dawned on me to bring it to your attention, but a week before he died, Barry told me that he couldn't stomach C&M's business practices and that the company did things that were illegal and immoral. He intended to gather evidence of what's going on—enough to send the executives involved to jail."

Abruptly, Reilly gripped my hand. The expression on his face signaled pure surprise.

"Did you ask Goodwin to describe the criminal activity?" he said evenly.

"Of course, but he refused to tell me. He said it would hurt people who had enough to worry about."

"Did he share his ideas with anyone else?"

"He definitely told his Wednesday night prayer group. That's as much as I know." I waited for several seconds while Reilly stared off into space. "Can I have my hand back?"

Reilly nodded. I tugged my hand free.

"It's so simple!" he said, a merry grin spreading across his wide face. "Goodwin talks about his suspicions to you, to his prayer group, probably to half of Ryde. Eventually the wrong person hears what Goodwin is saying and gets frightened because he or she knows that Goodwin is a loose cannon. Intelligent but unpredictable—which makes him a big risk."

"So he or she fakes Barry's suicide?"

"Easy as pie! You haven't seen the autopsy report. Goodwin had high levels of a prescription sleeping pill in his bloodstream. My colleagues presume that he knocked himself out to avoid feeling any discomfort from the carbon monoxide, but my gut says that the killer slipped him a Mickey, then fiddled with the furnace and faked the suicide E-mail."

"And made me the goat."

Reilly stopped smiling. "Whoever killed Goodwin is a genius. You became the perfect fall guy—the greedy headhunter who forced the loony chemist into the wrong job and drove him over the edge." He polished off the remaining item on his plate—a piece of dill pickle. "Eat the other half of your sandwich so we can get out of here. I have a ton of work to do."

The fresh wave of anger that poured through me took away what little appetite I had left. Not finishing meals in restaurants was becoming a habit. I flagged our waitress.

"Can I please have a doggy bag?"

Chapter Ten

ON MONDAY MORNING I found Gloria on her hands and knees scooping crumpled sheets of paper from the floor around her desk. She looked up at me like a deer in a headlight, then forced a smile.

"Rats!" she said. "I wanted to get this mess cleaned up before . . . well . . . you know. I had a great weekend. How about you?"

"You don't have to spare my feelings. I can imagine what those are."

Gloria let her faux smile fade. She scrambled to her feet, her fists full of litter.

"Our clients read David Friendly's article in the *Ryde Reporter*," I went on, "and are abandoning ship as fast as they can. The mail can be slow during the Christmas season, so they sent cancellation faxes. How many did we receive this morning?"

"Six. And there are two more stored in memory. The fax machine ran out of paper."

"Show me." I held out my hand. She gave me one of the larger wads of paper. I began to unfold and flatten it on her desktop and immediately recognized the distinctive logo on the first page: Talley

Manufacturing, a small but promising client. Hunnechurch & Associates had recruited a shipping manager for Talley the previous April. Gloria and I assumed there would be a string of new assignments as the company continued to grow.

"I'm sorry about attacking the faxes," Gloria said, "but I lost my temper. I did the same thing last night when I got back from training and saw the article. I used the *Ryde Reporter* as kindling in my fireplace."

"My copy is currently gracing the bottom of Winston's cage."

"I hope you fed him an extra helping of parakeet seed."

The Talley fax turned out to be a three-page letter, single-spaced—a lot of words merely to dismiss a headhunter. I suppose that Talley's lawyers insisted on giving me a thorough drubbing. Several nasty phrases caught my eye as I skimmed the pages: "This letter represents our formal notice that Philippa Hunnechurch & Associates is no longer our executive recruiter of record"; "We feel that we will be better served by an executive recruiter whose professional ethics match ours more closely"; and, "Please DO NOT contact any Talley Manufacturing personnel. If you have any questions or comments about this letter, address them to Nancy Owens, Esq., attorney at law, in the firm of McGuire, Owens, and Thatcher."

"You had the right idea!" I recrumpled the fax and tossed the wad into Gloria's wastebasket. "Any thoughts on what we should do next? We seem to have run out of clients."

"Yep. The first thing we need to do is raise a bulwark of prayer."

I heard a horn toot and moved to the window. A big truck making a delivery at the office building across the street had partially blocked traffic on Ryde High Street. I used the brief distraction to rein in the frustration I felt. I wasn't successful.

I spun around and snapped at Gloria: "While you are praying, you might ask God why he decided to lead me on a merry chase. I am totally bewildered as to why he destroyed my standing in Ryde, wrecked my business, and shattered my dreams. What purpose was served by allowing a criminal to use me as a fall guy—a diversion? Maybe you can get him to explain how making me miserable fits into his master plan for the universe."

To my surprise, Gloria didn't argue with me. Instead, she calmly said, "Tell me what's happened."

We sat together on the Victorian sofa while I recounted my conversation with Stephen Reilly. I described his suspicions about the suicide E-mail and his off-the-cuff theory of why someone might want to kill Barry.

"If Reilly is correct," I said, "I have been sorely used as a patsy—a convenient pawn in a brilliant scheme to camouflage Barry's murder." I added, "Of course, Reilly could be utterly wrong. He has no support for his notions at the police department."

"You think he's right?"

"I do. Barry was angry at other people on the day he died—not at himself."

"Murder changes everything," she said softly.

"How? Barry Goodwin is still dead. Will his mother really be happier to learn that someone else killed him?" I pointed at the wads of crumpled paper Gloria had left on her desk. "And Hunnechurch & Associates is still out of business. A reputation is like Humpty Dumpty after his great fall. All the king's horses and all the king's men couldn't put Humpty together again."

"Forget horses and men. Ask God."

"Why bother? Whenever I try to get closer to God, my life seems to come a cropper. My prayers simply don't get his attention."

Once again Gloria didn't challenge my words. "I've felt that way a few times too," she said, "but then I remember how often God *does* answer my prayers." She reached over and patted my hand. "By the way, did you tell God that you are mad at him?"

I hesitated before I answered. "On Friday night I offered a rather humble prayer, but last night I protested strongly—using quite colorful language. In truth, I was furious."

"I can imagine." Gloria chuckled. "I'll bet God gets yelled at a lot. It's easy to forget that he isn't the cause of evil and that he suffers along with us—"

Our front door, which I had neglected to lock, suddenly flew open.

Sophie Hammond stood in our doorway, her arms crossed, her back braced against the frame, her mouth bowed into a Cheshire cat grin.

"Shall I throw her out again?" Gloria asked me as she stood up.

"You'll both regret it if you do," Sophie said smugly. She held up an unfolded issue of the *Ryde Rebel*. My picture was on the tabloid's front page beneath an enormous headline that read, *A Shameful Rush to Judgment!*

I leaped off the sofa. Beneath the headline, in slightly smaller type, was a lengthy subhead I could read easily from six feet away:

> Philippa Hunnechurch was unfairly vilified when the communications executive she recruited apparently killed himself. The police seem satisfied that it's suicide, but why would a successful businessman busy making plans for his wedding fill his apartment with carbon monoxide? Our investigation shows that suicide was *not* an option for Barry Goodwin and that "Pippa" Hunnechurch, a conscientious local headhunter, was wrongly blamed for contributing to a suicide that never happened.

I blurted out the first thing that popped into my astonished mind. "Where did you get my picture?"

"From the Ryde Chamber of Commerce," Sophie said. "I would have sent our photographer over to take a new picture, but you weren't especially cooperative last week."

"Oh my! I didn't mean . . ." I began again. "What can I . . .?" I took a deep breath. "I apologize for the way we treated you."

Sophie shrugged. "It goes with the territory. Lots of people think I write stories about alien invaders and cows with two heads. The *Ryde Rebel* often gets a bum rap—just like you did."

"I can't tell you how foolish I feel."

"Foolish is better than irresponsible. My article lays out a detailed argument against Barry Goodwin's death being a suicide. I also rebut, point-by-point, most of the case against you that appeared in the *Ryde Reporter*. David Friendly is usually a good reporter, but he mishandled this story big time."

"I want to hear this," Gloria said.

"Me too!" I put in.

"My pleasure!" Sophie handed me her copy of the *Ryde Rebel* and looked around our reception room. "Nice digs. You guys have any coffee? If I'm going to give a lecture, I need to fuel up on caffeine."

"We've switched to tea," Gloria said.

"It's been years since I've had a cup of tea, but I'll give it a try."

Gloria filled three mugs. Sophie took a position of honor in the center of the Victorian sofa. Gloria and I moved visitors' chairs in front of her.

"You have to understand up front," Sophie began, "that the cops were encouraged to agree that Barry killed himself."

"By whom?" I asked.

"By the big hitters at C&M—namely Richard Campbell and Hilda McQueen. Barry's death came at a bad time for them." She blew across the top of her tea to cool it. "Do you know about the upcoming acquisition of C&M?"

"I've heard a few rumors, nothing more."

"I couldn't put the facts in my article, but I'll be happy to fill you in." Sophie grinned at me like a little girl bursting to tell a big secret. "They're going to announce the deal in mid-January. Hughes

Engineered Materials, a big conglomerate based in Minnesota, will pay two billion dollars for C&M."

"Blimey!"

"Oh yeah! A handful of long-timers at C&M are going to be very wealthy."

"Let me guess—Richard Campbell and Hilda McQueen."

"Sure. But don't forget Jerry Nichols and Sidney Monk. They also have a lot of C&M stock." Sophie sipped her tea. "Anyway, the last thing the folks at C&M want is a murder mystery that will generate a mountain of awkward publicity because the victim is a key manager. The path of least resistance is to believe that Barry killed himself. Hilda gave the cops, and any reporter who asked, a chronology of the weird things Barry did at C&M, and Richard repeatedly assured his friend, the chief of police, that Barry seemed suicidal during his last weeks on the job."

"He didn't seem suicidal to me," I said.

"Nor to lots of other people who knew him," Sophie agreed. "Trouble is, the cops stopped taking statements at C&M after they interviewed the senior executives. They would have heard a different story if they had delved deeper into the organization. I talked to three C&M employees who reported to Barry, to a half dozen salespeople who often went to Barry for marketing support, and to the other members of C&M's quality council, which Barry chaired. To a person they told me that Barry loved his job and was anything but depressed or anxious. Most described him as focused on the future and driven to get stuff done."

"Indeed! That is the Barry Goodwin I recruited last summer."

"But then he inexplicably changed," Sophie said. "Soon after Thanksgiving he became preoccupied and grew a nasty temper. No one I interviewed knew why." She peered at me for a moment, then asked, "Do you?"

I parried her question. "I promise to think about it."

"Karen Constantine said the same thing. I'm still waiting to hear from her."

"You questioned Barry's fiancée?"

"Yep. I tracked her down at her family's weekend cabin in the woods north of Frederick, Maryland. She's a highly intelligent woman. At first she figured that Barry killed himself, but that's because the suicide E-mail temporarily snookered her. Now she's changed her tune. They were busy planning a June wedding. On the Monday Barry died they talked about honeymoon destinations. A guy wrapped up in the future doesn't take gas."

"That makes sense to me," I said, "but do mental health professionals agree?"

"You mean the so-called experts like the tame shrink that David Friendly quoted in his article?"

"Precisely!"

Sophie gave a disparaging wave. "The lady read a few documents and said what David wanted to hear in order to get her name in the paper. I spoke to a psychiatrist on the Eastern Shore who actually treated Barry. He refused to give me specifics, but he was willing to acknowledge that he didn't consider suicide a significant risk when Barry was his patient. He also admitted to being surprised when he heard the news of Barry's apparent suicide."

"I wonder why David didn't talk to him," I said.

"David's not an investigative reporter. I figured out how to find Barry's shrink; he didn't."

"You make it sound difficult."

"It was a bear! Medical records are private."

"That's what I used to believe. Yet everyone connected with Barry seemed to know that he handled stress poorly. Only Gloria and I were in the dark."

Sophie frowned. "Time out! David's article says that Barry warned you about himself. David quoted Jerry Nichols to prove the point."

"The article is incorrect. Barry told me nothing about his limitations."

Sophie leaned back against a cushion. "Holy moley! That means David misquoted *two* sources in his article. I knew about Sheila Wade, but not Jerry Nichols."

The name rang a bell, but not loudly enough for me to identify its owner. "Who is Sheila Wade?"

"She was Barry's boss back when you recruited him."

I remembered. "Right! She owns Flynt Molding in Easton."

"Well, it turns out that she *wasn't* waiting for you to quiz her about Barry Goodwin's mental health. She told David that she was prepared to answer your questions in the event that Barry had revealed his prior problems with job-related stress."

Before I could stop myself, I said, "I cannot imagine David dissembling in print."

"You can't? How well do you know David Friendly?"

I glanced at Gloria, then back to Sophie. "We were good friends before he wrote the article."

Her eyes narrowed. "I see. . . ."

"No, you don't see. He was my friend, nothing more."

"Well, your *friend* certainly didn't do you any favors. His article jumps through hoops to prove that you were incompetent and that the suicide E-mail told the truth."

I couldn't help sighing. "I'm sure my performance seemed that way to many people."

"Not really. I spoke to several of your clients. They insisted that they liked Hunnechurch & Associates—that you did fine work—even though they won't do business with you any more."

I tried not to scowl as I thought about the many extra miles we had gone for our fair-weather clients—the out-of-town trips to identify candidates, the late-night meetings with recruits, the hard work on weekends to prepare candidate packages. Our excellent performance no longer made a whit of difference to them. All because of David's wretched article.

"Can I have another mug of tea?" Sophie asked. "Believe it or not, I'm beginning to like it."

Gloria took her mug. I pulled my chair closer to the sofa.

"Sophie, can I ask you a question?" I said.

"Shoot!"

"You've been remarkably open with us. What do you expect in return?"

She began to grin. "I was going to hustle you after I drank my tea, but since you asked, here it goes. I need your help. I want to know what was bugging Barry Goodwin during his last two weeks among the living. Barry did all of his shouting and complaining at C&M, so I figure his unhappiness must be connected to the company."

"Why would you care about Barry's demons?"

"Because they will lead me to the reason he was murdered." Her face seemed to light up as she talked. "My first story raised a lot of questions. I want to write a series of dynamite follow-up articles that deliver the answers. Tell me why Barry Goodwin died, and I'll obliterate the ideas that he committed suicide and that you did sloppy work. I'm offering you a win-win proposition. You help me scoop the stodgy establishment newspapers in Maryland, and I'll help put you back in business."

Gloria returned with a mug full of tea.

"Let me make sure I understand," I said. "You want me to investigate Barry's state of mind?"

"Hey, for all I know, a little birdie will whisper the whole story into your ear. I want facts I can work with, and I don't care how you get them."

"Why me? You seem to be a wonderful collector of facts on your own."

Sophie's expression darkened. "I am, except that I wore out my welcome at C&M when I cobbled the first story together. Richard Campbell sent a memo to every employee declaring me persona non grata."

I merely nodded, not wanting to tell her that Richard had probably done the same to me.

"Yeah. I can't get inside the building, and people hang up on me when I call them at home. That's why you're better situated than me to find out what made Barry go berserk."

"My earlier reply still holds. I promise to think about it."

"Don't think too long. The *Ryde Rebel* won't publish a stale story. Our deal is off if I don't have useful information by, say, Friday. That gives you five days, counting today."

Neither of us had much to say after that rather stark declaration. Sophie finished her tea and wrote her private cell phone number on the back of her business card. "I keep my telephone powered up twenty-four hours a day," she said. "Call me anytime."

When Sophie left, Gloria locked the door behind her and asked, "What do you think?"

"I think we can be sure what happened to Barry Goodwin. When one combines Reilly's theory with Sophie's details, murder is the inescapable conclusion."

Gloria nodded. "Two billion dollars is a whale of a motive."

Two billion dollars. An impressive sum for a small company. The "long-timers," as Sophie had called them, would each receive many millions of dollars for the stock they held, but the very size of the transaction made it fragile. Any hint of impropriety at Campbell & McQueen could sour the deal. Barry wanted to deliver more than a hint; he planned to blow a loud whistle. Whatever wrongdoing he discovered had almost certainly cost him his life, the poor soul.

Gloria shook my shoulder. "So, are you going to help Sophie?"

"Hers is the best offer I've received today. A series of articles that explain the truth might well change our former clients' minds."

"True, but if you begin to poke around at C&M, you could stir up a hornet's nest. You sparred with a murderer last year and didn't have much fun."

"Don't remind me." The experience hadn't been *any* fun. I had come close to being killed.

"Like it or not, though," I went on, "I don't have many choices. Sophie has invited me to go the second mile for Hunnechurch & Associates. Her scheme gives us a chance to remain in business. If I refuse her proposition, we might as well close up shop tomorrow."

"Where does Detective Reilly fit into all this?"

"He doesn't. I told him everything I knew. He is off on his own investigation."

"Are you going to tell him what Sophie is up to?"

"I can't. Reilly is too close to David and other reporters. Sophie would lose her scoop and not write her articles."

"OK—one last question: How do we begin?"

"We?" I began to shake my head. "This is my battle, Gloria. I got us into this mess; it is my responsibility to get us out."

"Hogwash! You may be 'Hunnechurch,' but I am the 'associate.' We walk our second miles together."

I went to the telephone on Gloria's desk and dialed Sophie's cell phone number.

"Hunnechurch here," I said when she answered. "I will find out what I can by Friday."

I rang off before she could say anything annoying that might make me change my mind.

Chapter Eleven

PRESUMABLY, THE JEWISH CHAP IN ANCIENT PALESTINE didn't have any out-of-pocket costs when he walked a second mile for a Roman soldier. Hunnechurch & Associates began spending money immediately.

"Telephone the detective agency you moonlight for," I said to Gloria, "and commission them to find out all they can about Barry Goodwin. I want to know the details of his life that don't appear on his résumé."

Her eyes widened. "That will cost us a bundle. Collier Investigations is not a cheap outfit."

I held my hand up like a school crossing guard. "Don't tell me how much. Pay whatever is necessary to do a thorough job."

She gave me a crisp military salute. "Yes, ma'am!"

"Next, visit the Web sites of local newspapers and TV stations and buy time on the Lexis-Nexis database. Download everything that's been spoken or written by the media about Barry since his death. Perhaps other reporters have been as enterprising as Sophie Hammond."

"Ditto!" After another salute, she said, "What are you going to do?"

"I will contact Diane Dupont. If anyone inside Campbell & McQueen might be willing to help, she's the one."

We both turned when someone knocked on our door and a booming male voice said, "Florist delivery for Pippa Hunnechurch."

I opened the door to find a vast bouquet of hardy blossoms—white lilies, white roses, and miniature carnations surrounded by Queen Anne's Lace and Christmas greens—all overflowing the arms of a short delivery man. The attached card bore a note that read: *Call my cell phone. Fondly, James.*

"Blimey!" I said. "I forgot that James arrived in Washington today."

Gloria signed for the flowers while I hurried to the phone in my office.

"Did you have a good flight?" I asked when James answered.

"I had a magnificent flight," he said in his most honeyed drawl, "because I thought about you once every mile in the air—all five-hundred-forty of them."

"Oh my!" I attempted a southern accent. "Kind sir, I do declare! You are making me blush and quiver."

"As a result of doing that much concentrated thinking about you, I immediately jiggered my calendar so that I can visit you in Ryde for precisely one hour. Are you free between eight and nine tonight?"

James misinterpreted my hesitation.

"I know it's hardly any time together, but my schedule for the next four days is immovable. Today, for example, I have four meetings before five, a dinner tonight that I can't get out of, and a projection equipment test that absolutely, positively must be done at 10:00 P.M."

"I didn't respond because I am speechless," I stalled. In truth, I felt uneasy about seeing James that evening. Would I be good company after all that had happened?

"Does that mean you can meet me?" he said.

"Let me think . . ."

Stop dithering, Hunnechurch. You've looked forward to James's visit for nearly a week.

"Correction!" I said. "I will meet you promptly at eight." I added, "Where?"

"How about the little plaza on Ryde High Street? The one with all the pigeons during the summer."

"A grand choice. The Chamber of Commerce Christmas tree is especially beautiful this year."

I hung up relishing the lovely mood I felt but knowing that I had to put James out of my mind until this evening and concentrate on Barry Goodwin. I dialed Campbell & McQueen.

"Pippa here," I said when I got through to Diane Dupont. "May I beg a favor?"

"What kind of favor?" she said cautiously.

"I want to discuss Barry's final week on the job."

"What for?"

I did not want to lie to Diane, but I couldn't tell her about my real mission. I compromised by evading the truth. "I feel I must understand the mistakes I made, so that I don't make them again."

"I'm supposed to avoid you, Pippa," she said. "In fact, I should report this phone call to Sidney."

"A brief chat is all that I ask. Say fifteen minutes?"

I held my breath as the seconds ticked by. She finally said, "We'll have to meet away from C&M. *Far* away. Somewhere you can bump into me—as if by accident."

"I know just the place. The bookshop across from Mulberry Alley. It opens at 9:00 A.M."

"OK. Tomorrow morning at nine. Near the children's books, where I will be shopping for a present for my nephew."

"Thank you, Diane. I appreciate your friendship."

She grunted, then said, "I hope you don't have to find me a new job."

When I put down the phone, Gloria thumped on the wall we shared. "Come and see your flowers," she called.

She had placed them in a large, plastic water carafe—the only item resembling a vase that we owned—that sat at the edge of her desk.

"Pretty nifty, huh?" she said.

"Indeed, except only you can see them."

She ignored my gibe. "So, are you going to drive to Washington to see him?"

"No. James is taking a hurried detour from his seminar activities and coming here. A single hour, from eight to nine."

Gloria whistled. "Oh, wow! A stolen rendezvous. Talk about romantic."

"I hardly think—" I began to say, but she interrupted me.

"Hey! My Wednesday night small group will meet from seven to eight tonight. Why don't you join us as a guest before your date?"

"May I remind you that today is Monday?"

"True, but I arranged a special meeting to talk about Barry."

"Oh dear! Please don't tell your group about our investigation."

"Of course not. I'll stick to the conclusions published in the *Ryde Rebel.*" She smiled at me. "But I may say a prayer—thanking God for giving Hunnechurch & Associates a surprising new beginning in the person of Sophie Hammond. I'd love for you to join us."

It's difficult to disagree with Gloria when she talks about prayer. Her rock-solid belief in God gives her an inner strength you can see at a distance.

"I want to be utterly honest with you," I said. "I have never be-longed to a small group, and I don't really know what members do when they get together. However, I suspect that the proceedings will be too *touchy-feely* for my tastes. We Brits are a reticent bunch who prefer not to be prayed over in public."

Gloria began to snicker.

I went on. "So, thank you for your invitation, but no thank you. As for Sophie Hammond, well, she may prove to be a miracle, but I prefer to reserve judgment—and my prayers of thanksgiving—until we know that her plan restores our reputation."

Gloria's snicker became a laugh.

"Please tell me what amuses you," I said.

"Sure! You have the silliest relationship with God I've ever come across."

═══════════════

While Gloria surfed the Web, I filled the rest of my workday pondering the sort of wrongdoing that Barry had discovered at Campbell & McQueen. Could someone have stolen money from the company? Was one of the executives involved in illegal insider trading of C&M stock? Did the company have a way to cheat the federal government when it sold plastic widgets that flew aboard military aircraft?

Enough speculation! You need facts, not surmises.

The only facts I had on hand were contained in the C&M file I had put together the previous summer. I reread the company's annual report, browsed through product catalogs, and skimmed over several trade magazine articles on plastics technology. I found nothing of value, but at least I felt the satisfaction of putting my mind in gear.

I went home at six, microwaved a Mexican TV dinner, and thought about James Huston while I ate—at first affectionately, but then analytically. I recalled the straightforward question that my sister Chloe had posed during a recent Sunday evening telephone tête-à-tête.

"How would you define your relationship with James?" she had asked.

"We are good friends," I had answered.

"No. 'Good friends' is not a sufficient response. I hear much more than friendship in your voice when you talk about James. I presume that the pair of you share deep feelings for each other; yet you have remained apart for more than a year. Can your state of noncommitment last much longer?"

"We speak to each other frequently."

"Over the telephone, which does *nothing* for your love life. You are not getting any younger, Pippa. Don't cut yourself off from the blessed possibility of having another child by waiting too long to remarry."

"How can you encourage me to marry James? You have never met him."

"He is interested in you, which amply demonstrates his intelligence, and you assured me that he is dishy. I trust your judgment in those matters completely."

I heard myself sigh. "Despite James's unabashed dishiness, we have some thorny issues to resolve."

"Ah, the thorny issues in our lives make excellent excuses for maintaining the status quo," Chloe had said. "As I see your situation, you have only *one* issue to deal with. James works in Atlanta, and you work in Ryde. I find it a pity that your careers, brilliant though they may be, should keep you apart."

At the time Chloe and I both assumed that Hunnechurch & Associates would continue rocketing toward success. Now, scarcely a month later, my "brilliant career" was on the verge of extinction. I could, if I so desired, forget about Sophie's article and relocate to Atlanta.

But do you so desire? How do you define your relationship with James?

The uncertainties leapt around my mind as I left Hunnechurch Manor.

Because Ryde is a colonial town, its streets are not laid out in a convenient grid. Magothy Street is a small C that nestles inside the larger C that is Ryde High Street. It took me about ten minutes—walking south on Magothy, then west on English Lane, then south on High Street—to reach Chamber of Commerce Plaza, a pocket-sized park next to the Ryde Chamber of Commerce building.

Even at this late hour, High Street was swarming with Christmas shoppers, but I had no problem picking James out of the crowd in front of the chamber's twenty-foot-tall Christmas tree. I folded myself into his arms. Even in the cold night air I could smell faint traces of his after-shave. It felt delightful to be hugged by a strong man, while hundreds of Christmas tree lights flickered nearby.

"It's wonderful to see you," he said. "I was afraid you might change your mind at the last moment—because of the events of last week."

It was hardly the greeting I had expected. I broke loose from his embrace. "Who told you about the events of last week?" I said more sharply than I had intended.

"You did—in a way. You gave me an airmail subscription to the *Ryde Reporter* as a Christmas gift last year. Remember? The issue with David Friendly's article arrived on Saturday morning."

I instantly felt foolish. "Oh, you read the article."

James offered me his arm. "Seeing that I am bigger than David, I will be happy to punch him in the nose if you so request."

"My former best pal deserves a thorough thrashing, but I intend to deliver it."

As we strolled north on Ryde High Street, I brought James up to date. I told him about Detective Reilly's suspicions that Barry was murdered, about Sophie Hammond's initial exposé in the current issue of the *Ryde Rebel*, and about the major mistakes in David's article.

"The bottom line," I said in conclusion, "is that David got much of the story wrong. His shoddy journalism cost me dearly. Hunnechurch & Associates currently does not have a single client."

"Poor Pippa." James kissed the back of my hand.

"To the contrary. Poor David! The man will soon eat crow—a flock of crows."

I explained that Sophie planned to prepare a follow-up article with additional evidence that Barry didn't commit suicide. I proudly added, "I am going to help her gather information."

James stopped walking. "I still have nightmares about the last time you dabbled in a murder investigation," he said. "Are we going to get shot at again?"

"Certainly not, James! This is a wholly different set of circumstances. Stephen Reilly and Sophie Hammond have the leading roles. I am merely a bit player, a walk-on character who will ask other bit players a few harmless questions about Barry Goodwin's state of mind. I don't intend to put myself at risk."

I spoke with complete conviction because I sincerely believed my own words. After all, where was the danger in visiting a handful of people who had been close to Barry Goodwin? My colleagues at the Ryde Chamber of Commerce use a quaint figure of speech to describe individuals who have an utter lack of perception about the reality of their situation. Such simpletons are said to "drink their own bathwater." That day, I consumed several gallons.

The glow from a nearby streetlight illuminated the dubious expression on James's face. "I hope you know what you're doing," he said. Then he asked, "Where does Gloria fit into this information-gathering scheme?"

"As always, she is my strong right arm. We both see Sophie's request as an opportunity to walk the second mile for Hunnechurch & Associates and also for Barry Goodwin's family. We need to restore our good name in the Ryde business community, and his family deserves to know what happened to Barry."

James looked at my quizzically. "I've never heard you talk about the second mile before. Do you know where the phrase comes from?"

"First Gloria, now you! Why does everyone want to give me Bible lessons?"

"You *do* know!" James put his hands on my shoulders. "In that case, I want you to attend my Wednesday morning seminar at the Waterside Hotel in Ryde."

"Your seminar? With respect, James, I have no intention of doing any international marketing in the foreseeable future."

"Marketing overseas is my topic on Wednesday afternoon and all day on Thursday. My leadoff session on Wednesday morning is, well, more closely related to the problems you currently face. Bring Gloria too. I promise both of you an interesting time."

James spoke with such enthusiasm that I couldn't help but agree, although I doubted that either of us would enjoy a three-hour lecture, even one delivered by the dishy James Huston.

"We will be there," I said with all the mock eagerness I could marshal.

"Splendid!" James gave a satisfied nod. "Now, to continue planning our week, what do you have in mind for Friday?"

"Pardon me?"

"Friday. The twenty-first of December."

It was James's little-boy expression that stirred my memory.

"December twenty-first!" I exclaimed. "Your birthday!" I recovered as best I could. "Gloria and I have your birthday festivities well in hand. That is all you need to know right now."

Happily, it was too dark for James to see me blush with embarrassment. I had completely forgotten my promise of a proper birthday celebration.

"Harrumph!" he said in an amused voice. "Since you are determined keep secrets from me, it's fortunate that I have to get back to work."

I glanced at my watch. "Oh dear! Our hour is up."

"My rental car is parked across the street. Shall I drive you home?"

"No. It's a *braw, bricht, moonlicht nicht* tonight. I'll walk home and think about you."

We kissed adieu and went our separate ways.

The question is still open, Hunnechurch. How do you define your relationship with James?

I hadn't thought of a good answer when I reached Magothy Street at a quarter-past nine and found three people huddling together in front of Hunnechurch Manor. "It's too early for carolers," I muttered to myself, but then I spotted a familiar swath of blonde hair beneath a pulled-down ski cap.

"Gloria?" I said. "Is that you?"

"Hi, Pippa," she said, a shiver in her voice. "We're positively freezing out here."

When I shepherded my unexpected visitors into my living room, Gloria said, "You know Dennis Marsh"—she gestured toward the tallest member of the trio—"but I don't think you've met Sharon Harrison. She also attends Ryde Fellowship Church."

I smiled at Dennis and extended my hand toward Sharon, a petite woman in her early forties who had just removed a pointy wool hat from atop her tightly curled brunette hair.

"I am the leader of the Wednesday night small group," she said. "It's a pleasure to finally meet you. Gloria has told us so many nice things about you."

"Has she now?"

"Oh, yes!" Sharon went on. "I insisted that we visit you this evening to explain that a small group is not at all touchy-feely."

I tried to catch Gloria's eye, but she was busy examining my ceiling.

Dennis jumped in. "I had an even worse fear, Pippa. I figured the meetings would be like group therapy sessions—you know, everybody moaning about their tortured childhoods. I was wrong. Our group is an extended family that helps us cope with the daily challenges of our lives and our faith." He winked at me. "When things go wrong in my life, I find it really helps to be prayed over in public."

"Come to our next meeting," Sharon urged. "See how a small group works."

"We-ell . . ." I began.

"I know that 'we-ell,'" Gloria howled. "She's going to come."

"You folks still look chilled," I said. "Shall I make some hot chocolate?"

"Thank goodness!" Gloria said. "I thought you'd never ask."

Chapter Twelve

With only seven shopping days left until Christmas, the retailers clustered on Ryde High Street near Mulberry Alley were full of customers at nine in the morning, even the Ryde Book Emporium, an old-fashioned bookstore that had managed to survive the coming of mega-book dealers in the outlying malls. The salespeople at the emporium actually read the books they recommended, and a tiny coffee bar in the back of the store (the emporium's only concession to modern bookselling practice) served delightful French breads and pastries.

The children's book department was a small alcove in the rear of the shop. I found that Diane Dupont hadn't arrived yet, so I made for the coffee bar and wolfed down a croissant and a double caffe latte to make up for the breakfast I had missed at home. I had awoken late that morning and spent more time than I meant to deciding what the well-dressed investigator should wear. My eventual choice was a gray woolen pantsuit that was professional, comfortable, and appropriate from morning to evening.

At ten minutes past nine I spotted Diane walking past the emporium's sizable collection of magazines. I waved to her; she waved back. Much to my astonishment, I saw that she had Jerry Nichols in tow. I had assumed that Diane would come alone—my first mistake of my investigation. I fought to keep a smile on my lips as I joined them in the alcove.

"This is your lucky day, Pippa," Diane said. "You'll get two opinions for the price of one. Jerry also agreed to ignore the directive against fraternizing with you."

"Many thanks, Jerry," I said. "It's nice to see you again."

Diane went on, "I figured that Jerry is the best person to describe Barry's final days at Campbell & McQueen. He knew Barry better than anyone else in the company."

We moved around a display rack overflowing with copies of *The Lion, the Witch and the Wardrobe* by C. S. Lewis. I stared at the cover illustration of Aslan and pondered the implications of Jerry's being here. I had planned a simple strategy: to ask Diane a few noncontroversial questions about Barry's bizarre behavior, then unobtrusively probe for the motive behind it. Could I do the same thing with C&M's master molder taking the lead? I suspected that was the real reason Diane had invited him along. She needn't fear losing her job with Jerry fielding my queries.

Ah well, all you can do is try.

"Jerry," I began, "as I explained to Diane yesterday, I am determined to learn from the mistakes I made recruiting Barry Goodwin. I hope to—"

Jerry didn't let me finish. "What mistakes? Barry sandbagged you like the rest of us. He was a certifiable nutcase. He fooled us for nearly two months, so it's no surprise that he fooled you for a couple of weeks last summer. I've seen you in action. You're a good recruiter, no matter what Richard Campbell and Hilda McQueen told you." He added, "I felt sick to my stomach at the inquisition we put you through. I stayed silent because nothing I could have said would have changed their minds. Somebody had to take the fall for causing us bad publicity, and you were the most convenient scapegoat."

"I take your point," I mumbled, wholly nonplussed by Jerry's unexpected candor. I needed a moment to recover my bearings and remember the subjects I wanted to cover. I took a deep breath and said, "Some people at C&M have described Barry's demeanor as angry rather than nutty, to use your word."

Jerry shrugged. "Barry did a little of everything. The side of him you saw depends on where you sat in the organization. He got mad at the senior executives and showed weird behavior to the rest of us." He frowned. "With one exception. Barry did have a big fight with our librarian a few days before he died, although I don't know how it started."

"I do," Diane said. "She came to me in tears to complain. It seems that Barry wanted to show Sidney Monk a copy of an article about plastic he had written for a technical magazine a few years back. That particular issue was missing from the library. Barry blew his stack and called her a worthless idiot."

I turned to Jerry. "Can you give me an example of Barry's 'weird behavior'?"

"I call it weird," he said, "because I'm not a shrink and don't know the right labels. Barry was hyper whenever I saw him. You know—jittery eyes, nervous hands, and shaky voice. He always seemed like he was ready to explode." He turned to Diane. "Is that what you remember?"

Diane sighed. "Barry rarely visited human resources, so I won't generalize, but he was definitely agitated last Monday afternoon when he threw a wastebasket through Sidney Monk's door." She looked directly at me. "Did you hear about that?"

"Unhappily, I did," I replied. "I wonder what could have provoked that much anger?"

Jerry stared at his hands. "My guess is that Barry lost his temper whenever things didn't go his way. He came from a small company where he could do whatever he wanted, but at C&M he had to sell his ideas to Richard, Hilda, and Sidney. Barry didn't like that."

Diane nodded in agreement. "His fight with Sidney had something to do with one of our products. I tried hard *not* to listen, but my office is next door to Sidney's. Barry was shouting at the top of his voice that Sidney had a responsibility to fix some kind of manufacturing problem. Sidney kept saying there wasn't any problem."

"What product would that be?" I hoped I didn't sound as excited as I felt.

Diane hesitated. "Our medical devices, I think."

"Do you mean C&M's artificial heart valves?" I asked.

"I'm not one hundred percent positive," she glanced at Jerry. "I heard Barry yell 'CM-7' a couple of times."

Jerry gave a dismissive wave. "It's another example of Barry's crazy behavior. Sidney has nothing whatsoever to do with our heart valves. Hilda McQueen designed the CM-7 and is personally in charge of their production. The CM-7 is the most precisely manufactured product we sell. The valves in use today were virtually handmade in my prototype molding shop by my staff. Hilda oversaw every aspect of production. If we had a manufacturing problem, which we don't, Hilda would be the first to hear about it. I'd be second."

What if Hilda refused to acknowledge the flaw that Barry had uncovered?

I dug into my memory for what Barry had told me during lunch at Maison Pierre. "You just don't get it, do you? Hilda already knows what's happening. I'm pretty sure that she's responsible."

As for the fight with Sidney Monk, perhaps Barry had heeded my advice and taken the matter to Sidney's attention. I could picture Barry exploding with fury when Sidney denied that a manufacturing problem existed.

Yes, it all makes perfect sense.

Barry Goodwin had stumbled across a problem with the CM-7 heart valves, but no one in Barry's chain of command would listen to him. Not Hilda, not Sidney Monk, not even Jerry.

Nonetheless, someone at C&M did listen. A person who worried that Barry's off-the-wall behavior might wreck the intended acquisition of C&M by Hughes Engineered Materials. The person who elected to fake Barry's suicide.

I decided to press Jerry and Diane a bit further. "By any chance, did either of you see the current issue of the *Ryde Rebel?*"

Diane shook her head, and Jerry nodded. "Hilda circulated a copy among the senior staff," he said. "You take a good picture."

"Did you read Sophie Hammond's article?"

"Yep. I agree with the stuff she wrote about you, but it's harder to swallow that Barry was murdered."

"The article makes it seem possible," I said.

"Of course, it's possible! Barry Goodwin was a sick puppy, crazy enough to kill himself or do something to get himself killed. Although . . ."

"Yes?" I prompted.

"Those of us who saw Barry walking around C&M with a wild-eyed look will probably vote for suicide. For what it's worth, I think he did kill himself."

Diane seemed to tremble. "They are two horrible alternatives," she said. "I don't know which is worse." She peered at her wristwatch. "Sorry, Pippa, but I have to get to work."

"Me too," I said. "Thank you both for throwing caution to the wind."

"Hang in there!" Jerry said. "You'll be off C&M's black list as soon as our heavy hitters forget about Barry."

We began to march single file toward the front of the emporium. As we passed the wall of magazines, I had a sudden thought. *What was in*

the technical article that Barry had wanted to show Sidney? Did it have any-
thing to do with heart valves?

I caught up to Diane. "Did the librarian ever find that missing technical magazine?" I asked.

"I don't think so," she said over her shoulder, "because Barry
brought his own copy to the office. He had it with him during his big
fight with Sidney."

"What happened to the magazine?" I asked.

It was my second mistake of the day. Diane and Jerry stopped walking and looked at me with puzzled expressions. It was too late to dodge
the subject, so I stayed close to the truth.

"I am grasping at straws," I said. "I will look at anything—no matter how implausible— that might shed light on Barry's frame of mind
in the days before he died."

Diane's face relaxed. "We shipped all of Barry's personal things to
his mother. I remember sticking the magazine into one of the corru-
gated packing boxes."

We exchanged our good-byes. As Diane and Jerry walked away, I realized that I would never work with them again. Jerry might be optimistic
about my future dealings with C&M, but I knew better. The executives
at C&M would forever associate Hunnechurch & Associates with the
damage done by Barry Goodwin—no matter what kind of follow-up
story Sophie wrote.

As for my other clients, I saw a glimmer of hope.

Sophie Hammond could weave a robust tale of faulty heart valves,
deception, and likely murder into a bombshell story that just might
help exonerate me if (and this was a big if) Barry had really found a
manufacturing problem with the CM-7 heart valve. What if he had
jumped to the wrong conclusion, however? What if his accusation was
merely a figment of his weird behavior? Sophie was smart enough to
want solid evidence. All I had were a few suppositions.

Perhaps Barry's magazine article will point you in the right direction.

A good idea, except, how on earth would I get Anne Goodwin's permission to browse through Barry's belongings?

━━━━━━━━━━━

I opted for the direct approach. I would visit Anne Goodwin and ask for her cooperation.

My cell phone was in my handbag that morning. I called Gloria and gave her a thumbnail sketch of my conversation with Diane and Jerry.

"Oh boy!" she said. "Campbell & McQueen ships heart valves around the world. Can you imagine the bad publicity and legal hassles if their valves are defective?"

"Indeed, which is why I need to know everything that Barry knew."

"Five bucks says that Anne Goodwin will refuse to see you."

"I will take that bet," I said. "Retrieve Barry's file and find Anne Goodwin's address and telephone number."

My Miata was in a parking lot on Ranger Street, a two-block walk from the bookstore. Halfway there the overcast sky began to spit snow, reminding me that I hadn't dressed for inclement weather. My investigator outfit, chosen mostly for comfort, included a pair of roomy leather-soled pumps and my lightweight Loden car coat.

Onward, Hunnechurch! Only a wimp would waste time and change.

The wind waggled my lightweight sports car as I crossed Chesapeake Bay Bridge, though my mind was too busy to register concern. It was scrambling to invent words that would reverse Mrs. Goodwin's clearly expressed dislike of me. The miles and minutes sped by. How would I change her mind about me when we stood face-to-face?

Anne Goodwin lived in an old clapboard Cape Cod halfway between Oxford and Easton, on a narrow, tree-lined road that backed against the upper reaches of the Tred Avon River. Snow was falling when I pulled into her driveway. An inch of undisturbed, fluffy powder had collected atop the gravel, but several lights were on in the house,

and someone had salted the walkway that led to the front door. Two
good signs that she was at home.

A gust of wind tingled my fingers and made me wish I had worn
gloves that morning. I jammed my hands deep into my pockets and
drew my coat tightly about my middle. It was more than cold enough
to see my breath. For no particular reason, I blew a vapor ring. I had
been a heavy smoker in England and an accomplished blower of smoke
rings until Simon had badgered me into throwing away my cigarettes
when I became pregnant.

Reminisce later. You have a technical magazine to find.

I followed the slush trail to the front door and worked the knocker,
still not sure what I would say when my knock was answered. I heard
movement inside the house. The door opened, and a flurry of inviting
smells—warm apples, fresh pastry dough, and savory spices—wafted
past me.

Anne Goodwin stood in the doorway, wiping her hands on a dishtowel. Her long apron was dusty with flour. I must have caught her
making pies for the holidays. She needed a moment to recognize me.
When she did, her features twisted into an expression of utter annoyance that made me take a step backward.

"You!" she hissed at me. "What do *you* want?"

"A few minutes of your time," I said evenly. "I need your help."

"Shoo!" She flicked her hand toward me as if I were a stray dog,
then slammed the door shut. I heard the deadbolt snick into place.

I stared at the doorknocker—a big, brass eagle—and decided to try
again. I worked the knocker hard, three times. *Bang. Bang. Bang.*

Mrs. Goodwin shouted at me through the door. "Go away, or I will
call the police."

Chilly air had begun to penetrate my pantsuit, and my feet felt icy
cold. I followed the slush trail back to my car, started the engine, and
switched the heater fan to maximum. I tapped Mrs. Goodwin's number
into my cell phone.

"Goodwin residence," she said cautiously.

"It's Pippa Hunnechurch. Please don't hang up."

She said nothing, but I could hear steady breathing. I worked the windshield wiper to sweep away a layer of snowflakes and peered up at the house. Anne Goodwin had pulled the curtain in the front window aside. She stared back at me, a portable telephone pressed against her ear.

"Why are you bothering me?" she said. "Haven't you done enough harm?"

"Can I come inside, Mrs. Goodwin? It's difficult to explain over the telephone."

"No, you may not come inside. I won't offer hospitality to the woman who killed my son."

I didn't reply immediately. I willed myself not to counter her hateful remark with angry words of my own.

"I understand your pain, Mrs. Goodwin," I said. "I miss Barry too. I assure you that I was shaken by his death."

"I expect you were!" She attempted a laugh, but it came out an ugly cackle. "Barry helped to expose your disgraceful occupation. I pray that his sacrifice will save the lives of other people."

"Your son didn't sacrifice himself, Mrs. Goodwin. He was murdered."

I heard her gasp and watched the curtain in the front window drop closed.

Idiot! You let your temper get the best of you.

I listened for the line to go dead, but she didn't ring off.

About thirty seconds passed before she finally spoke. "You said that to excuse your own incompetence." Her voice had shed much of its earlier rage.

I had no choice but to move full steam ahead. "Two people who have studied the facts carefully—one a policeman, the other a reporter—believe that Barry did not kill himself."

"I don't believe you."

I hadn't thought to bring a copy of the *Ryde Rebel* with me. I backpedaled as best I could. "A local newspaper in Ryde published an article about Barry. It explains in great detail why Barry was not likely to commit suicide." I added, "I will get you a copy."

More silence, then, "Why did you come here today?"

"Barry wrote a magazine article about plastic. I believe it might cast light on why he died."

Once again, I had spoken the wrong words.

"How dare you come to my home with crazy ideas?" she shouted at me. "Barry died because you stole him from the nice company he worked for. If you had stayed away from Barry, he would still be alive today."

"I'm sorry," I said. "I didn't mean to upset you."

Click. She hung up.

I drove back to Ryde empty-handed.

Chapter Thirteen

GUSTY WINDS AND BLOWING SNOW conspired to make the trip back to Ryde in my skittery, low-slung sports car seem interminable. I wanted to call Gloria, but I wasn't about to lift my right hand off the steering wheel for even an instant to retrieve my cell phone. I felt a surge of envy (mixed with annoyance) every time a heavy, four-wheel-drive vehicle whizzed past me and spattered my windshield with slush.

"My head is aching," I announced when I stepped into our reception room. "I am suffering from either eyestrain or hunger. Please point me to an aspirin *and* a sandwich."

Gloria sent out for both. Thus restored and refreshed, I dropped into the visitor's chair next to her desk and reviewed my morning's journey.

"It appears that I took two steps forward and one step backward," I said by way of summary. "Anne Goodwin remains angry at me, but she did listen to some of what I had to say."

"Does that mean you owe me five dollars?"

"Alas, yes, because I didn't return with the technical article we require. Can you suggest a promising Plan B to obtain it?"

"Well, I'm sure you made Mrs. Goodwin curious. Why don't we send her a copy of the *Ryde Rebel* and see what develops?"

"Great minds think alike," I said with a giggle. "I offered to provide her with a copy; do so immediately." I reached for Gloria's desk calendar. "Unhappily though, we cannot afford to wait for Anne Goodwin to have a change of mind. Today is Tuesday, and Sophie gave me a deadline of Friday to provide her with useful information."

"Will Barry's article really be useful? It's probably ten pages of technical gobbledygook."

"Barry considered his writing so relevant to his concerns that he started a major fracas at Campbell & McQueen because the librarian couldn't find it. I definitely want to read it."

"Hey, there's an idea. Why don't I call the Enoch Pratt Library in Baltimore?"

"It is worth a try, although"—I allowed myself an ashamed grin—"I didn't ask for the name of the publication. Barry might have written for a trade magazine, a scientific journal, even a technology newsletter. The author's name alone may not be sufficient to track down the article."

I ran my finger along the desk calendar. *Tuesday. Wednesday. Thursday. Friday.*

Wednesday! All at once I remembered James Huston's invitation.

"Is your morning free tomorrow?" I asked. "James invited us to sit in on his seminar."

"A seminar?" Gloria grimaced. "I'd rather have a tooth filled without the aid of anesthetic."

"I said much the same thing, but James's topic tomorrow apparently has nothing to do with international marketing. He assured me that we would both enjoy it."

"If you say so. . . ." Her expression announced great skepticism. "Nevertheless, I reserve the right to leave if I feel myself falling asleep."

"Fair enough." I leaned back in my chair. "Returning to matters at hand—how can we get our hands on Barry's article? What are our options?"

Gloria chuckled. "You know, if Barry were still alive, we could ask him. Authors usually have lots of copies of their work. But since he isn't—"

I shot upright. "I've been a blithering dolt. You are wholly correct. There are likely to be extra copies of his article in his apartment."

"Even if there are, how do you plan to get inside Barry's apartment?"

My answer was a Mona Lisa smile.

"No way!" Gloria bellowed. "I'm a good guy. A good guy doesn't help her boss break into an official crime scene."

"I hardly think that Barry's apartment is still a crime scene. It's been more than a week since his death." I increased my smile's voltage. "Of course, I am open to other suggestions."

Gloria frowned at me a while, then said, "Rats! I wish I had never learned how to pick locks."

———

Barry had moved to Ryde from Easton a week before starting his job at Campbell & McQueen. "The address is 1635 Spruce Siding," Gloria said warily. "It's an apartment building in the southwest corner of Ryde, a few blocks from Ryde Business Park and the C&M headquarters."

"Indeed! I remember now—you visited Barry's apartment on the morning he died."

She nodded. "All the streets in the neighborhood have cutesy names based on trees, like Birch Byway, Oaken Lane, Dogwood Copse, and Spruce Siding."

"I cannot imagine the stalwart seafarers who founded Ryde coming up with Birch Byway. It must be a new subdivision."

"Brand new, which means that it may be harder to break into." Gloria reached for her keys. "I'll drive, you navigate."

Gloria, worried that her truck was conspicuous, decided to park a block away from 1635 Spruce Siding. The new neighborhood looked unfinished, with large areas of cleared land waiting for homes to be built and countless young trees, none of them spruces, supported by wooden stakes. *They might offer decent shade in perhaps fifteen years,* I thought.

It had stopped snowing, but the temperature had fallen during the afternoon, creating patches of ragged ice on the streets and sidewalks. I needed Gloria's help to perambulate the slippery pavement. She was sensibly shod in winter boots; I was still foolishly wearing my leather-soled pumps.

Barry had lived in a three-story complex of shingle-sided garden apartments served by several exterior staircases. We saw nary a soul as we climbed to the second floor.

"Where are all the people?" I asked.

"This is a yuppie building," Gloria explained. "Everybody works— the place is uninhabited during the day."

Halfway down the inner corridor we found apartment 2-C. The engraved plastic nameplate beneath the doorbell button still read *Goodwin.*

"So far, so good," Gloria said. "I worried we might find yellow crime scene tape or some kind of notice on the door." She looked around. "You stand guard. I don't want to be surprised while I'm picking the lock."

"Is it a toughie?"

"Well, it has a deadbolt, but it shouldn't be too difficult. What concerns me more is an alarm system. I don't see any warning stickers, but you never know."

I kept my eyes peeled for approaching people while Gloria set to work with a lock pick she selected from a small leather pouch. In less than a minute I heard two soft clicks. She pushed the door slightly ajar and listened through the opening.

"There's no klaxon going off," she said. "I don't hear an automatic dialer calling the police, and I can't see an alarm sensor on the door. I think we're OK. Even so, I want to be out of here in no more than ten minutes."

I followed Gloria into a small foyer. Because Barry's apartment was an inside unit, its few windows faced in one direction—in this case, north. The half-closed Venetian blinds, coupled with the northern orientation and the bleak skies, made the rooms dark and uninviting.

Gloria closed the front door behind us and gave me one of the two flashlights she had brought along.

"Don't turn on any lights," she said, "and don't touch anything."

"Ah. Fingerprints."

"Exactly!" Gloria slipped her hands into tight leather gloves. "I'll do the lifting and touching. Let's move out."

We quickly determined that the apartment had a living room with a dining area, a kitchen, one bedroom (with its own bathroom), and a half bath (what we Brits call a "loo") accessible from the foyer. Mushroom-colored wall-to-wall carpeting covered the floors in the foyer, living room, and bedroom. The kitchen and bathrooms were tiled with off-white vinyl.

"Pick a room to do first," Gloria said.

I pointed to the living room and said, "We'll start there."

The white-painted walls were completely bare, giving the space an aura of austere emptiness. Barry's furnishings didn't help matters. Politely described, they were modest. To be brutally honest, they were pitiable.

He had placed two unattractive sofas, both upholstered in coarse brown tweed, at right angles to create an L-shaped conversation area that faced a TV set that sat atop a squat metal file cabinet. In the crook

of the L was a homemade coffee table—a square of plate glass supported by three short stacks of red bricks. A pair of tarnished brass floor
lamps stood behind the sofas. An inexpensive card table and four fold-
ing chairs were set up in the dining area that extended from the end of
the living room nearest the kitchen.

A waist-high, wooden bookcase stationed against the far wall held
a substantial collection of books and an inexpensive stereo. Atop the
bookcase was a framed color photograph inscribed "With Love from
Karen C." and an English ivy plant that was clearly dying of thirst.
Alongside the plant, a wilted fichus tree in a redwood pot was equally
parched. Standing in the shade of the tree was a chrome-plated tower,
nearly as tall as me, that held Barry's collection of CDs.

I leaned close to the sterling-silver picture frame to get a better look
at Karen Constantine. The photo was a portrait, not a snapshot, of an
attractive woman in her early thirties with lank hair of nondescript
brown and intelligent gray-green eyes. She had the same techie look
that Barry had. I could imagine them happily walking hand-in-hand
through the exhibit hall at a plastics convention.

"A rather curious mix of furniture, don't you think?" I said to
Gloria. "Barry may have lived here, but he didn't make it into a home.
The only valuable item I see is this picture frame."

"Single men of marrying age often have cheap bits and pieces from
different sources," she replied. "Chances are, he bought most of it at
thrift shops and borrowed the rest from relatives. The greenery undoubtedly came from Anne Goodwin. Mothers like to give their sons
houseplants to liven up their bachelor pads."

I walked to the bookcase and discovered that the titles were evenly
split between chemistry and management. "Barry didn't read for fun," I
began to say when a flash of color on the bottom shelf caught my eye.
"Eureka!"

"What did you find?" Gloria asked from across the room.

"A stack of magazines. The one on top is entitled *Plastics Technology.*"

"It *can't* be that easy."

"Flip through them. See if you can locate a feature-length article written by Barry."

"Where are you going?"

"To reconnoiter the kitchen. We Brits can't stand the sight of un-happy plants. I want to find a utensil I can use to water them."

"Do it quickly, and be careful what you touch."

"Absolutely!"

Barry's kitchen was compact but fully equipped. Someone had left a neatly folded dishtowel on a countertop. I wrapped it around my right hand as an improvised fingerprint shield, shifted my flashlight to my left hand, and pulled open the oven door. The interior looked factory-fresh and uncooked in.

I tried the refrigerator next. The interior was cold, but the shelves were empty and spotlessly clean. I looked in the freezer, thinking that Barry, like me, might have dined on frozen dinners. The freezer was empty, too, except for a plastic ice-cube tray filled to its rim with ice.

"Barry's refrigerator is bare," I called to Gloria. "I am astonished to think that he dined out morning and night."

"That's what bachelors with good jobs do," she answered.

"You seem to be bursting with practical information about bache-lors," I teased. "How do you explain that?"

"One can learn a lot by watching male friends who live closer than seven hundred miles away."

"Touché!"

A door next to the refrigerator looked like it led to a storage closet. I turned the knob and found a small utility room. Standing before me was the gas-fired furnace that had generated the carbon monoxide that killed Barry.

I took a moment to inspect the chimney pipe. It was a metal tube perhaps ten inches across that merely fit into a collar on the top of the furnace; I could imagine Barry's killer yanking it loose and redirecting the lethal flue gasses into the interior of the apartment. I couldn't help shivering as I closed the door.

One by one, I peered into the kitchen cabinets. They held expected things: four place settings of dinnerware (all seemingly unused), several drinking glasses, a few shiny pots and pans, and a small selection of cleaning products. The only edibles in sight were a goodly assortment of candy, potato chips, and pretzels—all in individual-serving bags.

I discovered a plastic pitcher in the cabinet below the sink and filled it with cold water.

"Any luck?" I asked Gloria, as I watered the English ivy.

She shook her head. "This pile includes nearly every issue of *Plastics Technology* for the past four years. I've looked at all the tables of contents. No byline by Barry Goodwin."

I moved to the potted fichus tree. "You said nearly every issue."

"Last February's issue is missing." She neatened the stack of magazines. "That could be the one we're looking for."

"*If* Barry's article was published in *Plastics Technology*. We don't know whether that is the case."

"Gosh, you limeys can be pessimistic."

"So true. Let's move on to Barry's bedroom." I added, "How are we doing for time?"

"We have four minutes left."

I returned the empty plastic pitcher to the kitchen and joined Gloria in the bedroom. The piece of furniture that caught our attention first was a large double-door mahogany wardrobe—what Europeans call an armoire—that stood against one wall.

"I'll bet his mother gave him that," Gloria said.

She looked through the shelves behind the doors and found a modest collection of underwear, socks, casual shirts, exercise clothing, and sweaters.

Barry's bed was a queen-sized mattress on a box spring pushed against one wall. Someone—I guessed the evidence technician who had searched the bedroom—had folded and stacked the bedclothes neatly on the floor.

Barry's one bedroom had doubled as a home office. His computer table was a cheap metal desk stuck in the corner. I realized that Barry must have been lying on the bed, drugged, while his executioner tapped away on the computer's keyboard a few feet away. I suddenly felt queasy.

"Hey! You're wobbling," Gloria shouted.

"I'll be fine, although I may splash some water on my face."

"Great. That gives you a chance to examine Barry's bathroom while I check his desk and browse through his closet."

"What do you expect me to find in a john?"

"Reading materials."

"Why didn't I think of that?"

The bathroom attached to the bedroom was a perfectly conventional American design: sink, toilet, and tub/shower. I wet my anti-fingerprint dishcloth and sponged my face. Almost by accident I pointed my flashlight beneath the sink and saw a fabric and wood magazine rack. I knelt down and reached inside. Instead of magazines, I grasped a thick textbook entitled, *The Techniques of Cardiac Valve Replacement.*

I riffled through its pages and near the back found a receipt that Barry had used as a bookmark. He had bought the tome on December fifth, from Baker's Used Professional Book Shop in Baltimore.

I opened the book to the marked pages. Someone, Barry I presumed, had used a fluorescent highlighter to underline a chapter title, "Anxiety Related to Potential Cardiac Valve Failure: The Medical & Legal Consequences."

A phone began to ring somewhere in the apartment. The bathroom door shot wide open.

"We have to get out of here," Gloria shouted as she grabbed my arm.

I didn't ask why. The heavy-duty concern on her face was all the explanation I needed.

We leapt for the front door. Once outside, Gloria stopped to relock the deadbolt. "I think we set off the burglar alarm," she said as she worked with her lock pick.

"You told me you didn't see an alarm."

"*I* didn't." She emphasized the "I" by touching her chest. "But *you* did. The keypad that turns the alarm on and off is on the wall in the kitchen. You walked right past it. The main control box is hidden inside Barry's clothes closet, behind his shirts. I'll bet that the sensors are motion detectors—possibly hidden in the light fixtures. We must have tripped them when we walked around the apartment."

"I apologize profusely." I scurried along the corridor in Gloria's footsteps. "Where are the police?"

"Most residential set-offs are usually false alarms. That telephone call was from the alarm service company to find out if anyone is at home. They'll notify the cops when no one answers with the right password. That should be happening right about now."

I held my breath as Gloria peered down the staircase.

"It's clear. Let's go."

I didn't need to be told twice. We flew down the stairs and race-walked toward Gloria's pickup truck, with me slipping and sliding along the icy sidewalk. Sixty seconds later we reached Maryland Avenue—the main thoroughfare that leads past the Ryde Business Park—in time to see a police car, its red and blue lights flashing, racing in the opposite direction.

"Blimey! We might have been arrested."

"That often happens to burglars who steal other people's property."

"Well, I admit that we burgled a bit, but we didn't take anything."

"Oh yeah?" Gloria pointed at my hands, which were clasped around the damp dishtowel, a flashlight, and Barry's textbook.

"Oh my! I didn't mean to walk away with his clobber."

"We ran away!" Gloria chuckled. "However, I don't think anyone has been prosecuted in Maryland for copping an old dishtowel. As for the book, where did you find it?"

"In the bathroom, as you suggested. It is a medical textbook. I believe that Barry considered it an important source of information." Once again, I opened the volume to the marked chapter.

"You didn't see any magazines or technical journals?"

"No."

"Neither did I. Not in his desk, not in his closet," she sighed. "So much for that idea."

"The idea was a good one, but we ignored the likelihood that someone else removed the publications that contained Barry's article."

"The killer?"

"The killer," I agreed. "I no longer have any doubts that Barry Goodwin was murdered."

"Sophie will be glad to hear that." Gloria poked my arm. "In fact, why don't you ask her to track down Barry's article as part of the research for her story? She is bound to have more resources than we do."

"Good idea . . ." I murmured. In truth, I was hardly listening to Gloria. I had begun to read the medical textbook on my lap. The chapter Barry had highlighted described the intense anxiety suffered by patients who learned that their replacement heart valves were poorly made.

The story was simple: A decade earlier, physicians realized that a widely used metal heart valve had a major problem—a critical weld could snap without warning. Sudden failures killed nearly two hundred patients around the world. The flawed design was taken off the market, and cardiac surgeons switched to newer, safer artificial heart valves.

What of the nearly one hundred thousand living patients who had potentially deadly devices clicking away inside their chests?

The obvious solution for many was to replace their imperfect valves. Unhappily, though, explanting, or removing an artificial heart valve and implanting a new one can be a highly perilous operation. Thousands of patients were advised to keep their dodgy devices because the risk of replacement surgery was greater than the risk of heart-valve failure.

The author of the chapter skillfully described the apprehension of living from heartbeat-to-heartbeat, knowing that a defective gadget inside your chest could suddenly fail—and kill you in seconds. It felt more like a horror novel than a medical textbook.

I wondered how I would react to the knowledge that I might have a time bomb attached to my heart. Would I be able to put aside all thoughts of faulty welds and lead an ordinary life? Or would my fear of sudden death dominate my life and turn every dream into a nightmare? The notion made me tremble.

The patients had sued the manufacturer and collected millions of dollars to compensate them for their fear. I doubted that any amount of money could recompense a life of perpetual uncertainty. The body eventually healed itself after surgery, but the anxiety of sudden failure stayed with the patient forever.

Gloria punched my arm. "You can stop looking worried," she said. "We made a clean getaway."

I closed the textbook and offered a makeshift smile.

"In point of fact," I replied, "I am thinking about defective heart valves and something odd that Barry said to me. When I asked him to explain the nature of his discovery at Campbell & McQueen, he said, 'I can't tell you the details without hurting people who have enough to worry about right now.'"

"And?"

"He was right to be circumspect. I am just beginning to understand the public turmoil that rumors of defective CM-7 heart valves would cause."

Chapter Fourteen

"JAMES IS *YOUR* BOYFRIEND," Gloria said grumpily. "Why does he want *me* to sit through his boring lecture?"

"He promised that you will have an interesting time. Those were his exact words."

"I wish he hadn't asked. I *hate* going to school."

Gloria and I were striding down Ryde High Street early on Wednesday morning, relishing the sunny, windless weather. We had both agreed it was much too lovely a morning to drive the two miles from our office to the Waterside Hotel, but the closer we got, the more fretful Gloria had become.

"You obviously don't hate all schools," I said. "I suspect that you have studied many things in the Maryland Army National Guard."

"That's different. The stuff they teach me in the Guard is useful. It's also interesting."

"Apparently many people find James Huston's seminars useful and interesting—he gives several each month, to increasingly large audiences."

"I'm sure you can find a few people here and there who actually enjoy listening to a consultant spout off, especially a consultant who talks with a dreamy southern accent. The trouble is, I'm not one of them."

"James will present a two-day seminar in Ryde; we have been invited to only the first morning. Nonetheless, if it pains you that much to attend, I will make your apologies."

She gave a little groan. "No. I have to go. I think James is a super guy. I don't want to hurt his feelings or yours."

"I'm glad you said that. I have an additional favor to ask."

"Please—not another seminar."

Now it was my turn to groan. "I am afraid it is more complicated than that. James's birthday is on Friday. I promised him a proper celebration. I even told him we were preparing one."

She brightened. "A birthday party! Now you're talking! Count me in."

"You have just put your finger on my problem. The *count* has me worried. You and I may be the only guests. I know that James has friends in Maryland and Virginia—he used to consult for the U.S. Department of Commerce—but I haven't a clue how to find them."

"I'll have plenty of time to figure out the solution at the seminar, while I'm bored out of my head."

The Waterside Hotel has a built-in conference center that can accommodate both small and large gatherings. James's seminar was assigned to the Broad Creek Room on the first floor. We followed two cardboard arrows that read "International Business Seminar," turned a corner, and came face-to-face with a three-foot photograph of James on an easel. The caption along the bottom edge read, "James L. Huston, Managing Director, Peachtree Consulting Group, Atlanta." I couldn't help but stare at James's craggy features and brilliant smile, his playful blue eyes, his thick head of dark, wavy hair. . . .

Gloria tugged my coat sleeve. "Maybe we can get a duplicate sign for our office? I'll hang it on the wall opposite your desk—you can drool all day."

"Very funny."

We gave our names to a woman seated at a table outside the Broad Creek Room and learned that James had preregistered us for the morning session. We left the table with plastic name badges hanging around our necks and went inside the meeting room. It was arranged classroom style with eight rows of tables—each row seating twelve people—facing a podium, and a screen at the front of the room. I estimated that two-thirds of the ninety-six available seats were already filled.

"Yeow!" Gloria said. "James's seminars *are* popular."

"Where shall we sit?" I asked.

"Near the back—in case either of us decides to leave. Lots of popular stuff is also boring."

"Point well taken."

We selected two chairs together in the seventh row, not far from an exit door. I scanned the room for James but didn't spot him. I wasn't surprised. He had once told me that his remedy for the mild stage fright he felt before a seminar was to look at himself in a mirror and do deep-breathing exercises.

"It works every time," he had said.

I chuckled at the thought of James huffing mightily somewhere close by.

Gloria swiveled in her seat and said, "Here he comes!"

James had entered the meeting room though a door on the far wall and was making his way to the podium. He spotted us and waved. I blew a discreet kiss in reply.

He pressed a button on the podium, and an electronic projector hanging from the ceiling threw a title slide on the screen:

The ABCs of International Marketing
Session 1: The Basic Principles of Business Success
Do the Right Thing, and Things Will Go Right!

"Good morning, ladies and gentlemen," James began. He introduced himself, then continued, "For much of today and all of tomorrow, we will consider the requirements for success when selling goods and services internationally."

Next to me, Gloria gave a small sigh of despair. "This is going to be brutal," she whispered. "I should have brought a book to read."

James continued. "Every journey must have a beginning. As businesspeople, our foundation for doing business overseas is a set of basic business principles that many of us apply every day in this country. I'll review them this morning." He paused for effect. "And yes—I really do believe the words on this slide. When you do the right thing, the chances are that things will go right."

James touched the button. New words appeared on the screen:

Principle #1
If You Recognize It's Wrong, DON'T DO IT.

"Is there anyone here today who *doesn't* agree with this simple notion?" James looked around the room, but no one disagreed. "Honoring this principle can keep a business person out of trouble everywhere in the world." He went on to give several practical examples of businesspeople who saved themselves grief by choosing *not* to do obviously wrong things.

I noticed that Gloria, despite her misgivings, had begun to pay attention. "You know something?" she whispered to me. "Principle number one is really the Golden Rule rewritten for business."

James brought up the next slide:

Principle #2
Let Your Own Sense of Right and Wrong Guide You;
Double-Dealers Always Fail over the Long Haul.

"The point here," James said, "is that you have to be faithful to what you know is the right way to do business. We see it again and again—people who abandon principle are sowing the seeds of their own destruction. Eventually, their duplicity gets them into serious trouble."

I felt Gloria's elbow dig into my ribs.

"Do you know what principle number two is?" she whispered excitedly. "It's a proverb from the Bible."

"I hardly think that James would quote Scripture at a business seminar," I whispered back as I rubbed my side.

"I'll prove it to you!" Gloria dug into her handbag and retrieved the pocket-sized Bible she carries with her everywhere. She flipped through pages furiously while James launched into a discussion of relevant examples of double-dealing disasters.

"I knew it!" She thrust the little Bible at me triumphantly. "Check out Proverbs 11:3."

I read the passage. "The integrity of the upright guides them, but the unfaithful are destroyed by their duplicity."

"Blimey! You are right. James is paraphrasing Bible phrases."

After that, James's seminar became a game to Gloria. She identified the scriptural sources of several other business principles as fast as James flashed them on the screen:

Give your customers everything they pay for. ("The LORD abhors dishonest scales, but accurate weights are his delight" Prov. 11:1.)

Pay fair wages to overseas workers. (". . . for the worker is worth his keep" Matt. 10:10.)

A good manager assumes that good times don't last forever. A company that can't survive adversity deserves to fail. ("If you falter in times of trouble, how small is your strength!" Prov. 24:10.)

Even I cackled out loud when James reminded us of the need to go beyond what our customers expect to receive. "A contract merely defines what you are *required* to do," he said. "But doing more for customers—going beyond the four corners of a signed piece of paper—is the way successful companies build the long-term relationships that help them to flourish."

"Ouch!" I yelped as Gloria gave me another poke in the ribs.

"It's Matthew 5:41—the second mile!" she bubbled. "Don't you recognize it?"

"Certainly! Moreover, I saw the connection *before* you pummeled my midriff."

Gloria had stopped listening to me. Her gaze was locked on the podium—and James.

"Do you see what I see?" she whispered.

"What do you see?" I replied, wary of her elbow.

"James has a Palm handheld with him at the podium. I think he's using it to time his presentation."

"Do you mean his cute little computer gizmo?"

Gloria delved into her handbag again and emerged with a silvery object the size of a pack of playing cards. "I didn't know he owned a Palm handheld. It looks to be the same model as mine."

"I've seen him use it on several occasions. He stores his appointments, and also names and addresses in it." I abruptly realized what I had just said. "Oh my! The names of his friends in Maryland and Virginia will be in it. Do you think we can get them out?"

She pointed to a tiny red window on the edge of her handheld. "These babies can talk to one another over an infrared light beam. If I can get my hands on James's Palm for thirty seconds, I may be able to copy his address files into my unit."

"A scheduled break is coming up. What if I distract James while you do your magic?"

"Let's do it!"

At ten-forty-five James declared a fifteen-minute "bio-break." Gloria scooted out the exit door on our side of the room as if she was bound for the ladies lounge. I waved at James; he obligingly trotted over to my table.

"Think of yourself as hugged," he said, his arms resolutely at his side.

"*Hmmm.* I can manage that." I added, "A very nice mental image indeed."

Out of the corner of my eye, I noticed Gloria slip through the door at the front of the room and advance stealthily to the podium. My job for the immediate future was to keep James Huston looking straight at me.

He began to smile slyly. "How do you like the contents of my seminar?"

"I can see that you think yourself a clever boots, but Gloria required less than two minutes to break your code. She translated each of your business principles into Bible verses within seconds of appearing on the screen."

He laughed. "Gloria is a Bible whiz. When would you have figured it out?"

I peered down at my hands and mumbled, "Not long after she did."

"I don't buy your timing." James crossed his arms like a schoolteacher prepared to scold an errant pupil. "Tell the truth."

"I freely confess that my knowledge of Scripture is less developed than it ought to be." I lifted my head and looked squarely at James. "Nonetheless, I am certain that the penny would have dropped when you reached the bit about going the second mile for one's customers."

James nodded, seemingly satisfied with my amended answer.

I didn't know how long it would take Gloria to transfer the names and addresses, so I kept talking to hold his attention. "However, in response to the initial question you asked me, I was awed and astonished by the contents of your seminar, as I am sure was Gloria. I find it both edifying and enlightening to discover that words of wisdom penned three thousand years ago can be applied today in the mercantile realm of international business."

James raised his hands and switched his southern drawl to full power. "Mercy, Miss Hunnechurch! I am a humble country boy who rarely hears fancy words like edifying and mercantile."

"In words of one syllable, I liked what you said."

He bowed gallantly. "Why thank you, ma'am. Now, with your permission, I must attend to a few details back at the podium."

I peeked around James's broad shoulders. Gloria was nowhere in sight.

"Certainly, Mr. Huston." I quieted my voice several notches. "Think of yourself as kissed."

"My, my, my! How can I teach a seminar with ideas like that bouncing through my brain? I may have to pour a pitcher of ice water over my head."

"Get back to the podium, or I will do it for you."

Scarcely seconds after James left, Gloria hove into view.

"The deed is done," she said. "James neglected to protect his name and address file with a password. I beamed the whole bunch into my Palm."

"I am glad you are on my side," I said earnestly, meaning every word.

She prodded her Palm handheld's screen with a little stylus. "We're in luck! James has a lot of Maryland and Virginia entries." She grinned at me. "What kind of birthday party are we going to throw for him?"

"I haven't given it much thought. Perhaps a classic, all-American birthday party, complete with party favors, silly hats, ice cream, a gooey cake, and forty-three candles?"

Gloria grimaced. "I'd shoot you if you did that to me. My ten-year-old cousin had an identical party last month."

"I yield to your experience and good sense. Do you have a better idea?"

"Well, is there such a thing as a birthday tea?"

"One can host a tea party on any occasion."

"A tea party is grownup, . . . it's different, . . . and it's English. James will love it."

I let the notion percolate for a moment. "Yes. It feels perfect," I finally said. "A birthday tea—with a goodly selection of sandwiches, cakes, and savories, and three different kinds of tea to drink."

"We'll hold it at my apartment, which is significantly larger than your house."

"We'll need a good cookbook, one filled with appropriate recipes for an English tea."

"I'll find one when I shop for the fixings, although I do have one question. What on earth is a savory?"

Any further planning was interrupted by James, who tapped his microphone and announced that he was ready to continue.

"I will explain savories later," I told Gloria.

James launched into a discussion of principle number nine. *No asset your company owns is more valuable than its reputation.* Gloria promptly identified the inspirational source as Proverbs 22:1: "A good name is more desirable than great riches; to be esteemed is better than silver or gold."

How true. And what better example than Hunnechurch & Associates?

"Our tenth and last principle is a favorite among management consultants," James said, "because we see so many business executives violate it—to their inevitable dismay."

He pressed the button that advanced the slide.

Principle #10
Hard Work "Invested" in a Sound Business Pays Off,
but It's Foolish to Waste Time on Hopeless Business
Strategies.

"Whew!" Gloria whispered. "That's a toughie. I don't remember any verse like it."

"Maybe it's not rooted in the Bible?"

She shook her head. "It sounds like a proverb; and furthermore, James isn't going to change the rules of the game in the last inning."

I tried not to smile as she attacked Proverbs, her index finger flying down the small pages, her lips quivering as she murmured one "No!" after another.

"Yes!" she suddenly said, loud enough to turn a few nearby heads. She handed me the Bible. I read the verse marked by her finger: "He who works his land will have abundant food, but he who chases fantasies lacks judgment" (Prov. 12:11).

James had been kind to the wishful thinkers in his audience. He had substituted the phrase "hopeless business strategies" for "fantasies." But when I glimpsed the men and women around me, I saw many remorseful expressions. They had plainly taken the principle to heart.

What about you, Hunnechurch? Don't you build castles in the sky?

I recalled my most recent business stratagem—my decision to support Sophie Hammond's scheme. Would it prove to be a fantasy? Or could the *Ryde Rebel* really offer Hunnechurch & Associates a road back to a pristine reputation? Sophie claimed it would, but her principal aim was to scoop the *Ryde Reporter* and the *Baltimore Sun*. She valued me as a source of information, nothing more.

What choice do you have?

There lay the rub. Sophie Hammond was my *only* hope to get back in business. Fantastic or not, I had to accept her proposal.

Gloria's Bible, open to Proverbs, was still in my hand. When I glanced down, my eye settled a few verses below James's final principle/proverb, on Proverbs 12:18: "Reckless words pierce like a sword, but the tongue of the wise brings healing."

I don't know why, but I found myself pondering the proverb. At first its meaning seemed perfectly straightforward. Poorly chosen words can hurt; well-chosen words can cure the injury. Barry Goodwin made a fine example of the former. His words had certainly been reckless—look at the damage they had done.

Then I felt a chill race along my spine as an impossible, ridiculous, absurd idea shoved its way to the front of my mind.

What if Barry had tried to be wise?

What if his goal had been to bring healing?

I pushed myself to remember the exact words Barry had said to me at Maison Pierre.

"I'm not leaving Campbell & McQueen until I have solid evidence of what's going on—enough to get the problem fixed, maybe even enough to send people to jail."

During our luncheon I had locked my attention on the word "jail" and ignored the more important phrase, "get the problem fixed."

All at once I knew what was "bugging Barry Goodwin," to quote Sophie Hammond.

It was so simple. Barry worried about the patients who had received faulty CM-7 heart valves. His chief concern was to repair the injury done to them. Sending those responsible to jail was a secondary matter.

He planned to blow the whistle, but only after he had gathered ir-refutable evidence of defective valves. A premature announcement would cause unnecessary pain to the very people he wanted to help. Barry understood that reckless words would pierce like a sword, so he continued to work at C&M. He bought a medical textbook on the sub-ject. He tried to prevent any patients from taking part in the news con-ference. He sought to enlist allies in his battle—Sidney Monk for sure, and possibly Jerry Nichols—although no one took him seriously. Everybody, including me, imagined him to be a loose cannon (someone likely to sour the acquisition of Campbell & McQueen by Hughes Engineered Materials) when, in fact, Barry had set out to go the extra mile for CM-7 heart valve recipients.

In the distance James was wrapping up the morning session by ex-plaining the source of his basic business principles. I heard people around me laughing, amused at being hoodwinked and pleased that lunch would soon be available; but all I could think about was Barry's single-minded campaign.

One thought in particular seemed to grow louder and louder in my consciousness. *Think about the future of Hunnechurch & Associates after you finish what Barry started.*

Chapter Fifteen

I MADE ANOTHER JAUNT across the Chesapeake Bay Bridge.

Each round trip cost two dollars and fifty cents for the toll, but I didn't mind the accumulating expense because traveling shore-to-shore over the five-mile-wide stretch of water unfailingly buoyed my mood. Not that I needed much cheering up that Wednesday afternoon. James and I had found a quiet alcove at the Waterside Hotel and said good-bye properly with a long hug and a kiss. Moreover, the weather became positively balmy. The temperature rose to sixty degrees—warm enough to melt the last chunks of snow against the buildings on Ryde High Street—while the absence of wind made it seem even warmer. I felt curiously energized by the two-step strategy that Gloria and I had conceived as we walked back to our office.

We would accelerate our efforts to learn everything that Barry Goodwin knew about CM-7 heart valves. Only then would we decide whether or not to share our findings with Sophie Hammond.

"We can't tell Sophie a partial story," I had said. "It has to be all or nothing. Anything less than a full revelation will leave hundreds of patients in a state of appalling worriment, wondering if their CM-7 heart valves are about to self-destruct."

Gloria had nodded. "I think you're right, but how are we going get the whole story?"

"Don't ask me questions I can't answer," I replied.

"Well, we should receive a preliminary report from the detective agency later this afternoon. I asked for everything available about Barry. It might point us in a new direction."

"While we're waiting, I'll visit Flynt Molding. Perhaps Barry's former boss has something to contribute—if she is willing to see me."

"In that case, I'll spend the next couple of hours inviting folks to James's birthday party." She flourished her Palm handheld. "I'll begin with the A's and work my way through the alphabet. I'll stop making calls when six people say yes."

"It sounds like a plan."

A half hour later I was driving along Route 50-301 toward the Chesapeake Bay.

I pulled to the side of the toll plaza on the western end of the bridge and dropped the Miata's top. I used the opportunity to call Sheila Wade.

I gave her my name and said, "I apologize for such short notice, but it is important that I talk to you. Can you spare thirty minutes?"

When I heard her hesitate, I feared that she might hang up. I relaxed when she asked, "Are you going to yell at me if I agree to a meeting?"

"No yelling—I promise. I want to discuss Barry Goodwin's fascination for plastics."

She chuckled. "Thirty minutes won't be enough time, but let's give it a try. We're north of Easton on Route 50, not far from the airport."

"I am a half hour away."

"I'll be waiting."

I drove ten miles an hour above the speed limit and soaked up the sunlight. Twenty-six minutes later I parked in front of an unremarkable cinder-block box with a flat roof, the kind of single-story factory one can find in industrial neighborhoods everywhere in the country. The moment I left my car, I began to smell the unmistakable scent of hot plastic resin. I followed my nose and a trail of "Office" arrows tacked on the exterior wall to a metal door on the right side of the building.

Flynt Molding's executive suite was a cluster of six small offices around an unmanned central reception area. The walls were painted eggshell white; the unexpectedly elegant office furniture was made of dark mahogany. A blue cloth banner the size of a bed sheet hung on the rear wall. Its large yellow letters proclaimed, *Flynt Molding Is Committed to Quality. We Are ISO 9001 Certified.*

I had begun to wonder how to make my presence known when a trim woman in a white lab coat poked her head out of the corner office and waved at me. Sheila Wade and I had spoken over the telephone the previous August, but we had never met. At the time I had pictured a younger person on the other end of the line, but this woman's short, dark hair was streaked with gray. I guessed her age to be about fifty-five. The last of my concerns evaporated when I saw that her light blue eyes were friendly and welcoming.

"Mrs. Wade?" I asked.

"Call me Sheila," she answered. "You must be Pippa Hunnechurch."

We shook hands, and I followed her into her office. The wall behind her desk was peppered with small objects that looked like drawer pulls.

She caught me staring and asked, "Do you know what they are?"

"No, although a few look vaguely familiar."

"They're knobs for radios and TV sets. My father, Raymond Flynt, manufactured a zillion of them during the fifties and sixties. In the days before handheld remotes and digital controls, you had to turn knobs to adjust the volume and change channels. Flynt Molding was one of the leading producers. We sold to Philco, Admiral, Zenith, Westinghouse, and a dozen other electronics companies that no longer exist."

"I never realized that knobs came in so many shapes and sizes."

"In our heyday we listed several thousand different designs in our catalog. My dad knew every model and variation. He was a man who loved plastic—not unlike Barry Goodwin."

A man who loves plastic. That was how Sheila had described Barry during our first telephone call. I remembered feeling surprised at her enthusiastic remarks. It's not often that a candidate gives me his present employer as a reference, but Barry had explained that Sheila accepted his decision to leave Flynt Molding. She had been unreserved in her praise for Barry's skills as a technologist and a business communicator. "I know that it's time for Barry to move on to a larger company," she had said. "He has outgrown our little Easton Shore operation." Her laudatory comments fully satisfied me. I didn't ask any penetrating questions about Barry, and the question of his ability to handle stress had never come up during our conversation.

Sheila perched against her desktop while I took an empty visitor's chair. "OK," she said, "what would you like to know about the *Prince of Peculiar Plastics?*"

"Pardon?"

"That used to be Barry's nickname in the factory because he spent most of his free time playing with exotic plastics." Her face broke into a nostalgic grin. "I still don't know why, but I allowed Barry to cost us a small fortune in lost production capabilities. You see, we don't have a separate prototype development shop. Barry would use factory machines after hours to experiment with unusual resins. More often than not, we would spend half of the next morning getting our clogged equipment back on-line."

Sheila turned away from me, but I had already seen the tears in her eyes. She sniffed and said, "Anyhow, Barry was truly fascinated with plastics technology, as you well know."

I chose my next words carefully. "Is it possible that his interest had become an obsession?"

She stared at her clenched hands for several seconds. "Oh my," she finally said, "how I wish you had asked me that question last summer. It seems rather late in the day to roam around in Barry's psyche. Nothing can change the fact that he's dead."

"No, but several hundred other lives may be at risk—lives that Barry wanted to protect."

Sheila lifted her head. "*Whose* lives are at risk?"

I gave her an abridged account of Barry's final days at Campbell & McQueen, relating all I had witnessed and learned about his bizarre behavior, but leaving out the theory that he didn't kill himself. I would need much more than a half hour to explain why I believed that Barry was murdered.

"As near as I can fathom," I said, to wrap up my narrative, "Barry was convinced that he had found a flaw in the CM-7 heart valve and that the company was not taking action to correct the problem."

"I can't imagine *anything* that would upset him more." She jumped to her feet. "Wait a minute! Why tell me tales about Campbell & McQueen? Even if what you say is true, when did the CM-7 heart valve become your problem?"

"That's a fair question. My answer is that I feel a growing responsibility to finish the job that Barry started. Many people believe that I did wrong by Barry last summer. Despite what you may have read in the newspapers, I was completely unaware of his mental health issues."

Sheila took a deep breath. "I advised Barry to tell you about his condition, but he refused. He wanted the C&M job more than you could have imagined. I have never seen him more excited than he was the afternoon he returned from talking to you. Essentially, you offered candy to a hungry baby."

"Barry certainly seemed eager during our first interview. To be frank, I assumed that he was unhappy at Flynt Molding. He kept asking how soon the job would be available at C&M."

Sheila sighed. "I suppose I had better fill in the missing pieces for you. How much do you know about plastics?"

"Alas, very little."

"Have you come across a plastic called Hevlan?"

"I recall hearing the name at C&M, although I don't remember anything more."

"Hevlan is a high-quality resin made in Germany. It's superstrong and highly stable but very finicky about molding temperatures, which makes it hard to work with in an ordinary facility like ours. However, it's virtually inert inside a human body, which is why Campbell & McQueen chose Hevlan for its CM-7 heart valves." Sheila sat down again on her desktop. "Hevlan was Barry's favorite plastic. Some people might say he was obsessed with finding new ways to apply it. Most of his experiments in our factory involved Hevlan."

"I take it that Flynt Molding doesn't use Hevlan?"

She shook her head. "My father stayed in the radio and TV knob business too long. When I took over the company, we were almost bankrupt. We've survived as a plain-vanilla plastics molding shop. We mold plastic mugs, housings for power tools, small carrying cases—lots of useful products but nothing that calls for the remarkable properties of Hevlan."

"On the other hand, C&M does use Hevlan," I said.

"Tons and tons of resin each month. Hevlan is an ideal material for high precision parts—for aircraft, space satellites, military equipment, and people. In fact, one of C&M's executives is a world-class expert on Hevlan chemistry, and the master molder probably knows more about manufacturing Hevlan components than anyone else in the country."

"You must mean Hilda McQueen and Jerry Nichols?"

"They're the ones! Barry idolized them. He was especially ecstatic at the thought of working with Jerry. I think Barry had a secret dream. He

wanted Jerry to say, 'Forget public relations and come back to the prototype development shop where you belong.'"

"Are you saying that Barry wanted out of corporate communications?"

"Barry never stopped being a plastics person. Communications was
a kind of fallback position after his . . . well, breakdown."

I heard myself yelp, "Barry had a *breakdown?*"

"It wasn't an official nervous breakdown, although he was hospital-
ized for a few weeks." Sheila crossed her arms. "Look, Barry joined us
ten years ago as a plastics engineer. Five years ago I made the mistake of
promoting him to plant manager. Six months later he fell to pieces. Barry
wasn't crazy; he was simply a high-strung individual prone to anxiety
and depression because he was lousy at juggling several tasks at the
same time. He'd get angry dealing with the small details. He couldn't
cope with a stressful job."

"So he changed careers."

She nodded. "After his breakdown, Barry's shrink managed to convince him that technical work didn't fit his personality—a diagnosis I
never agreed with. The short of it is, Barry went back to school for his
MBA. He finished in only sixteen months, then rejoined Flynt Molding
as our communications and marketing manager. That's when his love
affair with Hevlan began." She added, "Deep down inside, he didn't
want to stop being a plastics technologist."

"Is that when Barry became a part-time boffin?"

Sheila's expression changed to puzzlement.

"Excuse my slip of the tongue," I said. "'Boffin' is affectionate British
slang for a research scientist."

She smiled. "Part-time boffin is a perfect label for Barry. He convinced himself that playing with Hevlan in the factory was a form
of market research. He also became a champion of quality and customer satisfaction. Thanks to Barry's hard work, we standardized
the processes we use to make our products. We virtually eliminated

product defects and, along the way, became an ISO 9001 certified company. It's a source of great pride to my other employees."

An idea arose in my mind. "I am beginning to understand why Barry became so upset. He suffered three simultaneous disappointments—one with the plastic he loved, another with the product quality he espoused, and a third with the company he respected."

"Exactly! A defective Hevlan product sold by Campbell & McQueen would push three of Barry's emotional hot buttons at the same time."

"Let me add a fourth button. What if Jerry Nichols—the master molder he venerated—refused to acknowledge his discovery?"

"Barry would have gone ballistic." Her face went grim. "Is that why he killed himself?"

The only answer I could give with reasonable honesty was a noncommittal shrug.

———

Driving past a decoration-bedecked shopping mall on Route 50-301 triggered my memory. *You don't have a birthday present to give James at his tea party.* The sight of the overflowing parking lot made me groan, but I flipped my turn signal and followed a long string of Christmas shoppers down the access road. I finally found a narrow parking spot near a dumster a good quarter of a mile away from the mall's side entrance.

I had bought James a cashmere sweater for Christmas. My first thought was to purchase another cashmere item—say a bathrobe—for his birthday. However, all notions of clothing vanished when I walked past an electronic gadget shop just inside the mall. A big sign in the window read: *Pre-Christmas Sale. DVD Players. The Perfect Gift for Loved Ones Who Travel.*

One look and I was hooked: a book-sized device with its own miniature TV screen and two little speakers that could play a DVD anywhere—in an airport, on an airplane, in a motel room.

True, the cost was significantly more than I had intended to spend, but it seemed so right for James. I reached for my credit card.

Gift in hand, I stopped at the coffee counter in the food court for a double cappuccino. I managed to find a vacant two-seat table and dawdled awhile, mentally replaying my talk with Sheila Wade.

Now you know what made Barry Goodwin tick.

I tried to imagine myself in Barry's shoes, my frustration growing, my fury building because neither Jerry Nichols nor Sidney Monk will believe that C&M's flagship Hevlan product—the CM-7 heart valve—is defective and that Hilda McQueen is responsible. People's lives are at risk, yet I seem to be the only one in the company who cares about quality.

Jerry probably frowns and says, "I don't believe you."

"Then I'll bring you solid evidence!" I answer, although I know it will take time.

Why is it going to take time, Hunnechurch? For that matter, what kind of "solid evidence" was Barry talking about?

Blast! Every time I answered one question about Barry Goodwin, two more cropped up.

I tossed my empty paper cup, reached for my cell phone, and called Gloria.

"I'm glad you checked in," she said. "Collier Investigations delivered Barry's dossier an hour ago. Nothing jumped off the pages when I gave it a quick scan, but I may not know what to look for." She shifted subjects. "How was your visit to Flynt Molding?"

"Productive."

"Good. You can fill me in later. I have to go shopping."

"Ah. The tea party."

"Yep. Six guests are invited. I made it halfway through the Os in James's names and address list. The last invitee is a bubbly gal in Alexandria, Virginia, named Lesley Oppendahl, who thinks it will be a hoot to attend."

"You are an associate more precious than rubies."

"True. However, I am not clairvoyant. You still haven't told me what a savory is."

"The foods one serves at an English tea party can be divided into two categories, sweet and savory. While many savory dishes are simply not sweet, my favorites are actually quite spicy—for example, sausage rolls, Welsh rarebit on toast, cold meats with pickle or chutney, and sandwiches with a savory filling—oh, something like anchovy paste."

"Everything sounded delicious until you mentioned anchovies. Yuck!"

"Have you ever eaten an anchovy paste sandwich?"

"Thankfully, no."

I heard her mutter, "Boy, and I thought army food was creepy." An instant before she rang off, she said, "By the way, don't forget that our small group meets tonight in my apartment. We begin at seven o'clock sharp."

Bother! I had forgotten.

Why on earth did you agree to go? You're not a small-group person.

I looked up at the mall's glass skylight and was astonished to see darkness. Night had arrived while I lingered over my coffee.

Of course it's dark, Hunnechurch. The nights are long when the winter solstice is less than forty-eight hours away.

All at once I felt hungry and tired. This had been a busy day—the kind that should end with me curled up on my sofa with a good book. The very last thing I wanted to do that evening was to participate in a small group meeting and listen to other people complain about their problems. I had too many of my own to deal with.

I called my office again, but this time Gloria didn't answer. I dialed Gloria's mobile number and was told by a computer voice that "the subscriber you called is unavailable." Her cell phone was probably sitting in the Dodge's glove box. Finally I tried Dennis Marsh at Campbell & McQueen. He answered on the fourth ring.

"You caught me going out the door," he said.

I dove in without preamble. "Please make my excuses tonight. I won't attend the meeting."

"I'm sorry to hear that, Pippa. Can I ask why?"

"I don't feel ready to be part of a small group."

"You can't get away from us that easily. We'll pray for you even if you don't come."

"That would be lovely," I mumbled as I broke the connection, although I hoped they would forget about me that evening. I still felt uncomfortable with the idea of people talking to God on my behalf.

```
┌─────────────────────────────────┐
║        Chapter  Sixteen         ║
└─────────────────────────────────┘
```

I ARRIVED AT MY OFFICE on Thursday morning feeling uneasy. How would Gloria react to my not attending her small group meeting the night before?

"Good morning," I said to her.

"Good morning," she said back.

"Lovely day, isn't it?"

"Lovely—although a bit colder than yesterday."

"I trust you are fine this morning."

"I am. And you?"

"Equally fine."

"That's nice."

I smiled and asked, "Did you make a pot of tea?"

She smiled back. "You can stuff your tea pot in your ear."

I held up my hands in surrender. "I'm sorry about last night. I apologize. Forgive me."

"You have nothing to be sorry about. A small group represents a serious commitment to other people, so going or not going has to be your decision. I'm not supposed to criticize you or even call you a jerk for chickening out at the last minute."

"Thank you for your forbearance."

"I'm especially not supposed to tell you that I cursed out loud when I learned that you called Dennis Marsh instead of me."

"I tried your cell phone, which was turned off."

"But not my home phone, which has a perfectly good voice mail service."

"Oh, dear. I didn't think about your voice mail."

She glared at me for a second or two, then handed me a pink "While You Were Out" slip. "I give you this reluctantly," she said, "because it will probably make you feel good. It's from Anne Goodwin. I took it off your office answering machine. She called at ten 'til seven."

The message consisted of nine words: "I am willing to receive you early this morning."

"You had better go now," Gloria said, "while it's still early."

I checked my wristwatch. It was eight-forty-five.

"Surely I have time for one hot cuppa."

"Hit the road, Hunnechurch! If you get comfortable, you won't feel like another trek to Easton."

"How true," I said with a sigh.

The journey itself was less than memorable. Traffic was unusually heavy. I ended up in the slow-moving lane at the toll plaza. I crossed the Chesapeake Bay Bridge behind an enormous moving van that spewed diesel smoke at me. Worst of all, I had repeated opportunities to ponder the fact that I would be "received" by Anne Goodwin, not welcomed. Why did she want to see me? There hadn't been enough time for the postal service to deliver the copy of the *Ryde Rebel* that Gloria had mailed her. Perhaps she wanted to give me another tongue lashing?

At half-past nine I found myself staring once again at the big eagle doorknocker. The brass bird stared back, daring me to lift its tail. I steeled myself and gave two polite taps.

The door flew open, and Anne Goodwin, a determined expression on her face, projected a rush of words at me. "I had hoped to see the last of you, Miss Hunnechurch, because I don't like what you do for a living. If you had left Barry alone, he would be alive today. That is the unvarnished truth. Nothing you can say to me will ever change it. However, now that I know what you are doing and why you are doing it, I am willing to talk to you."

She had obviously rehearsed her opening speech, and once she spoke it, she relaxed. She took two steps backward and said, "You can come in."

I stepped into a small living room full of bold hues. The wallpaper displayed large red and pink roses on an ecru background. Two easy chairs upholstered in plush velvet the color of an eggplant sat catty-corner to a blue-green sofa and made a cozy conversation cluster opposite a brick fireplace. Anne was wearing the same long apron as before, but this time it was clean and there were no apple pie smells in the air. She gestured for me to take one of the easy chairs. She sat down on the sofa.

"You have me at a disadvantage, Mrs. Goodwin," I said. "May I ask what you believe to be the purpose of my investigation?"

"You're helping the *Ryde Rebel* so that you can save your business and rescue your career."

I hid my surprise. "I take it that you spoke to Sophie Hammond."

She scowled at me. "What if I did? The things we talked about are none of your business."

I kept silent and looked at her with all the friendly expectation I could paint on my face.

"What I *will* say," she went on, "is that Miss Hammond told me that you are acting as her assistant. I know it's your job to gather information that will make clear why Barry became so upset during the week before he . . ."

I held my breath while she paused to blow her nose.

"In any case," she continued. "I consider that a useful thing to do. What information do you require from me?"

"It has to do with Barry's work in plastics technology."

"How can *you* comprehend anything about plastics?" she said with a sneer. "Sophie told me that you don't even have a real college education. No wonder you never understood a sensitive scientist like Barry."

Hold tight, Hunnechurch! Don't let her get to you.

"I learned a good deal about plastics when I began to work with Campbell & McQueen," I said. "I know that Barry experimented with a plastic called Hevlan."

"Hevlan!" She shouted the word like an obscenity. "Barry talked and talked about Hevlan. How strong it is, how versatile. If it wasn't for Hevlan, he would still be working at Flynt Molding. He would be alive today . . ."

She squeezed her eyes shut when she realized what she had said. She clenched her fists and began to hit the tops of her knees. She began to speak in a hissy whisper. "You lured Barry away from home with Hevlan. That's why I blame you for his death. Now do you understand?"

"I understand," I said softly.

"Good." She blew her nose again and gazed at me blankly. I decided to start again, this time with a different opening statement.

"There are two ways you can help my investigation, Mrs. Goodwin. The first is to give me your permission to enter Barry's apartment in Ryde."

"Why?"

"I want to look through his books and papers."

The expression on her face changed from bewilderment to comprehension. "Oh, yes. That makes sense. Barry had a shelf full of books and papers in his apartment."

"By any chance, do you have the key?"

Slowly, Anne raised her hand and gestured toward a cherry wood secretary across the room. "Look inside the leftmost cubbyhole," she said.

I fought back the excitement I felt and moved slowly to the small, elegant piece of furniture. An ordinary white business-letter-size envelope was tucked into the cranny. I opened the flap and discovered a three-by-five-inch file card with a key taped neatly across its middle. Barry had carefully printed instructions on the card: *The burglar alarm keypad is on the kitchen wall near the refrigerator. The access code is 7221.*

I smiled at Anne. "I will return this to you no later than tomorrow afternoon."

She gave an indifferent shrug. "What's the second way I can help?"

"I want to read an article that Barry wrote—possibly for *Plastics Technology* magazine."

"Oh yes . . . his article. It was published last winter. He was very proud of it."

"Do you have a copy?"

Her face grew dark again. "He gave me one, but I put it in the fireplace last week. The article was about Hevlan."

"Ah."

"Maybe you'll find a copy in his apartment."

"Perhaps I will," I agreed, although I knew better. "Getting back to Barry's books and papers—I believe that Campbell & McQueen sent you some items that Barry had in his office."

Anne pointed at a coat closet near the front door. "I left the box in there."

I walked to the closet. Inside, on the floor, was a white cardboard box—the kind that holds ten reams of copier paper. I removed the lid. Inside was the usual assortment of tools people keep in their desk drawers: pens, pencils, a sheaf of business cards, a stapler, a calculator, a ruler. I found several brochures about plastic resins and the February issue of *Plastics Technology* magazine. The article Barry had written was on page forty-eight: "A New Look at Hevlan: Can a High Performance Resin Find a Home in Low Performance Products?"

Ta da!

A timer bell rang in the distance.

"I promised to bake five pumpkin pies for my church today," Anne said. "My pie crust dough is chilled enough to roll." She stood up and walked to her kitchen.

I was about to replace the box's lid when I saw a Palm handheld buried under the brochures.

I called out to Anne, "I am going to borrow a magazine and Barry's handheld computer."

She suddenly appeared at the kitchen door. "Borrow anything you want from the box, then show yourself out. You can do me a favor in return. If you find anything in the box made out of Hevlan, toss it away."

———

I had called Gloria as soon as I fired up the Miata. "We have Anne's go-ahead to explore Barry's digs, but she seemed flaky enough this morning to change her mind. Let's check out the apartment immediately."

I parked in front of 1635 Spruce Siding, behind Gloria's truck. She was waiting for me near the steps that led to Barry's apartment. With her hands in her pockets and her coat collar turned up to within inches of her blonde hair, she looked like the *femme fatale* from a 1950s spy movie. I gave her the envelope with the key and alarm code.

"You deal with the locks and the keypad," I said.

"Big deal! It's not much fun if we have permission."

The first thing we did was to lift the Venetian blinds and turn on the overhead lights, which made the apartment feel much less gloomy than it had the previous Tuesday. I was pleased to see that the English ivy plant and the fichus tree were on the road to recovery.

Gloria walked from room to room like a general surveying a battlefield. "Two days ago we looked for a copy of Barry's article," she said. "What's our objective this afternoon?"

"I don't know what we're looking for."

"You can't be serious!"

"However, I have every expectation that one of us will enjoy a *you'll-know-it-when-you-see-it* moment."

"That's ridiculous!"

"I presume you have a better idea?"

"You bet. We'll work together to perform a systematic search of the apartment. I'll do the digging; you look over my shoulder and do the analyzing. That way, we both see everything."

"Your approach works for me. Onward! Leave no leaf unturned."

Gloria mumbled something about "silly British amateurs" that I didn't quite catch, then began searching in earnest. It took us nearly a half hour to complete the living room. We began with a thorough probe of Barry's file cabinet/TV stand, which contained nothing but carefully organized receipts and instruction manuals. Next we tackled the bookcase, wherein Gloria removed, opened, and shook each book. All we exposed was sufficient dust to make Gloria sneeze. In quick succession, she looked inside the frame that held Karen Constantine's photograph, patted down the sofa cushions, felt for bulges under the carpeting, and browsed through Barry's collection of CDs.

"He's got enough Reba McEntire, Shania Twain, and Trisha Yearwood CDs to fill a bushel basket," she said. "Who'da thunk that Barry was a country music fan?"

"More likely a country *diva* fan."

She began to open the CD "jewel cases."

"Are you going to put on some music?" I asked.

She shook her head. "Nope. A CD album package is a good place to conceal a computer CD-ROM, if you are so inclined. Maybe he hid a bunch of data or documents?"

Barry hadn't. All the CDs matched their album covers.

We moved on to the bedroom. We started by looking through the closet we hadn't had time to inspect on Tuesday because the burglar alarm had gone off. Gloria reached into every pocket, felt inside every shoe, opened every suitcase, patted down every tie and hung-up shirt. Happily, Barry had not lived in the apartment long enough to build a collection of cardboard boxes on the top shelf. The only box in sight contained brand-new Christmas tree ornaments, three still-wrapped strings of lights, a package of tinsel, and—at the very bottom—a receipt dated ten days earlier.

"Hey! We never noticed," Gloria said. "Barry doesn't have a Christmas tree."

I felt an urge to apologize for Barry. He had died on December 10, rather early in the month to set up holiday decorations. After all, today was December 20—and I still hadn't bought a Christmas tree or the necessary trimmings.

"Now that I think of it," I said, "this box of ornaments is additional evidence that Barry was murdered. He thought ahead to the end of December, something a suicidal person wouldn't do."

It took another ten minutes for Gloria to squeeze the clothing in the wardrobe and feel along the shelves. Nothing was hidden inside.

"Where do we look next?" Gloria asked. "Barry's desk, bathroom, or computer?"

"Perhaps Barry's kitchen. All this looking over your shoulder has made me thirsty."

"OK—let's take a break."

We went to the kitchen. I remembered which kitchen cabinet held a few drinking glasses. I retrieved two and filled them at the sink.

"I hate tap water without ice cubes," Gloria said.

"If I recall, ice is the one thing that Barry does have." I reached in his freezer, pulled out the ice cube tray, and handed it to Gloria. "Cubes for the lady."

She took the tray—and (no pun intended) froze.

"What's wrong?" I asked after several seconds of watching her stare down at the tray.

"There's something in the tray other than frozen water. Actually some *things.*"

Two days earlier, when I had glanced at the ice cube tray with the help of a flashlight beam, I had seen only ice. Now, however, in the bright light cast by four fluorescent tubes in the ceiling fixture, I could make out shadowy blobs inside four of the ice cubes.

"Let's thaw them out," she said.

I looked for a mixing bowl to hold the ice cubes, while Gloria cracked them loose from the tray. We filled the bowl with lukewarm tap water and watched as the ice slowly dissolved, revealing four curious round objects.

Gloria spoke first. "They look like Ritz crackers wearing skirts."

Indeed they did. The "cracker" part of each object was a cream-colored disk a bit more than an inch across. The "skirt" was a wider ring of soft white fabric securely attached to the central disk.

I picked up one of the objects and discovered that the "disk" was actually a ring that supported two half-round hinged flaps. Each flap could open and close like a tiny barn door.

"I give up," Gloria said. "Do you know what they are?"

"I suspect we are looking at Campbell & McQueen CM-7 artificial heart valves. Barry, for reasons unknown, squirreled away four of them in his freezer compartment." I began to pat the valve dry with a twin to the dishtowel I had commandeered during our unauthorized visit. "We seem to have stumbled upon what we didn't know we were searching for."

"One of the four is broken," Gloria said. "See—a flap is missing on this one, along with a big chunk of the nearby edge. I wonder why?"

I looked at the damaged device. Someone had used a Dremel motor tool or a similar cutting device to neatly carve away the piece of the ring that included one of the hinged barn doors.

"I am clear out of ideas and speculations," I said. "It is obvious that the first thing we need is an expert who can answer our questions after he or she confirms that these are real artificial heart valves—not mock ups, toys, or who knows what?"

"How about Joyce Friendly? She's an operating room nurse. Chances are, she's handled a heart valve or two."

"Joyce would be ideal, but . . ."

"But?"

"I can't ask Joyce to keep a secret from her husband. I certainly don't want David to get wind of what we know—I trust him less than I do Sophie Hammond."

"Just ask her to identify the doodads. Don't tell her where we found them." Gloria took the dishtowel from my hand and set to work drying the other valves. "The alternative is to telephone every heart surgeon in the book until one of them agrees to see you."

I thought a moment and made the practical choice. "Joyce it shall be. Help me find something we can use to wrap the valves."

We settled on the plastic Ziploc sandwich bags that Gloria discovered in a kitchen drawer. We were bagging the fourth valve when I heard her stomach rumble.

"What do you expect?" she said, her words accompanied by a sheepish grin. "The sandwich bags made me think about sandwiches, which reminded my stomach that it's lunch time."

My wristwatch read 12:35.

"Now that you mention it, I am hungry too," I said. "I think we can safely leave without perusing Barry's computer for two reasons. First, his Palm handheld is in my trunk, waiting for you to examine. Second, I feel confident that we unearthed his treasure trove."

My cockiness that afternoon knew no bounds.

"In fact," I went on, "I believe that Barry's magazine article, plus his Palm, plus the valves he hid away will give us all the raw material we need to reconstruct Barry's concerns about the CM-7."

They did.

Alas, one of the items also aroused the interest of a murderer.

Chapter Seventeen

A STIFF BREEZE zipped through the employee parking garage built alongside Ryde General Hospital as I stood shivering in the chilled pre-dawn air, swaddled in my quilted goose-down parka and sheltered by a concrete column a few feet away from Joyce Friendly's dark green Subaru station wagon.

I had arrived at the garage at 6:00 on Friday morning and promptly located Joyce's car on the second floor. The sky looked black as coal— an appropriate sight on the longest night of the year. At six forty-five I noted that a narrow sliver of gold had begun to glow on the eastern horizon.

I knew that Joyce worked the night shift at Ryde General, but I wasn't sure when it ended, and I didn't want to explain myself over the telephone. I suppose I also feared that she might refuse to see me because I had rebuffed her invitation to Christmas dinner. Therefore, I decided to stake out her station wagon in person.

It had seemed like a good idea the day before.

Gloria and I had eaten lunch at the Ryde Diner after leaving Barry's apartment. We returned to our office after consuming a pair of "50s Classic Superburger" platters and pored over our loot. We locked away two of the undamaged heart valves in the back of a file drawer full of old résumés. As the day progressed, I tried to understand Barry's magazine article while Gloria examined the contents of his Palm handheld. I also read the preliminary report on Barry prepared by Collier Investigations. I already knew most of the content: Barry was born in Easton; he didn't have a police record; he had never been married; he held a valid driver's license.

One odd fact did intrigue me, however. Collier had managed to obtain the transaction log for Barry's personal credit card. On the Monday that Barry took me to lunch, he also had enjoyed an expensive breakfast at the very same restaurant—Maison Pierre. He had, however, used his own credit card—rather than his C&M company credit card—to pay for the earlier meal. I made a mental note. *Find out whom Barry took to breakfast.*

Later, Gloria and I did some last-minute planning for James Huston's birthday tea party, which was scheduled to begin at four o'clock on Friday afternoon. James would arrive in Ryde after lunch on Friday and check into a small bed and breakfast located at the bottom of Magothy Street. I had told him nothing about the tea party.

"Your sole responsibility, Mr. Huston," I had said during a telephone chat on Thursday evening, "is to present yourself at Gloria Spitz's apartment tomorrow at precisely 4:00 P.M."

"Yes ma'am," James had answered, "although I would surely like to see you earlier in the day."

"You cannot! I have every waking hour scheduled, starting at six in the morning."

"I am impressed."

"So am I. I plan to arise at five tomorrow morning."

I had, which led to my standing on the second floor of a window-less parking garage for nearly an hour.

Joyce Friendly emerged from the stairwell at 6:55, looking tall even in her winter topcoat. She seemed tired after a long night's work and lost in thought.

"Hi Joyce," I called when she was thirty feet away. I didn't want to frighten her.

She stopped and peered at me. "Pippa?" she said, her voice full of astonishment.

"Good morning!" I walked toward her. "I need a moment of your time. It's quite important."

"It must be for you to stand out here in the cold. Your cheeks are an unhappy shade of blue." She took my arm. "Let's go to my car. It has electric seat warmers."

I eagerly climbed into the passenger seat. Joyce cranked up the engine and flipped a switch next to the gearshift lever. Seconds later I could feel heat rising though my seat cushion.

"I'll call home while you are thawing out," she said as she retrieved a cell phone from her purse. "I have to tell David what's happening. He's expecting me home for breakfast at seven."

I pivoted in my balmy seat and stared determinedly out the window while she spoke to him, but, of course, I heard every word.

"I'll be a few minutes late this morning, hon," she said. "I'm still at the hospital—Pippa Hunnechurch is with me." She listened a while, then said, "I'll tell her. Bye, sweetie."

I pivoted back when Joyce snapped her phone shut and dropped it into her purse.

"David hopes that you're well," she said.

"Convey my thanks when you see him."

"With pleasure. Now, tell me why you ambushed me in a garage."

I had brought two of the probable heart valves we found in Barry's apartment with me—one undamaged, the other mutilated. I handed the Ziploc bag containing the intact valve to Joyce and said, "I believe this a medical device. Can you identify it for me?"

Joyce switched on the Subaru's dome light, and her eyes widened. "Where did you get this?"

I had a ready answer. "I can't be specific, but I can tell you that it came into my possession yesterday."

"Well, tell whoever swore you to secrecy that this is a prosthetic heart valve, specifically a Campbell & McQueen model CM-7. In medical parlance it's called a bileaflet valve. Two leaflets hinged to an orifice ring swing open and shut to permit blood flow in one direction but prevent it in the other. I think that this particular prosthesis is designed to replace a diseased aortic valve. The artificial mitral valves have a slightly different configuration."

She opened the Ziploc bag and held the valve between her fingers. "It's funny," she continued, "but I haven't been up close and personal with a CM-7 before, even though I assisted at several valve replacement operations. Each valve comes packed in a sterile container, attached to a carrying handle. I've never unpacked a valve or carried one to the surgeon."

"Are you sure it's a real CM-7?"

"Positive. Ryde General is one of the hospitals that participated in the testing program to win FDA approval. There's a big CM-7 poster hanging in the operating room nurse's lounge. This happens to be one of the most advanced artificial heart valves in the world."

"I have been told that it's made of Hevlan plastic."

"Yes. But a very special formulation that can be polished to a high luster. That's because the surfaces of an artificial heart valve have to be extraordinarily smooth. Any roughness might encourage clots to form as the heart pumps blood past the leaflets."

Joyce weighed the CM-7 in her hand. "Did you notice that this device seems heavy for a small object made out of plastic? Campbell &

McQueen adds a small amount of powdered tungsten to the Hevlan so that the valve will be visible when the patient is X-rayed."

"It seems like a straightforward device."

"It is. Only two moving parts. But keep in mind that those parts must swing open and shut with absolute reliability for as many as a million heartbeats a year. It takes skill to design an artificial valve that physicians will trust."

"May I ask what the cloth ring is for?" I asked.

"It's called a sewing cuff. The surgeon fastens the prosthesis in place with sutures that sandwich the cuff between the heart and the aorta."

Joyce dropped the valve into the Ziploc bag and gave it back to me. "You've made me terribly curious, Pippa—and more than a little bit uncomfortable."

"Actually, I have something else to show you. A damaged CM-7."

I lifted the other plastic bag.

"That's weird! Someone cut a piece out of the orifice ring."

"Can you think of a reason why?"

"None whatsoever." She added, "I wish you'd tell me where the valves came from."

"I can't tell you, Joyce. Not yet."

"You sound just like David. When I ask him about a story in the works, his usual reply is 'I'm not ready to talk about it.' Oh, how I hate those words." The exasperation left her voice as quickly as it had arrived. "Speaking of David, when are you and he going to make up?"

I shrugged. "I don't have an answer."

"Neither does David. I ask him at least once a day." Her eyebrows moved downward as she frowned. "You two are alike in so many ways—no wonder you became friends. It grieves me to see you angry at him."

"I have a right to be angry at David."

"He didn't realize how much pain his article would cause you, but he is too proud—and too stubborn—to beg your forgiveness. You may have to take the first step."

"I hardly think so. I am the injured party."

"Remember what Paul wrote in his letter to the Colossians. 'Bear with each other and forgive whatever grievances you may have against one another. Forgive as the Lord forgave you.'"

"I'll mull it over," I said, hoping to end the discussion about David and me.

She reached over and gave me a hug. "Do more than mull, Pippa. *Pray* about it. And please reconsider your decision to boycott my Christmas dinner. We both want you come. Honestly!" She moved her hands to the steering wheel. "Now, can I give you a lift to your car?"

"That would be lovely. I'm parked on Major Sutley Road, around the corner from the hospital."

It was ten minutes past seven when I thanked Joyce, wished her a Merry Christmas, and slipped out of the Subaru. As I watched her drive away, I thrust my hands in my pockets. My fingers closed around two Ziploc bags and the CM-7s inside.

Why, I wondered for the umpteenth time, had Barry hidden them in his refrigerator?

━━━━━━━━━

I had one more person to see that morning before I could begin to help Gloria prepare for James's party. Now that I knew the valves were real, I wanted to show them to Hilda McQueen. The CM-7 was her pet project; the time had come to find out whether she had been aware of Barry's concerns.

How are you going to get Hilda to see you, Hunnechurch?

I pondered the problem as I drove to Campbell & McQueen's headquarters. The only solution I came up with involved a heavy-dulie. I knew it was wrong, but I was steeling myself to deliver it when

I spotted the big copy board sign in front of C&M. It usually announced a help-wanted requirement. Today it announced: *C&M is closed for Christmas. Open again on Tuesday. Have a great holiday!*

Blimey!

I pulled to the curb and called Gloria at home.

"Is there any way you can find out where Hilda McQueen lives?" I asked. "Ideally in the next fifteen minutes."

"How about in the next twenty seconds?" she said smugly. "Barry downloaded the entire Campbell & McQueen phone directory into his Palm handheld. I guess he thought that the director of communications might have to reach company people after hours. Anyway, Hilda's address and home phone number are readily available because I cleverly carried the Palm home with me last night."

"I bow to your shrewdness. Please access the information."

She did—in less than the promised twenty seconds.

Hilda answered her phone on the second ring.

"Good morning," I said cheerfully. "This is Pippa Hunnechurch. I want to meet with you this morning."

Her response began with a profound sigh. "I am leaving for a two-week European vacation in a few hours, Pippa. I am simply too busy to meet with you this morning. Even if I were free, I don't see how either of us would benefit from meeting. You and I have nothing more to discuss. I plan to sign C&M's agreement with Nailor & McHale when I get back in January."

"This isn't about Hunnechurch & Associates working for Campbell & McQueen. I want to talk to you about the hidden defects in the CM-7 heart valve. Before Barry Goodwin died, he told me that the CM-7 heart valve is, to turn a phrase, unfit for human consumption."

"Nice try, Pippa, but I've heard all about Mr. Goodwin's inane accusations. He attempted to convince Sidney Monk that I concealed a manufacturing problem. The man was a lunatic."

"Perhaps . . . but Barry was sane enough to give me a CM-7 valve that he considered defective. He told me to send it to a reporter at the *Baltimore Sun.*"

"Now I'm sure that you are lying. CM-7 distribution is tightly controlled. Each heart valve has a serial number; every valve is accounted for. We store new valves under lock and key. Goodwin didn't have access to our CM-7 inventory. He *couldn't* have given you a sample."

"I'll show it to you when we meet, Hilda. I have it with me in my pocket."

"I don't think so."

"Let me describe it to you. A cream-colored orifice ring. Two cream-colored leaflets. A white cloth sewing cuff. Smoothly polished surfaces. A curiously heavy feel in the hand."

"Those facts prove nothing. We publish photographs of the CM-7 in our product brochures." Her tone had changed; I could hear concern in her voice.

"Fifteen minutes, Hilda. That's all I ask."

Another deep sigh. "I'll give you fifteen minutes if you can get here in five."

Hilda lived in a grand, old, two-story colonial on a large wooded estate northwest of Ryde. I parked my car next to a midnight blue Cadillac, in front of a covered entryway with a wrought-iron chandelier hanging from its ceiling. Large clay planters, empty now except for the leaves that had blown into them, stood like giant ashtrays on either side of the glass-paneled front door. I pressed the button and heard a muffled *ding-dong-ding* from inside.

Hilda greeted me with a curt nod and a dour expression. I countered with a friendly smile. She merely let out a fresh sigh. I followed her inside.

She was dressed in a loose black pantsuit and frilly off-white blouse—a comfortable outfit for a trans-ocean flight. Her brunette hair had a fresh-from-the-salon appearance. I caught a whiff of expensive

perfume as we strode through a marble-floored foyer and into a surprisingly masculine room with walls of bookshelves, leather-covered
furniture, shuttered windows, earth-tone color scheme, and a huge
walnut desk.

"Welcome to my library," she said. She pointed to an armchair wide
enough to hold two of me. I sat down. She took an elegant wing chair—
in Hepplewhite style, I guessed—upholstered in an unusual oriental
floral fabric. "If you really have a CM-7 in your pocket, show it to me."

I lobbed the undamaged valve, still in its Ziploc bag, into her lap.

Hilda's face went white.

"Oh Lord!" she murmured. "This can't be."

I said nothing while she fumbled to open the bag. She held up the
CM-7 and examined it in the light that streamed through the window
behind her chair.

"You said that Barry Goodwin gave this to you?"

"That's exactly what I said," dodging the direct question.

"Well, it *is* a genuine CM-7. I don't know of another plastics company that has the ability to do this quality of work with Hevlan." She
looked at me. "I can't conceive where, or how, Barry Goodwin got his
hands on a production CM-7. The serial number tells me it was from
one of the six initial production batches we manufactured three months
ago. That was before Goodwin joined the company."

"Are you sure of the timing?"

She nodded. "I'm sure about the date, but I'm baffled how one of
our valves could fall through our accounting system. We are *very* careful about inventory."

Not one valve. Four.

I now understood why Barry had taken extraordinary precautions
to hide the valves. He didn't want anyone to know that he had them—
not even his cleaning lady.

"I'll give you the errant valve in exchange for answering two questions," I said.

"Fair enough."

"My first question is obvious. Are there any manufacturing defects in that valve?"

"None that I can see. It seems to be an ordinary production CM-7, mostly handmade by Jerry Nichols's team, which means that it's flawless in every way. What's your second question?"

"Barry Goodwin thought himself a Hevlan expert. Could there be a manufacturing defect that somehow involves Hevlan?"

Hilda looked intently at the CM-7 in her hand. I could almost see the wheels turning in her mind. "You're asking me," she finally said, "if there could be a Hevlan-related manufacturing fault *not* visible to the naked eye."

"Is such a thing possible?"

She shook her head. "I can't imagine how. I can tell that this valve is made of Hevlan. No other plastic has the same luster—Hevlan almost glows. If anything had gone wrong during the molding process, the surface would be grainy. Besides, we do extensive quality testing of every valve we mold before it gets its serial number." She flipped the CM-7 into the air like a silver dollar and caught it in her palm. The leaflets made a clacking sound. "You can *feel* a valve that has an internal defect—say an air bubble deep inside the orifice ring. This CM-7 is perfectly balanced. No flaws, no defects—inside or outside."

Hilda spoke calmly, but I could see a shadow of anxiety flicker across her face. She hadn't told me the whole truth. She was holding something back.

Barry had discovered a flaw in the CM-7.

"Thank you for your time," I said.

"Thank you for the CM-7." She made a point of looking at her watch. "I really do have to get back to my packing." We stood up, and she continued. "There has to be a simple explanation for how Barry Goodwin came into possession of this particular prosthesis. I'll track it down and let you know—when I return from my vacation."

I drove away from Hilda's house sure of only one thing: I didn't have a "whole story" about heart valves to tell Sophie Hammond. The cell phone service was spotty in this part of town. I waited until the outskirts of Ryde to dial Sophie's office.

"I'm sure glad you called, Pippa," she said. "The *Ryde Rebel* goes to press at midnight, and I'm pulling words out of the air for my follow-up story. What do you have for me?"

"Alas, nothing,"

"*Nothing?* You've been beating the bushes since Tuesday."

"True, but I can't say with certainty what upset Barry Goodwin during the last days of his life."

"I don't need certainty. I'll settle for conjecture and possibilities. Tell me what you think."

"I can't do that. Not until I am sure of all the facts."

I regretted my words the moment I spoke them.

"That means you uncovered something big!" Sophie shouted. "Come on, Pippa. I shared with you—you share with me."

"Good-bye, Sophie."

I stuffed my cell phone back into my handbag. It began to ring almost immediately. I ignored the persistent bleats all the way to Gloria's apartment.

Chapter Eighteen

A MEDLEY OF FAMILIAR SMELLS surrounded me as I walked into Gloria's apartment. I recognized the friendly aromas of warm scones, hot sausage rolls, and sharp cheddar cheese. They brought me back to the many afternoon teas I had enjoyed in Chichester.

"Have you had breakfast yet?" Gloria asked.

"No." I sniffed the delicious air. "And after a whiff of this place, I realize I'm starving."

"Good. You'll make a perfect guinea pig. I whipped up test batches of the hot dishes for the tea party. You can tell me if I got them right. Pour yourself a hot cuppa and join me at the kitchen table."

When I sat down, she said, "Tell me why melted-cheesy stuff is called Welsh rabbit. It doesn't have long ears or a fluffy tail."

"You have made Welsh *rarebit*—which is often pronounced rabbit—although it's too early in the day to split hares."

I ducked as she flung a toast wedge at me.

"It smells grand," I said. Gloria gave me a slice of toast she had covered with the melted cheddar mix then broiled for about thirty seconds. "Yum. It tastes even better."

Gloria had prepared two other English teatime classics. We moved on to her sausage rolls ("I would add a *soupçon* more spice," I said.) and finished with scones with jam and *double Devon cream* ("Perfect!").

After breakfast Gloria gave me a tour of "Tea Party Central," as she dubbed her living room. Gloria lived in the northwest corner of Ryde, on Poplar Road, in a two-bedroom apartment that had begun life as the second floor of nineteenth-century gingerbread Victorian. The old house had been restored and sectioned into flats ten years earlier. Her principal living room furniture consisted of four overstuffed armchairs surrounding a glass-topped coffee table. Today she had placed the four chairs from her dinette set in between the armchairs to create seating for eight.

"We have invited a total of nine people," I said.

"True, but I expect that you or I will always be standing, continuously replenishing the goodies on the coffee table."

"An excellent point."

"We also have to hand out these things."

"These things" were English party crackers. Gloria lobbed one at me.

She went on. "I thought you were talking about biscuits—until the man in the party store showed me how they work. These things are *ordinance*. I bought the extra-powerful variety. Let's set this baby off."

The cracker looked like a big piece of hard candy enclosed in fancy wrapping paper. I knew there was a cardboard cylinder inside, which was about two-inches across and four inches long. I poked my fingers into one end of the wrapping, and Gloria took charge of the other end. We each yanked a cardboard tab.

Bang! The "snap"—a tiny explosive charge—snapped, and out popped a tissue-paper birthday hat and a tiny ceramic dog.

"There's a different toy in every cracker," Gloria said.

"Indeed, there is. I had an extensive ceramic menagerie when I was a child."

I dropped into one of the armchairs and found myself staring at the splendidly decorated Christmas tree in the corner. Gloria had obviously been waiting for me to notice it.

"My tree looks different, doesn't it?" she asked enthusiastically.

"Yes, but also strangely familiar."

"That's because all the decorations are retro. It's the kind of tree you and James might have had when you were kids. Red, green, and blue glass-globe ornaments, genuine tinsel made of metal foil, traditional candy canes, and antique blinking lights."

"Please define *antique.*"

"I used ordinary light bulbs rather than light-emitting diodes or fiber-optic sprays." She added. "I think they're pretty, in an old-fashioned way."

"The tree trimmings of my childhood do *not* qualify as old-fashioned."

"Whatever."

Showing a domestic nature I hadn't seen in action before, Gloria fluffed pillows, straightened napkins, and centered a cluster of candles on the coffee table. Then she prodded me out of the chair.

"Rest later—after we cook like crazy."

Gloria marched me into the kitchen, dropped an apron over my head, and pointed at two loaves of sliced bread—one white, the other brown. "We'll start by making those little tea sandwiches that don't have crusts."

"With what fillings?"

"Egg salad, cucumber, and Marmite—for the truly adventurous."

"Who told you about Marmite?"

"The man in the gourmet food store. He said that Brits like to spread the stuff on buttered toast. He even called it a savory."

"*Some* Brits do. Marmite is made from spent brewer's yeast and has a rather . . . *uh,* distinctive flavor."

We lopped the crusts off the bread, made sandwiches, cut them crosswise, and arranged the triangles on two large platters. Gloria adding sprigs of parsley for decoration. We worked until we had created a small mountain of sandwiches. We also talked about my visits to Joyce Friendly and Hilda McQueen.

"I still have more questions than answers," I said, "but I feel confident about several things.

"One . . . Barry did indeed discover an imperfection in the CM-7— something related to Hevlan, the plastic used to manufacture the valves.

"Two . . . Barry understood the enormous risks of making his findings public before he completely understood the extent of the problem. Simply put, he didn't want to scare the stuffing out of the hundreds of patients who have already received CM-7 valves until he was absolutely sure of his facts.

"Three . . . Barry set out to gather compelling evidence about the defect. He managed to get hold of four real CM-7s despite Campbell & McQueen's elaborate security.

"Four . . . Hilda has an inkling of what the flaw might be. I could see as much in her eyes.

"Five . . . Barry erroneously concluded that Hilda was responsible— or else I am a terrible judge of people.

"Six . . . someone who wanted the defect to remain a secret murdered Barry.

"Seven . . . we still don't have enough information to go public with the story. We would start the very same panic that Barry was determined to prevent."

When Gloria didn't respond to my litany, I looked up from my sandwich making. She had a half-eaten Marmite sandwich in her hand and a curdled expression on her face.

"I can't believe that Brits actually like this stuff," she said. She gave me her unfinished sandwich and reached for a glass of water.

"I tried to tell you that Marmite is an acquired taste." I began to nibble contentedly.

"From now on, I'll hang on every word you say."

———————

The doorbell rang at five minutes 'til four, while I was in the bathroom combing my hair and touching up my makeup. Gloria tapped on the door and said, "A fellow named James Huston is here. He's asking to see you."

I raced into the hallway and into his arms. I caught a peek at Gloria out of the corner of my eye. She gave me an animated thumbs up.

"How is the birthday boy?" I asked when we finally untangled ourselves.

"A tad anxious, ma'am. I'm wary of birthday parties."

"You will love this one." I grabbed his arm and tugged him to "Tea Party Central."

"Have mercy!" he said. "You ladies have created a banquet."

"I promised you a proper celebration, and a proper celebration you shall have, but please direct your amazement toward Gloria. She did the lion's share of the work."

He bowed at the waist. "*Ah* am overwhelmed by your kindness, Ms. Spitz. Although I fear you have set out enough food to feed an army."

"Not an army," she said, "just six of your local friends."

James's eyebrows sprang up. "My friends? How is that possible? I've never told you who my Yankee friends are."

"We merely applied the power of modern technology," I said. "In any case, one should not look a gift horse in the mouth."

The doorbell rang again. Gloria gave James a gentle push. "I suggest you answer that," she said. "It's definitely for you."

A moment later we heard him laugh. "Howard! Ray! How on earth did they find you fellas?"

I gave Gloria a high five. "Nice work, pardner."

Two men, one considerably younger than James, stepped into Gloria's living room.

I collected their coats while James did the introductions. "Pippa Hunnechurch and Gloria Spitz, meet Howard Lockwood and Ray Crosby. They were colleagues when I consulted for the U.S. Department of Commerce." I noticed that Ray (a ruggedly handsome man about thirty) held Gloria's hand a remarkably long time. She didn't seem to mind.

James tapped my shoulder. "Who told you about Howard and Ray?" he asked.

"One can't keep secrets from a headhunter," I said smugly as I hung up the coats I was holding.

The doorbell rang again before he could reply. I found two women and a man on the doorstep. James made introductions, and I took coats. Their first names (all I managed to remember) were Janice, Sherry, and Kevin.

Gloria shooed the trio into the living room while James whispered urgently in my ear, "Tell me how you did this! I am dyin' of curiosity."

"The answer, James, lies inside your Palm handheld," I said.

He blinked as he understood what we had done. "The address list inside my Palm! Gloria hacked my handheld! Talk about a duo of devious female—"

"Now, now James!" I interrupted. "Wait until your party is over before you insult us."

"I suppose you're right." He gave a pained laugh. "Well, that will teach me not to use a password. Nothing is sacred from you Yankees."

I kissed him on the cheek. "Let's join our guests."

James and I arrived in time to hear Gloria switch to her most artificial British accent and announce the "essential rules" of an English tea party. "It's very simple," she said. "You sit stiffly on the edge of your chair with tea cup held firmly in right hand, pick up food with left hand, take teeny bites, and talk like your mouth is stuffed full of cotton balls." She paused to take a breath. "Of course, this is an English *birthday* tea party, which gives you additional responsibilities. For example, you find an array of English party crackers on the table in front of you . . ."

The next forty-five minutes was great fun as everyone—especially James—tried to follow Gloria's instructions. We exploded party crackers, donned the yellow, pink, and green tissue paper hats they released, and tucked into the food. The Welsh rarebit and sausage rolls were great hits with the men. Janice and Sherry gobbled up scones. I did most of the serving because Gloria had become locked in rapt conversation with Ray Crosby.

I felt guilty disturbing them. "The birthday cake, . . ." I whispered to Gloria.

"The cake?" She looked at me blankly for a moment. "Oh yeah, the cake."

In keeping with the tea-party motif, the "birthday cake" Gloria had chosen was actually an oversized fruit tart. It took us more than a minute to light the forty-four candles (including one for good luck) we had placed around the tart's perimeter.

"I guess that Lesley Oppendahl, the lady from Virginia, is not going to show up after all," Gloria said. "She seemed so excited about James's birthday when I invited her."

"Five out of six invitees are more than enough. James is clearly having a good time."

I shuffled into the living room holding the flaming tart, vaguely afraid that if I fell I would start a major fire.

James beamed like a little kid as Gloria dimmed the lights. He blew out the candles in one breath, and we sang "Happy Birthday." After Gloria had helped James cut up the tart, I tapped my teacup with a spoon and stood up.

"James," I said in a somewhat formal tone, "I am sure you have noted that no one brought you a birthday present today."

"Now that you mention it . . ."

I kept talking. "Gloria specifically instructed your friends and colleagues *not* to bring gifts. That, of course, is in keeping with the Huston family tradition."

"Howsoever, my daddy used to say that not all family traditions are worth honoring."

"Quite right! Therefore, I decided to break with custom and provide *one* present for you to open."

I had hidden the miniature DVD player under the coffee table. Gloria retrieved it while I was speaking. "Something digital, for a man who likes gadgets and travels a lot."

James tore away the wrapping and stared at the box for several seconds. "I am speechless," he finally said. "This is the finest birthday gift I've ever received."

The doorbell rang.

"I'll go," I said.

I opened the front door to a strikingly attractive woman. She stood about five-foot-five, was buxom where it counted, and slender elsewhere. She had blue eyes, blonde hair, and finely sculptured features. She was perhaps a year or two older than me.

"I trust I have found the Spitz residence?" she said in a syrupy southern drawl that matched James's accent.

I stuck out my hand. "You must be Lesley. I am Pippa Hunnechurch."

"Is that a fact?" Her eyes flashed. She looked me over head to foot. "My, my! Jimmy Huston is the most unpredictable of gentlemen. His tastes are as changeable as the weather in Maryland. Lead me to our birthday boy."

I stepped aside. She glided through the apartment with the hip-swiveling smoothness of a centipede and stopped in front of James. He was on his feet and no longer smiling. In fact, his face had become a mask. I couldn't tell whether his expression signaled amazement or alarm.

"Hi there, Jimmy H.," Lesley said. "Long time no see."

"Not long enough, Lesley," he snapped. "Why are you here?"

"*Ah* was invited to help celebrate your birthday by a charmin' person named Gloria Spitz. How could I stay away?"

Gloria jumped up so quickly, her dinette chair tipped over.

James spun around. "Why did you invite her?" he asked Gloria.

She began to blather. "Well . . . I . . . the truth is . . . she was . . . actually . . ."

Lesley moved closer to James. "Huston, do we have a problem?"

"I thought that was a corny joke ten years ago, Lesley. I still do today." James's voice got louder. "Why did you accept Gloria's ill-advised invitation?"

"How could I resist the opportunity to meet your current lady friend? I assume that is her." Lesley fluttered her fingers at me. "We may be apart now, Jimmy H., but I am still interested in your life. We did have five outstanding years together."

My heart missed a beat.

James had a hangdog look on his face. "Lesley is my former wife."

I heard an audible gasp and soon realized that I had made it.

"Your *former wife?*" My words came out as soft squeaks.

Lesley turned to me. "He didn't tell you he was married before? How shameful! Men can be so duplicitous. For all these years *Ah* thought Jimmy was a true southern gentlemen."

"Shut up, Lesley," James said. Then he said to me, "We never had an occasion to talk about my life ten years ago. My former marriage is certainly not a secret."

Lesley ignored James. "I wouldn't trouble myself about it, Pippa. I am definitely not interested in Jimmy any more. He is yours. Do with him as you wish."

I ignored Lesley and spoke to James, "If it's not a secret, why didn't you tell me?"

"You never asked," James said.

"I didn't know I was supposed to ask. I told you about Simon without prompting."

Lesley jumped back in. "No, Pippa. Now I disagree with you. You should have assumed that Jimmy H. had been married before. You can't be naïve enough to believe that a hunk like James Huston would not have been snapped up in his prime."

"I'm still in my prime, Lesley," James said.

"*Ah* am afraid not, sugar." She spoke to me. "Pippa, you should have seen James in a swimsuit when he was twenty-eight. A wondrous sight to behold!"

"Shut up, Lesley!" James said again. He stepped between Lesley and me. "None of this would have happened, Pippa, if you and your nosy sidekick hadn't snooped in my Palm handheld."

"Feel free to peruse my old-fashioned address book," I shot back. "I don't have any previous husbands listed."

"No, but you probably have a former boyfriend or two." He shook his head heavily. "You did worse than invade my privacy. You were careless with the information you stumbled across."

"Perhaps I should stumble around some more. Is Lesley the *only* former wife I don't know about?"

Lesley moved out of James's shadow. "I really do hate to see good friends fighting over a foolish misunderstanding. Y'all must kiss and make up. I insist."

"Shut up, Lesley!" James and I said simultaneously.

"I need to cool off," James said to me. "I had better leave before I say—or do—something I'll really regret."

"Nonsense. This is your party with your friends. I shall leave."

Before James could stop me, I picked up my handbag and raced out of the apartment. Halfway down the stairs I realized I had forgotten my coat, but I kept going. I managed to keep far enough ahead of James to slide into the Miata and lock the door before he arrived.

"This is silly, Pippa," he shouted through the convertible top. "Where are you going?"

"To think about things. I'll be back in thirty minutes. Make my apologies to your guests." I started the engine, shifted into gear, and switched the heater to maximum.

I had told James the truth. I needed some time alone to absorb the fact that he had been married to Lesley. I also needed a chance to ponder my sins. James had been right; the wretched episode had been my fault. I had asked Gloria to pinch his address list, but I had failed to take notice of the "friends" she had invited to the party. Why did we assume that everyone on James's address list would be welcome? It was yet another example of Hunnechurch & Associates not going the second mile.

Why did you assume that James would not have an ex-wife?

Should I have guessed? Or should I have asked? Or should he have told me?

I tried to weigh the various arguments, but I found it difficult to concentrate because of the traffic around me. My plan had been to make a quick circuit of my favorite curvy road—the misnamed Romney Boulevard—a narrow country lane north of Ryde that is barely wide enough for two cars to pass in opposite directions. Alas, I had forgotten about rush hour. It was only a few minutes after five. Poplar Road was crowded, transforming my relaxing drive into a stop-and-go slog. At this pace I would need twenty more minutes just to reach Romney Boulevard.

Stop being childish, Hunnechurch! I decided to head back to Gloria's apartment.

Because the traffic on Poplar Road made a U-turn impossible, I turned right onto Edwards Lane with the intention of making two more rights and a left. That's when I noticed the flash of high-beam headlights in my rearview mirror. I accelerated, hoping to put more space between my low-slung sports car and those blinding lights. I was about to punch the accelerator again when the car behind me slammed into my rear bumper. I couldn't tell the make or model, but I knew it was a full-sized sedan—twice the weight of my little vehicle.

The steering wheel jerked out of my hands; my roadster lunged to the right and climbed the grass verge. I straightened the wheel, tromped on the brakes, and skidded back onto the road. An instant later the big car hit me again. Much harder.

My Miata flew across Edwards Lane on two wheels, with one side off the ground. I thought it might flip over, but the airborne wheels came down hard when I reached the opposite curb. I remember wondering, *How much road does a road hog need when a road hog hogs the road?*

Momentum carried me forward onto a lawn and toward a huge tree. I heard the sound of metal tearing. Something exploded in front of me. I felt pain in my chest. Then everything became dark as the night.

One final thought went through my mind. *Hunnechurch, you are still wearing a ridiculous pink tissue-paper hat.*

Chapter Nineteen

I HEARD MY SISTER'S VOICE.

Chloe has a distinctive voice—bold, self-assured, and commanding—with a robust accent that most Americans would describe as "very English."

"Still sleeping," I heard her say. "But that could be the effect of the many medications. She *seems* to be getting proper care, but how can one be sure." A pause. "Certainly, Stuart, I shall call as soon as the situation improves."

That's my Chloe. Always confident, always able to take charge of the situation.

What situation?

You must be in England, I thought to myself. Visiting Chichester.

I moved my hands and felt sheets and a thin blanket.

I am lying in bed, in Chloe's guest room. Except—where are Chloe's goose down duvets?

I heard her voice again. "I love you too, Stuart. Take care, and best of luck with the sermon tomorrow."

How nice! Chloe loves Stuart.

I attempted to say, "That's nice, Chloe," but managed to generate only a few garbled peeps.

"Pippa!" Chloe said. "Are you finally lucid?"

I opened my eyes. Her face was high above, beaming down at me. I made an effort to smile back. "Hello, Chloe," I croaked.

"Don't talk loudly," she said. "Your throat is parched because there is an oxygen thingamajig on your nose. And try to keep still."

"Keeping still is nice."

I suppose I fell back asleep, but I woke up again when my bed sagged and I felt a sharp pain in my side. "Ouch!" I said.

"Sorry, dear—but now that I'm sitting on your bed, I can understand all that you say."

"Chloe—when did I arrive in England?"

"You aren't in England, Pippa. I am in Ryde."

I tried to fold my brain around the notion that Chloe had traveled across the ocean. Only one explanation seemed to make sense. "Oh, I'm sorry, Chloe. You don't like your Christmas gift. You came to Ryde to exchange it."

"I am sure my gift is lovely, dear. I haven't opened it yet."

She turned to speak to someone beyond my range of vision. "Would you please tell Joyce Friendly that Pippa is awake?"

Like an outboard motor slowly starting and accelerating—*put-put-put*—my mind began to put words and concepts together. Bed. Pain. Oxygen. Joyce Friendly. Chloe.

Chloe?

I hurtled toward full awareness. "Chloe? Is that really you?"

She reached across and pushed my hair from my forehead. "In the more-than-ample flesh."

"Where am I?"

"In hospital. In a lovely private room." She added, "Don't try to move."

I tried to raise myself up on my elbows. Big mistake. Pain slashed through my chest and shoulders. I turned sideways to ease the hurting, and my left-side ribs erupted in fire.

"Arrgh!"

Chloe held my hand, then clucked her tongue. "There is nothing like an object lesson to convince a banged-up patient to lie still."

The pain had one positive effect. It finished the job of clearing my muzzy head.

"I had a car crash," I said. "A big car struck my rear bumper. I tried to get out of the way, but I lost control."

"You hit a maple tree head-on. But don't worry; the tree survived intact. You put a few gouges in its bark, nothing more."

"What happened to my Miata?"

"Hang on, let me think. James Huston used a curious term to describe the condition of your wee vehicle. Ah yes! *Totaled.*"

"Blimey! I loved my little roadster." I had another thought. "Good heavens, Chloe. You flew all the way from England to sit by my side."

"Yes, well, your friends gave me a bit of a fright when they told me you arrived at hospital unconscious." She hesitated a moment. "They assured me you would recover, but I booked my flight immediately—to make certain that you hadn't totaled yourself too."

"I'm glad you came."

She squeezed my hand. I squeezed back.

I glanced at the window to the side of my bed. The shade was partially drawn. I could see night.

"What day is today? What is the time?"

"It is Saturday, December twenty-second. It is approximately 6:00 P.M."

"You mean that I slept for twenty-four hours?"

"Not quite. I watched you drift in and out of consciousness this afternoon."

"I don't remember a thing."

"The doctors said you were not quite ready to awaken fully, although"—Chloe frowned—"a rather abrupt policeman named Reilly suggested that I give you a hearty shake."

"Reilly was here?"

"He wanted to talk to you about your *incident,* as he called it. He even claimed to be your colleague." She sniffed. "Fortunately, I was by your side and able to safeguard your best interests. I soon sent him away with a flea in his ear."

"How?"

"I stood my ground and paraphrased Job. '. . . till the heavens are no more, Pippa will not awaken–or be roused from her sleep.'"

I couldn't help but chuckle at the notion of Reilly being forced to retreat by the Scripture-toting wife of Stuart Hunnechurch-Parker, the vicar of All Souls Church in Chichester, Sussex, England.

"Poor Detective Reilly," I said. "I didn't have the opportunity to warn him that you can be as formidable as a mother bear protecting a cub."

"He is fully aware of that now," she said with another sniff.

Chloe is (though she doesn't like it said aloud) my older sister—five years older, to be exact—a difference in age that she eagerly exploited when we were children. Chloe took on the role of elder, wiser, sibling-in-charge, and she steadfastly refuses to relinquish that mantle. We have a sisterly resemblance, though her mouth is fuller than mine and her face more rounded. She, like me, has dishwater blonde hair, but her favorite styles run to the short and curly. She is my height, but with a stockier build that would befit an Amazon and an innate poise that exudes authority. When Chloe talks, everyone listens.

"You've certainly caught up on everything that has happened," I said. "How long have you been here?"

"I arrived at Baltimore-Washington International Airport late this morning. James was kind enough to pick me up."

"Where are you staying?"

"Hunnechurch Manor, of course. Gloria Spitz restocked your larder for me and made up a bed in your guest room."

"Impossible! My second bedroom is still full of Mum's old furniture that you shipped me two years ago."

"James and Gloria did some judicious rearranging and stacking. He, by the way, is a very charming gentleman—not to mention good-looking. I cannot fathom why you haven't yet taken him out of circulation. What *are* you waiting for?"

"Chloe, for the zillionth-plus-one time, I am not in a rush to get married again."

"So you keep saying. If you really feel that way, you should inform James and cut him loose. It is clear to everyone and his cousin that James is wholly smitten with you, although he seems as reluctant as you to confirm the fact."

"You asked James how he felt about me?" Raising my voice caused sufficient pain to make me flinch. I let my head fall back on the pillow.

"Someone had to ask. Both of you have been locked in this shilly-shallying relationship for more than a year. Why are you wasting precious time? Obviously, you are as smitten as he—or else you would not have run off like that."

Chloe poured a cup of water for me, then unwrapped a bendable straw so that I could sip without lifting my head. "One of you had better show some initiative—soon."

"James and I have not yet . . . *ah,* discussed our relationship." I suddenly recalled our shouting match on the day before. "Although after what happened at his birthday party, we may never have the chance."

Chloe gave a little snort. "I presume you are talking about the regrettable episode of the former wife from hell? I have been fully briefed by Gloria."

I nodded. Over the years Chloe has demonstrated a remarkable ability to become "fully briefed" on all aspects of my life. It makes no sense to conceal anything from her.

"I handled things so stupidly," I said. "I became upset because he hadn't told me about his first marriage." I began to sniffle into my bedsheet. "I said hateful things to him, and he'll never trust me again because we snooped in his Palm handheld."

Chloe pried the bedsheet from my fingers and handed me a tissue. "To the contrary. James is even more distraught than you are. He has already forgiven your clumsy snoopery. Further, he admits that he should have told you about Lesley months ago but did not for fear that you would think less of him because he had been divorced. Lastly, he blames himself for sending you into the night—and into harm's way."

"That's *not* what happened. He tried to stop me, but I ran off. Besides, how can James feel responsible for a careless accident?"

Chloe's face abruptly took on a grim expression.

"Another motorist witnessed the incident and called the police," she said. "Detective Reilly is convinced that you were intentionally run off the road. That is why he is so anxious to speak with you."

I tried to feign surprise, but my memory was now working well enough to for me to recall that my "incident" was anything but an accident. The big sedan had purposefully hit me twice.

Someone tried to kill you, Hunnechurch. Probably the same person who murdered Barry Goodwin.

I didn't want to think about it just then. Nor did I want to deal with Chloe's piercing gaze.

Happily, Joyce breezed into the room, an enormous grin on her face, and asked, "How does the wide-awake Ms. Hunnechurch feel?"

"Achy," I replied.

"I'll bet." She shoved a digital thermometer under my tongue. "I wanted to see you before my shift in the operating room begins. As long as I'm here, I'll check your progress." Joyce checked my pulse, measured my blood pressure, and reviewed the chart at the foot of my bed.

"Everything's approaching normal," she went on. "You were lucky. Your air bag and seat belts worked as advertised." She sat down on the side of the bed, across from Chloe. "I'm supposed to let your doctor tell you, but your injuries are not serious—two broken ribs, which is why you are wearing a tight chest binder, and a series of remarkably color-ful bruises that run from your knees to your neck."

"Why did I sleep for twenty-four hours?"

"You were sedated. A nice, long sleep is often part of the pain control protocol with rib fractures."

"When can I go home?"

"Today is Saturday. I would guess you'd be discharged on Monday. You should be much more comfortable by then—and in a perfect frame of mind to attend my Christmas dinner."

I opened my mouth to object, but Joyce touched a finger to my lips. "Don't argue! The matter is out of your hands. James Huston, Chloe Hunnechurch-Parker, and I have declared a state of truce between you and David. Gloria Spitz has also agreed to dine with us, which removes your last possible objection. To cut a long story short, you will eat fried turkey at my house—even if you choose to glare at David throughout the meal. Now . . ."—she stood up—"three concerned people are waiting to see you. Your doctor has requested one nonfamily visitor at a time, for no longer than fifteen minutes each. Who shall be first?"

I thought quickly. "Gloria first. She wears the same color lipstick as I do. I must look awful."

Chloe gave me an appraising glance. "Well, I have seen you looking better."

I pointed to the doorway. "I beseech thee as a fellow Hunnechurch—bring me Gloria."

"*Hmmm.* One wonders if perhaps your head was injured after all."

I threw my empty paper cup at Chloe as she left the room.

"Can I be cranked up?" I asked Joyce.

"Certainly. Tell me when it hurts."

Joyce pushed a button on a pendant control box, and I rose like Venus on her seashell out of an ocean of light blue bedding. My midriff began to stab at an angle of sixty degrees. Joyce saw the grimace on my face and lowered me a notch.

"I never realized that broken ribs hurt so much," I said.

"Wait until someone makes you laugh."

Scarcely a moment after Joyce left, Gloria bounded in and squinted at me. "Can I hug you, or will you break?"

"Hug away—gently!"

After delivering a gentle squeeze, Gloria pulled one of the metal armchairs in the room closer to my bed and sat down. "The word is, you're going to be fine," she said, "although, to quote your sister, you look like you've been run over by a lorry—whatever that is."

"A lorry is a big truck."

"Wow! I thought *I* was blunt."

"I need lipstick and a mirror, on the double."

Gloria displayed a small canvas tote bag. "Lipstick, foundation, blusher, mascara, and—if you can stand the view—a magnifying mirror. A complete tool kit."

"Bless you. Let's go to work."

Gloria held the mirror. I began the refurbishment.

"Speaking of blessings," she said, "our small group is praying for you. I also put you on the church's prayer tree. You're in the best of hearts."

"Thank you." I realized that I really meant it.

"Moving to another subject. What's left of your Miata is sitting in the police impound lot. Reilly wants the evidence team to inspect it."

"Perhaps I will buy myself a huge truck like yours in anticipation of the next round of playing bumper cars."

"There won't be another round." Gloria lifted the bottom of her sweater. I could see the top of a pistol tucked into a waistband holster.

"When you go home, I'll move in with you. I intend to watch your back until Reilly catches the creep."

I had seen the gun before—a Walther PPK automatic, Gloria had called it—and I knew that she had a permit to carry a concealed weapon. Nonetheless, the sight of the blue metal pistol put a chill down my spine.

She continued, "Reilly wants to talk to you. Really bad. He asked me a bunch of questions earlier today. I batted my eyelashes like a dumb blonde and told him I had no idea why someone would want you dead. I don't think he believed me."

"I may have to play dumb with Reilly too. I can't talk about heart valves—not yet."

Gloria gave me a skeptical look. "I don't think he'll believe you either. If you don't throw him a small bone, he'll keep bothering us."

"What kind of bone?"

"Maybe a hint about Barry's concerns."

"We'll see." I started to apply my lipstick so I wouldn't have to say anything more on the subject. When I was finished, Gloria held the mirror in position to give me a wide-angle view.

"An amazing restoration," I said. "I am ready to entertain gentlemen callers."

"Not a moment too soon," Gloria said. "James Huston and David Friendly are pacing the floor of the waiting room like expectant fathers. They both feel guilty, so now's the time to ask for favors."

I forgot Joyce's warning and let myself laugh.

"Arrgh!"

"Suck it up, Hunnechurch. I cracked ribs during two different National Guard training exercises two summers ago. The trick is to embrace the pain. Make it your friend."

I pointed to the door. "Happily, the end of your compassion coincides with the end of your fifteen minutes. Depart!"

Gloria backed out of the room making funny faces. I managed to giggle rather than laugh.

James Huston approached my bed looking contrite. He didn't ask permission to hug me. He simply did.

"I apologize profusely," he said. "Please forgive me. I should have told you about Lesley."

"Yes, you should have, but on the other hand, I now feel sorry for you. What did you have in mind when you married *her?*"

"What do you think?"

I couldn't stop a small laugh. "Arrgh!"

"Am I hurting you?"

"No. I felt a little twinge when I shifted position. Hug me tighter—it will go away." I turned slightly in his arms. "In any event, you are forgiven."

We chitchatted about a dozen different things until the fifteen minutes were up. His birthday fruit tart. His upcoming seminars. Christmas in Georgia. My sister Chloe. The power of prayer. Both of us preferred to avoid *the* subject—our relationship.

At last we heard a rap on the doorframe. Chloe's head appeared for an instant. "Time, gentlemen. Time!" she said.

"Arrgh!"

"What's going on?" James asked.

"It hurts when I laugh, and everyone has decided to be amusing." I wriggled out of James's arms. "'Time, gentlemen. Time.' was what pub owners used to say when it was time to close."

James shrugged. "I presume I missed the punch line."

"The idea of Chloe as a pub landlord is downright hilarious—to me."

James reached for my fingers and kissed them. "You are a strange lady," he said as he left, "but then, I seem to attract them."

I didn't even wince at his joke.

David Friendly waited in the doorway, holding a globe-shaped cactus in a black pot. "A peace offering," he announced. "This is a golden barrel cactus with lots of spines. I will gladly sit on it before I write any more feature stories about a murder victim."

I managed to transform my Arrgh! into a passable "OK!"

David clasped my hand. "I made a cub reporter's mistake when I didn't give you the opportunity to rebut those negative allegations in the article. I hate to admit that Sophie Hammond is right, but I did make a rush to judgment." He smiled cautiously. "Please forgive me."

"I forgive you," I said.

David kissed my forehead. "You told me that more words in the *Ryde Reporter* couldn't undo the damage. Well, I intend to try. I convinced Lenny Smithson to let me write a follow-up article that will revisit your relationship with Barry Goodwin. OK?"

When I didn't answer, David asked again. "OK?" Then he added, "David calling Pippa! You seem to be lost in thought."

"Quite so. I was pondering your description of Barry. You called him a 'murder victim' a moment ago."

He nodded. "I had a chance to talk to Stephen Reilly today in the waiting room. I agree with him; a direct attack on you eliminates any remaining possibility that Barry Goodwin committed suicide. The motive for Goodwin's murder is obvious too. Get rid of a noisy whistle-blower before he could damage a two-billion dollar acquisition."

"Detective Reilly has become an astonishingly chatty policeman."

David ignored my flippancy. "Reilly plans to interview you in a day or two. In the interim, he asked me to give you some advice. There's only one reason for the person who killed Goodwin to try to kill you. Somehow you, too, have managed to learn enough to threaten the acquisition—which puts you in the same danger as Goodwin."

David paused to let his words sink in, then reached into his pocket for a slip of paper. "Reilly asked me to write down everything he said, so that I would get it exactly right." He began to read. "Pippa

Hunnechurch conducted a four-day-long investigation aimed at learning what was bugging Barry Goodwin before his death. It looks to me that she found out more—maybe even why Goodwin died. Trouble is, she hasn't shared any of her discoveries with the police, and that's dumb because hanging on to those secrets could get her killed. Please remind Miss Hunnechurch that there are dozens of dark streets in Ryde—and hundreds of big maple trees."

I began to feel an ache in my ribs even though I wasn't laughing.

Chapter Twenty

I WAS ANNOYED TO BITS and whining loudly by Sunday afternoon. I felt that I had recovered sufficiently to go home, but my doctor urged—and James and Chloe insisted—that I spend one more night in Ryde General. I might have argued successfully with the doctor, but Chloe and James—*never.*

I resigned myself to a Sunday dinner of institutional food.

However it wasn't the prospect of bland cooking that troubled me that afternoon. Chloe had talked my doctor into lifting the previous day's visitors' restrictions. With Gloria's help, she had orchestrated an unending parade of friends, neighbors, and business colleagues "to cheer me up." Visitors came from our office building, from the Ryde Chamber of Commerce, from Ryde Fellowship Church, and (surprisingly!) from two local companies that had ceased doing business with Hunnechurch & Associates. With the one-visitor-at-a-time rule gone, they showed up two and three at a clip. Chloe played "mother" and dispensed candy, soft drinks, and a warm welcome to anyone who appeared at my door. James Huston sat in the corner, smiling benevolently, watching my world go by. The pair of them had become thick as thieves.

Alas, I didn't need cheering up.

What I truly wanted was time alone with Gloria so that we could talk about the "advice" Detective Reilly had delivered to me via David. Reilly had assembled his message carefully. To foreclose any evasion I might try about my activities, he reminded me that I had conducted a "four-day-long" investigation . . . that I had been looking for "what was bugging Barry Goodwin before his death" . . . and that I probably found out "why Goodwin died."

The latter two items were the exact phrases that Sophie Hammond had spoken to me a week earlier. She probably had had a tape recorder in her purse that captured all that she and I said.

Only one conclusion made sense. Reilly had played me for the simpleton. He had been in cahoots with Sophie from the start. His startlingly detailed recitation during our lunch at Ruth's guaranteed that I would take Sophie seriously when she came to see me.

Reilly assumed that I would jump at the opportunity to salvage my business. He expected me to throw my lot in with Sophie and to learn things about Barry that he couldn't. After all, folks at Campbell & McQueen and on the Eastern Shore might be more willing to talk to good old Pippa Hunnechurch than to a Ryde cop on a fishing expedition.

Except you didn't allow for the possibility that I might change my mind.

I chuckled at the thought of Reilly's frustration when Sophie relayed my Friday-morning decision to decline her proposal.

I could easily guess what Reilly would do next. He would apply his only leverage and try to frighten me into telling him what I had discovered. However, he would also move ahead with his own investigation. Stephen Reilly and Sophie Hammond made an efficient team. Working together, they would quickly surface Barry's Hevlan-related concerns about faulty CM-7s. I doubted that Sophie would have any qualms about revealing that Barry Goodwin died because he thought the CM-7 was defective.

Like it or not, I was in a race with the *Ryde Rebel*. The only way to head Sophie off at the pass was to convince Reilly that he should sit on the incomplete story and not share it with her.

I had no idea how I would accomplish that neat little trick.

My private tête-à-tête with Gloria began when she drove me home on Monday morning. Her pickup truck has two bucket seats with a fold-down storage gizmo in between; she rarely carries more than herself and one other person.

"Reilly is a clever dude," she said when I described the significance of his warning.

"I should have realized what he was doing," I said. "Coppers never share information without a good reason."

"You'll get your chance to give him a piece of your mind this after-noon. He called me at home at 7:00 A.M. and said he would drop by Hunnechurch Manor after lunch."

"I expected as much. The trouble is, I don't know how to handle Reilly. I have to assume that anything I say will be relayed to Sophie Hammond."

"Tell him *nothing!*" Gloria said.

I glanced at her. To my astonishment, she was grinning at me.

"You want me to stonewall the good detective?" I said. "The other day you advised me to toss him a bone. What made you change your mind?"

"I read that chapter in Barry's textbook." Her smile vanished. "We have no choice. We can't let Sophie turn the story into an exposé that will terrify those patients. We can't put out any word until we are con-vinced beyond a reasonable doubt that Barry found a potentially dangerous defect. Even then, we have to make sure that the news causes a minimum fear factor."

"There is the trifling matter of *my* fear factor. As Reilly is sure to point out, a villain *did* try to run me off the road and into a tree."

"Hang tough!" She patted her midriff. "Mr. Walther and I will watch over you."

"We also have the issue of Hunnechurch & Associates to deal with." I let myself sigh. "Keeping silent will do nothing to restore our tarnished enterprise. Quite the contrary—people will think we are guilty as charged in Barry Goodwin's suicide note and David's original article."

"Like the Bible says, 'There is a time for everything, and a season for every activity under heaven.' This seems to be our time to focus on heart valves. Our business can wait."

"Bless you, Ms. Spitz. I feel a hundred-fold bolder than I did an hour ago." I muttered to myself, "I hope my boldness stays with me when Reilly turns up the heat."

We bustled into my house at a quarter past ten. The lovely morning air felt icy and harsh during the quick walk from truck to front door—yet another sign of my semi-invalid status. My doctor had advised against climbing stairs for a day or two, so we decided I should spend the next few nights in my living room, sleeping on my overstuffed sofa. Gloria would kip upstairs in my bed. She helped me settle in a comfortable armchair and went to put on the kettle.

"I am in the mood for Darjeeling tea today," I called.

Winston, who lives in my kitchen, began to chirp.

"Bird alert!" I heard Gloria call through the wall. A moment later a whir of blue wings propelled Winston to my side. He circled my head a half dozen times, then made a perfect landing on my shoulder.

"That parakeet went ape," Gloria said. She had returned from the kitchen with a handful of diced apple. "He tried to batter down the little drawbridge door in his cage when he heard your voice."

"Poor Winston," I cooed as I fed him an apple chunk, "you nearly became an orphan on Friday."

Winston abruptly launched himself off my shoulder and flew to a curtain rod. He began to screech noisily.

"I don't believe it!" Gloria said. "I swear I saw a huffy look on his face."

"It was mean of me to say what I did. Birds are clever, sensitive creatures, especially members of the parrot family." I held the dish of apple pieces aloft and began to whistle softly. Winston flew down and perched on the rim.

Gloria lay on the sofa and scrunched into the cushions with her body. "I suppose it'll do for a few nights," she said, "although it may be too soft. You don't want to flex those ribs."

"Flexing is not an option. I was rewrapped tighter than an Egyptian mummy this morning. I can barely bend enough to sit in this chair."

I had a thought. "I've been home for ten minutes and have not yet been overwhelmed with kindness. Where are James and Chloe?"

"Out and about—although they should have returned by now."

"What's going on?"

"They are preparing a surprise for you. I've been sworn to secrecy."

We heard a commotion at the front door. I struggled to my feet in time to see James wrestle a hefty Christmas tree into my narrow hallway. Right behind him was Chloe, toting two overstuffed shopping bags. She tipped one forward; I could see it was full of ornaments.

"You bought me a Christmas tree!" I squeaked.

"And a hard job it was to find a proper one on the day before Christmas," Chloe said. "We searched from one end of Ryde to the other—"

"Before we found a beauty only a half mile away." James winked at me.

"There is a widely held psychological theory," Chloe said, "that the kind of decorations used on a Christmas tree accurately reflect the owner's personality. What does *not* having a Christmas tree tell the casual observer?"

"Undoubtedly, that one's youth was dominated by a bossy sister," I said.

"Excuse me, ladies!" James said. "This spruce is heavy as blazes. Where do you want it?"

I waved my hand haphazardly toward the rear corner of my living room. "Over there, I suppose."

"I think not," Chloe said. "The front corner will provide a superior vista when you are seated on your sofa."

I surrendered without a fight. "The front corner it is."

James maneuvered his burden into the corner, then rotated the stand so that the fullest side of the tree faced outward.

In seconds Chloe had torn open several boxes of ornaments and plastic tinsel. "Help me trim," she said to me in a tone that made refusal impossible.

"Bah humbug," I muttered, then said to Gloria. "Give a hand too."

"I would, but I can't," she said. "I am off."

"Aha!" James said. "Another last-minute Christmas shopper."

Gloria hesitated. "I have a . . . *ah,* date with Ray Crosby," she said to me. "We're meeting for a Monday brunch."

I needed a moment to link the name with the handsome laddie I had met at James's tea party.

"You're a fast worker."

"We intended to go out on Saturday, but your collision changed our plans. James and Chloe can be your bodyguards until I return."

It took the three of us nearly an hour to trim the tree to Chloe's satisfaction. I couldn't raise my arm above shoulder height, but I could hang ornaments on the lower branches. I have to admit; it wasan impressive sight when the time came to turn on the twinkly lights. Everything seemed in perfect balance—the different kinds of ornaments, the thickness of tinsel on the branches, the amount of green still visible beneath the strings of colored bulbs and glass globes.

I looked around the room. "Where has Chloe gone to?" I asked James. "This is the moment of triumph. She should throw the switch."

"I'm talking on the telephone to Stuart," she called from the kitchen. "Come and say hello."

"Of course."

She handed me the receiver. "I'm terribly sorry about your accident, Philippa," he said. "Praise God you were not badly injured."

"Praise him indeed."

We slipped into our usual risk-free chitchat. Put delicately, Stuart and I were not the closest of in-laws, mostly because he didn't approve of my resettling in America after Simon and Peggy died. Stuart was a family man through and through; he couldn't accept the notion of starting a new life three thousand miles away from one's sister and mother. We used impeccable politeness to bridge the divide of opinion between us.

"How's Mum?" I asked when we had emptied our small-talk reservoirs.

"Mum is in fine health. She's looking forward to Chloe's return and wishes that you could come home too."

"Perhaps I'll be able to make a trip at Easter."

A nice thought, that. But the way your customers have fled, you will be penniless by spring.

Stuart must have read my mind. "Pray about coming home, Pippa. If it is God's will, he will provide the means."

A silly question shot through my head. *Does God issue frequent flyer miles?*

Chloe and I returned to the living room, where—with due solemnity—she pushed the switch that illumined the tree. My small living room changed color as the Christmas lights projected reds, green, and blues into crevices and corners.

"Wow!" I said. "That's super!"

We stood there enthralled, watching the lights blink on and off. I even managed to stop worrying about Detective Reilly's looming visit. When the three of us had oohed and ahhed sufficiently, James kissed my cheek. "I will be in the kitchen playing with my fabulous birthday present," he said.

No sooner had he gone than Chloe said, "Do you have a moment to talk?"

The spell cast by the tree went *poof!*

I spun around. "I know you have been waiting patiently for the perfect opportunity to give me a big-sister lecture, Chloe, but I don't need one. Not about safety, or marriage, or the tick-tocking of my biological clock."

The smug-mixed-with-hurt pout on her face told me that I had made a tactless mistake.

"Blimey!" I said. "You really do want to talk."

She nodded slowly, then took my hand. "I'm delighted to see that you are clearly on the mend. You no longer need me sitting by your side, and so I booked a seat on the four o'clock flight to London. My plane lands in England before dawn on Christmas morning. I will arrive in Chichester in time to share Christmas dinner with Stuart and Mum."

"You're going home *today?*" I took a breath to restore my voice to its normal pitch. "I assumed we would have Christmas together."

"I admit that I was tempted to spend Christmas in the company of Joyce, David, Gloria, and James, but I belong in Chichester as much as you belong here."

"I suddenly want to return to England with you."

"Nonsense! Anyone with half a brain can see that you've made a successful life in Ryde."

"It's not as successful as you imagine," I said softly.

"You say that because you still gauge achievement in terms of your profession. The loyal friends you've made are much better measures of your success. I am proud of you, Pippa."

Tears welled in my eyes, and I hugged Chloe for what seemed like five minutes.

"When do you have to leave?" I eventually asked.

"James will drive me to the airport after lunch."

The doorbell rang—a long sustained ring that told me who was there before I opened the door. There stood Stephen Reilly, holding a rolled-up copy of the *Ryde Rebel* as if it were a policeman's baton. He did not look happy, but then his sour expression might have mirrored my own.

"Good!" he said. "You're back among the conscious."

"It's not yet afternoon," I replied. "This is an awkward time for us to meet."

"Give me a break, Miss H.!" He pushed past me with sufficient vigor that not even Chloe was prepared to dispute him.

"Why don't I make a fresh pot of tea," she said cheerfully. "I'll be in the kitchen with James if you need me."

Reilly unfolded the tabloid. "Hot off the press. Note the front page."

The central element was a large photograph of my car squashed against the maple tree. Small photos of Barry Goodwin and me were inset below. The headline above the wreck proclaimed: *Former Headhunter Attacked By PR Man's Killer.*

"I'll save you the trouble of reading the whole article," he said. "The gist is that the attack on you proves that Goodwin was murdered. You became a target when you stumbled upon the nature of the criminal activity at Campbell & McQueen that Goodwin uncovered in the weeks before his convenient suicide."

"'Criminal activity' is a phrase that Sophie Hammond got from you."

Reilly frowned. "What?"

"You used the term 'criminal activity' during our lunch at Ruth's. It is not an expression I employ in everyday conversation."

Reilly threw up his hands. "Don't be a moron! *Of course,* I have Sophie on a string. She was part of the perfect plan I invented. Something for everyone. Sophie gets to prove she's the greatest muck-raking journalist since Walter Winchell; I get to reopen the Goodwin homicide investigation; and you get a good-as-new, totally vindicated reputation—not to mention a mountain of free publicity guaranteed to rebuild your business."

Reilly rerolled the *Ryde Rebel* and hurled it like a javelin at my sofa.

"As I said, a perfect plan," he went on, "except *you* blew it, big time. You decided to keep secrets and ended up hurting yourself." He plopped into my armchair. "My investigation is alive and well, but you won't get credit for helping. Sophie published a pretty good article, but she labeled you a 'former headhunter' to emphasize that your business is kaput. As for you—well, you lost your car and were almost killed."

I didn't say anything for a while. The kettle whistling in the kitchen sounded unusually loud, so did the splash of water pouring into the teapot.

Reilly looked at me expectantly. I finally spoke. "I have some insight into Barry's concerns but not a full explanation of the facts. Sophie Hammond would inadvertently do horrendous damage if she wrote an incomplete story."

"What kind of damage? To whom?"

"I can't answer those questions unless you promise not to tell Sophie Hammond."

"I promise not to tell Sophie Hammond."

I tried to smile as I shook my head. "I apologize—but I won't take the risk."

"Is that a fact?" Reilly offered a sarcastic grin. "Let me tell you about risk. There's a clever murderer out there who has you on the top of his list. The only way to make him lose interest is to tell me everything you know *before* he kills you." Reilly stood up. "The information you gathered might even help me catch him. And who knows? Maybe I'll decide *not* to charge you with obstruction of justice."

"Before you leave," I said, "I have a favor to ask."

Reilly looked at me as if I had lost my mind.

"In a day or two," I continued, "you will discover for yourself every-thing I know. When you do, I urge you to think long and hard before you share your finds with Sophie Hammond. Ponder the consequences to people who have enough to worry about right now."

Reilly began to laugh. His laughing grew louder as he walked down my hallway. He turned when he reached my front door.

"You are a piece of work, Miss H," he said. "Not very bright—but funny as all get-out. I'm really going to miss you when you're dead."

Chapter Twenty-one

WHEN REILLY LEFT I returned to my armchair and felt a gush of pain in my side that took my breath away—a not-so-subtle reminder that I had allowed my four-hour pain pill to wear off.

You were warned, Hunnechurch. Take 'em like clockwork or they stop working.

I had assured my doctor that I was going home to restful quiet—a day of reading, TV-watching, pill-taking every four hours, and (assuming I felt up to it) a brief outing to Ryde Fellowship Church for the early Christmas Eve service. We had shaken hands on my covenant, and I had every intention of keeping my promise.

Chloe came to my rescue with a glass of mineral water. I swallowed another pill, shifted my mind to neutral, and assumed that the busiest part of my day had passed.

Silly me.

Although I retired to my armchair with the best of intentions of keeping the promise I had made to my doctor, a parade of visitors that afternoon and evening repeatedly brought me to my feet.

———

12:28 P.M. Gloria flew through the front door, yanked me out of my chair, and gave me a bear hug that peeled apart the Velcro ties on my chest binder. Happily, my analgesic pill had begun to kick in.

"What's the verdict on Ray?" I asked unnecessarily.

"He has . . . definite possibilities."

"Does that mean he owns a machine gun?"

Gloria was too psyched up even to notice my feeble attempt at satire.

"No," she said, innocently. "Ray likes shotguns. He shoots skeet and trap with a 12-gauge."

———

1:04 P.M. Chloe trod down my staircase suitcase in hand and announced that she was ready to leave for the airport.

"I hate good-byes," she sniffled.

"I loathe good-byes," I agreed.

We proceeded to snivel away in each other's arms while tears streamed down our cheeks—hers of farewell, mine of pain, because her powerful elbow was pressing against my side.

"Ah well," she finally said, "I had best be off."

I replied through clenched teeth. "Call me the instant you get home."

Chloe, bless her heart, didn't offer any advice about my dealings with Detective Reilly, although she and James had heard our whole conversation while having tea in the kitchen.

"I trust your judgment, Pippa," she said. "You must do what you think best." She sniffed. "Although, a spot of prayer would certainly be in order."

I stood in the doorway breathing shallowly to ease the pain as Chloe ever so slowly climbed into the passenger's seat of James's rented

Ford Taurus. We blew kisses at each other until the car was nearly out of sight.

———————

2:21 P.M. James returned from the airport and—finding me alone in the living room—proceeded to give me an earful about "the foolish risks you seem to be determined to take for no apparent reason. Your sister may trust your judgment, but I prefer Reilly's. We've been down this path of noncooperation with the police before, and it leads to scary people who want to kill you." He gestured mightily and changed subjects. "And another thing! You assured me you were only a bit player in this charade. How did you get promoted to *next victim?*"

Naturally, I couldn't take James's bombast sitting down. I stood up and inadvertently put pressure on my ribs.

"Yikes!" I managed to say as I clutched my side.

"I rest my case!" He stormed off, leaving me alone again.

———————

3:18 P.M. My doorknocker slammed. James called from the hallway, "You have guests bearing gifts, Pippa." I listened to the different voices while James took coats, and I soon realized that the leaders of Gloria's small group had descended like the Assyrian hordes.

Blimey! What now?

The voices moved into the kitchen. I stood up, put down the novel I was reading, and "embracing" the twinge in my ribs, joined the throng. Dennis Marsh and Sharon Harrison were sitting at my dinette table. Gloria was browsing the titles of my cookbook shelf. James was fiddling with my teakettle.

"They've brought you get-well cookies," James said. "All of them chocolate chip. *I* intend to eat them with milk, but I know *you* prefer tea."

Sharon Harrison placed an enormous tin on the table. Big gold letters on its lid announced: *"The Universal Rx for Whatever Ails You! Take*

One (or Two) as Necessary to Sweeten Your Disposition and Help the Medicine Go Down."

"Thank you," I said in my most genial tone, although I still had no idea of what was going on. I took the empty chair next to Dennis.

Sharon hesitated as if to find the perfect words, then began, "I hate to bother you because I know that you just got out of the hospital and that you aren't a big fan of small groups, but the group needs some help that only you can provide."

She spoke so sincerely and sounded so regretful that I couldn't bring myself to refuse. "It's no bother, Sharon. Please tell me how I can help."

"It's like this. Ryde Fellowship has a New Year's Eve celebration in the church social hall, but you've probably heard about the party."

I nodded, but not enthusiastically. When I had seen the event mentioned in the church bulletin, I had immediately pictured a clone of the lackluster gatherings that Chloe and Stuart attended each year—an evening full of stodgy participants, dreary music, and indigestible food.

Sharon went on. "The theme of this year's party is 'A Movable Feast.' We'll have lots of different foods from around the world—all prepared by church organizations. You know, the women's circles, the small groups, the deacons, the youth groups—"

"I get the idea," I interrupted. "Every group is asked to prepare a dish."

"*Two* dishes. One hot and one cold. The organizing committee came up with a list of foods, then we drew lots to see who cooks what. Our cold dish is easy—Greek stuffed grape leaves." She paused again to assemble her thoughts. "They told me that our hot dish is English, but it has a strange name. It's called bubble and squeak."

I burst out laughing, despite the pain in my side. Winston heard me and began to chirp along.

"Do you know what it is?" Dennis asked.

"Of course," I answered. "Bubble and squeak is an old-fashioned English concoction of cabbage and potatoes fried together—traditionally in beef drippings, but these days in butter. The name, it is said, comes from the different sounds the ingredients make. Cabbage bubbles, and potatoes squeak—or perhaps it's the other way around."

"Can you get us the recipe?" Sharon asked.

Gloria chimed in. "I can't find one in any of Pippa's cookbooks."

"One hardly needs a recipe," I said. "The dish only has two main ingredients. However, I can't imagine a less festive food. Take it from an Englishman, you don't want to serve bubble and squeak at a New Year's Eve party."

From behind me James said, "What if we gussied it up for the party, like Cinderella?"

"Pardon me," I said, being too astonished to say anything else.

"Well, I assume we are going to this New Year's Eve shindig, and since I enjoy cooking, I figure we can bring the bubble and squeak. We'll make a party version, with plenty of spices and ingredients that give it some color."

What could I say? I had to agree, even though the thought of spending New Year's Eve in a church basement eating beautified cabbage and potatoes seemed the height of absurdity.

James grinned like a loon. "We'll have a grand ole time."

4:35 P.M. A tinny rendition of "Flight of the Bumble Bee" signaled the arrival of a call on the cell phone clipped to James's belt. We were both in the living room—he sitting on the overstuffed sofa, me in the armchair—reminiscing about Christmases past. I looked at the phone enviously as James flipped the lid open; my cell phone had been smashed in my car wreck.

He was amiable at first—"Hello, Todd!" "Merry Christmas" "How is the weather in Canada"—but then the conversation took a nasty turn.

James abruptly stood up and walked into the kitchen. Even a room away, I had no difficulty hearing him shout: "No way!" "Forget it!" "Not this country boy!"

Then things quieted down again, and James's voice became an indistinct mumble.

He returned five minutes later, looking like a kid who received a failing report card.

"It seems," he said, "that I spoke too soon when I told you I was free for the *entire* holiday period." He inhaled deeply. "It seems that the contract I signed to do a series of seminars in Canada in mid-January requires me to be available for promotional activities." He inhaled again. "It seems that the public relations person working with my Canadian associate was able to schedule a brief spot for me on a Canadian version of the *Today* show. I will be part of a panel of experts talking about the future of international trade, which, of course, is a great opportunity for me."

I cut in when he drew yet another deep breath. "If you say 'it seems' once more, I will hurl my empty mug at you."

"OK. Here's the story. She booked me to appear during the seven-thirty segment on Tuesday, January 1. That means—"

I interrupted. "That means you have to arrive in Toronto the day before. So you won't be able to attend 'The Moveable Feast,' after you signed me up to go."

"There's *some* good news. My friends in Toronto, Todd and Pam Stimson, are hosting something called a"—James began to enunciate slowly—"Hog-OH-Mony."

I leapt to my feet.

"The word you are trying to say is *Hogmanay*—pronounced **hog-man-ay**—a fabulous Scottish-style New Year's Eve party. Now I really am furious."

James beamed. "The good news is that you are invited too."

"I am?"

"Todd was very accommodating. His wife grew up in Kent, England; she would love to meet you. They have an extra guest room in their house."

"What about the bubble and squeak?"

"We'll make up a batch before we head north. Gloria can tote it over to the church."

I sat down slowly, seeking a position that eased my aching ribs.

"I'll think on it," I said.

━━━━━━━━

6:00 P.M. James and I arrived at Ryde Fellowship Church for the family Christmas Eve service. The sanctuary, filled with poinsettias, looked splendid. Banners depicting nativity scenes hung from the arched ceiling. We stood. We sang. We sat. We prayed. We listened, once again, to the series of familiar lessons taken from Luke. We took joy in the birth of our Savior.

When one of the church's families stood together to light the "Christ candle," I thought about Chloe flying high over the Atlantic Ocean. I even managed to pray a silent, *Godspeed*. My ribs had stopped hurting, and for the first time in weeks, I felt completely at peace.

My bliss lasted until the end of the service. I was easing out of the pew when Gloria whispered into my ear, "I'll take you home in my truck."

James asked the obvious question. "What's wrong?"

"A red Honda with Virginia license plates followed your Taurus to church this evening," she said.

A jolt of fear tightened my muscles; and my side began to throb. Gloria had ridden shotgun during our drive to the church. She had positioned her tall truck a block behind James's rented car. If she said we were followed, we were.

"Did you get a look at the driver?" James asked.

She shook her head. "Too dark, but I think it was a woman." She patted her handbag. "I wrote down the license number."

"I agree we don't take any chances," James said to me. "You ride with Gloria. I will take a slow drive through the distant precincts of Ryde before I return to the Waterside Hotel, in case the lady decides to follow my car again."

I kissed James goodnight in the shadows next to the church while Gloria stood guard and a brisk northerly wind whipped underneath my wool skirt. It wasn't much of a smooch because my mind kept conjuring up images of faceless females in red Hondas. *Why*, I wondered, *would a woman from Virginia want to follow me?*

———————

7:34 P.M. Gloria parked her truck in front of my house then transferred her pistol from its holster to her coat pocket.

"Just in case," she said.

Gloria got out of the Dodge first and came around to my side to open the door. I stepped down to the pavement and began to walk quickly toward the front door, eager to get inside where it was both warm and safe. I caught a hint of movement out of the corner of my eye. Gloria pushed me toward the truck. I stumbled but managed to stay on my feet, despite a fresh spurt of pain in my ribs. I heard scuffling sounds behind me and Gloria saying, "Hold still, or you'll break your wrist."

When I recovered my balance and turned around, I found Gloria applying some sort of martial-arts arm grip to a woman who was grimacing as much as I was. She had a slender body on an average-sized frame. It took me a moment to realize I had seen her face before in the picture frame on Barry Goodwin's bookshelf.

"My goodness!" I said. "You are Karen Constantine, Barry's fiancée."

"Please ask your friend to let me go." She sounded frightened.

"First, I'm going to free your arm," Gloria said to Karen. "Then, while you stand as rigid as a department store manikin, I'm going to make sure you aren't carrying a weapon. It's OK for you to talk. In fact,

I want you to start talking by telling Pippa why you followed her to church this evening."

"I followed you because I have to speak to you in *private*," she said to me, although her eyes stayed fixed on Gloria. "You've been surrounded by people all day. I hoped you would be alone this evening. I know it's Christmas Eve, but I can't wait any longer. My conscience won't let me."

"Here I am. Talk."

"Can we please go inside? I'm freezing out here."

Gloria had finished patting down Karen's coat and was about to search her handbag. I began a benign conversation to pass the time.

"I'm terribly sorry about your loss," I said. "Barry was a wonderful man."

Her eyes filled with moisture that the streetlights made glisten. "Thank you. Barry was wonderful. It's because of him that I'm here."

I recalled her license plate. "You live in Virginia, I presume."

She started to nod, then glanced at Gloria and stopped. "I live in Arlington, Virginia, because it's close to where I work."

"No weapons," Gloria said.

"Of course not!" Karen snapped, regaining some composure.

"Where did you park your red Honda?" Gloria asked.

"In a driveway down the street. The house is completely dark. I think the occupants are away for the holidays."

Gloria grunted. "Very clever—that's why I didn't spot it on the street."

We marched into Hunnechurch Manor and settled in the kitchen. I looked in the teapot and found it filled with a lukewarm brew we had infused a few hours earlier. Gloria nuked two mugfuls in my microwave oven; I took another pain pill; and Karen sat down at the dinette table and folded her hands like a polite child in kindergarten.

"I'll be in my bedroom," Gloria said. "Holler if you need anything."

"When should I start?" Karen asked after we heard Gloria tramp up the stairs.

"Go to it," I replied. "The floor is yours."

Karen began with a long and slow sigh. "I met Barry when he returned to school for his MBA—I'm still working on mine. He had a technical background; so do I. We were very much alike, except I can be more stubborn than Barry. Once I make up my mind about something, hardly anyone can make me change it."

I couldn't think of how to acknowledge her confession, so I merely smiled.

"We spent the weekend before Barry was killed at my parents' cabin in the woods. We talked about you a lot. You see, Barry had found evidence of wrongdoing inside Campbell & McQueen. He wanted to show it to you, but I told him not to. Barry tried to change my mind, but I refused. I reminded him that you are a consultant—that the company pays your bills, not him." She shivered, as if challenged by a vivid recollection. "The funny thing is, now I want your help, and I have to share stuff that I advised Barry not to tell you."

She stared at me intently. "Pippa, can I trust you to keep a big secret?"

"Many people have."

She looked around the kitchen—a final check to make certain we were alone. "Barry discovered that the artificial heart valves C&M sells are made of the wrong kind of plastic."

"The valves are made of Hevlan, I believe," I said evenly.

"Uh-huh, but not the kind of Hevlan that's approved for medical use by the Food and Drug Administration."

"Are you certain?"

"Well, Barry was positive, and I believe him. He was an expert on Hevlan. Medical-grade Hevlan can survive all the chemicals and other goop inside a human body. Some of the other grades of Hevlan can't."

"So a valve made of the lesser sort of Hevlan might fail?"

"Barry wasn't sure what would happen, but he didn't want to worry the patients until he had dotted all the Is and crossed all the Ts—if you know what I mean?"

"I understand completely. Incomplete information might needlessly frighten hundreds of people."

"Barry asked me to hack into Campbell & McQueen's on-line purchasing system. He wanted copies of the invoices of all of C&M's purchases of Hevlan resin during the previous six months. He kept saying, 'The invoices are the smoking gun—the last piece of the puzzle.'"

"Do you know how to hack into a computer?" I asked.

"My undergraduate training is in computer science. I suppose I know enough to hack into a system that's reachable from the outside company, but C&M's on-line purchasing system is only accessible inside the company—there's no way to reach it via the Internet. I told Barry he would need a computer person inside the company to help him."

An insider who understood computers? Dennis Marsh immediately sprang to mind. Had Barry asked Dennis to give him access to Campbell & McQueen's on-line purchasing system?

"Do you think he succeeded? Was Barry able to access the system?"

Karen shrugged. "I don't think so. He would have told me—unless it happened on the day he died."

"You said you wanted my help. . . ." I let the tone of my voice add a question mark.

"I should be mourning Barry's death, but I can't," she said. "I keep remembering that the problem Barry found is still out there. I keep thinking about people with heart valves made of the wrong plastic." Her features hardened; I saw a tiny shudder. "I imagine them clutching their chests and keeling over."

Karen reached out and clasped my hand.

"I don't know anything about C&M," she went on. "You do. I need you to tell me what to do next."

Chapter Twenty-two

I GLANCED AT THE CLOCK on the wall above my kitchen table. Eight-fourteen on Christmas Eve. Santa Claus was on his way; children would soon be dreaming of sugarplums; the rest of us should be settling down to our winter naps. This was hardly an appropriate hour to accelerate an investigation.

Dare you wait until after Christmas?

Now that I understood the specific CM-7 defect that Barry had uncovered, my race with the *Ryde Rebel* took on new impetus. The wrong kind of Hevlan was a problem made in heaven for Sophie Hammond. It was easy for readers to understand, fearful to contemplate, and imposs-blefor Campbell & McQueen to explain away. It was the sort of flaw that would attract media attention around the world—and propel Sophie to the front ranks of investigative reporters.

How far behind me were Stephen Reilly and Sophie Hammond? I didn't know, but their combined resources dwarfed mine. Sooner or later they would close the gap.

Don't ignore the question, Hunnechurch. Can you risk waiting until after Christmas?

I realized that the answer was really another question: Whom else had Barry told about his discovery?

He had refused to share the specifics with me or with his small group, but he had enlisted Karen Constantine's help and told her everything. What if Barry had also sought assistance from other experts and detailed his concerns to them? I suddenly pictured Barry speaking to physicians, plastics gurus, product liability attorneys—whole rooms full of people who, in turn, might be interviewed by Reilly or Sophie.

I decided that we had to move ahead—on Christmas Eve.

I spoke to Karen. "I want you to tell your story to someone else."

"To whom?"

"To the only person at Campbell & McQueen I still trust."

I shouted up the stairs. "Gloria! Where is Barry's Palm handheld?"

"With me—in the guestroom," she shouted back.

"Please bring it down."

"*Now?*"

"Please."

Gloria arrived with the Palm handheld in her right hand and a bemused expression on her face. She was wearing pajamas, a bathrobe, and slippers.

"My apologies," I said. "We have to go out again tonight."

"We? As in Pippa and Gloria?"

"We—as in all of us, including Karen."

"Out where? Everything is closed on Christmas Eve."

"Not necessarily. Please do your thing with the Palm handheld—find Diane Dupont's telephone number at home."

═══════════

"This is too unreal for words," Gloria said as she watched Karen doing jumping jacks to keep warm. "I hope Chloe never finds out that I let you leave your sickbed on a freezing night."

"I don't have a sick bed."

"Don't kid me! I can see the look on your face. You are hurting."

The three of us were waiting outside Campbell & McQueen's security gate, hoping that Diane Dupont would arrive before the gusts of cold wind transformed us into popsicles. It was going to be a nippy Christmas in Ryde.

"My ribs are throbbing a bit," I admitted. "I brought a painkiller pill with me; I'll take it when we're inside the building."

"*If* we ever get inside!" She batted her gloved hands together. "I still don't understand why we had to park my truck around the corner and wait outside in the cold."

"As I patiently explained an hour ago, Diane fears that a large, distinctive vehicle parked next to the gate on Christmas Eve might tempt a passing policeman to call the security firm that watches over the building. She would rather our comings and goings remain unnoticed."

Diane had sounded incredulous when I reached her at home.

"You want to break into our on-line purchasing system *tonight?*" she had asked.

"It's the only way to get to the bottom of Barry Goodwin's allegations."

"But I'll be risking a job I love."

"It is precisely *because* you love to work at Campbell & McQueen that you must help us. Imagine what a story in the *Ryde Reporter* would look like. *PR Man's Phony Suicide Linked to Company's Sale of Defective Heart Valves.*"

She hesitated. "Are you sure you've told me the truth—about what Barry told Karen Constantine?"

"She will be happy to tell you herself."

I gave the telephone to Karen. She gave it back a minute later.

"Holy moley!" Diane said. "Karen sounds like a completely credible witness. The kind of news story you dreamed up could wreck C&M."

"Indeed! It would ruin your reputation and stop the upcoming acquisition cold. Hughes Engineered Materials would have to abandon you for fear of endless product liability lawsuits."

"Holy moley!" Diane repeated.

I pressed forward. "When can you get us into the C&M building?"

"Give me an hour."

"Done!"

"One thing though," Diane said. "Whether or not you find corroboration for Barry's claims in the on-line purchasing system, I intend to notify Hilda McQueen. The Hevlan heart valve is her baby. They don't pay me enough money to carry a load this heavy by myself."

"I have no objection." How could I? I had no doubt in my mind that Hilda knew about the defect. I recalled the anxious look on her face when she examined the CM-7 valve I had found in Barry's ice cube tray. She had recognized immediately that something about the Hevlan plastic didn't look right.

As I mused about Hilda, the mystery of the "mutilated" heart valve explained itself. Barry had probably cut a piece out of its orifice ring for testing. He had sent the fragment off to a consultant equipped to perform a chemical analysis of the plastic resin.

Diane eventually arrived—ten minutes late, wearing a look of utter trepidation on her face.

"Get in."

We bundled into her big Buick while she poked an access card into a slot. Subterranean motors propelled the tall security gate open. Diane accelerated and drove to a small door on the side of C&M's building.

"This is the entrance our night-shift people use," she said. "I don't know the alarm code for the front door."

As we exited the car, Diane said. "A security camera inside the little lobby takes pictures twenty-four hours a day. Try not to look suspicious; act like a C&M employee. Lots of our people work odd hours, even on holidays."

Diane used a key to unlock the outside door. She led us into a tiny vestibule; the TV camera she spoke of was hanging below the ceiling. I stood self-consciously in its gaze while Diane performed the two steps necessary to unlock the inner door. She slipped her access card into a reader, then entered a series of numbers on a keypad. Clearly, C&M took a belt-and-suspenders approach to physical security.

The building was fairly dark inside; only one light fixture out of every four in the corridor was lit. We walked single file behind Diane to C&M's executive suite—a long row of private offices with desks for an administrative assistant outside each office door.

"I don't have access to the purchasing system," she said, "but Sidney Monk does. You'll have to use his computer."

Diane unlocked the door to Sidney's office. Karen sat down at his desk; Gloria pulled a visitor's chair alongside Karen to watch her work.

"Is there any way I can help?" I asked.

Gloria gave me a *you-don't-know-beans-about-computers* look that encouraged me to leave the pair alone with their bits and bytes.

I found Diane outside Hilda McQueen's office shuffling papers atop a desk that belonged (according to an old-fashioned bronze nameplate) to Carol Cooper.

"Carol is Hilda's administrative assistant," Diane said. "She's not the most organized admin in the building, but she's bound to have a copy of Hilda's vacation itinerary."

After a few more seconds of rummaging, Diane said, "Bingo!"

She scanned the sheet of paper. "Hilda is supposed to be in Paris, at the Hotel Ambassador on Boulevard Haussmann and Rue La Fayette. Sounds lovely. Let me see if I can get a hold of her."

Diane dialed a lengthy international number and asked for Madame Hilda McQueen, *"s'il vous plait."* Diane covered the receiver with her hand, "You have heard the extent of my French vocabulary."

Diane suddenly frowned. "Of course she checked in!" she said. "She flew to Paris three days ago." A pause. "You have heard nothing from Mrs. McQueen?" Another pause. "I see. Well, thank you . . . I mean, *merci."*

Diane put the phone down slowly. "Hilda never checked in," she said. "No one canceled her reservation. The hotel has no idea where she is."

"Try her house," I said. "Perhaps she changed her mind at the last minute."

Diane gave me a look that said, *Would you cancel a trip to Paris?* Nonetheless, she redialed the phone.

"Her answering machine picked up," she said. "I'll leave a message—just in case."

Diane had the receiver loosely against her ear; I heard the machine beep too. "Hilda," she said, "this is Diane Dupont. Please call me ASAP. It's very important."

Diane looked at me nervously as she rang off. "Well, I guess I could call Jerry Nichols or maybe even Richard Campbell. What do you think?"

"I think we keep our own council until we fully understand the extent of the Hevlan problem."

Diane nodded—her full-blown expression of trepidation renewed.

"I wonder how the computer whizzes are doing?" I said.

We looked into Sidney's office. Karen was merrily clicking away on the keyboard. Gloria seemed exceedingly impressed.

"Any progress?" I asked.

"Lots!" Gloria answered. "Karen is terrific. She's a step away from logging onto the purchasing system in Sidney's name. Give us ten more minutes."

I turned to Diane. "I can suggest something useful to do while we wait."

"Like what?"

"I want to compare the different grades of Hevlan. I presume you keep a supply of each in your prototype molding shop."

She sighed. "Why not? It's only a quarter-mile walk to and fro."

I managed to keep up with Diane's long strides, although my side was stinging. I had fibbed to Gloria. I had no intention of taking a pain pill for fear that it would make me sleepier than I already felt.

Diane led me to a laboratory table in the rear of the molding shop and pointed to a shelf laden with small glass jars full of resin beads. "One of our quality assurance people sits here. He has samples of all the resins we use."

The jars were carefully labeled. I quickly found "Hevlan Resin 3077A—Medical Grade" and "Hevlan-Resin 3077B—Industrial Grade." At first glance both seemed to be full of identical cream-colored resin beads.

"Do you need anything else?" she asked, a touch sarcastically.

"Alas, yes. A magnifying glass."

Diane went off, mumbling words I felt happy not to hear, and returned with a large, round magnifying glass—a classic model that might have been owned by Sherlock Holmes. I arranged two groups of cream-colored resin beads (about a dozen of each variety) side by side on the laboratory table. I switched on the table's powerful overhead lamp, adjusted its moveable arm to position the shade directly above the beads, and commenced to study the two kinds of Hevlan.

Each piece of resin was shaped like a tiny soup can: a cylindrical pellet—scarcely a tenth of an inch tall—with a flat top and flat bottom. Even under a magnifying glass, medical-grade and industrial-grade Hevlan appeared indistinguishable to me. I asked Diane to have a look.

"They're *almost* the same," she said.

"You can see a dissimilarity?"

"Yep. It's like the difference between a vanilla milkshake and a vanilla malted. One kind of Hevlan is a tad darker than the other."

I peered through the magnifying glass again. Diane was right. The color of industrial grade Hevlan seemed a shade darker. The minor color shift had been too subtle for me to notice, but a Hevlan expert would twig to it immediately. A mother knows the difference between identical twins; Barry or Hilda would recognize different grades of Hevlan on sight.

"I want to take these resin samples with me," I said.

"No problem." Diane pulled opened a drawer in the laboratory table. It was full of empty plastic vials, the kind druggists use. "Knock yourself out."

———

Gloria was working at Sidney's computer when we returned to his office.

"The purchasing system is an easy application to figure out," she said to me. "It keeps track of purchases, invoices, and inventory. What kind of information do you want me to retrieve?"

"I want to see purchases of Hevlan resin for the complete year. I am especially interested in 3077A resin—that's medical-grade Hevlan."

Gloria poked at several keys, then worked the mouse awhile.

"OK!" she said. "I searched on Hevlan and ordered the report to be sent to Sidney's printer."

The laser printer sitting on Sidney's credenza began to hum. It promptly spit out three sheets of paper covered with details of Hevlan purchases.

"Blimey! You folks buy a lot of Hevlan," I said.

"Duh!" Diane replied mockingly. "Have you forgotten that C&M is a leading manufacturer of precision Hevlan components?"

Gloria came to my rescue. "Let's narrow the search to purchases of medical-grade Hevlan."

This time a single sheet of paper emerged from Sidney's printer. It cataloged eight separate purchases of 3077A Hevlan resin for the year.

"I can decipher the listings for you," Diane said as she moved beside me. "In January we bought a small batch of medical-grade Hevlan. We didn't need much resin early in the year because we were still building prototype valves and refining our production techniques."

"Understood," I said.

Diane continued. "We started to mold initial production valves in June—about a hundred each month. We purchased six batches of Hevlan—in June, July, August, September, October, and November.

"Then in December we ordered a really big batch of 3077A Hevlan because we are going to start full-scale production of CM-7 valves in January."

I studied the purchasing report for a moment. The abbreviations on the page began to make sense.

"I think I've got it," I said, and I pointed to the November purchase. "The November shipment was ordered on November 23."

"Correct," Diane said.

"By Jove, I think she's got it!" Gloria shouted in her mock English.

"However," I said, "the other monthly shipments were ordered on the first of each month."

"True," Diane said.

I started to ask why the ordering dates were different, but Gloria let loose with "By Jove, she's *really, really* got it!" Diane multiplied the silliness by launching into a falsetto rendition of "The Rain in Spain." I joined in, and the question evaporated from my mind.

Karen restored us to sanity by asking, "Did we find Barry's 'smoking gun?'"

I frowned. Gloria arched her brows. Diane shrugged.

"The list of purchases looks fine to me," Diane finally said. "I don't know what Barry was thinking, but his accusation doesn't make sense. There's simply no reason *not* to mold the valves out of medical-grade resin. We obviously had plenty of 3077A Hevlan on hand, and the stuff costs only a few dollars a pound more than the industrial grade. Besides, the cost of the resin is peanuts compared to the hand labor that was necessary to make the initial run of valves."

"Maybe Barry made a mistake?" Gloria said.

Karen threw back her head. "No!" she shouted. "Barry is dead! He was murdered because of what he discovered. I'm sure of it!" She began to sob softly.

"I think Karen makes an excellent point." I said. "Barry believed he had uncovered criminal behavior at C&M. Too much has happened to assume that Barry was mistaken." I added, under my breath, "Including an attack on me."

Diane sat on the edge of Sidney's desk. "Does anyone have any bright ideas? As long as we're here, are there other systems we should break into?"

"I have a thought," I said. "I have a hunch that Barry was in contact with a person who could test the various grades of Hevlan resin. Is there a way to review his telephone calls?"

"Piece of cake!" Diane said. "I can access his telephone log on-line."

Diane took over the computer. "It says here that Barry worked for the company a total of fifty-one days and that he made a total of eleven-hundred and fifty-six outside calls—which certainly proves that PR people talk a lot." She added, "Do you want me to print the list for you?"

"We don't have time to review that many calls. Let me browse over your shoulder."

The owner of each telephone Barry called appeared next to its number. Diane paged through the list while I tried to spot names of interest. The vast majority of the calls were local—to newspapers, radio and

TV stations, printers, freelance writers, restaurants in Ryde, and the Waterside Inn. All were obviously job related. I even found three calls to Hunnechurch & Associates.

"He made a few dozen calls to Carlson Networking in Virginia," I said.

Karen raised her hand. "That's where I work," she said.

"He recently made several calls to Western Maryland Technical Institute."

Diane and Karen both said simultaneously, "WMTI was Barry's college."

"One of the calls to WMTI was on the Monday he died. That may be significant because he made only two other outside calls that day— one to Karen at Carlson Networking and the other to Simonette Resin Corporation."

Diane spoke first. "Simonette is the Hevlan distributor."

"That call was made at 3:32 P.M."

"Right after Barry's fight with Sidney," Diane said. "I'll bet that he tried to duplicate the purchase information we found in the on-line system."

I reached for Sidney's telephone. "I'll dial the number at WMTI," I said. "Perhaps the school has a voicE-mail system."

It did.

A silky, slightly accented voice said, "You have reached the telephone of Professor Barbara Salazar. I'm sorry to miss your call. Please leave a number and a brief message. I will call you back soon. Good-bye."

The voice was familiar. I had spoken to Barbara Salazar five months earlier when she had provided one of Barry's job references. Professor Salazar was head of the WMTI's Materials Science department and an expert in plastics in her own right.

I wondered if she had attended Barry's funeral. I wondered if Sophie Hammond had come across her name. I especially wondered if Professor Salazar had told anyone else about the chunk of cream-white plastic that I felt sure Barry had sent to her.

Chapter Twenty-three

THE THUMPING ON MY FRONT DOOR began at seven-thirty on Christmas morning. I tried to ignore it in the hope that it would stop. When it didn't, I rolled off my overstuffed sofa—to minimize the ache in my ribs—and slowly rose to my feet.

I started down the hallway, but Gloria beat me to the door. She worked the lock and turned the knob.

"Mer-r-r-ry Christmas, sleepyheads!" James boomed at us. He was wearing a red Santa Claus hat and holding a sprig of mistletoe. "*Ah* see that you were both sleepin' in today."

Gloria, standing out of James's sight, behind the door gave me a "what's-going-on?" look. I replied with an "I-haven't-the-foggiest-idea" shrug.

"A Happy Christmas to you, James," I said, "but why are you here so early—without warning?"

"It's hardly early, Ms. Hunnechurch. Every kid on Magothy Street has been awake for an hour. Now, as for my reason for comin' unannounced, I am here to give you and Ms. Spitz an extra Christmas present." He pointed to two large brown paper shopping bags at his feet. "I have brought the makings of a genuine southern breakfast. Orange juice. New Orleans style coffee with chicory. Fried eggs. Genuine country ham. Biscuits. Sausage gravy. And, of course, grits."

James couldn't see Gloria's grimace or her pretend heave. I managed not to laugh out loud.

He moved toward me and gave me a kiss. "I made some compromises of course," he went on. "The biscuit dough comes in a cardboard tube, and the orange juice is not fresh squeezed, but I expect you will enjoy them nonetheless."

James picked up the bags and marched past us toward the kitchen. I wiped the sleep out of my eyes and tried to clear my head.

Gloria and I had arrived home from Campbell & McQueen well past midnight, my side throbbing sufficiently that I decided not to climb upstairs. I changed into my pajamas, tightened my chest binder, took a pain pill, and curled up on my sofa. It took hours—and a big glass of milk—to fall asleep because I couldn't stop my mind from pondering the new posthumous dilemma that Barry Goodwin had brought me.

On the one hand, I believed Barry. I accepted his claim that the CM-7 was made of the wrong kind of Hevlan. His murder and the look I had seen on Hilda McQueen's face were evidence that Barry was right.

On the other hand, I believed Diane Dupont. It made no sense for C&M to use lesser breeds of Hevlan and, in fact, the company had purchased plenty of the medical-grade resin.

The next morning it felt like James had arrived only seconds after I finally drifted off.

Gloria tugged me aside. She waited until we could hear the sounds of groceries being unpacked, then said, "Are you going to tell James about our junket to C&M last night?"

"Not unless he asks a question that forces me to admit it. James would certainly disapprove of our visit. I am not in the mood to defend my decision or to explain what we found. . . . *Blast!*"

"What's wrong?"

"The printouts I took from C&M are on the kitchen table."

I strode into the kitchen as fast as my ribs would allow. James was busy lining up ingredients on my countertop.

"Do you use sequential order or alphabetical order?" I asked.

"Proper organization is the hallmark of any successful endeavor. I suspect this is why there are more famed male chefs than female chefs."

"Let's not go there."

"*Ah* agree." He gave me a cool, appraising look. "Not that I mind the sight of you walkin' around in pajamas, but can you disappear while I cook breakfast?"

I filled my voice with pseudo indignation. "*Well!* If that's the way you feel, I shall get dressed."

I took a backward step toward the kitchen table, whirled about, and deftly scooped up two sheets of paper: the list of C&M medical-grade Hevlan purchases, and the log of telephone calls Barry made during his final six working days.

"Breakfast will be ready in exactly thirty minutes," James said.

"Yes sir!" I replied.

I made for the walnut buffet table in my hallway and stuffed the papers into my handbag.

Twenty-nine minutes later—showered, dressed, and coiffed— Gloria and I reappeared in the kitchen.

"Now, before we dig into our southern breakfast," James said as we sat down, "I would like you ladies to contemplate a simple truth. You could eat this well *every* morning if you lived in the South."

"Talk about a heart attack on a plate," Gloria said with obvious awe. "I've never seen so many fatty foods on one table. The heart association must have your name on their Ten Most Wanted list."

I scanned the profusion of yummy calories that James had set out on the table.

"Are we really expected to eat all that?" I said.

James looked at me with wide-eyed innocence. "How can you do justice to the fine Christmas dinner that Joyce Friendly is certain to prepare on an empty stomach?" He started to grin. "Who wants to say grace?"

"Definitely me!" Gloria said.

We joined hands. "Father in heaven," Gloria began, "we have a lot to thank you for on this special day, the day of your Son's birth. We give thanks that Pippa is mending nicely . . . and that James was able to be with us today . . . and for the fabulous breakfast he prepared. We also ask your special blessing as we dig in. Lead us not into temptation and deliver us from overeating. In Jesus' name, Amen."

Not all prayers are answered.

═══════════

"I really wish Pippa was in shape to walk to the Friendlys," Gloria said as we piled into James's rented Ford Taurus at a quarter past one on Christmas afternoon. "A hearty five-mile hike on a cold day like this one would begin to work off that ridiculous breakfast."

"Even if my ribs didn't hurt, I'd be too full to walk." I leaned back against the headrest and closed my eyes. Perhaps I could sneak in a brief nap.

"Stay awake," James shouted. "I don't know the way."

"It's easy," Gloria said from the backseat. "Find my apartment, drive two more blocks along Poplar Road, then turn right on Forest Road. You'll go past a handful of working farms and eventually see the Dells on your left."

I added, "The Dells is a charming subdivision of perhaps thirty houses."

We drove. I drifted until I heard the ratcheting sound of James setting the Ford's emergency brake.

"Are we there?" I asked.

"Nope," James said. "Gloria and I decided to make a short detour to Edwards Lane."

My eyes popped open. James had stopped in front of the maple tree I had hit.

"Let's take a look," James said.

There wasn't much to see three days and nights after my "incident." The lawn around the tree was mangled. "That was done by the paramedics and the tow truck," Gloria explained. The tree had an area of damaged bark not much larger than a dinner plate.

"The silver lining in this dark cloud," James said, "is the opportunity for you to buy a real vehicle—not a minuscule two-seater that I could barely fit into."

"I think Pippa should buy a truck," Gloria said.

"A compact pickup," James agreed.

Gloria: "With four-wheel drive."

James: "And leather seats."

Gloria: "And a premium audio system."

James: "A *fine* choice. Lots of ladies drive compact trucks in Georgia."

"Except . . ." I said to Gloria, "I don't want a pickup truck. And . . ." I said to James, "I live in Maryland, not Georgia."

"That is a circumstance easily changed," James replied. "I promise you'll find the drivers down south less . . . deadly."

I smiled as if James had make a joke, but all of us, including Gloria, knew that twice that day he had offered a veiled invitation that I leave Ryde. She had a wistful look on her face when we returned to the car.

Blimey, Hunnechurch. James seems to have made a decision. How are you going to respond?

We drove in silence to the Friendly's house—a neat Cape Cod about a quarter mile off Forest Road, hidden behind a natural bulwark of scrub oak and pine trees.

The elaborate Christmas dinner Joyce Friendly served offered another opportunity to overindulge—a deep-fried turkey and a spiral-
cut ham complete with oodles of trimmings. Then we had two
desserts—a big helping of pumpkin pie and a small slice of the
miniature Christmas pudding I had made months earlier. David shut
off the lights and Joyce carried in the flaming pudding while the rest
of us applauded.

After dinner we gathered in the family room. Everyone insisted that
I take the comfy sofa.

Gloria swooped in with Peter—the youngest Friendly, nearly five
years old—who looked like a Christmas elf in the green pants and
matching red-trimmed vest his grandmother had sewn. He leapt out of
her arms and dive-bombed the cushion next to me. The sofa bounced
and I winced.

"What's wrong, Aunt Pippa?" Peter said.

I touched my ribs. "I hurt my side, but it's getting better."

He nodded, then shifted gears. "Did you like what Santa brought
you?"

"As a matter of fact, Santa was most kind." Gloria's gift was a one-
year membership to the Ryde Rifle and Pistol Club (along with a promise to teach me how to shoot); the Friendlys gave me a gift certificate to
my favorite boutique in Mulberry Alley; and James presented me with
exquisite gold and pearl earrings—perhaps the most personal gift I had
ever received from James.

I felt myself blush as I held one of the earrings against a lobe for
everyone to see. Gloria and Joyce were grinning goofily. They, too, had
read the signals that James was continuing to send me.

As the afternoon faded, so did we.

"It looks to me like our merry band is falling asleep," Joyce said. "I
prescribe caffeine all around. I'll brew some Kona coffee and make a pot
of Russian Caravan tea."

"Our sleepiness is the revenge of the turkey," David said. "Turkey meat contains a natural tranquilizer. We ran an in-depth story about it last week."

"I ate more ham than turkey," James said. "How do you explain my lethargy?"

"Whatever the cause," I said to Joyce, "make mine a tall *mug* of tea."

Gloria peered at her wristwatch. "I wish you had had your hot cuppa earlier," she said to me.

The odd comment—plus the curious edge in her tone—made me suspicious. I checked my watch; it was almost four o'clock. When I glanced up, I realized that Gloria, James, and David were gazing at me expectantly—and fighting back smiles.

"What have you cooked up now?" I asked.

"Absolutely nothing!" Gloria replied much too quickly.

The eager looks and almost-smiles continued until a little white box on the coffee table in front of me began to beep.

"Answer it!" Gloria screamed. "It's for you."

I opened the box and found a tiny cell phone scarcely larger than a candy bar.

"It's your new personal phone," James said, "to replace the one that was smashed."

"James and I bought it for you as a bonus present," Gloria said. "The latest technology."

"I don't know what to say . . ." I began.

"Stop wasting time!" Gloria shouted. "Answer the phone before they hang up."

I gingerly flipped the phone open and said, "Hello."

An unmistakable voice boomed, "Merry Christmas, Pippa! It's Chloe."

"Chloe! Where are you?"

"In Chichester, of course. With Stuart and Mum. Steady on, Mum's picking up the telephone in the study."

It seemed only a few moments to me, but the call timer on my new cell phone calculated that I spoke to Chloe, Mum, and Stuart for thirty-three minutes. I might have spoken even longer, but the battery-discharged warning signal began to beep.

"We didn't give it a full charge," Gloria said. "Who knew you would talk forever?"

Gloria and James set up the phone's recharging cradle while I recharged my own batteries with a cup of strong tea.

Shortly before six, David stood up and announced, "Eggnog time!"

"Impossible!" James said. "I, for one, have reached the point of absolute fullness. I can't accommodate another item."

"Me too," I said.

"Ditto," Gloria concurred.

David ignored our pleas. He disappeared into the kitchen and returned with a tray of glass mugs. "Christmas is not complete without a large helping of Friendly's Special-Recipe Holiday Eggnog." David gave me a mug and a wink. "I know you don't drink, but eggnog without rum is like . . ."

"A Christmas pudding without a bit of brandy." I winked back. "I shall attempt a sip or two."

With the group's attention focused on eggnog, I was able to retrieve my new cell phone and slip away to David's home office for a brief interval. I hoped that a good hour-and-a-half in the recharge cradle had put sufficient energy in the battery to make two phone calls.

My first call was to the information operator in Hancock, Maryland.

"Information for what city?" she asked.

"I don't have a full address. Please look for listings in the vicinity of Hancock. The name is Salazar. Barbara Salazar."

"I have a Dr. B. Salazar in Westberg, Maryland."

"That must be her."

I punched the number into my phone but hesitated to press the *Send* key. Professor Salazar had been cordial, even friendly, during the summer, but would she be annoyed by a call at home on Christmas afternoon? I decided to chance it. Perhaps her celebration, like ours, was nearly over.

Six rings. "Hello."

"Merry Christmas, Professor Salazar. This is Pippa Hunnechurch, in Ryde."

A moment to catch her thoughts, then, "Ah, yes . . . the headhunter."

"Forgive me for disturbing you on Christmas, Professor, but I am working under a severe time constraint. I have a question about Barry Goodwin."

"You may ask it."

"Did Barry send you a piece of plastic to examine?"

Silence.

"Professor Salazar?" I prompted.

"In person, perhaps, I will answer your question. Face-to-face, not on the telephone."

"You want me to visit you?"

"Yes. Come to my office at the college on Thursday afternoon at one o'clock, and bring . . . proof."

"What sort of proof?"

"You seem to know a fact that Barry considered a secret. I ask myself, how is this possible? I come to only one conclusion. You have discovered Barry's concerns about a certain . . . *ah,* device. Convince me that this is true—that you understand what Barry was trying to do— and I will tell you about the piece of plastic I examined."

"I understand perfectly. I have the proof you want."

She rang off just as Gloria shouted, "Pippa! Come see the snow."

David had switched on the floodlights that illuminated a large patio beyond the family room. Joyce had drawn back the draperies that covered a wall of sliding-glass doors. Peter was standing with his nose against the glass, watching fat snowflakes collect on the redbrick paving.

"I know a little boy who is going to try out his new Christmas sled tomorrow," I said.

Peter nodded, too caught up in the moment to say anything.

"The six o'clock news just started," David said. "I'll check the forecast." He worked a remote control to turn on a large-screen TV.

We heard Veronica Nelson, Channel 11's roving reporter, an instant before we saw her—standing in front of a large house that had a wrought-iron chandelier hanging in its covered entryway.

". . . the victim died of multiple gunshot wounds. According to one source who asked not to be named, Ryde police theorize that Dr. McQueen was shot as many as four days ago, possibly last Friday, and that her body remained undiscovered until early this afternoon."

All of us moved closer to the TV.

The image on the screen switched to footage of Hilda photographed at C&M's news conference. Veronica Nelson talked on:

"Dr. McQueen, age fifty-eight, a well-known scientist and businessperson in Maryland, was cofounder of Campbell & McQueen, a manufacturer of precision plastic components based in Ryde. Dr. McQueen also served on the boards of three local charities and was an ardent supporter of her alma mater, Johns Hopkins University.

"Associates of Dr. McQueen told Channel 11 that she was scheduled to have left for a European vacation last Friday. Police confirm that she held reservations on a flight to Paris that departed Dulles International Airport at three forty-five on Friday. The reservations were never cancelled."

The picture changed again—to a wide shot of Hilda's house that must have been taken earlier in the day. Several police cars and an ambulance were out front.

"Dr. McQueen's body was discovered when Ryde police conducted a routine check on her house at the request of C&M senior executives. A C&M spokesperson, Mr. Sidney Monk, told Channel 11 that Dr. McQueen's failure to notify the company of her whereabouts was totally out of character and immediately raised concerns."

Gloria tugged my sleeve. "You visited Hilda on Friday morning," she whispered to me. "You may have been one of the last people to see her alive."

I didn't respond—not wanting to say even in a whisper what I was thinking. My visit had prompted the killer to shoot Hilda. Why else would the same person have tried to run me into a tree a few hours later?

Chapter Twenty-four

DETECTIVE REILLY DESCENDED ON ME like a London fog at seven o'clock on Wednesday morning. Gloria left us alone in my living room glaring at each other. He didn't say hello, and neither did I.

"I consider you a material witness," he finally said as he unbuttoned his topcoat. "You belong in jail—to encourage your compliance and for your own safety. I'd be doing you a favor to arrest you."

Courtesy triumphed. I pointed to an armchair. "Please sit down, Detective. Can I offer you a cup of tea?"

"No. But you can tell me about your meeting with Hilda McQueen. Why did you find it necessary to visit a C&M executive on a day when the company was closed?"

I tried to bluff. "What meeting do you have in mind?"

Reilly's expression became a mixture of scorn and amusement. He began to itemize on his fingers:

"First, the meeting you arranged when you used your cell phone to call Mrs. McQueen on Friday morning.

"Second, the meeting you traveled to in your late, lamented red Miata, which was observed parked in Mrs. McQueen's driveway at approximately eight-thirty in the morning by a neighbor who honors her civil responsibilities by cooperating with the police.

"And third, the meeting that was, in fact, memorialized by Mrs. McQueen herself, who scribbled seven words on a Post-It note we found next to the telephone in her bedroom. The words were, 'Pippa Hunnechurch,' 'Valve?' and 'Here in five minutes.' Your name and arrival time were easy to understand, but we're definitely puzzled as to why she wrote the word valve, then underlined it and added a question mark. Do you have an explanation?"

I felt my cheeks flush. "I really can't say."

I thought furiously. The police hadn't found the CM-7 valve I had left with Hilda . . . *ergo* the killer had taken it . . . *ergo* here was more evidence that Barry had discovered a genuine defect.

Reilly sighed. "You still won't tell me what you know."

"I still *can't.*"

I had seen Reilly on television that morning, announcing that "Given the death of a second C&M executive in less than two weeks, we are reexamining our conclusion that Barry Goodwin's death was a suicide." A mob of reporters were sticking microphones in his face. If he even muttered the phrase "heart valve," it would become today's big story.

I had a thought. "You knew I called Hilda on Friday morning. Did you check whether she made any calls after I left?"

Reilly leaned back in the armchair until it groaned under the strain. "Of course, we did. She made more than a dozen calls after you left—mostly to C&M personnel. We're trying to interview them."

"Trying?"

Reilly's face darkened. "C&M has surrounded its people with lawyers. You're not the only pain in my posterior today."

I felt cheered by the news that other potential witnesses were stonewalling the police. Perhaps the parade of corporate lawyers would slow Reilly down long enough for me to finish the investigation that Barry started.

"C&M wants to limit the publicity because of the acquisition," I said. "Billions of dollars are at stake."

"So everyone keeps telling me. All I care about is the murderer roaming around Ryde."

"I said something to you the other day that bears repeating. When you get to the bottom of Barry Goodwin's motives, think long and hard before you tell Sophie Hammond, or any other reporter. You don't want to hurt people who have suffered enough."

This time Reilly didn't laugh at me. He levered himself out of the chair and asked, "I still don't have the vaguest idea what you are talking about. Maybe if you explained, I'd come over to your side."

"Give me two more days, and then I may be able to tell you the whole story."

"Why are you doing this, Miss H.? What's in it for you, other than a pair of broken ribs?"

"Nothing tangible, if that's what you mean. It's more of a second-mile thing. Many people reminded me that I didn't go the extra mile for Barry when he was alive. I have the chance to do it now that he's dead and finish up a project he started, something that was important to him."

"A project that got him killed and sent you to the hospital."

"I suppose that proves how important it is."

"Yeah . . . something important enough to die for—and to kill for."

Reilly buttoned his coat.

"Thank you for not arresting me as a material witness," I said.

Reilly shrugged. "Hilda McQueen was known to be alive three hours after you left her house. I couldn't make the case that you have relevant information about the circumstances of her death. I don't even have solid evidence linking Hilda's death with the attack on you."

He gave me a little wave. "I tried my best, but the state's attorney refused to throw you in jail. Go figure!"

━━━━━━━━━━

Gloria thawed leftover scones for our breakfast. I stared at the mutilated CM-7 valve in its plastic Ziploc bag, hoping all the while it would stimulate a burst of inspiration.

"You look gloomy," Gloria said.

"I am. I still can't make heads or tails of the conflicting information we have. Moreover, I don't want to waste today. I am plum out of ideas for useful things to do."

"If you should have a brainstorm, remember that whatever you do, *we* do together. I'm not letting you out of my sight until Reilly catches the killer. I also have a new security rule. No trips anywhere after dark. When the sun goes down, I want you in this house with the doors locked."

"I wouldn't have it any other way," I replied.

The two intact valves we had found in Barry's apartment were still safely tucked away in a locked file cabinet. The damaged CM-7—the valve with part of its orifice ring cut away—was the proof I would take to Barbara Salazar on Thursday—the source of the Hevlan sample she had received from Barry. I lifted the valve to eye level. How, I wondered as I studied its polished surface, had a device designed to save lives become a motivation for two murders?

Gloria dished up the scones with butter, a jar of raspberry preserves, and a bowl of yogurt.

"Are you still interested," she asked, "in who had breakfast with Barry at Maison Pierre?"

"Goodness! I'd forgotten all about it."

"You said you were curious, so I called the facts into Collier Investigations. They sent an E-mail reply this morning. Barry's guest was a guy named Mark O'Brian, the *former* director of corporate communications at Campbell & McQueen. Barry was his successor."

"How on earth did Collier track down those bits of trivia?"

Gloria smiled. "Terry Collier called Pierre and asked if he remembered the day when Barry ate two meals at the restaurant. It turns out that Barry and Mark O'Brian were both great customers—frequent expense-account diners at Maison Pierre."

"We could have asked Pierre," I said.

"Yep. Investigating is rarely rocket science."

"Do we know how to find this Mark O'Brian?"

"Let me check Barry's Palm handheld. Maybe we'll get lucky again." We did.

Gloria read me the details. "Mark O'Brian is director of media relations at the Marshall Agency." She peered at me. "Ever hear of it?"

"Indeed I have. An especially trendy advertising and public relations firm. Once upon a time, I harbored fond hopes of making it our client."

"I see no reason why you can't give O'Brian a sales pitch while you question him about his suspicious breakfast with Barry."

I threw half a buttered scone at Gloria.

Mark O'Brian agreed to see me at his office at ten-thirty.

"We better leave the house at ten," Gloria had said. "Last night's snowfall dropped a good four inches on Ryde. It's probably a mess downtown." And so it was—especially in Ryde Old Town where the Marshall Agency was headquartered. Snow had been pushed to the curbs of the narrow streets, making it difficult for two vehicles to pass abreast.

Marshall's home was a lovely, renovated four-story townhouse on Cove Street in Ryde Old Town. A brass plaque to the side of the front door proclaimed the edifice to be on the National Register of Historic Buildings. A second, smaller plaque explained that the townhouse had been built in 1793 by Callard and Hortense Edwards, the founders of a Maryland family noted for its abolitionist fervor a half-century later.

Marshall was one of the "boutique firms" among our local advertising agencies; it specialized in developing quirky, innovative, and above all, entertaining, "business-to-business" advertising designed to sell high-technology products. Virtually everything its writers and designers produced appeared in technical and industry magazines or graced booths at conventions and trade shows. Marshall's rapid growth would soon prompt its relocation to a bigger building, but for now, the cobbles and gas-fired streetlights on Cove Street seemed a perfect backdrop for the agency's creativity.

Mark O'Brian was shorter than me, round in the belly, and outgoing. He had an unruly head of light brown hair and an infectious grin. I pegged his age as near forty. He led us up two flights of stairs to the former housemaid's bedroom that served as his office. The floors were varnished pine planks, partially covered with a red, black, and gold oriental rug. Three of the walls were painted a brilliant white; the fourth, behind Mark's small desk, was dusky red and covered with framed advertisements, awards of achievement, and membership certificates in advertising and public relations organizations.

Mark offered me a chair at a tiny round conference table next to a window that seemed to have its original eighteenth-century glass panes. It overlooked a small rear garden that had been converted into an eight-car parking lot. Gloria had managed to maneuver the four-wheel drive Dodge onto a snow pile in the corner. She was now standing guard just outside the office.

Mark lifted an errant lock of hair off his forehead. "Your phone call this morning puzzled me. What exactly was your relationship with Barry Goodwin?"

"I placed Barry at Campbell & McQueen. In your former job."

He nodded. "That's what you said earlier. I guess I don't understand why a headhunter is still interested in Barry. Being buried makes him a poor candidate for a new job." He shook his head. "And now that Hilda McQueen is dead, well, let's just say that C&M would not be my first choice for a client. Hilda had a trace of character; the other executives at C&M are liars and backstabbers."

I was surprised at the intensity of Mark's outburst, even though I knew he had been fired by C&M. Mark had rebounded to a fine job at a first-class agency that might seek C&M as a client someday. He gained nothing but a poor reputation by badmouthing his former bosses to another member of the Ryde business community.

Perhaps I could exploit his attitude? I had planned to tell Mark as much about my investigation as I dared, then ask him to recount his breakfast conversation with Barry. The odds of success were slim. I took a deep breath and made a roundabout change in my strategy.

"As I believe you know, Barry was also unhappy with C&M management. He told me that he met with you at Maison Pierre and shared his concerns about . . . a certain defective product."

Mark's wonderfully blue eyes blinked. "He told *you* about the CM-7?"

I made a nonchalant gesture. "Nothing but hints, really. Barry was cautious—the soul of discretion."

"I'll say. He refused to give me specific details. You would have thought Barry worked for the CIA the way he kept secrets."

"Let me be frank." I leaned as close as I could to Mark. "I, too, have been treated shabbily by C&M. In a nutshell, I will probably have to take the company to court to recover the fee I earned to recruit Barry."

"Yep!" Mark scowled. "That's the C&M I remember."

Mark swallowed my first fib, so I proceeded to offer up a second.

"My attorney suggested that I conduct an informal investigation to build my case. My goal is to reconstruct Barry's state of mind before his death. If you have no objections, I would like to know the substance of your discussion with Barry."

"I don't object, although I don't think it will do you much good. He wanted to know three things. Why was I fired? How come Jerry Nichols is such agony to work with? And, did I know an unofficial way to get a few sample CM-7 heart valves to play with? Actually, he asked the questions one at a time. If he didn't like my first answer, he wouldn't have asked the second question." He added, "Of course, the first and second questions are closely related."

"How so?"

"I was fired because I stood up to Jerry Nichols. He refused to make himself available for media interviews or to answer reporters' inquiries about C&M products. Jerry behaves like one of those baseball players who loves being idolized but refuses to take time out to sign autographs for kids."

Mark laced his hands behind his head. "I kept complaining to Hilda. I told her that I couldn't do an effective public relations job if C&M's leading technologist wouldn't pull his weight. Reporters expect access to key personnel; Jerry didn't give a hoot."

"I take it that Hilda didn't resolve the problem."

"She tried, but Jerry went around her. He ordered Richard Campbell to fire me."

"*Ordered?* Richard is the chairman of the board."

"Jerry, as they say, is a legend is his own eyes. He thinks he's indispensable to C&M. Unfortunately, Richard Campbell agrees with him. He called me into his office and gave me the big push—three days before I was scheduled to present my new, improved advertising strategy for C&M's medical devices business."

"Oh, dear."

"Happily, my strategizing didn't go to waste."

Mark pointed to the windowsill next to me. "Grab that doohickey that's shaped like an eyeball."

I picked it up. "What is it?"

"A glass eyeball! I leave it on the sill to drive the pigeons bananas. They think that someone is constantly looking at them through the window."

I examined the prosthesis. The front was eerily accurate—a perfect eye, complete with tiny red veins. "Amazing," I said.

"I took the communications plan I developed at C&M," Mark said, "replaced 'heart valve' with 'glass eye,' and never looked back."

"Good for you!"

I placed the glass eye on the table.

"Take it! I have lots more." He began to smile. "Isn't there someone you'd like to keep an eye on?"

I groaned, as he expected me to, and slipped the eyeball into my pocket. If the prosthesis intrigued pigeons, how would a parakeet react?

Mark returned to his story. "Richard pushed me off the bridge, but Sidney Monk helped to justify my departure by claiming that only a corporate communicator who loved and understood plastics could get along with Jerry, which is pure twaddle! *Nobody* can get along with Jerry. His head is as big as his reputation. Both are getting bigger every year."

"Is Jerry as good as they say?" I asked.

"He's probably better. Jerry Nichols may be the best molding technologist in the United States—at least that's what several reporters told me."

Mark tilted his chair back against a white wall. I noticed several scuff marks; he had done the same thing many times before.

"Enough of Jerry . . ." Mark went on. "Barry and I spent most of breakfast talking about his third question—where to get sample valves? Naturally, I asked why he wanted them. He told me that he had spotted a critical defect in a CM-7 valve. I told him he was crazy, that Hilda and Jerry were perfectionists who also knew what they were doing."

"Barry didn't agree?"

"Nope. He said that he noticed the flaw in mid-November. It seems he had been escorting a group of foreign VIPs through the prototype molding shop. They stopped to watch a CM-7 valve being molded.

According to Barry, he could barely contain himself during the rest of the tour."

"I can well imagine."

We sat without speaking for several seconds. I conjured up an image of Barry bursting at the seams.

I finally broke the silence. "I have been told that C&M has an elaborate accounting system to track CM-7 inventory."

"Not quite. The company is eagle-eyed about heart valves *before* they reach the shipping department. After that, nobody watches real hard. I told Barry it would be easy to glom onto a valve or two from an order about to be packed. Hospitals generally order a bunch of valves at a time. If a shipment arrived one valve short, the hospital would assume that somebody made a careless mistake and tell C&M to send a replacement. It would take C&M months to figure out that someone pinched a valve."

By then Barry would have the irrefutable evidence he wanted and be long gone from the company.

I stood up.

"Thank you for you candor," I said.

Mark escorted Gloria and me down the stairs. He handed me a business card when we got to the front door. "Marshal is the fastest growing ad agency in town. We sometimes call on headhunters to find us people. You seem savvier than most. Send me your marketing package."

I felt wistful as I took the card. Hunnechurch & Associates would never work for Mark O'Brian—not after he learned how convincingly I had fudged the truth.

Chapter Twenty-five

Perhaps we now had the answer to one of the tricky questions that had been lurking in the back of my mind. Barry had obtained the four sample valves by stealing them from Campbell & McQueen's shipping department sometime in November.

"What did you think of Mark O'Brian's explanation?" I asked Gloria, as we drove back to Hunnechurch Manor.

"Makes sense to me. C&M was getting ready to ship three thousand heart valves around the United States. The shipping people must have been up to their hips in CM-7s. Who would notice if four of the last batch got lost?"

Gloria made an unexpected turn on to Arundel Lane.

"Where are we going?" I asked.

"To the Ryde Food Mart. You need to buy the makings of bubble and squeak."

"Blimey! I blessedly forgot about New Year's Eve." The penny dropped. "Hold on! Today is only the twenty-sixth of December. I have oodles of time until the thirty-first."

"No, you don't. James promised to invent a gussied-up party version that's bound to take a few hours of work in the kitchen. You're tied up tomorrow, and his schedule is unpredictable. Do it this afternoon."

"Grumble, grumble," I muttered, but I knew that Gloria was right.

Gloria wheeled into the parking lot and found an open slot next to the shopping cart return station. She pulled a pad and pencil from her handbag. "What ingredients do you need?" she said.

"Cabbage and potatoes, of course. And butter."

"Anything else?"

I drew a blank. "In truth, I am not completely sure."

Gloria and I shouted simultaneously, "Call Chloe!"

I flipped open my new cell phone.

"Good heavens," Chloe said when I told her what James planned to do. "A Cinderella version of bubble and squeak. What an outlandish concept!"

"You've not come across such a thing?"

"Certainly not. The essence of bubble and squeak is simplicity. Would you paint polka dots on red bricks? Or add chocolate syrup to English breakfast tea?" She answered her own questions. "Of course you wouldn't!"

"James hasn't proposed the end of civilization as we know it, Chloe. He merely wants to concoct a more elegant form of a rather crude English side dish—one suitable for a New Year's Eve party."

I heard her sniff. "I will give you the proper recipe for a wholly English bubble and squeak. Let it be on your head if your southern friend chooses to abuse it."

Chloe's recipe served six people and was remarkably straightforward: Melt three tablespoons of butter in a large skillet. Sauté a chopped, medium onion until soft. Mix in one pound of cooked mashed potatoes and a half-pound of thinly sliced cabbage. Fry over medium heat until brown. Salt and pepper to taste. Some cooks add a half-pound of finely chopped beef or ham for additional flavor.

"That is the recipe in its entirety," she said. "Bubble and squeak is unpretentious, robust fare—an easy-to-make dish invented to use up leftover potatoes. I frankly doubt that even a misguided American can ruin it."

We said our good-byes, and then I called James at the Waterside Hotel.

"What are you doing today?" I asked.

"Working on a marketing presentation and thinking about you."

"Be that as it may, I require your presence this afternoon. Present yourself at my kitchen at 2:00 P.M. Be prepared to deal with cabbage and potatoes."

He paused. "Oh. Right! The New Year's Eve food thing."

"The very same. Your body may be at a Hogmanay in Toronto on Monday evening, but your prettified bubble and squeak will be on display at the Ryde Fellowship Church."

———

Gloria let James in at two. He whooshed through my front door on a wave of cold, damp air that suggested we were in for another round of snow.

"It's freezin' out there," he said as he unsnapped his collar, unwrapped his scarf, and peeled off his leather gloves. He pulled me against him gently.

"Watch the ribs," I said.

"I would love to."

Bother! He's at it again.

Gloria relocked the deadbolt. "You guys have fun. I'm going upstairs to catch a few soap operas on the TV set in your bedroom."

"I assumed you would want to help," I said.

"Ever hear of having too many cooks in the kitchen?"

James chuckled, but I could tell that Gloria was completely serious. *Oh dear. What would it be like to cook together with James?*

I had laid out the basic ingredients on my kitchen counter in no particular order. James immediately began to arrange them by height.

"Unhand my cabbage and onion, sir! You are here today in the roles of scullery maid and creative consultant."

I had captured Chloe's basic recipe on a piece of Gloria's paper. I showed it to James.

"Sounds simple enough," he said after he read it. "I had best begin peeling and cutting."

"An excellent suggestion."

"Where do you keep your chef's knives? I prefer a ten-inch multi-purpose blade."

I pointed to a drawer. "The few blades I own are in there."

"Unbelievable!" James said as he examined my motley handful of knives. "How can you cook with these dull strips of edgeless metal?"

"Whenever possible I *don't* cook," I said louder than I had intended.

"I feared a certain amount of stress today. Here! I saw this in the hotel gift shop and purchased it for precisely this eventuality." He produced a rolled up fabric object from his pocket and let it unroll like a window shade. It was an apron with bold lettering on the front: I am a Maryland Crab!

"Very amusing," I snapped. "Can the jokes. We have a ton of work to do."

James peeled and sliced the potatoes. I cut up the cabbage and chopped the onion.

"I have a plan," he said. "We make a batch of everyday bubble and squeak and divide it into six small portions. Then we can improve the end product by experimenting with additional ingredients."

"Such as?"

"How about maple syrup? Or Parmesan cheese? Or heavy cream and nutmeg?"

"Yuck! Chloe may have been right about you."

"I beg your pardon?"

"Never mind. Keep cutting."

James set the potatoes to boil. I delved in the drawer beneath my stove for my ancient cast-iron skillet, which I had purchased at a garage sale three years earlier.

"Now there's a classic utensil!" He unexpectedly frowned. "For shame, Miss Hunnechurch! You haven't seasoned your skillet. I can even see tiny bits of rust." James examined the iron surface with the concentration of a diamond cutter. "I believe I can save it."

Uh-oh. This is going to be a long afternoon.

James scrubbed the skillet with a steel wool pad, rinsed it in hot water, dried it thoroughly by heating it on the stove, then tenderly rubbed the interior with vegetable oil.

"Now, we bake it for at least a half hour in a 350-degree oven to complete the seasoning process," he said as he set the digital oven timer. "A well-seasoned skillet is a magnificent cooking tool—and the mark of a skillful cook."

I had watched James's frenetic activities to save the skillet while I sat at my kitchen table and sipped a mug of tea. He had raced hither and yon—from sink, to stove, to counter—with unbridled determination. He came to a sudden stop next to my table.

"I am being ridiculous!" He gave the tabletop an angry thump with his palm. "I can become a pompous jerk when I get nervous. I apologize for my nonsensical behavior."

"What are you nervous about?" I knew I had asked a foolish question the instant the words left my mouth.

James sat down next to me and took my hand. "The time has come to talk about *us*."

"Oh."

The house seemed to fall silent. Even Winston had stopped his preening and stood stony still in his cage. The lone sound I heard was the soft tick-tocking of the quartz clock on the wall above my head.

"It goes without saying that I love you."

"You can say it."

"I will—later. After I talk about our 'thorny issue.' Chloe told me that's what you call it."

"Ah. I live in Ryde, Maryland. You live in Atlanta, Georgia."

"True. Except you have it wrong."

"I do?"

He nodded. "Atlanta isn't really my home anymore. It's become a base of operations for me. I could operate my consultancy from anywhere. Chicago, New York, Washington, D.C. . . .""

"Ryde, Maryland."

He smiled. "Even Ryde, Maryland."

"Does that mean we *don't* have a thorny issue?" I asked.

He sighed. "I'm afraid we have a lulu."

"Oh?"

"I have to tell you about my marriage to Lesley."

"Please do."

"I met Lesley in college. At Emory University. We got married when I graduated. Nine years later we divorced."

"I see."

"Do you?" James let my hand slip out of his. "If I said that our marriage didn't work out, I wouldn't be lying, but no failed relationship can ever be summed up that succinctly. The sad truth is that Lesley left me because I couldn't live up to her expectations. She wanted a husband who worked nine-to-five . . . who would be home on weekends . . . who could plan two-week vacations . . . who someday might become an involved parent. In short, she wanted a conventional American husband like all her friends had."

"You weren't a conventional husband?"

"Far from it. I decided to become an international marketing consultant, which meant I was constantly traveling. Three-week trips overseas to visit foreign trade offices. Cross-country jaunts in the United States to go to conventions and conferences. Last-minute appearances on Canadian TV shows that upset the plans she made for New Year's Eve."

"I get your drift," I said. "I can even sympathize with Lesley's distress. One must work long and hard to make a business succeed. I doubt that Simon would have endured my schedule at Hunnechurch & Associates without complaint."

James's face clouded. "*Now* you have put your finger on the thorny issue. Nothing has changed with me, Pippa. I am still a travelin' man. On top of that, you have your own business—with your own meetings to attend and trips to make. If we got married, we might be apart weeks at a time." He shook his head dejectedly. "Long separations made Lesley bitter, and I wouldn't want that to happen to you."

If we got married! Had James proposed to me? For that matter, did I want him to? His straightforward explanation of our thorny issue was difficult to challenge. Would I be happy in a marriage punctuated by long absences?

"I take it that you haven't come up with a solution," I said.

"I've thought about it. I've prayed about it. I've examined it from all sides." He took my hand again. "I'm stumped."

We stared awhile at the oven timer, at the green numerals counting down the seconds. Less than fifteen minutes to a well-seasoned skillet, but no deadline for the uncertainties we felt.

Gloria knocked on the doorframe. "I crave milk and cookies. Can I come in?"

"Certainly," I said. "The tin of chocolate chip cookies is in the cupboard next to the stove."

"How's the delectable British dish?" she asked.

"Charming as ever. The bubble and squeak is coming along too." James's face brightened at the corny joke he had made.

I chortled—and squeezed James's hand.

Gloria smiled. "For a minute there, I was getting worried. You two were moping, big time."

"We've been wrestling with a difficult subject," James said. "Two independent careers versus one shared future."

"Seems like old news to me." Gloria took a moment to pry open the cookie tin. "You guys have been juggling two careers and two cities for more than a year now. I thought you had it all worked out."

"We haven't resolved anything," I said. "We take each day at a time."

Gloria found a jug of milk in the refrigerator. "Not a bad approach when you think about it." She grinned at us. "Therefore do not worry about tomorrow, for tomorrow will worry about itself. Each day has enough trouble of its own. You could look it up—Matthew 6:34." She poured a glass of milk and dunked a cookie. "You might also want to consider Romans 8:28. And we know that in all things God works for the good of those who love him."

"It can't be that simple," James said. Then he glanced at me. "Can it?"

"What would you do if we ceased worrying about our respective careers?" I asked.

James exaggerated his southern drawl. "Why, I would move to Ryde . . . profess my undyin' love for you . . . and humbly ask for your hand in marriage. How about you?"

I boosted my English accent to turbo-power. "I, sir, would reciprocate your declarations of perpetual affection and favorably acknowledge your kind offer of matrimony."

"Now that we've sorted that out," Gloria said, "please cook the stupid cabbage and potatoes."

"Kissing first," James said. "Then cooking."

"On that note, I'm outta here."

The next several minutes passed much too quickly, and then the oven timer beeped.

"Do we really have to make bubble and squeak?" James asked.

"You committed us."

"Kick me if I should ever make a similar mistake."

I unwound myself from James's embrace. "With both feet."

I drained the cooked potatoes. He retrieved the skillet.

"Is that what seasoned cast iron looks like?" I said. "I freely admit—you have achieved an amazing improvement."

We melted the butter and tossed in the onions.

"So far, so good," James said. "I love the smell of fryin' onions."

The aroma changed dramatically when we added the cabbage and potatoes.

"I suddenly remember that I don't care for fried cabbage," he said.

The contents of the skillet neither bubbled nor squeaked—no matter how vigorously James stirred, mashed, and scooped.

"Did I do something wrong?" James whacked his wooden spoon on the side of skillet, dislodging a large blob of cabbage-permeated mashed potatoes.

"I'm afraid not. You are looking at the bubble and squeak I remember."

"This stuff reminds me of something my grandmother used to feed the hogs when I was a boy." James's nose twitched. "It's too petrified to be prettified."

"Far be it from me to say, I told you so!"

"What are we going to do?" There was a hint of panic in his voice.

"Scratch the bubble and squeak. We'll bring sausage rolls instead."

"From my tea party?" James smacked his lips. "Now, *they* were delicious."

"I will throw myself on Gloria's mercy and beg that she whip out a few dozen."

"Or, you can give me the recipe. I love to cook."

"And I love to eat."

"Yes, ma'am," James said as he tightened his arms around me. "I can tell that this is the beginning of a beautiful relationship."

We forgot about the bubble and squeak.

Chapter Twenty-six

GLORIA BEGAN OUR TRIP to western Maryland with a barrage of questions.

"I've been waiting all morning to talk to you alone. Did you tell Chloe? Did you set a date? When is he going to buy you a ring? Did he eventually propose to you properly? Did you accept?"

"Yes, this morning. . . . Not yet. . . . We haven't discussed a ring yet. . . . Yes, James proposed to me last night with great panache. . . . And yes, I accepted most appreciatively."

"What's a panache?"

"Panache is the style and confidence one would expect from James Huston."

"Then how come you're not bubbling over with excitement?"

"I bubble calmly." In fact, the speed of our betrothal had given me the willies. I needed a bout of solitude to absorb all that had happened. Alas, I had planned a day where other people would surround me.

We had left Hunnechurch Manor at eleven, after another festive brunch. Once again, James had arrived early with the fixings—this time including crumpets, English "banger" sausages, kippers (better known as oak-smoked herring on this side of the pond), and Scottish bitter-orange marmalade. He planned to spend the afternoon in my house, he had said, "polishing my marketing presentation, experimenting with Gloria's sausage roll recipe, and mostly pining for you to return."

"Let me add another chore to your list," I said. "Clean up the bubble and squeak."

In our elation the night before, we had ignored the skillet full of butter-fried cabbage and potatoes. It now sat cold and congealed on my countertop.

James had smiled wryly. "I feel uneasy discarding the first meal we cooked together as an engaged twosome. Some couples talk about 'our song.' We have 'our casserole.' Maybe we ought to get it bronzed?"

My parting words had been, "Away with the bloomin' mess!" But fortuitously, James forgot all about the pan of foul goop that morning.

The slate-gray sky had begun to spit light snow as we left Ryde—no challenge at all for the off-road tires on Gloria's truck. She was in high spirits and not the least bit concerned about the weather. We had a two-hour drive ahead of us, and I didn't want to spend the trip gabbing about my engagement.

"It's been days since I've checked the answering machine in my office," I said to Gloria. I rummaged in my handbag for my new cell phone.

"Speaking of the office . . ." Gloria said. "I'll leave you with James when we get back and pay our end-of-the month bills."

I couldn't help but grimace. Hunnechurch & Associates was depleting its meager financial resources as efficiently as the salt truck ahead of us on Route 70 was spewing salt on the road.

To my astonishment, I found a message from Sidney Monk when I entered the access code: "Good morning, Pippa. Merry Christmas. It's about ten o'clock on Thursday morning. Please call me at your convenience, but the sooner the better."

I dialed Sidney's number. Diane Dupont answered.

"What's up, Diane?" I asked. "I received a message to call Sidney."

"Beat's me! He's been closeted with Richard Campbell all morning. They told me to transfer your call to Richard's office."

Two clicks and a squawk later, Richard answered.

"Pippa Hunnechurch here," I said.

"Pippa! Thanks for calling back so promptly. Don't go away. I want to put you on the speaker phone so Sidney can join in."

The line went silent for a moment, giving me a chance to ponder the cordiality—the unqualified joy—I had heard in Richard's voice. He had chaired the kangaroo court that expelled me from Campbell & McQueen. When—and why—had we become fast friends?

Richard came back, sounding as if he was deep inside a barrel.

"Hi again, Pippa. Merry Christmas."

"Merry Christmas to you," I said cautiously.

"I won't beat around the bush, Pippa. You're the kind of consultant we want to do business with in the future. We have an immediate assignment for you."

"You do?" My voice soared at least an octave.

"Absolutely!" Sidney said. "We've decided that you understand our business much better than Nailor & McHale ever will. We want you to find us another director of corporate communications."

"I see," I said, although I was completely bewildered.

Richard came back. "We applaud the kind of discretion you've shown this week, Pippa. We take good care of team players at C&M. I've ordered the disputed invoice paid in full, and I can promise you a steady stream of new recruiting assignments."

It took me a few seconds to grasp the between-the-lines meaning of Richard's largesse.

My fee was a reward for not telling the police about faulty artificial heart valves.

The new assignments would ensure I remained a "member of the team."

According to Reilly, after I had left Hilda's home she made "more than a dozen calls, mostly to C&M personnel." She undoubtedly called Richard and told him that I had shown up with a defective CM-7 in hand. However, Richard (who had friends in high places—the Ryde Police Department) also knew that I had refused to explain my visit to Stephen Reilly.

I imagined the pair of them sitting in Richard's office, unsure of my motives but confident that they could buy my silence permanently. I doubted their generosity would survive when the story of the CM-7's defect was finally revealed.

There are other ways to guarantee your silence, Hunnechurch!

Did one of them try to drive me off the road after he killed Barry and Hilda? I had to admit the possibility. No one would lose more than Richard if the upcoming acquisition stumbled, but Sidney also owned a healthy portfolio of C&M stock.

I cleared my throat and said, "I understand perfectly, gentlemen. I will be in touch."

I rang off, feeling proud that I hadn't delivered the terrible string of curse words that had gathered on the tip of my tongue.

West of Frederick, Maryland, Interstate 70 rises away from the coastal plane and starts a slow climb into the foothills of the Piedmonts. This is the start of the Blue Ridge Province, a region underlain mainly by folded and faulted sedimentary rocks. I know this because four months earlier I had recruited a corporate attorney for Lorenzo & Hart, a company that does highway maintenance on I-70. A brochure the company gave me claims that you can see these rocks exposed in a fold in the terrain between Catoctin Mountain and South Mountain. We were, however, zipping along I-70 at too great a speed to provide a good view.

"Don't you think that seventy miles an hour is a tad fast in falling snow?" I asked Gloria.

"Not with my tires," she replied, "or my driving skill."

"I certainly hope the information Professor Salazar has for me is worth all this peril."

"Whatever."

We left I-70 ten miles beyond Hancock, stopped to refuel, and learned that Western Maryland Technical Institute was eight miles "straight ahead."

The roads in this corner of Maryland have a distinctly English flavor—high hedgerows along narrow, winding lanes. Gloria drove the Dodge confidently at a steady forty miles per hour through the inch or so of snow on the pavement. Halfway to WMTI, a minivan slid past us, engine roaring. The spray from the rear wheels splattered our windscreen. Gloria swerved. The Dodge's tires held tight.

"Blithering idiot!" Gloria screamed at the van's taillights. She muttered, "That's not going to happen again," and increased her speed to a rather alarming fifty-five.

Ten minutes later, our windscreen caked with slush, we passed through an ornate, black-iron gate and soared across a snow-covered speed bump with a frame-shaking shudder.

Western Maryland Technical Institute was established in 1956, on the grounds of a defunct nineteenth-century orphanage. Many of the old institution's redbrick edifices, dormitories, dining halls, and classroom buildings were renovated. They became the pretty buildings on campus. The recent additions were utilitarian cement structures that seemed ungainly by comparison, even under a blanket of snow.

The Materials Science building where Professor Barbara Salazar worked was the ugliest of the bunch. We found a parking spot a few paces from the entrance and trudged up the front steps. The faculty directory on the wall announced that Salazar's office was on the third floor.

The stairwell was empty and the third-floor hallway deserted, as one would expect in the middle of the Christmas break. Professor Salazar's office door was open. She was sitting in an armchair near the window, tearing up sheets of paper. I knocked on the door frame.

She glanced at me. "Ah—Miss Hunnechurch. Come in. We meet face-to-face at last."

She was dark and super-model thin—probably in her mid-forties—with exotic cheekbones, glowing black hair, and extraordinary brown eyes that made me feel I was being x-rayed. She was wearing a WMTI sweatshirt and blue jeans.

I introduced Gloria. The professor didn't try to rise and shake our hands—the floor around her feet was a sea of papers, folders, notebooks and what might have been old homework assignments.

She threw a wad of paper into a plastic garbage bin. "I have begun my spring cleaning early. Every decade or so, I bow to administration pressures and shovel out my office."

She turned on a luminous grin. "I am known as the champion pack rat on the campus . . . and you are known as—how shall I put it?—an executive recruiter of questionable skill. My bad reputation is well deserved; yours may be highly exaggerated."

"You've spoken to Sophie Hammond?"

"And to a policeman named Reilly. They asked if either you or Barry had been in contact with me." She shrugged. "I told them nothing—they didn't have the proof I require. Do you?"

I held the mutilated CM-7 valve between my thumb and forefinger. "Barry cut the sample of Hevlan he sent you from this artificial heart valve."

"Bravo!" She leaped over the peaks of paper and became instantly hospitable. "Please call me Barbara. Kick aside this foolish paper and find chairs. Can I offer you a warm drink?"

"I would love a cup of tea."

Barbara opened a cupboard in her bookcase. "My private stock of instant coffee, teabags, and hot chocolate—all taken from the school cafeteria."

On the lowest shelf was an electric teakettle—identical to the one Mum owned when we were children.

Salazar read my mind. "As a matter of fact, I bought the kettle in England."

Gloria took the kettle. "I'll fill it with water."

"May I examine the valve you brought?" Salazar extended her hand. I dropped the CM-7 into her palm.

She paused, then went on. "Not much doubt, is there? The color is off. This device is made of the wrong Hevlan resin."

"Did you test Barry's sample scientifically?"

She smiled again and asked, "How much do you know about WMTI?"

"In truth, not much."

"We are not the finest technical university in the world, but we *do* have recognized expertise in a few areas. If I may be allowed some immodesty, plastics technology is one of our strengths. In addition to teaching several practical courses in plastics processing and design, I direct a polymer testing and characterization laboratory that is widely recognized as one of the best in America. I often testify in product liability lawsuits. Barry told me to prepare myself to be an expert witness against Campbell & McQueen."

She sat down at her desk, pushed papers off the cluttered top, held the damaged CM-7 close to her desk lamp, and studied the valve from all angles for a good five minutes.

"An exquisite piece of work," she finally said. "This is as good as molding gets." She sighed deeply. "To answer your original question— yes, I tested the sample cut from this device. We have several different testing technologies at our disposal, but I chose the best—molecular spectroscopy—to compare the materials with other examples of Hevlan

I have on my shelf. This valve is made of industrial-grade Hevlan, not the required medical grade."

The teakettle began to whistle. Gloria made instant coffee, I brewed tea, and Barbara prepared hot chocolate.

"Tell me about Hevlan," I said while we fiddled with our cups.

"A magnificent plastic. Strong. Resilient. Almost indestructible, if used properly. But difficult to work with."

I nodded. "So I've been told. However, Barry thought it had many applications in everyday products. He wrote a technical magazine article about Hevlan—"

Barbara cut in. "I know. 'Can a High-Performance Resin Find a Home in Low Performance Products?' He asked me to review his draft before he submitted it for publication. I told him that he had provided a superb comparison of the different grades of Hevlan and that the article demonstrated his profound respect for Hevlan. Unfortunately . . ."—she shook her head sadly—"most of his conclusions were wrong. Hevlan will never be used for consumer products."

"Too expensive?"

"*Much* too expensive. To use Hevlan in, say, a plastic sink faucet, would be like serving caviar as cat food. You can do it. The cats will love it. But no owner in his or her right mind will pay the bill."

"Getting back to heart valves . . ." I said. "Did Barry ask you for a written report?"

She picked up the CM-7 again and turned it in her fingers, looking at one side then the other. "No. Not a formal report. He wanted a memo that detailed my findings. I spoke to Barry early on the Monday he died and told him that the memo was finished. He instructed me not to mail it to him. He planned to drive here—to bring me additional samples for testing."

"For what purpose?"

"To nail shut the Campbell & McQueen coffin. Those are his words. Barry felt very strongly about the deceit he had uncovered."

"I don't understand the need for more tests."

"The little piece of plastic he sent me proves nothing by itself. It might have come from anywhere." She squeezed the CM-7 tightly in her hand. "Even this defective heart valve is not conclusive evidence that a defect exists across the whole product line. One bad valve might be a fluke—a sloppy error made during production that doesn't represent the thousands of valves that C&M has shipped. To prove a wide-scale defect I would need to examine several intact valves."

"Would a total of four valves have been enough?"

She thought for a moment. "Four examples would have made an excellent start. A good lawyer could use my analyses and conclusions as a justification to demand even broader testing."

A wave of sadness rolled over me.

Barry hung around Campbell & McQueen longer than was necessary— long enough, in fact, to get himself killed.

Mark O'Brian had told Barry how to acquire his sample valves several days before his public fight with C&M's librarian . . . and the fateful news conference . . . and his battle with Sidney Monk that ended with a thrown wastepaper basket. Barry would be alive today if he had simply walked away from C&M with four production CM-7s in his pocket.

Why had Barry kept pushing *after* he gathered his "solid evidence" against C&M?

For the same reason you are gnawing on the same bone, Hunnechurch. Barry was worried about those hundreds of patients.

"One last question, Barbara, if I may."

"Certainly, Pippa."

"Do you think patients are in danger if their replacement heart valves are made of industrial-grade Hevlan?"

Barbara leaned back in her chair. "That would depend on the kind of Hevlan used to mold the valves. My analysis proved that the sample Barry sent me wasn't medical-grade Hevlan. I didn't try to identify the specific grade."

"I can help you there." The two pill vials full of resin beads I had taken from C&M's prototype molding shop were in my handbag. I had used a marking pen to label their caps. I handed them to Barbara.

"Well, if the valves are made out of Hevlan 3077B resin, one of the best industrial grades, I'd say there's a very low risk of deterioration inside the body. It's still against the law—and I wouldn't want a heart valve made of the wrong material inside my chest—but I doubt you will see any patients die from a sudden catastrophic failure."

Chapter Twenty-seven

IT WAS SNOWING STEADILY when we left the Western Maryland Technical Institute at three o'clock. The two-lane road leading back to the Interstate was snow-packed and icy in spots—not much fun to drive, even in a big, agile four-wheel-drive pickup. Gloria and I raised shouts of joy when we reached I-70 and joined the stream of glittering headlights moving east. I let myself relax.

I suddenly felt Gloria poking my arm.

"Wake up, Hunnechurch," she said. "I'm tired of your sleeping."

I looked up. It was still snowing, but now it was dark.

"What time is it?"

"Nearly five o'clock."

I stretched. "Where are we?"

"A few miles east of Frederick."

"How much longer until we get home?"

"We're moving along at a steady thirty-five miles an hour. I'd guess another hour and a half of driving." She added, "Are you hungry?" I heard a noticeable tinge of yearning in her voice.

"Not at all. I may not eat for another week, not after the huge brunch we consumed this morning."

"Well, I'm starving. Driving through snow is hard work; it burns up lots of energy. I'm thinking of getting off at the next exit for some coffee and a light supper."

I did the arithmetic in my head. "If we keep going, we'll be home by six-thirty."

"That may be too early. James is kinda busy right now."

"I thought he was working on a presentation."

"Nope. He's preparing a romantic candlelight dinner for two."

"He is?"

"Yep. It's a surprise."

"Then why did you tell me?"

"So you won't say something silly, like 'I would have been happy with cheese and crackers,' and make him feel dumb for planning a lovely surprise." She turned to me and grinned. "You've been out of circulation for a while. You may have forgotten that guys' feelings are easy to hurt."

"Point well taken." I had a thought. "Then you don't actually plan to work at the office tonight?"

"No way! That was my excuse for leaving you alone with James. Assuming, of course, that you'll feel safe alone with him for three hours?"

"Ha, ha, ha!"

"So do we stop, or what?"

"We stop."

Gloria followed the knife-and-fork restaurant icon at the next exit to a roadside eatery named Harvey's Diner. The place, obviously new, had been built to resemble a traditional American diner from the '40s or '50s. Its metal-clad walls gleamed like silver in the blue-white beams of a dozen mercury-vapor flood lamps. A huge red neon arrow atop the roof flashed on and off in a fiery welcome. Inside the arrow, a blue clock announced the time: five forty-five. Instead of numbers, the clock's face had letters and spaces that spelled out: TIME-TO-EAT!

The dining aisle was nearly full with other travelers seeking a break from the tedium of driving on a snowy evening, but we managed to snare an empty two-seat booth next to the lunch counter.

A waitress old enough to have worked in an original 1950s diner wiped our table with a damp cloth and plunked down paper placemats decorated with green-and-red Christmas trees.

"You gals ready to order?" she asked.

I was about to ask for a cup of tea, but I spotted a box of mediocre teabags on the stainless-steel shelf behind the counter. "I will have a large cup of coffee," I said.

Gloria ordered the deluxe crab cake sandwich platter with fries, a large coffee, and a vanilla milkshake.

"I'll also have a donut," I said, "to keep my friend company."

The waitress returned with two steaming mugs. The coffee inside was hot and strong; I took several sips and began to wake up.

"I've been wondering . . ." Gloria said as she emptied a second package of sugar into her coffee. "We've run out of people to talk to. Do we know the whole story yet?"

"A good question, that. Let's review what we do know." I found an old ballpoint pen in my handbag.

"Can I borrow your notepad again?"

"It's empty. I forgot to buy a replacement pad."

"Then I'll use my placemat." I turned it over.

"Our story begins," I said, "with Barry Goodwin, who has recently accepted the position of director of corporate communications at Campbell & McQueen. While escorting visitors on a factory tour, Barry accidentally discovers that the company he respects deeply is producing heart valves made with industrial-grade Hevlan resin. Barry concludes that this is a shady business practice—a conspiracy that probably involves C&M's senior executives."

I scribbled on the back of the placemat:

1. *Barry discovers CM-7s are defective*

2. *Senior execs involved in conspiracy???*

"But Barry is not your ordinary corporate communicator." Gloria said. "He is a techno-geek who loves plastic, adores Hevlan, and is devoted to quality. Barry gets mad at the people responsible. He decides to collect enough evidence to send them to jail—including four sample valves."

I wrote:

3. *Barry infuriated; feels personally betrayed*

4. *Starts gathering evidence of crime*

5. *Steals four CM-7s*

6. *Sends chunk of valve material to Barbara Salazar for analysis*

"However," I said, "Barry empathizes with the patients who have received faulty valves. He recognizes that ill-timed public disclosure of the problem will cause massive anxiety."

7. *Barry fears public disclosure*

8. *Strives for secrecy; hides sample valves in ice tray*

I must have frowned because Gloria asked, "What's bothering you?"

"I'm puzzled," I said. "If Barry wanted to keep the heart-valve defect secret until he finished gathering conclusive evidence, why did he start so many public fights at Campbell & McQueen? Diane Dupont heard Barry railing at Sidney Monk about a manufacturing problem involving the CM-7."

The waitress arrived with Gloria's crab cakes and my doughnut. She sighed when she noticed that I had transformed my placemat into a writing surface. She handed me the plate and offered an exasperated look that said, *You* figure out where to put it down.

Gloria picked up a french fry and said, "I can think of an answer to your question. Maybe Barry wanted C&M to fix the problem?"

"You're a genius!" I drew a big smiley face on the placemat. "Once Barry read the medical textbook, his concerns for the patients became more important to him than his desire for vengeance. He tried to make the situation known inside C&M, but his own bad behavior got in the way. No one would listen to him! No one would take him seriously. That explains his bizarre behavior at the news conference and the shouting match with Sidney."

I wrote:

9. *Barry launches campaign to fix problem*

10. *Barry confronts Jerry and Sidney—they don't believe him*

11. *Barry shows magazine article to Sidney to prove that he (Barry!) is a Hevlan expert*

12. *Barry becomes upset at the news conference when patient with heart valve is introduced*

13. *Barry, wholly frustrated at lack of progress, fights with Sidney*

14. *Barry murdered . . .*

I stopped writing.

"Why was Barry murdered?" I asked.

Gloria swallowed the piece of crab sandwich she had eaten. I tried a piece of my donut; it was stale.

"That's easy." Gloria said. "The killer wanted to ensure the acquisition of Campbell & McQueen by Hughes Engineered Materials. He, or she, was afraid that bad news about a key C&M product would make Hughes think twice."

I frowned on purpose. "The so-called loose-cannon theory. Eliminate Barry before his bizarre behavior can damage a two-billion-dollar transaction."

"You sound skeptical."

"I am skeptical. I've never been comfortable with the notion. To begin with, who would kill Barry to protect the acquisition?"

"Someone who stands to gain a lot of money when the deal goes through."

"Scores of C&M employees fall into that category. Give me names."

"Richard Campbell is an obvious candidate."

"Richard is a wealthy man today, the chairman of a successful company. Richard tried to buy my silence this morning; that's his modus operandi. He's not the type of fellow likely to arrange an ersatz suicide." I doodled a big C&M on the placemat. "Frankly, I can't imagine anyone at C&M killing Barry for being a wild-eyed sick puppy, as Jerry Nichols described him. Even if Hughes chose not to acquire C&M in January, another buyer was bound to come along."

"I don't know about that." Gloria said. "The possibility of an enormous product liability lawsuit might frighten other companies away. Not to mention the stupidity factor."

I took one of Gloria's french fries. "The what?"

"When the story finally gets out that C&M shipped heart valves made of the wrong plastic, the company and its executives will look *really* stupid."

I returned to my doodling and drew a bold line under the C&M. "I agree that the specter of costly lawsuits poses a serious problem for C&M, but equally so does the loss of Hilda McQueen. It *might* make sense to protect C&M by eliminating Barry Goodwin, but Hilda wasn't about to blow the whistle on a C&M manufacturing defect. Why kill her? She was an irreplaceable asset."

"For that matter, why try to kill you?"

"I've been wondering the same thing. What links us together, besides the obvious facts that I hunted his head and that he reported to Hilda?"

Gloria's milkshake arrived. She unwrapped a straw and plunged it into the glass, then stirred the creamy concoction and began to sip.

"Barry, Hilda, and me," I murmured. "What else do we have in common?"

"How about heart valves?"

"Pardon?"

"Barry stole four . . . you found them in his ice tray . . . you gave one to Hilda."

"And the killer took it!" I said loudly enough to attract our waitress's attention. I smiled and shook my head; she turned away.

"You're a *double* genius today!" I half-whispered to Gloria. "I've been a dunderhead. Hilda was shot, and I was attacked *after* she told other people about the defective CM-7. The murderer appropriated the valve from Hilda and then tried to kill me because I had given the device to her."

"If you're right, we've come around in a big circle. We're back to the idea that Barry and Hilda were killed to keep the CM-7's defect a secret from the outside world."

"True. Unless . . ."

"Unless?"

My mental tumblers clicked into place. All at once I understood.

"Unless what you called the stupidity factor is alive and well."

"Someone didn't want to look really stupid?"

"Precisely! These murders occurred because a person made a careless mistake. Someone got a bit sloppy and perhaps neglected to go the second mile."

"You mean the wrong kind of Hevlan?"

I opened my handbag. Below my wallet, keys, cell phone, lipstick, compact, tissues, and a clipped-together stack of Chesapeake Bay Bridge toll receipts were the two sheets of paper I had crammed to the bottom on Christmas morning. I unfolded and smoothed the list of C&M's purchases of medical-grade Hevlan and shoved Barry's telephone log back inside.

"Barry told us," I said, "to look for the 'smoking gun' in C&M's on-line purchasing system. We failed to see it."

Gloria attacked her milkshake in earnest.

"Imagine," I said to her, "that it's your job to mold a batch of five hundred artificial heart valves every month."

"OK—call me Ms. Molder."

"The work goes swimmingly for five months, Ms. Molder, but then, at the start of the sixth month you make a frightful discovery. You don't have enough medical-grade Hevlan on hand to finish the production run—probably because you made a duffer's mistake and forgot to order replacement supplies. What do you do?"

"I quickly place an order for another batch."

"Alas, you've waited too long. The order won't be filled until the end of the month."

"Ooops!"

"More than ooops—you face disaster. Your company is driving hard to finish its initial production run of three thousand heart valves. A news conference has been scheduled. Orders have been received from across the United States. Everyone expects the valves to be shipped the very instant the FDA gives its approval."

"Oh boy! What do I do now?"

"You search your production facility. Lo and behold, you see tons of a virtually identical industrial-grade plastic resin. Not only does it look like medical-grade Hevlan; you suspect it will probably work as well too."

"I'm saved! So what if a few hundred valves are made of the wrong kind of Hevlan? They'll probably work fine. Who will even notice?"

"There's the rub. Someone did notice."

"Barry Goodwin."

"Exactly! Barry Goodwin. A man who loves Hevlan. A man who can spot the difference between a vanilla milkshake and a vanilla malted. A man who cared enough to go the extra mile."

"I don't want people to know what I've done."

"Certainly not, Ms. Molder. You have your world-renowned reputation to consider."

"So I eliminate Barry Goodwin by faking his suicide."

"Indeed."

"Then I make it look like he was crazy all along . . . that he should never have been hired . . . that the headhunter who recruited him was incompetent."

I nodded. "However, you underestimated Barry Goodwin."

"Rats! He secretly stole four of the bad valves."

"No. You don't know that. How could you? What you do know is that on the Friday before Christmas the president of your company calls up and tells you, 'You'll never guess what a pesky headhunter just presented me—a heart valve made of the wrong kind of Hevlan.'"

"Double rats! Now I have to eliminate the company president *and* the headhunter. Trouble is, the headhunter is a real pain to get rid of. She always has people around her."

Gloria slurped up the last bit of her milkshake.

"Stupidity is a terrible thing," she said.

"I only wish, Ms. Molder," I said as I folded my notated placemat and stuffed it in my handbag, "that the real killer wasn't so bloody intelligent."

Chapter Twenty-eight

MAGOTHY STREET had not yet been plowed when we stopped in front of Hunnechurch Manor at a few minutes after seven. The sidewalk next to my little row house, illuminated by the coach light above my front door, had an undisturbed coating of snow perhaps three inches deep. James's rented Ford Taurus, parked out front, was completely covered.

"I like a man who stays home and cooks," Gloria said. "You always know where he is."

"Are you sure you won't have dinner with us? You must be exhausted after a three-hour drive through a snowstorm."

"I'm fine. It's stopped snowing. I'll be home in five minutes. Give me a call on your cell phone when you're done eating."

"Are you sure?"

"Hunnechurch, you got engaged last night. The last thing you need right now is me sitting at your dinner table. Besides, the hugging and kissing you two do will probably spoil my appetite."

"You are a princess among women."

She leaned over and kissed my cheek. "Don't keep him waiting. James Huston is one of a kind."

Only after the big Dodge had disappeared around the corner did I notice that my front windows were dark. I keep one of my living room lamps on a timer switch that comes on at four every afternoon. Perhaps the bulb had burned out? Then I remembered—James had prepared a candlelight dinner to surprise me. I wondered if he had darkened the house to intensify the effect of the candles.

I let myself in and slid the deadbolt in place. It felt cooler than usual inside the house, as if someone had left a window open. I could smell wondrous aromas coming from the kitchen. A pork roast, perhaps. Freshly baked rolls. A sweet-pungent smell I couldn't identify.

"I'm *ho-me*," I yelled.

I heard Winston chirp a welcome from the kitchen. It was dark. So was my wee dining room. I tried the living room. "James—where are you hiding?"

A voice I instantly recognized answered from the darkest corner. "James is with me, Pippa. We've been waiting for you. Please join us."

My eyes had begun to adjust to the bit of light from Magothy Street that filtered in through the front windows. I could make out James sitting on the sofa. He had his hands raised. I turned and saw Jerry Nichols standing in the blackness next to my Christmas tree.

"Your boyfriend has been very cooperative," he said, "but then, there's nothing like a Colt Python .357 magnum to focus a man's attention. I keep it loaded with exceptionally compelling hollow-point ammunition. One shot is all it takes."

"I'm sorry, Pippa," James said. "I left the kitchen window open a few inches because of the heat from the stove."

"And I climbed in when he left the room," Jerry said with a dull laugh. "Nothing to it. That's how I'm going to leave when I'm finished."

I sat down next to James.

Jerry's voice had become cold, wholly emotionless. I had no doubt that he planned to shoot us. He had killed Barry and Hilda. What were two more deaths on his scorecard?

"For crying out loud, Jerry," I said evenly. "You don't have to do this." I was amazed at how calm I sounded, how rational.

"This is all your fault, Pippa. All you had to do was leave well enough alone. Barry Goodwin was dead and buried. Why did you have to stir things up at Campbell & McQueen?"

I reached for James's hand, but he had moved an inch or two closer to Jerry while I was talking. I decided to keep talking.

God, give me strength . . . and a glib tongue.

"Is your reputation as a plastics guru really that important, Jerry?"

"What do you know about my reputation? I'm a master molder—the best in the country. No one can handle Hevlan better than me."

"Your days of molding Hevlan are over, Jerry. You shouldn't have killed Barry and Hilda."

"Who says I did? There's no proof that I killed anyone. I'm very careful. This gun, for example, has absolutely no connection with the bullets they dug out of Hilda. And if the lights were on, you'd see that I'm wearing latex gloves."

"What happened to the lights?" I asked.

"I pulled the fuses. It's much cozier in the dark. Don't you agree?"

James had moved a few inches more toward the other end of the sofa. I tried a new tack.

"Well, no matter what happens tonight, Jerry, your reputation is kaput, gone, belly up. You left a smoking gun where everyone can find it."

"What's that supposed to mean?"

"You aren't as careful as you think, Jerry. You forgot about Campbell & McQueen's on-line purchasing system. Its electronic brain contains the full story of your rank stupidity. Imagine! C&M's master molder lets the prototype molding shop run out of medical-grade Hevlan."

"That doesn't prove a thing." At last I heard concern in his voice. James had moved some more.

"However, your biggest mistake," I said, echoing my words to Gloria three hours earlier, "was the wretched way you underestimated Barry Goodwin. He acquired several of the defective valves you made. They were hidden in the refrigerator in his apartment. He even had one tested by a technique called"—I hoped I got it right—"molecular spectroscopy. No surprise! It was made of industrial-grade Hevlan."

"I don't believe you. Every valve is accounted for." More concern.

"Funny, that's what Hilda McQueen said, but she was wrong. I remember how I described each valve to her. A cream-colored orifice ring. Two cream-colored leaflets. A white-cloth sewing cuff. Smoothly polished surfaces. A curiously heavy feel in the hand." I paused. "Do you want to know how Barry got them?"

"How?"

"He took them from C&M's shipping department. He simply walked away with them. Do you want to know where they are now?"

"Where?"

"Locked in my office. My associate will turn them over to the police—and the *Ryde Rebel*—if anything happens to me. Like I said earlier, your reputation is toast."

My telephone rang.

The wall phone in the kitchen, the table phone in the hallway, and the cordless phone in my bedroom upstairs filled the house with sound.

"Who cares if you have a dozen valves?" Jerry said, his voice emotionless again. "No one will ever find them. I'll make sure of that."

His arrogance was back in full bloom, and I had run out of good doubt-builders.

"That's probably Gloria," I said. "She knows I'm here. If I don't answer my phone, she'll come running."

After four rings the telephone answering machine in the hallway switched on. We heard my voice saying, "You have reached Pippa

Hunnechurch. I'm sorry I'm not able to take your call right now. Leave a message, and I'll get back to you when I can. Please wait for the beep. Thank you."

The beep, then the voice I prayed to hear.

"Hi, Pippa. It's Gloria. When you guys finally get un-lip-locked enough to return this message, give me a call."

Jerry moved toward the door leading to the hallway.

The room erupted in light and noise. When my head stopped ringing, I realized that Jerry had shot my answering machine.

"She doesn't seem that eager to hear from you," he said.

The shot he had fired would probably wake the neighborhood. Someone was bound to call the police. Jerry knew that. He was getting ready to act. We had to act first.

I remembered my cell phone. Darkness cuts two ways. Jerry didn't see me ease open the lid and gingerly touch the buttons to enter Gloria's cell phone number. I set the open phone next to me on the sofa. I couldn't talk to her, but with luck she would hear our voices. Could she get here in time?

Jerry pulled back the hammer of his revolver.

Lord, if you have a miracle up your sleeve, we definitely need it now.

James had reached the end of the sofa.

James suddenly moved in a way I had never seen him move before. He seemed to soar toward the Christmas tree. In an explosion of tinkling, colored bulbs and glass globes sprayed in all directions and shattered against whatever they hit—walls, floor, and furniture. I watched the tree swing in a broad arc and knock Jerry over.

Jerry fired his gun again. The bullet tore into my sofa, exactly where James had been sitting a few heartbeats earlier, and exploded against the springs. The acrid smell of burned gunpowder filled my living room.

James tried to lift the Christmas tree and swing it again, but its branches were caught against the side of an armchair. Jerry managed to roll away from the tree and raised his arm. I realized he was pointing the gun at me. I had been selected as his new target.

I dove for the floor, trying to ignore the searing pain in my ribs. Another brilliant flash assaulted my eyes. I screamed as the bullet whizzed by, inches from my cheek. It shattered an occasional table and tore through the living room wall into my hallway. I hoped it wasn't powerful enough to reach the house next door.

Thank you, God!

I skittered sideways, behind my other armchair. I fought back a sob and shook my head to clear it. I could almost feel the adrenaline pumping through my veins. The fight or flight response. But where could I flee to and how could I fight?

James suddenly pulled me to my feet and propelled me into the dining room with such force that I slid halfway toward the door that opened into the kitchen.

"Run, Pippa!" he shouted. "Get out."

I could hear sounds of scuffling behind me, from the living room. Curses. Furniture breaking.

Jerry fired at me again. I heard a crash in the kitchen—the sound of falling metal and breaking glass. The bullet had gone through two walls and smashed into . . . *Winston's cage.*

I ran into the kitchen. The cage was lying on the floor; I could hear Winston was squawking and screeching angrily.

Chin up, matey! You'll be fine.

I felt a chill breeze. The slightly open window was in front of me. James had urged me to run—had pushed me to safety. I could lift the window and be running down the street in seconds.

No way! I won't leave James.

I needed a weapon, something to use against Jerry. I felt around in the dark. My fingers touched something cold and hard. The skillet— still full of bubble and squeak—was on the stove where we'd left it. I found the handle. It must have weighed ten pounds.

I ran back to the living room. James was trying to move behind the sofa. Jerry, sitting on his knees, had his gun pointed directly at James.

Dear God, no!

I swung the skillet as fast as I could. The pain in my side made me gasp, but the noise I made was overwhelmed by the sound of cast iron hitting muscle—a gratifying thunk that reverberated throughout the little room. Rancid cabbage and potatoes flew everywhere.

Jerry pitched forward under the blow to his back but immediately started to raise himself up again. I realized I had hit him with the flat bottom of the skillet.

I repositioned the skillet in my hands and swung again—this time harder. The edge of the skillet hit high on his gun arm. I heard an appalling crunch as bone shattered. Jerry crumpled to the floor. His head struck the edge of my coffee table, and his gun clattered near his feet.

James kicked the gun into a corner, then felt the pulse in Jerry's neck. "He's alive but probably in shock. You smashed his upper arm good and proper. Lord knows what he did to his head. I better get the lights turned on."

James jogged to the kitchen.

A few moments later the lights came on.

I heard a moan and a scraping sound next to me. I looked down. Jerry—his face covered in blood—was pulling himself along the floor with his good arm. He was a few feet away from the gun.

"Don't make me hit you again," I screamed.

Jerry kept moving.

I raised my skillet high in the air.

The window behind me crashed open.

Gloria rolled into the living room, grabbed Jerry's big revolver, and sprung to her feet like a gymnast.

"Wow!" she said. "This room smells funny."

Epilogue

I HAVE NOW DINED AT MAISON PIERRE—the most expensive restaurant in Ryde, Maryland—a total of four times—most recently in late January, when Gloria and I took Diane Dupont to lunch to celebrate her promotion to director of human resources at the new C&M Plastics Division of Hughes Engineered Materials. We had to eat quickly because Diane had a 1:00 P.M. meeting with the division's newly named president. (Richard Campbell had retired within hours of the sale of Campbell & McQueen and was somewhere in Europe, enjoying his new multimillions.)

"I personally want to shake the hand that beat the stuffing out of Jerry Nichols," Diane had said.

Diane was being melodramatic. Jerry was in much better shape than he deserved to be. I had broken his right arm and chipped his left shoulder. Falling against my table had opened up a gash in his scalp that required thirty-five stitches. He bled a river, but it caused no permanent damage inside his head other than the defects that led him to commit murder.

The police had confiscated my skillet. "You'll get it back after the state's attorney is through with it," Stephen Reilly had said. I couldn't quite imagine how it would be used at Jerry's trial:

And, did you, Miss Philippa Elizabeth Katherine Hunnechurch, use a frying pan full of rancid English food to cosh the accused, Mr. Gerald Nichols, about the arm and shoulders?

I did, m'Lord.

═══════════

Actually, a trial never took place. Jerry copped twin pleas to shooting Hilda McQueen and running me off the road. He was sentenced to life in prison with the possibility of parole after fifteen years. There wasn't sufficient evidence to prove that Jerry had fed Barry Goodwin knockout pills and sabotaged the furnace. Despite Reilly's best efforts to reopen the case, Barry's death remains on the books as a suicide.

═══════════

As Diane also reported at our sumptuous lunch, corporate justice was swift and merciless. A week after Jerry Nichols was released from the hospital and indicted for murder, a cleanup team from Hughes corporate headquarters emptied out his office and painted over his name on his personal parking space. A few hours earlier the same team had performed the same rites for Sidney Monk, who had been asked to tender his resignation.

Sidney took the fall for not listening to Barry Goodwin.

"See what happens when you don't go the extra mile?" Gloria had said.

═══════════

"And see what happens when you do," Diane said as she polished off a ramekin filled with Coquille Chesapeake. "I wasn't able to get Hunnechurch & Associates its full fee. Barry, after all, did not complete his sixty days on the job. However, my masters have agreed to pay half your invoice in recognition of your exceptional efforts on the division's behalf."

"Hear! Hear!" I said. "It sounds to me as if Hughes Engineered Materials is a class act."

"True," Diane said. "If you need more proof, they've promised to consider me as a candidate for vice president of human relations."

"Rats!" Gloria said. "I had hoped we would get the assignment to replace Sidney."

Happily, Diane laughed at Gloria's little joke.

"Speaking of assignments," she said, "I want you to search for Barry's replacement, and we also need a master molder as soon as possible—a plastics whiz to replace Jerry."

Barbara Salazar immediately sprang to mind. I will present her candidate package next week.

I enjoy recruiting good people for Hughes because the company did, indeed, show itself to be a classy corporate citizen. Hughes took responsibility for the heart-valve fiasco and did the right thing. When the bad batch of CM-7s was recalled, it turned out that only thirty-nine prostheses had actually been implanted into patients. The affected patients were compensated; twenty people chose to have their valves explanted at Hughes's expense. A number of editorials complemented Hughes for "going the extra mile."

Philippa Hunnechurch & Associates is almost back up to speed, thanks to David Friendly and the series of "corrections" he ran in the *Ryde Reporter*. Our former clients are beginning to call again with assignments, and our bank balance is on the rise. Nevertheless, we had to cancel the office furniture that Gloria ordered in December. Alas, I was forced to spend my limited budget for replacement furniture elsewhere.

Specifically, my sofa at home was beyond repair. James helped me choose a new one—a little longer, a little fluffier, and a lot more comfy.

My well-worn oriental rug went to the cleaners. Jerry's blood was easy to remove. The real challenge was the stale grease.

I brought in professional cleaners to eliminate the bubble and squeak pong from my living room. Two guys in bio-suits attacked the mess with vigor.

I hired a carpenter to repair the window Gloria had crashed through. He also patched the various bullet holes, except for a crater the size of my fist in the rear wall of the living room. I decided to hang a picture over it and create a conversation piece.

Chloe—have I shown you my bullet hole?

That particular bullet hole, of course, was made by the slug that knocked over poor Winston's cage. Happily, my faithful budgie lost nothing more than his dignity and a few feathers. He seems pleased with his new cage and will be fully to his former self after his next molt.

Incidentally, anyone who reads the *Ryde Rebel* regularly will probably remember seeing a picture of Winston sitting on my shoulder in the follow-up article Sophie Hammond wrote before she left our small city. To no one's surprise, Sophie landed a plum job with one of the large national tabloids. Her specialty is the creepy crime story.

━━━━━━━━

On the subject of creepy crimes . . . Stephen Reilly and I are experiencing a certain friction over his contention that Gloria and I removed evidence related to a crime from Barry's apartment. He chooses not to accept the two perfectly logical arguments we offered:

1. The dishtowel and the medical textbook don't count.
2. We took the frozen CM-7 valves after the police were done with the apartment, when we had Mrs. Goodwin's permission to be there.

Reilly and I are still sort-of friends, although our budding relationship has been set back a few notches.

On the subject of budding relationships . . . it's quite a sight to see Gloria and Ray Crosby side by side at the gun range, wearing shooting glasses and earmuff sound protectors, blasting away at side-by-side targets. Their common interests in shooting and Christianity prompted me to point out that they "praise the Lord and pass the ammunition."

Gloria replied, "We will pray for your sense of humor."

In fact, several people pray with me (and for me) regularly. I'm now a regular at a Wednesday night prayer group, though a different group from the one Gloria belongs to. Despite my initial concerns, I have grown to love my group—and the seven new friends I've made. I feel sure that I'm stumbling less on my faith walk, and for that I praise God.

I really do feel that God has poured his blessings on me. Little by little I'm coming to understand what it means to trust in him.

My business, which was hanging by a thread, is on the road to recovery. Praise God.

My friendship with David is back on track. We have promised to trust one another, so that nothing like this ever happens again. Praise God.

My friends are steadfast and faithful, especially Gloria. Praise God.

I am living life abundantly, in a way I never imagined possible. Praise God.

I have found a man to marry, a male I can invite into my life who doesn't have feathers. Praise God.

═════════

James and I are making plans—quietly and without guidance from our relatives.

Much to Chloe's chagrin, I have not yet chosen a ring. Nor have we decided where we will be married. She is lobbying intensely for Chichester, England, and a service conducted by Stuart (not a bad idea, actually). She has also urged me (us) to adopt a hyphenated last name.

"'Hunnechurch-Huston' has such an international ring to it," she said.

"I categorically refuse to become Philippa Elizabeth Katherine Hunnechurch-Huston," I said. "I prefer not to carry business cards twice the usual width."

═════════

James is following through with his promise to relocate the headquarters of Peachtree Consulting Group to Ryde, even though there's nary a peach tree in sight. It turns out that his burgeoning seminar business in Canada has shifted its center of gravity. Maryland is now at the center of his consulting and teaching activities.

Who would have guessed?

═════════

One reason for James's new teaching opportunities in Canada was the exposure occasioned by his appearance on the New Year's Day morning TV show, which generated a lot of interest in his seminars. James flew to Toronto on the afternoon of Monday, December 31. He returned to Ryde on January 2, bearing gifts supposedly for me (an elaborate set of chefs' knives made in France), a videotape of the broadcast, and several snapshots of him enjoying a *Hogmanay* party hosted by Todd and Pam Stimson. He looked far too merry for my tastes.

═════════

Back in Ryde, Gloria and Ray went to the Moveable Feast at Ryde Fellowship Church on New Year's Eve, carrying a huge batch of English sausage rolls that James prepared before he went off to Canada. Gloria freely admits that James's sausage rolls are even better than hers—an extraordinary compliment.

———————

Over Gloria's loud objections, I decided to stay home on New Year's Eve and watch TV with Winston. I threw a blanket over the holes in my sofa and curled up with a mug of Darjeeling tea. In truth, I felt too sore to do anything but watch other people celebrate.

To my amazement, Chloe called at two minutes past midnight to wish me Happy New Year.

"Good heavens, Chloe," I said. "It's barely five o'clock in the morning in Chichester."

"After your recent sojourn in the hospital, I sensed a need to keep closer tabs on you."

"Actually, I'm making arrangements for a full-time tab watcher on this side of the pond. Your work is done."

"You and James?" she shrieked. "Tell me everything!"

Our call lasted an hour and twenty minutes.

The phone rang again seconds after I put it down.

"I don't know about this," James said. "A man should be able to reach his fiancée at 12:01 on New Year's Day; yet your phone has been busy *forever.* Are there other admirers I need to worry about?"

"Not a one."

"In that case, Happy New Year, sweetheart."

We talked until I heard a rapping on my front door.

"Open up, Pippa!" Gloria called. "We come with *dozens* of sausage rolls."

———————

Gloria, bless her heart, is one of those people who walk the extra mile for others without thinking about it. I'm doing my best to learn. Sometimes I succeed, sometimes I fail. And when I do fail, there's grace.

ABOUT THE AUTHORS

Ron Benrey grew up in New York. He has written six non-fiction books and more than a thousand magazine articles. He holds degrees in engineering, management, and law.

Janet Benrey grew up in Kent, England. She was a photographer and and executive recruiter before turning to writing and literary agenting. She holds a degree in communication.

Ron and Janet began writing together in 1989, when they founded Benrey+Benrey, a marketing communications firm that supported many of America's leading companies. Their first Pippa Hummechurch mystery, *Little White Lies*, was published in 2001.

When they are not planning new adventures for Pippa Hunnechurch, Ron and Janet enjoy sailing on *SeaSaw*, their small sailboat. They live in Columbia, Maryland, in easy reach of the Chesapeake Bay.

You can contact them by visiting Pippa's Web site, www.pippahunnechurch.com.

Pippa Hunnechurch parted company with God seven years ago.

Today she needs a miracle.

Pippa Hunnechurch scoffs at the idea that God cares about her future. So with economic hard times on the horizon, Pippa concludes she is on her own. But Pippa does have one ally. A genuine Christian soldier, who understands that in the midst of a battle to save her business, her reputation, and ultimately her life, Pippa needs most to put the Lord back in her life again.

Praise for *Little White Lies*
"In their debut novel, the Benreys spin a brisk Christian murder mystery . . . fast-paced and liberally seasoned with flavorful bits of British culture and dry humor."
—Publishers Weekly

". . . a strong spiritual theme as well, but the authors skillfully avoid falling into preachiness and pat answers."
—Amazon.com's Best of 2001

BROADMAN & HOLMAN PUBLISHERS